PENGUIN BOOKS

WRAP IT IN FLAGS

Robert Terrall is the author of some fifty novels, several of them under his own name, many more under the pseudonyms Robert Kyle, John Gonzales, MacLennan Roberts, and, most notably, Brett Halliday. Under the latter name he has written twenty-four "Mike Shayne" paperback mysteries, from 1957 to 1976. Over the years the paperback sales of his novels have reached 25 million copies. A graduate of Harvard University (where he was the president of the *Lampoon*), he has held only one salaried job in his postgraduate career: a brief stint as a film critic for *Time*. He lives in Sharon, Connecticut, with his wife, Martha.

———

To Ann Bogart

It was lovely to spend time with you, exchange tales of your world and ours, and see your talented company in motion

Robert Terrall
July 11 '97

Wrap It in FLAGS

Robert Terrall

 Penguin Books

PENGUIN BOOKS
Viking Penguin Inc., 40 West 23rd Street,
New York, New York 10010, U.S.A.
Penguin Books Ltd, Harmondsworth,
Middlesex, England
Penguin Books Australia Ltd, Ringwood,
Victoria, Australia
Penguin Books Canada Limited, 2801 John Street,
Markham, Ontario, Canada L3R 1B4
Penguin Books (N.Z.) Ltd, 182–190 Wairau Road,
Auckland 10, New Zealand

First published in Penguin Books 1986
Published simultaneously in Canada

LIBRARY OF CONGRESS CATALOGING IN PUBLICATION DATA
Terrall, Robert.
  Wrap it in flags.
  I. Title.
PS3539.E69W7   1986   813'.54   85-12244
ISBN 0 14 00.8045 7

Grateful acknowledgment is made to Warner Bros. Music for
permission to reprint portions of lyrics from "I Get a Kick
Out of You" by Cole Porter. Copyright 1934 (renewed) by
Warner Bros. Inc. All rights reserved.

Printed in The United States of America by R. R. Donnelley &
Sons Company, Harrisonburg, Virginia
Set in Aster

For Martha

"You couldn't sell that fish to the Poles if you wrapped it in flags."

—STEFA SALKIN, *Lublin Days*

Wrap It in FLAGS

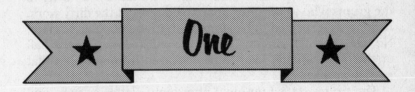

There is no accounting for starlings. Why should they pick the one site where they will create the maximum amount of inconvenience for everybody and return to it year after year, when there are more suitable places only a few minutes' flight away?

One spring, early in the 1970s, they descended on Fort Belknap, Virginia, in piney woods at the foot of the Blue Ridge. Originally Fort Schuylkill, renamed for Grant's controversial secretary of war, it had commanded this broad valley since before the Indian Wars. In recent years it had been used for backers' auditions, and when important congressmen were flown out to be shown some glamorous new weapons system and then were unable to land because the place was overrun by nasty, disagreeable birds—well, it embarrassed everybody.

Starlings are notoriously hard to count. Ornithologists estimated that at its most crowded, the rookery contained between three million and nine million individual birds. An insufferable number! Luckily the Defense Department was between wars at that moment, and if we couldn't impose our will on a few million unarmed, if fanatical, starlings, the rest of the

1

world would look down on us (in a phrase that was popular then) as a pitiful helpless giant.

So a task force was organized, comprising elements from all services—Operation Icarus in the histories, Doody Duty to the grunts who were called upon to do most of the dirty work. As long as it seemed to be going well, it was popular warfare. No one, whether stepping out of the enlisted men's mess hall or the officers' club, likes to be criticized from above in that particular way.

The troops stayed up night after night clattering pans and setting off firecrackers. To get a good night's sleep, all the starlings had to do was move a few miles in any direction, but they were never able to make the connection. They wanted this one stand of pines, and damn it, the Army had got here first.

They departed finally, in their own good time. Next year they were back, but now the soldiers were ready for them. During the winter, Unconventional Warfare had come up with a foul-smelling liquid which Air Assault choppers sprayed on the pests on a frosty mid-April evening. The stuff ate through their natural weatherproofing, and all but a few froze to death. In Washington, the Joint Chiefs opened champagne. Saigon had fallen and they needed a win, for their own self-esteem.

But the surviving starlings busied themselves, and the next spring there they were again, as raucous as ever. If anything, filthier. The spray planes were waiting, but somehow the birds had acquired an immunity during the winter. They hopped around grooming each other. The chemical mixture seemed to give them quite a nice high.

The trees were electrified that year, at considerable expense. (But this was Pentagon money, which differs in many respects from money as the word is understood in the ordinary world.) By April the upper branches were hot enough to barbecue a chicken. The Chiefs themselves flew out, and watched anxiously as the advance guard swirled up from the southwest, circled and came down. Sparks flew. It was like those backyard mosquito zappers. *Psst!—psst!* It seemed to be working. Then the main force arrived, and blacked out all of western Virginia, parts of Delaware and Pennsylvania.

The system was redesigned at a lower voltage. The starlings took a few weeks to adapt, but adaptability is those birds' middle name. The constant play of electricity kept them awake and lively, and seemed to have the effect of raising the birthrate. Next year's flock was *enormous*.

All right, artillery. A five-mile-square target area was placed under round-the-clock Harassment and Interdiction, using canisters packed with flechettes, those evil little barbs that can put a hole through three-quarter-inch plywood. But the news leaked. The Audubon chapters mobilized. Nostalgia was a big thing that year. A whole college generation was troubled with vague longings for the old movies, the old groups, the great demonstrations. From all parts of the country, young people poured into Washington. Protesters are even harder to count than starlings. One hundred thousand? Two? A lot, anyway. Between the birds at Fort Belknap and the demonstrators circling the Pentagon, the Chiefs had every reason to consider that they themselves were the endangered species.

And they choked.

They canceled the H. and I. and cooled out the birds, humanely, with repeated applications of nerve gas. Now what to do with the bodies? It was your basic toxic-waste problem—no community could be found that was willing to accept between three and nine million stoned starlings. Finally they were dumped on Yucca Flat, north of Las Vegas, Nevada. Maybe they would pick up some stray radioactivity or something.

Meanwhile, in the hollows and swamps and the estuaries, new flocks were gathering. At their wits' ends, the Chiefs did what they should have done in the first place—they consulted Michael Mirabile, the resident think-tanker.

Only one thing to do, Mirabile told them immediately. Cut down the forest.

How could they have failed to see—? Of course! So when the birds showed up that year, a nasty surprise awaited them. Instead of friendly pine-covered hillside, they found nothing but stumps and sawdust. For a moment the great disciplined army broke into a mob of confused and quarreling individual birds. Their squawks were sweet music to the task-force cadre.

3

Now a long shudder washed from one edge of the flock to the other. Never mind, the United States is a big country. And an instant later they were gone, complaining, defecating, to make a nuisance of themselves somewhere else.

Colombia. Not the university, the country.

For the last two or three decades, its government has been reasonably pro–United States, but that part of the world has never seemed terribly important to North Americans. Few tourists go there. When, after a brief period of destabilization, new people took over, only a handful of Washington pedants could have supplied the name of the newly deposed president. A portly scoundrel with the hanging jowls that are the mark of rich dinners and little domestic opposition, General Maxímo de Santamaría Schmidt forgot who his true friends were and neglected to look over his shoulder. After a ceremonial exchange of gunfire, he fled to a prepared refuge in Miami Beach, to join a distinguished exile community.

A three-man junta replaced him, colonels, one each from the army, air force and intelligence community. Now, three-man Latin American juntas have a way of dwindling to two-man juntas, then to a single strong man; and indeed, in the first photographs the colonels seemed to eye each other with more than usual suspicion. Only the army's man was wearing a hat, a helmet liner with a decal of a condor grasping a thunderbolt. The chairmanship—the hat as well, presumably—would rotate monthly, if all went according to the communiqué.

Gonzalo Alvarez Blanco was the chairman's name. A hero of the Korean War and the antiguerrilla struggle, he had been dashing as a youth—photographs existed that proved this—but too many important muscles, psychological ones as well, had let go at the same time. He combed his few remaining hairs from west to east, in the manner of the late North American general, MacArthur.

Each colonel had his own little list of relatives and clients. During the first day or so there was some strenuous jockeying, which took place, appropriately, at the Jockey Club in downtown Bogotá. They sat in the upstairs library, in leather armchairs which had creaked beneath generations of Colombian leaders. The mixture of odors in the room had been building for a century and a half. The lightest touch on a bell would bring a tottery steward with brandy and cigars, or the *Financial Times*. There was one pale rectangle over the fireplace, where a bad likeness of their predecessor, in oil, had been taken down. Their own joint portrait had been commissioned, but the artist was waiting for U.S. recognition of the new regime before beginning.

The Conservatives, who had avoided the Jockey since De Santamaría's downfall, were beginning to venture back. Now and then one blundered into the library. Seeing the colonels with serious faces, Yankee-style dispatch cases leaning against their chairs, clipboards on their laps, they apologized and tiptoed out.

The chairman's ball-point had arrived at the name of a newly promoted captain, the son of an old comrade. Rather than asking for a post, this Iluminado Castillo was asking to be relieved of one. He had been ordered to Counter Coup school in Washington, one of the international academies funded by the Pentagon out of its public service account. Attendance was not compulsory, certainly not, but unofficially, every country on the U.S. team was expected to send a promising young officer on pain of being overlooked at check-signing time. Someone would have to go, but Castillo considered himself insufficiently qualified.

"He has had his present command for so short a time," the chairman explained, "he hates to leave before he gets his boots dusty, so to speak. Ministro?"

The intelligence colonel, Hernán Vega González, was attempting a bubble glass for perhaps the first time in his life, and he had taken too large a bite of his brandy. He had not been a Jockey member before the coup, but his election had been automatic, the blackballs in the box being overlooked by the Governing Committee. He was widely feared, in the belief that anyone so self-assured must have secret sources of revenue, ties to important embassies.

5

"Quite O.K., thanks," he replied when he was able to stop sputtering. "As for Iluminado Castillo, I have received nothing but glowing reports of this young man. It is important to send our best people at the beginning. By how well they do, the regime will be judged."

"I agree, you know," the chairman said, "but if he lacks that enthusiasm, that 'fire in the belly'—" (He used the English expression.) "You had a candidate, I believe, Colonel?"

"My nephew as it happens. The lad will have a brilliant career, I feel sure, but let me be candid with you. At the moment, he has a small complexion problem. Our first appointments should set a certain—tone."

Leather complained as he sat forward. Vega had been trying to cultivate an implacable look to go with his new status, but he could only sustain it for eight or ten seconds. He kicked out his feet to pick up the highlights on his new Argentine riding boots. As far as his colleagues knew, he had never been on a horse.

"To speak to the matter of motivation. Counter Coup, granted—one boring lecture after another, all theory and no practice, which can be torture for a mettlesome young man. I am thinking along these lines. Our five-sided friends to the north have permitted us to know ridiculously little—nothing at all, actually—about the high-technology barrier they are planning to erect across the Panama Isthmus, one day's stroll from our frontier. A working model is undergoing field tests at Fort Belknap, where certain of the Counter Coup exercises are scheduled to take place. Merely suggest to young Iluminado that he keep his eyes open, ask the occasional naive question. That there is an element of danger may appeal to him. A motorcyclist, is he not? And refuses to wear a helmet? There might be a decoration in it, nothing too grand, say the Knight's Cross of the Order of the Condor."

The chairman studied the ash that was threatening to fall from his cigar. "It is possible that that might make a difference. He reads constantly; it is one of his least attractive traits. A devourer of Le Carré novels."

"You go to the farm tonight. Suppose you swing around by way of Cartagena, drop in on the boy and sound him out. Discreetly, Colonel, with the door locked and the water running. For as I am sure you're aware, Washington swarms with other readers of spy novels, and if some unfriendly service gets wind of the hush-hush aspects of the mission, he will be closely watched and otherwise hampered."

The ash dropped, and the chairman, though still doubtful that he could persuade his young protégé, agreed to make the attempt.

The session continued, three old comrades-in-arms dividing the spoils and the opportunities. When the chairman's aide looked in to remind him that the airplane was waiting to carry him north for the weekend, good-byes were said cordially.

"*Ciao*," Vega told him, carrying it off well.

The others stayed to finish their brandies. The air force colonel, known in his own service as "Animal" because of the ferocity of his political opinions, went to the door to check for eavesdroppers.

Coming back: "I confess I don't understand you, Ministro. Have I been misinformed? I was given to believe that glances have been exchanged between"—he left a blank for the name—"and this same young Iluminado Castillo."

The reference was to the chairman's handsome wife, Doña Gabriella, who read *Time* in English and was ambitious to jostle the capital into the twentieth century before the twentieth century was altogether over. Hernán Vega, ignoring his colleague's question, was still trying to get brandy out of his bubble. This time he achieved a decent mouthful without choking. He sat back, smiling. The feat was not as difficult as it looked.

The other continued: "So it would be prudent, would it not, a matter of common sense, for the husband to want to pack the young man off to Washington before the marriage is dishonored? Is it already too late, is the question people are asking."

The intelligence colonel continued to smile. Such secrets as these were his specialty.

"According to my informants, it is some months too late. More than glances have been exchanged, on numerous occasions."

"Then why, in God's name," the Animal demanded, "this implausible story of an intelligence mission, the Order of the Condor? If you had asked my opinion, I would have said excellent, let the young man stay in Colombia under the señora's eye. Her finca is less than one hour's drive from Cartagena by the four-lane. While her husband is busy in Bogotá, headaches will keep her home, the headaches of a woman of forty with a passion for a young man half her age. As the adventure continues, they will become careless, perhaps. With those 'bugs' of yours, your tiny cameras, would it be so difficult to organize a scandal?"

"Causing our friend Gonzalo, this month's chairman of the Council of Ministers, to withdraw from public life."

"Precisely. You have convinced me that solo leadership is his goal, and unless we strike preemptively, strike with *power*, it is you and I who will be given thirty minutes to catch the plane to Miami."

"My dear colleague." Before the recent upheavals, Vega González, with his Indian grandmother, would never have spoken so familiarly to a Jockey Club member. But now, of course, he was a member himself. "You may not know that it was the señora, and no other, who arranged for her lover's North American orders. She is unaware that he has asked for this cancellation. And you have guessed correctly, in the interests of state security I have been tapping telephone calls. She has rented an apartment in Cartagena as a hideaway. She phoned the young man two hours ago and commanded him to meet her this evening. Not possible, he told her. He must prepare a lecture. But she is determined to see him and I believe she will go to his room at the hotel. For she has a present to give him, along with last-minute words of advice."

"A present?"

"In fact a uniform, specially tailored. A total surprise. And she will want to make sure it fits. I imagine the following 'scenario.' She will wait until after dark to knock on his door. 'You will be away three months, see what I have brought you. Undress at once and try it on, I order you.' Presently, another knock on the door. The husband! He will have his entourage with him, including, perhaps you know him, a constabulary sergeant named Luis García."

The other's face cleared. "I'm beginning to follow you. You aren't thinking in terms of a twenty-four-hour scandal, but of confrontation. García, yes, I've heard of him."

"And devoted to me as it happens, for I've snatched him away from the firing squad more than once. With a little luck the lovers will be discovered naked in bed. And won't this reckless young motorcyclist have his own pistol under the pillow? Bullets will be flying around, I think I can guarantee you, and one or two, I am confident, will strike our esteemed temporary chairman and carry him off into another and possibly less competitive world. Will anyone worry who fired these rounds, the young lover or some 'hit man,' as the Yankees have it, in the bodyguard? I expect not, for as minister of public safety, I will be in charge of the investigation."

The Animal was beaming. "It is skillfully planned, Ministro. My congratulations."

Two

It was the most brilliant marriage of that season. The bride-groom, the future chairman of the Council of Ministers, was just back from Korea, and he looked like a recruiting poster, his chest splendid with ribbons. But he came of a porcine family, and before the contours could change, Doña Gabriella made sure he was photographed in various masculine poses.

He was popular with his fellow officers because he was so clearly one of themselves, uncomplicated, foul-mouthed, without guile. As for the guile, that was provided by Gabriella. Her family had money and memberships, a great house in Bogotá, everywhere cousins. At her little dinners, she forced herself to be pleasant to the despicable De Santamaría, who would press his leg against hers under the cloth and breathe heavily, in a way men of that class consider sentimental. She smiled into his eyes and returned the pressure, flustering him pleasantly, and Gonzalo would be promoted ahead of his age group. At her insistence, Gonzalo took lessons in speaking into a microphone, and learned how to banter with unfriendly reporters. In public, in full uniform, with his medals, he still managed a certain sparkle. At home, only the two of them, he was dull, dull. Dear God, he was dull.

He refused to jog or play golf, and forbade all discussion of the rights of women to sexual fulfillment. Gabriella's North American magazines advised her to speak to him frankly, explaining that sexual pleasure had to be mutual; if she enjoyed herself more he, too, would enjoy himself more. The experts who gave that advice had obviously had little experience with colonels in the Colombian army. One anniversary followed another. Finally, one night after wine, in the seventeenth year of the marriage, she experienced a very faint flutter. This was success in a way, she supposed, but could it be described as a *climax*?

To exercise her English, she applied for membership in the Book-of-the-Month Club. She was accepted. Unfortunately for her mental tranquillity, the Yankee novelists were taking advantage of the new freedom to describe the sex act in detail, frequently from the female point of view. A citizen of a Catholic country, a good Catholic herself, Gabriella sometimes despaired. Gonzalo visited a mistress three times a week, at four thirty in the afternoon, and in a rational world this would seem to entitle his wife to a similar freedom. Not so, however. True, the men in her circle occasionally gave Gabriella that look which says "I beg you to accept my explosion, beautiful lady. Let me throw you down on this grass (on the floor, on the bed, on the sofa) and we will do unprintable things." Unprintable— they ought to glance into some of those North American novels.

Once or twice, oh, five times at the most, always at the same point in her menstrual cycle, she said to herself, Very well! and sent the look sizzling back. To the man's consternation! For she was Doña Alvarez Blanco, the wife of the nation's one authentic hero, unofficial leader of the loose anti-De Santamaría conspiracy.

So she made her peace. The coup preparations, the breakfasts and phone calls and endless discussions, kept her busy. After accepting her final bonus selection, she resigned from the Book-of-the-Month Club. One can live without magnificent orgasms. Undoubtedly most people do.

Then young Iluminado Castillo showed up on her doorstep with his letter of introduction, in an unsuitable haircut and blue jeans, a necktie of an unfashionable width. He was squinting angrily, not sure if the person who had answered the door was the lady of the mansion or one of the servants, and Gabriella went head over heels in an instant, *tronado*, as they say; she could hear the mutter of thunder.

His father had been a childhood friend of her husband, a fellow student at the U.S. academy in Panama City (he was also, as a matter of fact, one of those men who had given Gabriella the look). While the older Iluminado pursued his fortune in Rome, in Washington—even, when nothing better suggested itself, in Bogotá—the son lived uneventfully with his mother in a small town in the Department of Norte de Santander. He was educated by Jesuits, who gave him their version of history and an ability to speak fluent English, with World War II idioms and a slight Boston accent.

Suddenly the modern world arrived in the neighborhood, in the form of a magnificent highway, being built from Pamplona to the coast with great speed and panache by a crew of mad Yankees. Iluminado fell in with these people. There was a girl, Gabriella found out later, one of several who held a red flag during the day and at night drank aguardiente and smoked native-grown dope elbow to elbow with the men.

Iluminado had always intended to become a tank commander like Patton, like Gonzalo—like his own father, for that matter, who had risen to captain before having to resign his commission as a result of a misunderstanding involving his commanding officer's wife. Now, to his mother's dismay, Iluminado announced that he meant to make his career on the highway. It seemed that they needed a payloader driver. He had fallen in love with these quirky and powerful machines. His mother, such a meek woman as a rule, said no emphatically, under no conceivable circumstances, and packed him off to the capital with a letter to his father's old classmate. Couldn't Colonel Alvarez Blanco do something to help this deserving young man?

To be logical again, why should the older man–younger

woman combination be acceptable, while the other way around is considered ridiculous? (The young woman Gonzalo visited, for example, was certainly no more than eighteen.) It was a classic situation, well documented in the literature of all countries: the young man from the provinces, ignorant of the world but eager to learn, the older woman with a husband who falls asleep night after night in front of television. She asked Iluminado to cocktails a few times to meet the necessary people. Seeing him across the room gave her a sensation like hunger. Her stomach growled uncontrollably. One afternoon he came to thank her for his lieutenant's commission. Unluckily, it was the dangerous moment when her warm flow was about to begin. He looked charmingly awkward in the new uniform. And suddenly, without intending it in the least, she gave him the look!

He was rocked by it. Some minutes later she manipulated him into her bedroom, and some minutes after that, into herself.

Their ostensible errand was to look at the famous picture of Gonzalo in helmet and fatigues, climbing out of his tank. Her fingers were damp, for whatever reason, the photograph slipped from her grasp and the glass shattered, a symbol for what she now hoped would happen. He cut himself on the glass and had to sit on the edge of the bed while she put on the Band-Aids. Her breasts swayed centimeters from his face. A touch, a quick grappling collision, a jarring, out-of-control kiss. Because of his cuts he couldn't unzip without help. A beautiful aroused object burst into view—her hands felt the heat.

But something still held him back.

"My sweet darling, I know!" she said with a shiver. "If Gonzalo found us together, he would send one bullet through us both. So hurry, hurry."

The implication being that the man whose marriage he was being invited to dishonor, a believer in the traditional Hispanic values, might walk into the house at any moment and find them together. As a matter of fact, Gonzalo was in Manzanilles, cultivating the commander of the Third Division. Iluminado was still young enough to doubt his own courage. Extremely pale,

13

the big artery in his neck pulsing visibly, he advanced into her embrace.

It was completed in an instant. She could have excited him again, she was confident, but she couldn't confess the truth, that Gonzalo would be away for three days. She had to bundle him out, with many passionate kisses and promises, whispering at the door, "Tomorrow at four thirty."

On succeeding afternoons he improved, but he could never let go completely. It was all there on his face:

"How lovely she is, one would never suppose she has a son nearly my age. So expert at this. She must have had a long succession of lovers, or have read many novels. The perfect breasts grazing my chest with the urgency of their nipples. The fingernails at the base of my spine. And yet! The wife of my father's oldest friend, a war hero, wounded in battle. Who tracked the guerrillas sometimes for sixty consecutive hours without food or sleep. Who commanded the detachment that stormed the bottling plant held by De Santamarístas." (For by this time the coup had been brought off with total success, the officer corps had been purged and Iluminado was about to receive his promotion to captain.) *"Who has dared to make the nation great again, so it is no longer necessary to apologize for being Colombian—"*

And at that point, if not earlier, his body would interrupt the harangue and he would collapse like a struck tent. As for poor Gabriella, she would feel *something*, usually, but compared with his masculine pyrotechnics it was merely a faraway tingle.

Seeing clearly what was needed, she told him about Gonzalo's wound. It had, in fact, been inflicted by a can opener. True, he had scoured the countryside looking for guerrillas, but he had never caught up with any. As for the already-famous attack on the bottling plant, that had been arranged in advance. The defenders had aimed their guns at the heavens, creating a great deal of commotion for the seven o'clock news. Casualties? Amazingly low, in fact zero. And as for the coup itself, with its carefully crafted slogans—well, it so happened that a certain North American corporation had undertaken to sell Colombia much-needed airplanes, and De Santamaría had de-

14

manded consultant's fees in the amount of ten million dollars, to be deposited to his account in Miami. The colonels had offered the same deal for considerably less, so good-bye De Santamaría.

Iluminado was smiling. "It's so obvious why you are telling me this. Every schoolchild knows the story of how the colonel was wounded. By a Red Chinese bayonet, on the banks of the Yalu."

"By a P-38 can opener! One of those wicked folding ones the Yankees supply with the field rations. They have disabled whole regiments."

But he would have to learn for himself, it seemed.

The Cartagena garrison needed a commanding officer. Gabriella compaigned successfully on Iluminado's behalf, without telling Gonzalo her true motive: how conveniently Cartagena could be reached from the old farm she fled to whenever she couldn't smile through one more state dinner or other formal occasion. She found an apartment in town, furnished it charmingly, and went on with her young man's education. But patriotism continued to get in their way, and one night, to her consternation, he ground his teeth unpleasantly and announced that duty, honor, country, the soldier's trinity, demanded that they stop stealing off to these secret meetings. A soldier, he was forbidden tears except for the death of comrades, but Gabriella, when she understood that he meant what he said, shed a few.

What to do? The solution came to her while Gonzalo was shuffling names on his patronage lists. Washington! There, if anywhere, Iluminado would discover the true nature of the world.

His father had friends there who gave (he had told Gabriella) dull but glittering dinner parties. Iluminado would be invited to embassies, where fashionable women would look him over like a horse they were thinking of buying. (But she would have to do something about the ill-fitting uniform.) And these would be women, Gabriella was sure, who knew all the sexual tricks, who routinely achieved the nearly continuous spasm. How she would miss him, how she would burn with jealousy. But when he returned, stripped of his old-fashioned illusions, he would see the advantages of coming back to that almost sinfully comfortable bed, with its silk sheets and its piled-up pillows, and there she would be his student.

A group of fourth-generation philanthropists (gringos, needless to say), with more money than sensible projects to spend it on, had funded a two-year study of the floundering Colombian economy. Only one way for the hard-up nation to make ends meet, the experts concluded: make itself more attractive to tourists.

So a national campaign was undertaken to persuade the natives to smile more when doing business with visitors from hard-currency countries. A primitive Motilone Indian village was reconstructed on the Río de Oro, modeled after the famous Rockefeller promotion, Williamsburg, Virginia. The flush toilets were state-of-the-art but everything else was true to the period. Visitors were helicoptered in from Barranquilla, on the coast, and rowed ten kilometers upstream by muscular coca-chewing young men wearing only a penis sheath. Penis sheaths became one of the fastest-moving items in the thatched-roof village boutiques, being outsold only by shrunken heads.

The big reenactment, a weekly fertility rite, was a smash hit from the start, popular with participants and spectators alike. A popular Amazonas witch doctor was brought in to do love spells and cures. His methods proved to be particularly effective against headaches. A meek, inoffensive-looking person until he put on the mask and feathers, he stamped around a twig fire in a spooky clearing, waving the leg bone of a jaguar and kicking up phosphorescence while a backup group worked the drums and rattles and uttered the pain cry of the howler monkey. Meanwhile, the headache victims crouched in the shadows, tormented by insects, perhaps wishing they hadn't come. Hours later, the old man sprang at them unexpectedly, and with a loud shriek rapped them smartly across the side of the head with his bone. In a surprising percentage of cases, it worked. The results were reported in the North American alternative-medicine press, and presently charter flights to the Río de Oro were being organized from Los Angeles and other Yankee cities, though mainly, of course, from Los Angeles.

The other gringo-assisted project, a gambling casino in Cartagena, was less successful. Built by technicians on loan from the U.S. Army Corps of Engineers, it announced itself to passing ships with the gaudiest display of neon south of downtown Las Vegas. Historically, this was the corps' first casino, and they did their usual workmanlike job. You would never suspect that the ancient fortress of San Felipe de Barajas, which had outlived its usefulness when the last pirates were hanged, had once stood on the site.

Not everybody in town was happy about this. The authors of the study had overlooked the fact that one out of five inhabitants of Cartagena made a living, a scratchy one to be sure, selling lottery tickets to each other. The opening ceremonies were marred by deliberate traffic jams, stink bombs, emetics in the soda dispenser, sabotage of the slot machines.

Because of disaffection among the police, the Cartagena garrison, under the command of the youthful Iluminado Castillo, moved out of barracks and took over two floors of the hotel. The Syndicate of Lottery Ticket Salesmen continued to boycott and agitate, but they had the sense not to try any funny business in the gaming areas, knowing that most of the shills were actually soldiers, who would be glad to beat on a few heads to interrupt the monotony. Allowed to drink nothing but glass after glass of iced tea, making shills' bets with make-believe money, they found the nights incredibly tedious. Still, as soldiering went in this corner of the world, it wasn't bad duty. The pits were air conditioned. Whenever a cruise ship was in, it was possible to meet women—usually schoolteachers or widows, however.

Doña Gabriella, accompanied by her skinny Barranquilla cousin, Ana, parked the Olds in the underground garage and took the elevator to the casino floor. Passing beneath a neon sign—AYUDE A NUESTROS NINOS A LEER–APOSTAR ("Help Our Kids Learn to Read, Gamble")—the ladies purchased a stack of hundred-peso chips and strolled into the blackjack pit.

Gabriella wore spike heels and diamonds, a halter dress of black silk, descending so low in back that it exposed the full length of her spine, all the way to the bottommost knob and the umlaut. She knew that her presence here, on Iluminado's final night, would be reported to her husband's enemies, but never mind, it was patriotic to frequent the Bolívar. Seventy percent of its net win, not that there had been any so far, had been pledged to the anti-illiteracy campaign in the country-side.

She sat down and because she was hoping to lose her stake quickly, immediately began to win. Chips piled up and spilled. Finally, impatient to get on to the real reason for this visit, she invited her cousin to play a hand or so, and to cash her in.

She returned to the garage for the suit box. Coming back up, she found herself sharing an elevator with a crop-headed U.S. major labeled, tersely, "Sadowski." These Military Assistance majors were thick with various slippery people in the capital, Colonel Hernán Vega González for one, whose fingers had definitely been crossed when he pledged allegiance to the junta. All the North American's transmitters were sending. He admired her diamonds. He admired her clearly marked cheekbones and hipbones, the curve of her abdomen.

"Do you speak English?" he wanted to know.

As a matter of fact, Gabriella did speak English. She used an expression she had picked up during her membership in the Book-of-the-Month Club.

"Piss up a rope."

He goggled. A moment later, her heart beating lightly and rapidly, she was tapping on Iluminado's door. Footsteps. He opened for her holding a hand grenade.

"Gabriella! But I didn't expect—"

His matador's haunches were concealed beneath OD underwear—olive drab, that depressing color the United States has imposed on all the armies of the Western world by the simple means of giving the uniforms away free. The shorts

18

were all he was wearing. She touched his face lightly and sailed in.

She was seeing this room for the first time, and she was enchanted with it. He had made changes in the usual casino-hotel decor. A riot-suppression manual, small arms and an assortment of crowd-control weapons were arranged on one of the beds. An aerial map of Cartagena was tacked to the flocked wallpaper, with an acetate overlay marked up with greasy pencil. Goya's naked duchess, a good color print, was still on one wall. On another, Iluminado had added a large glossy photograph of a North American actor, looking extremely pleased with himself, in the role of the late General George S. Patton, Jr. Stuck in the mirror were snapshots of Iluminado's sad-eyed mother, his father in a beautiful white suit and a white planter's hat, a dark-haired girl in front of a bulldozer (was this perhaps the girl Gabriella had heard those rumors about?).

His boots had been buffed until they gave off a soft glow, like the heads of saints in old paintings. Side by side on the luxurious carpet, one leaning tipsily under the weight of a sheathed knife, they filled Gabriella with tenderness.

She picked up a gas mask and clapped it on. "Do I frighten you, darling?"

"You frighten me constantly," he assured her. "We agreed it was too dangerous for you to visit me here."

"I won't stay twenty minutes. Don't worry, I've been gambling with my cousin Ana. If there is gossip about it, I can tell Gonzalo it was Ana, not I, who loves you to distraction and had to see you."

"Who would believe that? Ana, my God, she's nothing but bones and hair."

She touched his arm, causing the muscle to rise against her palm. "You haven't said if you like my dress."

She revolved for him, letting him savor the full extent of her nakedness, and ended in his arms. They kissed. It was teeth against teeth, diamonds against flesh. Nine days since she'd seen him! He took the air out of her lungs.

The wafflelike grid of the hand grenade was grinding against her. When she pulled back he almost dropped it.

"Is that thing alive?" she exclaimed.

He, too, she was happy to see, was suffering from severe shortness of breath. He added the grenade to the lethal display on the bed.

"An adjustment has to be made before it will detonate. Called a guava for the obvious reason. Usually part of a CBU, Cluster Bomb Unit. In the U.S. army everything is known by initials. Two hundred steel pellets, killing radius ten meters. Gabriella, these last days have been—"

He put his fists together and twisted them apart. "I try to study and I can feel your fingers. I must memorize all this by oh-nine-hundred hours tomorrow, CS, LZ, WP and on and on and on—and my mind runs to our times together, our conversations. I talk to you, I try to explain. Each day it gets worse. But we can't go back to the way we were because that was torment."

"For me," she said calmly, though she hadn't really felt calm since the young man entered her life, "it wasn't torment at all, it was lovely. In any case, you're off to Washington tomorrow, where I think you may manage to forget me a little."

"Is it possible you haven't been told? I'm not going."

"Of course you are going. No one would dare take your name off the list."

"I asked them to send someone else. There are dozens who are anxious to go."

"But I don't understand you, darling," she said, frowning. "You agreed it was necessary."

Embarrassed, he turned away.

"I didn't expect to have visitors; I have nothing to offer but powdered coffee."

"Nothing, thank you. Answer me."

"Well—there are two U.S. majors here, Major Grimes, Major Sadowski. Major Sadowski is the serious one. He has served in Honduras, Peru, Bolivia, and he says I am the first halfway decent line officer he has worked with in Latin America. Halfway decent—that doesn't sound like much, but coming from him it's a compliment, trust me. The men are beginning to resemble soldiers. Their salutes are much better, though as the

20

major says, still far from Quantico standards. I learn all the time but there is still so much I don't know. I thought it would be embarrassing for me at the Washington school, to be unable to field-strip a machine gun, for example—"

"I'm sure that school is nothing but printouts and push buttons," she said sharply. "Look here. I brought you a good-bye present. Shall we open it, even so?"

The suit box came apart when she unfastened the handle. Iluminado unfolded the tissue paper, his expression carefully blank. Uniforms are supposed to be identical, that's what the word means. But within the guidelines there are many things a good tailor can do. Her beautiful young man was trying hard not to react, but his lips parted when he saw the supernova pinned to the left breast.

"Gonzalo's," she explained, "he won't miss it, he has been given so many. A Finnish order, Knight Commander of the White Rose."

"I am not entitled to wear it."

"In Washington, dear, who would know? It is English cloth, do you like it? Our own Indian ladies from Chiquinquirá worked the braid. Put it on, I fear it may be tight across the shoulders."

His mind, as usual, was working very close to the surface. He liked her present, but he would have to be tortured before he would admit it. She watched him twist and turn at the narrow mirror, with the wary look of all men trying on clothes. Her elegant centaur—half man and half officer.

"Does it pinch under the arms?"

"No, it seems fine. Chiquinquirá braid. I'm sure it cost you a fortune. So I must go to Washington, it seems. Otherwise I might do something to embarrass you, such as killing the new lover you are undoubtedly thinking of taking. I'll tell the major that I find the training too harsh. What is the purpose of these midday marches? Fifteen kilometers today under full-field packs and helmets. Five men collapsed on the sand. Whereas in Washington! My father considers it one of the few pleasant cities left in the world. Everything air-conditioned. Women outnumbering men three to one."

"My love, why do you always get angry when I bring you a present?"

"What makes you believe that I'm angry?"

Not angry? He was snorting with fury. And something came to life inside Gabriella, like a tiny nibbling animal. He had always been so respectful, and that might be why—

"Another lover, what an excellent idea. Our beautiful apartment sits there empty, rent paid until the end of the quarter."

She let her head touch his shoulder.

"No, my dear, there won't be another. You are the first and the last. If you go to Washington, I'll run around and keep busy, and try not to think by how much the women outnumber the men there. But *if you stay*," she said ominously, starting to undress, "you must get over these honorable scruples and make love with me! Or you'll make me an enemy, I warn you."

"The powerful Señora Alvarez. I wouldn't want that."

Having less to take off, he was ready first, prepared to punish her for bringing him such a magnificent present. If his penis had been the minute hand of a clock, the time would now be five minutes before the hour.

"I predict you will be a success in the United States," she said lightly, though a little frightened, as always, "if in the end you decide to go."

The bed had been made up army-style, tight as a drumhead. He attempted to enter her immediately, something which only women in backward countries allow to happen. But Gabriella, who did her yoga every morning like a saint, was not completely helpless.

"Darling, you're crushing me."

He never apologized, on principle, but the rebuke caused him to lose fifteen minutes of elevation. As an ex-Book-of-the-Month-Club member, she knew how to remedy that. It took courage; always before, she had lost heart at the last minute. But she had promised herself tonight when she came that this was to be his real going-away present. She got the hang of it almost at once.

She looked up after a time.

22

"This is called fellatio in English. Do you like it?"

"I—think so."

"It's one of the most popular ways in the United States, I believe."

She rearranged herself, and welcomed him inside her. She had charmed his anger away, and he was being careful again. Too careful, alas! Yes, Washington is the place for you, my dear, she thought, where there are more women than men and cynicism is the agreed-upon attitude.

She felt something toward the end, but it was faint, faint.

"I was too fast again," he murmured, slipping away.

"No, *niñito*, you were perfect."

She was running her hand along his flank: satin over steel. Baby, she had called him, but he only looked like a baby when he was sleeping, and that she had seen just once. (In seven months, once!) As an officer, he was forced to wear one of the silly military haircuts. Gabriella had been present at the shearing, and had moaned as the ringlets dropped onto his lap and shoulders. He had a fine straight nose, the little mustache she had suggested to make him look older, a blinding smile which in her opinion he released all too seldom, the legs of a middle-distance runner, scarred here and there from high-speed skids and cracked-up motorcycles. Keep busy, she had said. She would have to keep *furiously* busy or go mad. And yet it had to happen.

She spoke gently. "Darling, Cartagena is not a good place for you at this moment, believe me."

"I must believe you, I suppose, but tell me why."

"These marches in the heat, who orders them?"

Surprise brought him up on one elbow. "The training schedule was developed by the major but I approve completely. For to fight a tough and determined enemy—"

"My dear, what enemy?"

"I admit," he said stiffly, "the guerrillas have been inactive lately, but let them see us become soft and lazy—"

"Guerrillas, guerrillas. They are of no significance whatever and you know it. I'm talking about our esteemed fellow conspirator Colonel Vega González. He has interested himself, I

23

happen to know, in these same North American majors, and I strongly suspect that he is the inspiration for these crazy marches and so forth."

"I'm sure the minister of public safety has more important things—"

"How little you know about politics, my love. If there is dissension in your command, it will reflect on the judgment of the people who gave you the promotion."

"No, you are wrong for once, Gabriella. Dissension? Far from it. It's been a slow process but I am beginning to win their respect. I run the obstacle course with them, make the same marches. I came in today carrying two rifles, a mortar plate, a second helmet as well as my own."

"You are marvelously fit, I know. But you are also both beautiful and lucky, and your men are neither. A captain's bars at your age—someone high up in the regime must surely be looking out for you. That elegant watch is undoubtedly a gift from some wealthy lady. In such circumstances, where your soldiers practice with live hand grenades, a sensible commanding officer orders siestas, you know, not marches."

"But isn't this," Iluminado said skeptically, twirling a finger absently around her nipple, "merely part of your campaign to persuade me that the world is corrupt, and nothing is the way they taught me at school?"

She asked him to trust her, to believe that she wouldn't be urging this separation unless it was necessary. While she talked he kept up the contact with her nipple, and the little fox awakened inside her. Iluminado, too, was showing signs of resurrection—he was wonderful in that regard. But before she had a second chance to achieve, to *feel*, the phone exploded on the table between the beds.

Three

Her cousin's announcement rushed into her ear.

"It's Gonzalo! Asking for the number of Iluminado's room!"

In her nakedness—she had even taken off her eyelashes—Gabriella rose like a flushed bird.

"Hold him in the lobby for three minutes and you can have my new bracelet."

Much to her surprise, she saw that Iluminado, who must have heard that her husband was on his way, was starting a cigar.

"I knew this was how it would end."

She was wriggling into her dress. Underwear? Not necessary. "*Querida*, get dressed at once."

He rotated his cigar to be sure it was burning correctly, then picked a grenade out of the clutter of weapons on the second bed. He was tremendously excited, she could see.

"Put that down this minute," she ordered.

"He fought in a war. Our one chance will be to take him by surprise. Attack first, explain later. A saying of Patton's."

How lovely and foolish he was, out of some earlier century.

Gabriella's fingers worked quickly. With a little luck, she could be on the fire stairs before the elevator reached this floor. Every time Gonzalo tried to do something on his own, he bungled it badly. If he had consulted her beforehand, except how on earth could he, she would have advised him to phone ahead for the room number, and come straight up.

"Iluminado, don't you hear me?"

"Or the pistol, perhaps. Get it over with at once. Fire as the door opens."

"Then we would all die, you ninny. He travels with body-guards now, so this is no time for such masculine foolishness. Let him come in and find you at work. The señora? No, you haven't seen her all week."

"You won't ask me to do anything dishonorable."

"No, niñito. It is permissible to lie to husbands, in all countries, at all periods of history."

She could do the rest on the stairs. Telling him again to be sensible, for once, she opened the door.

A figure in raincoat and dark glasses stood under the red light marking the exit, holding a dispatch case in an unnatural position, as though it might not be a dispatch case at all but a camouflaged submachine gun. This was Luis García, who had been glimpsed not long ago by a good friend of Gabriella's, in the back seat of a parked car with Vega Gonzáles. Only her muddle-headed husband refused to believe that there was anything suspicious about this, for he and García had campaigned in the mountains together, as though that meant anything.

He sent her a flash of teeth.

"Señora, with respect. Return to the room, please. The colonel will be joining us in a moment."

She stepped back and slammed the door.

"A Vega agent," she said. "And that means—"

"That this has been planned in Bogotá," Iluminado supplied, "by someone who knew you were coming to see me."

"So if you're really dying to kill somebody—"

"I think so," he agreed. "But in silence, not to bring people out of their rooms. First some willy peter, I think. Slang for

WP, in other words white phosphorous. Confuse him with smoke."

He consulted the manual to be sure he was making the right choice. A grenade in his hand, he stopped with his hand on the doorknob. To gather his courage? No, he was thinking.

"Shouldn't we, darling," she said nervously, "before anyone else arrives—"

"*L'audace*," he told her, probably quoting some other authority. "Attack with audacity, but make sure you attack in the right direction. Stop dancing about, Gabriella. There is no particular hurry. Wherever the colonel goes, people want to shake hands with him and ask a favor. If I knife this man openly it will be a declaration of war."

He returned to the phone and ordered the switchboard girl to page the North American major, Sadowski.

"He plays twenty-one in the casino, for hours and hours," he said aside to Gabriella, "and always loses. He will go home a poor man."

Shouldering the phone, he prepared his big officer's Colt. Snap, slide, click, snap. Gabriella continued her nervous movements. Terrible pictures ran through her mind, scraps of dialogue, pleas, shouts, sound effects. The plight of a woman in a masculine world!

"Major!" Iluminado snapped in a tone she had never before heard him use. "Captain Castillo talking. Listen to me carefully. Suicide detachments from the Lottery Ticket Syndicate are about to attack the casino. This is hard information. Do you understand me? The lottery ticket salesmen, who threw the firecrackers and rotten eggs during the ribbon cutting. No, no, I'm not drunk."

The major was sputtering, like the admirals who looked out the window at Pearl Harbor that long ago December morning and couldn't believe the change in the weather.

"And Blessed Virgin!" Iluminado exclaimed. "Here they come now."

He touched the phone with the pistol muzzle and blew it apart, sending a fan of shrapnel across the bed they had used for their lovemaking. He gave his happiest laugh, the one he usually saved for his moment of orgasm.

Gabriella brought her hands together. "Oh, how I love you."

"And I you," he replied automatically. "The lottery ticket salesmen, those devils, they wouldn't try to take us by storm, they would do something underhanded and sneaky."

He picked up the grenade he had been committing to memory when she arrived, the "guava," and took it to the window, where he knocked out a pane. They were on the seventh floor. The Avenida de la Republica was choked with its usual twilight traffic. Excellent, Gabriella thought; a grenade dropped in that tangle would be a difficult thing to ignore.

But having been a soldier for less than a year, Iluminado hesitated.

"There will be casualties."

"True," she said, "but in this way, perhaps not including you or me."

"No, here is a better idea."

He armed the grenade, counted from one to six—much too slowly, in Gabriella's opinion—and leaning far out, lobbed it across the face of the building.

And a very pretty thing happened.

A sudden bang, a fireball, and the enormous sign, BOLIVAR, winked out in a rush of neon, leaving only a blackened armature and a few hanks of wire. Below, pelted with bits of glass and grenade fragments, cars went out of control. One long Detroit sedan climbed the curb and attempted to get into the casino through the revolving door. People were running and screaming.

Gabriella hugged her young man from behind. "What did I do to deserve—"

The clocks continued to run, but she was no longer trying to hurry him. It was clear who commanded the troops in this bedroom.

He was making a selection of weapons.

"CS," he announced, "to bring tears to their eyes. How lucky that I had the class to prepare for tomorrow. Plastic explosive. A cattle prod."

28

He swept it all into a shopping bag.

"And masks? Yes, definitely masks. You also, Gabriella."

They were ready in a moment. Peering out through the goggles, she beheld a terrifying figure, wand in one hand, grenade in the other. The pistol holster rode low on his hip. Smoke already seemed to be rising around him. Her little fox was snapping at her insides. If he made love to her in that costume—

She pulled him against her and their mouthpieces clashed.

She threw the door open at his signal and he bowled the grenade. Their adversary, the evil García, darted forward to send it back. He fielded it cleanly, on a short hop, but the throw had been perfectly timed. It went off in his hand.

The one thing Major Chester Sadowski didn't like about this Colombian deal was the fact that so many Colombians pretend they don't understand English. Whenever Sadowski felt called upon to give a soldier a piece of professional advice, he liked to stand toe to toe with the man, and watch the words take effect. He didn't entirely trust his interpreter, a four-eyed Colombian youth with long hair and *much* too long fingernails. The boy's name was Angel, and in Sadowski's opinion, he was deliberately letting those fingernails grow, to show his contempt for American values.

The major had all the usual gambling superstitions including one that had already caused him to lose a good bit of money: that it is possible to outfox a twenty-one dealer by counting the pictures and tens as they fall from the deck. Unfortunately (unfortunately for Sadowski, fortunately for the casino), he believed in hard soldiering during the day and hard R and R at night. After his fourth or fifth frosted daiquiri, which were furnished free to high rollers like himself, the ten-count had a tendency to disappear in the refrigerated fog rolling down from the air conditioning.

Another subtle distraction: as in most stateside casinos, the girl dealers wore damned little except eye makeup north of the navel. The previous night, leaning far forward to give him a provocative glimpse of pink areolae, the bitch had busted him with what had to be the fifth queen in that deck. Was something subtly anti-American going on here?

Tonight a Japanese tour was in, so they had some authentic customers for a change. Sadowski's own current baby-doll, Consuela, stood close behind him, one warm hand on his shoulder, to show the foreign competition that this exciting hunk (who in addition to being all-male, as they could see, was paid every month in dollars) was already spoken for. To madden his little interpreter—Consuela and Angel had been bedmates before the arrival of the American mission—Sadowski slipped his arm around her waist and gave one of the ripe melons there a lingering squeeze. She boogied a bit, to show that she liked it. Angel, shilling in third base, one seat away, was liking it considerably less.

"Shape up, trim an inch and a half off those fingernails," Sadowski wanted to tell him, but he'd be wasting his breath.

"Hit me," he told the dealer, who was standing there popping her nipples. "Lightly."

She flipped him a card, for a fourteen total. While he was running numbers, one of the saucily-dressed cocktail chicks handed him a cordless courtesy phone.

Sadowski couldn't hear because a mob in the craps pit was trying to influence the tumble of the dice with prayers and Japanese imprecations.

"Who?"

Some practical joker was claiming to be Captain Castillo, one of the few officers in this drag-ass outfit who gave any impression of understanding what Sadowski was trying to get across. Sadowski knew for a fact that the captain had gone up to his room, like the fine young officer he was, to master the study materials for a class on internal suppression options.

Key transfer points in Sadowski's cognitive system had been frosted over by too many daiquiris. Something about lottery tickets, something about rotten eggs. All at once a thunderclap came out of the phone and nearly tore off the top of his skull. He started back and looked at the phone in horror.

The dealer was waiting.

"Hit me," he said without thinking, and to nobody's surprise including Sadowski's, she snapped off the queen of spades, the exact same lady she had murdered him with the night before. How could he be expected to concentrate when people—

The building rocked, as though struck by a meteorite or runaway airplane. Sadowski could feel Consuela's gluteal muscles tighten under his hand. Stacks of chips sprayed out across the green felt.

His soldier's blood surged upward, melting the frozen connections, and he heard what Castillo had been attempting to tell him. The lottery ticket salesmen! Yeah! The Commie rats who had tried to bankrupt the casino by fixing the slot machines so every play was a jackpot.

"A rocket," he remarked, with authority.

"Sir?" his interpreter said, doubting him.

"Seven point two. Incoming."

As a matter of record, although he had been a marine for more than three decades, Major Sadowski had never come under hostile fire. During Vietnam, when the reputations were made, the Corps had decided that he could best serve his country at a recruiting desk. Because he *looked* so much like a marine—the sucked-in gut, the beer-keg torso and tiny pig eyes, the short nails and the haircut, the bellicose squint.

But he had known that the good Lord wouldn't let that expensively acquired know-how go to waste. He heard a patter of falling glass and felt the familiar blood-pressure warning. What the mothers had done, they had blown the sign! And that made him *mad*, because whenever he turned onto the avenue and saw those huge letters, of an incandescence no other nation has yet been able to achieve, his eyes filled, he felt a prickling in his nasal membranes, and he was so proud to be an American.

Tires screamed, and the building took another hit from some large object or large-caliber weapon. Sadowski swept up his chips, including those he had just lost to the spade queen, and bellowed, "Weapons platoon! Form on me!"

Most of his fellow gamblers, in spite of their distinctly unmilitary appearance, were actually soldiers, but he couldn't seem to get anybody to meet his eye. What these guys needed was a little American leadership in the shape of a good kick in the ass.

He had left his sidearm upstairs. He bulldozed his way to the nearest security guard.

"Loan me your weapon."

The man looked back at him suspiciously from the far side of the language barrier. Losing his patience quickly, Sadowski nailed him with a right hand and picked his .38 out of its holster. His men still wouldn't look at him. To get their attention he fired into the chandelier, and the crowd spooked for the doorway.

His interpreter, little Angel, was trying to sneak past. The first commandment in Military Assistance is never to lay a finger on a soldier of the host country, but fuck that, emergency procedures were now in effect. He clamped a come-along on the Colombian's elbow.

"Tell these assholes to stop behaving like assholes and start behaving like soldiers."

And to his astonishment, the little shit-sack tried to bite him. His face distorted by some kind of perverse Latin emotion, he actually clicked his teeth a quarter inch from Sadowski's windpipe. Disgusted, Sadowski let him go and clambered onto a craps table.

"Juan! Andrés! Leopoldo!"

He felt tears start to his eyes, not, this time, sentimental ones. Sweet Jesus, if the bastards had tear gas— Somehow, knowing only the most primitive bedroom Spanish, he had to make his men understand that unless they could lay down some kind of suppressive fire, they would be slaughtered like beef cattle. Something exploded in the depths of the building. Had the attacking force fought its way into the below-ground garage? Machine guns were talking from all four directions, and these were M-60s, unquestionably, a weapon Sadowski knew and respected. He understood all at once, really for the first time ever, that the purpose of fifty-caliber bullets, their single purpose and justification, is to kill people.

An elderly Jap—armed only with cameras, however—came

to attention and asked if an ex-kamikaze pilot could make himself useful. Sadowski shouted, though he had never liked gooks of any description, "The more the merrier!"

The street entrance to the lobby proved to be blocked by an automobile. Sadowski's trained mind made the necessary jump. The main assault elements would come through the parking lot.

He directed the Japanese to start building a breastwork of slot machines.

Jack Grimes, the second Military Assistance major, was on his usual perch, a stool in the ground-floor lounge, in his usual excellent humor. He was very short, as they say—he owed his country just thirteen more days, and he meant to spend them right here, among people he knew and trusted.

He was flanked by two in-house hookers who were hoping to entice him upstairs. They kept jabbing fingers at his eyes, trying to make him blink, but Grimes was able to turn off that reflex at will. For five years, until the psychiatrists sensed that he was losing his motivation, he had flown nuclear standby out of Omaha. Riding around on top of all those multiple warheads, you learn to do nothing impulsive.

An explosion rattled the bottles on the back bar. It would take louder noises than that to rattle Jack Grimes. Presently the lights dimmed and he thought he heard jack-hammers. Strange. Sadowski would explain it at breakfast. Now there was a man who walked around with a question mark up his ass.

One of the girls—only a child, really—had her hand inside his shirt, to find out if he was ticklish. No, dear. He was an ex-nuke-jockey. Ticklish was something else he was not.

Jaime, the bartender, observed, "They're shooting in the casino, Major."

Over the long evenings, without saying much to each other, Grimes and Jaime had developed a kind of mutual regard. Grimes supposed he'd better go find out what was happening.

In the pit, shills, cocktail ladies, stickmen and pit bosses

33

were milling around like drunks in a burning nightclub. Red in the face, nearly purple, his truculent colleague Sadowski was up on a craps layout, stamping about in his jungle boots and waving a pistol. He gestured to Grimes to come join him. Grimes flinched, his first real flinch since the fall of Saigon, and faded backward.

The ominous clatter continued. Not jack-hammers, he realized. The casino management was pretty security-conscious, had to be, but Grimes hadn't known they had fifty-calibers. Well, they would have to do it without him.

Shooting was everywhere now. No direction seemed safe. Smoke poured from the air conditioning. He saw running figures, portly men in hard hats carrying submachines. He yanked open a door that was ordinarily kept locked. This led into the cage, the casino's heart. The cashier and count men, Americans, had locked up the cash and run to emergency stations.

Grimes turned off the lights and sat down to wait. The machine guns rattled on frantically, about to go into hysteria. Another big bang somewhere, followed by a siren.

And people said nothing ever happened in Cartagena.

Angel, Sadowski's interpreter, didn't see the major coming until it was too late.

"Gotcha!"

Together they began working the room. Whenever Sadowski cornered someone who looked vaguely familiar, he tightened his grip on the interpreter and told him to tell the chicken-balled bastard to stop shitting his drawers and stand tall, like a man. Perhaps it lost some of its edge in translation. Far from standing tall, they continued to skulk and sidle, and claim he was confusing them with somebody else, which of course was always a possibility. He found a group of seven or eight hiding in the men's room. Face it, they had signed up for rice and beans; they hadn't bargained for gunfire.

He was frantic to think that he still wasn't part of the fire fight that was developing outside. Seeing a group of uniformed figures near the keno lounge, he hauled Angel that way. The uniforms were Colombian—that is to say, they were United States Army, basically, but tarted up in various ways to gratify the Latin love of ostentation. Sadowski's adrenal glands spurted like fire hoses as he recognized Colonel Gonzalo Alvarez Blanco, *el caudillo*, the Man to See, definitely higher-higher. Instinct told him to salute, but his saluting hand was fully occupied holding the interpreter. Feeling the grasp on his elbow slacken, Angel made a new twist for freedom. And somehow—no way to explain it except that the queen of spades had brought him seven full minutes of bad luck—Sadowski's weapon discharged.

The odds were very good that the bullet would go into the floor. Or it could have shattered the keno board, or gut-shot one of the piled-up slot machines. Instead, under the influence of the baleful black queen, it threaded its way through the crowd and struck down this month's chairman of the Council of Ministers.

Of course there were people in the capital who wouldn't be too unhappy about this, Hernán Vega for one, who had recently stood Sadowski a bourbon at the Jockey Club and pressed him to accept his unlisted phone number. But it was also true that from Vega on down, if it became a case of saving their own skins, they wouldn't hesitate to lighten the balloon by throwing Sadowski to the polar bears. Major hoping to make lieutenant colonel—and you don't get points toward promotion by shooting one-third of a ruling junta—Sadowski decided not to wait around for the ballistic people to dig out the slug and start confiscating handguns. He sauntered away. For a man of his natural command presence, it was hard to look anonymous, especially with little Angel continuing to give trouble. But the mishap had dispelled what was left of the daiquiri fumes, and he began to think strategically instead of by the seat of his pants (the same spot, as it happened, where his wayward bullet had struck Colonel Alvarez Blanco).

The one time these peon retards had shown any gung-ho capability was when they uncrated the new M-16s. They did love to line up the sights and feel the oiled walnut against their cheeks. Up to now it had been all dry runs and nomenclature.

35

So all right! Live ammo, live targets. They would appreciate that.

When the garrison had moved into the hotel, the combined orderly and supply room took over one of the gift shops. It was locked for the night, and Sadowski had to shoot the door open, which got a little esprit going at last. The supply sergeant bustled in and began raising bureaucratic objections. With civil wars in every Central American country, an M-16 could be sold for $450 on the illegal market. He wanted to see orders from Captain Castillo, and every gun had to be signed for.

Sadowski gave him the Marine Corps response, a karate chop to the larynx.

He found himself in command of a fifteen-man force. It was the cream of the company, augmented by a small contingent of Japanese. They didn't have much of an army back home and they seemed to miss it. Sadowski bawled out an order and they came to lopsided attention. He was proud of these guys. They acted the civilian most of the time, *mañana, mañana,* go away, don't bother me, but deep down, all they had needed was someone to show them the way.

The real surprise was little Angel. He, too, wanted a rifle.

"No, Angie," Sadowski told him. "Your place is with me."

But Angel wanted to get in on the scrap, and he was so full of martial enthusiasm that Sadowski finally gave in. He got a real belt out of the loving way Four-Eyes handled that gun. It was nearly as tall as he was. One of the soldiers showed him how to take off the safety, and what to press to make bullets come out.

Each man drew a Claymore, for Sadowski had decided they should booby-trap the swimming pool apron, which the attackers would have to negotiate in order to enter the casino. He himself walked point. As the ragged formation approached the boutique arcade, it went by a huddle of women, cocktail chicks in the main, who were *so* relieved that the army had succeeded in pulling itself together. Consuela was among them, doing her wriggle as always. The look she gave Sadowski added inches to his upper-body statistics. Then she looked elsewhere in the column, smiling scornfully, and Sadowski recalled abruptly that she and Angel had once lived together. And Angel, through what Sadowski now saw may have been a tactical error, had been issued an M-16 and shown how to use it. Too late to do anything about it now.

According to Iluminado's manual, one WP-109 grenade will generate enough smoke to fill a fifteen-meter cube. He plunged into this cube, keeping close to one wall. He knew what to do, having attended a demonstration by Major Sadowski on silent kills with the knife. But García's clothes were on fire! He had dropped the dispatch case. Enveloped in smoke, screaming, he slapped at the flames with both hands.

And instead of killing him at once, as he had had every intention of doing, Iluminado snatched a fire extinguisher out of a wall bracket. Later he was ashamed of the impulse, for Gabriella had made it clear that this man was a Vega spy, part of a conspiracy to bring about her disgrace and her husband's downfall. If he lived, he would be able to testify that yes, indeed, Señora Alvarez had stood in the doorway, wearing only one earring, holding her high-heeled shoes in one hand. So Iluminado should have backed off and let him continue to burn.

No matter. Looming up through the smoke, grotesquely masked, Iluminado must have looked like an avenger from some distant, more righteous planet. Misunderstanding, the sergeant fled in terror, to throw himself through the window at the end of the corridor. He went down like a shooting star, and came to a melodramatic end at the edge of the swimming pool.

Behind them, they heard the click of a closing door. Through the thinning smoke, Gabriella and Iluminado looked at each other. They had locked themselves out.

She was all right, but Iluminado had been trying to remember too many things at the same time, and the lower half of his new uniform lay in tissue paper on the other side of the locked door.

Gabriella flew to the fire stairs, but García had locked it to make sure that his quarry was properly trapped.

The noises in Iluminado's head made thinking difficult. With a few crumbs of C-4 he could blow the door. But Gabriella was gesturing. The elevator, hurry, the downstairs garage. In their masks no one would know them, and there was a spare pair of warm-weather slacks at their apartment, just three blocks away.

But for any of this to happen, a car going down had to arrive at their floor before the car coming up, bringing her husband and his armed retainers.

They waited in a fever of impatience. With two little pings, both lights came on at once. Iluminado activated another smoke grenade and rolled it between the doors.

The Down car, first by a tick, already carried a passenger, one of the middle-level casino executives. Hosts, they were called, or pit bosses. They ate little except steak and baked potatoes with sour cream. They all carried too much weight and had a spicy odor from after-shave lotion. This one was wearing the usual uniform, a funeral director's black suit, dark blue tie with horseshoes, the whole thing topped off with a hard hat. He was holding an Uzi, the excellent Israeli submachine gun.

Two frightful masked creatures came in at him. One, a woman, squirted Mace in his eyes, the other took his weapon, made him remove his pants, and using a cattle prod, drove him out of the car.

He was supposed to be able to handle himself, that was part of the job description. He was so deeply ashamed about how easily he had been disarmed that he went back to his room for new pants and never spoke a word to anyone about the experience.

The elevator had been told to stop at the lobby, and they couldn't countermand that. The door opened on a turbulent scene. To add to the confusion, Iluminado rolled his tear gas grenade into the crowd. Reaching out, he slapped the lump of C-4 on the outside of the door before letting it close.

They dropped to the garage. He came out firing.

The valets were local youths with no reason to risk their skins defending somebody else's casino. They had left a half acre of unattended automobiles, all with keys in their ignitions. Iluminado advanced, firing short bursts with one hand, trying to hold up the overlarge pants with the other. Gabriella's own car, an Oldsmobile with government plates and flags on the front fenders, was wrong for people hoping not to be noticed. He motioned her into a Jaguar two-seater. If this car was as fast as it looked, it could outrun anything on the highway, and she could be home watching the evening news before her husband had sorted things out and started from Cartagena.

The family car while Iluminado was growing up had been a rust-eaten Fiat. Until he had an Uzi in his hands, he hadn't realized just how much he had always resented these big Fleet-woods and Imperials, the Ferraris and BMWs. He emptied the clip at random, shattering glass and leaving scribbled graffiti across the gleaming flanks and snouts. As the Jag roared up the ramp, he tossed his final M-67, fragmentation, over his shoulder. The blast assisted them to the street.

Gabriella peeled up her mask.

"Darling, you were like a symphony orchestra. Oh, I love you!"

He braked and swung. There would be time to trade compliments when they reached the big road.

"Now we must agree on a story—" she began.

Too late, he saw blinking lights. It was Eyewitness TV, rushing across town toward the Bolívar to get action coverage before the action was over. Only one lane was really open. Shapes hurtled toward him, all hard, some jagged.

"And I you," he remembered to answer before he lost consciousness.

Currently, the Bolívar's four sets of books—one for the Colombian tax collectors, one for the IRS, one for the dummy owners, one for the true owners—all showed a loss. Not to worry. As soon as the competitive situation could be clarified, the profits would come.

The people who were feeling the real pain were the resident managers, Joey Rizzo and Alvin Kraus. The owners—the true owners—considered them reasonably honest. But the gambling business, like every other, has its traditions, and nobody would be too upset if Rizzo and Kraus moistened their fingers with Elmer's before counting the paper money. Unfortunately, no win, no skim—an old Vegas saying. First you work off the nut.

The spic lottery ticket peddlers, whose business had largely been wiped out by the Bolívar's five-peso slots, didn't want to adjust. Some wild threats were flying around, "drive-you-into-the-sea" kind of thing. One look at those nerds and you knew they wouldn't drive anybody into the sea, but Rizzo and Kraus put their heads together and came up with a way the thing could be milked—milked for real money. Forwarded the most inflammatory leaflets, with English translations, to the people back home. Got the authorization. Everybody agreed that the local army detachments, even with the majors handing out that good American advice, wouldn't be a hell of a lot of help if the local soreheads ever made serious trouble. One oddity of the casino business is that no one who has been convicted of a gambling offense in the other forty-eight states can be given a license to gamble in Nevada or New Jersey, where that activity is not only legal but strongly encouraged. Drawing on this pool of seasoned professionals, Rizzo and Kraus recruited a fine group of middle executives. Great guys, totally loyal. Acquainted with guns. The Corps of Engineers, in a rut after all those dams, had put up a real solid dam of a building, without one ground-floor window. In the worst-case scenario, the garrison could button up in the pit till Air Assault got there. They had steaks in the freezer. A fifty-caliber machine gun was mounted in each of the third-floor corner suites, commanding all approaches. Ex-CIA men contributed the tactical concept and arranged for the purchase of the heavier weapons. Everything was ready.

The talk continued in town. That was all it was so far, talk, an occasional shaken fist as Rizzo or Kraus drove past in his big gringo car. Coincidentally, that same afternoon, the very afternoon that Gabriella was driving in to pay her surprise call on Iluminado, Rizzo and Kraus had been discussing getting things rolling by blowing up a small truckload of dynamite in the parking garage, one idea, or how about giving the shills some real Scotch for a change instead of iced tea, see what that led to? And then some helpful person came along and blew up the sign.

Within minutes, all the floodlights were on. The machine gunners raced to their posts and ripped off a few bursts to clear their weapons and let the phantom attackers know that the odds, as always, favored the house.

Rizzo, after making sure that the sign had really been carried away, went looking for Kraus. Kraus, meanwhile, was looking for Rizzo. They met at the baccarat ladder. Thinking about money, they were untouched by the panic that was sweeping the gambling floor.

"Yeah, they took out the sign," Rizzo said.

"Bastards. PR-wise, you know just a nameplate might have been better."

"Going for the bankroll, I'd say," Rizzo said, keeping a straight face on the chance that someone was eavesdropping.

"Which you wouldn't want to get yourself killed over, would you, considering that the guys have got it insured."

"Why don't you pull the lights, Alvin, make it a little harder for them, and I'll get the switchboard."

They went different ways. In the lobby, people who might have just broken out of a mental hospital were piling up slot machines. Rizzo had no time to stop and point out their error. Didn't they realize those things were *delicate*? Fuck them up even slightly and you could never trust them again.

When the lights went off, he stepped into the phone room, moved the girl roughly aside and pulled the spaghetti out of her board. She was screaming, and in the sudden blackness, with the smell of terrible things in the air, she wasn't the only one.

Rizzo carried a breast-pocket flashlight, on the off-chance that something like this might happen. With its help, he picked his way to the cage.

Kraus was already there, and he had brought a prepared satchel containing a little vial of the real stuff, a percussion cap and a fuse, some empty bags to carry the cash. Any casino's bankroll fluctuates according to how well its customers have been doing, but here at the Bolívar, as a matter of policy, it was never permitted to fall very far below $1.2 million. Nothing will aggravate a customer more than to come off a hot streak and be told that the casino can't pay off till the banks open the next morning. At $600,000 apiece, Rizzo and Kraus would finally be getting some payback for all the hard work and headaches.

A sense that something was wrong made Rizzo swing his flashlight. They understood that there was someone else in the room.

"Don't mind me," Major Jack Grimes said from the couch.

Don't mind *him*! Unfortunately, that was no longer possible. He had heard enough to know that the casino's joint managers, who were, after all, crooks, were about to take advantage of the uproar to help themselves to $1.2 million of somebody else's money.

For the same reason that Rizzo carried a flashlight, Kraus carried a handgun. With all the fifties and M-16s banging away, with the shouts and the hissing flares and the sirens, no one, Kraus was sure, would remember hearing a quiet unobtrusive little pistol shot in the cage.

Four

Ana, the skinny cousin Gabriella had persuaded to chaperone her on her dangerous visit to the casino, brought bad news of what was happening in other parts of the hospital.

"That toad Vega—he's been in Gonzalo's room for the last twenty minutes. And you know what they're doing, Gabby, they're deciding your future. How do you think you can talk your way out of this? Iluminado in another man's pants, a much bigger man. When they lifted you out of the wreck everybody could see how little you were wearing under your dress. Why do I say little? You were wearing precisely nothing."

"Sometimes I don't, Gonzalo knows that, and he hates it. Tell me what people are saying."

"You don't want to hear."

But bad as it undoubtedly was, she had to know. And some crazy theories were running around. She wished it could wait till morning, for she could hardly raise her head from the pillow, but she couldn't risk it. Gonzalo had to be given a story he could believe, or at least pretend to believe. And her brain had completely stopped working. What plot were those two devising against her? She moaned faintly, the first time she had ever allowed anyone to hear her make such a sound. Why had she let the gorgeous young man attract her so fatally?

Luckily Ana carried a purse as well stocked as a pharmacy. She scrabbled around and brought out two purple pills, which she persuaded Gabriella to swallow.

Gabriella saw floodlights and orbited briefly. When she returned to earth she borrowed Ana's comb and eye makeup and prepared herself for what she knew would be a difficult encounter.

"If he tries to read me a lecture," she said grimly, "I'll bring up that slut on Saint Catherine's Street, see how he likes that."

The guard outside Gonzalo's door, who must have been listening to the gossip, shuffled uneasily before letting her in.

Vega had gone. Gonzalo, lying on one side in a nest of pillows, showed her a baleful eye.

"Don't talk to me, whore."

"*What!*" she exclaimed. "Do you understand what you're saying?"

She made sure the door was securely latched and advanced on the bed, as high as a 747 thanks to the purple pills. Gonzalo was as pale as the sheet, poor donkey, and in the demeaning hospital garment entirely lacking in dignity.

"Whore," she repeated more quietly. "I'll ask you to explain that in a minute. Is there much pain?" she thought it would be diplomatic to ask.

"Spare me your crocodile sympathy."

She moved a chair. "Perhaps you should tell me first just what you're doing in Cartagena."

"I thought I would drop in unannounced and catch you in bed with your paramour."

"Boyfriend, we call them now."

"Boyfriend, exactly. A boy half your age."

"I see," she said, perhaps overdoing the reaction a little, "you're talking about young Iluminado. Because we were in the collision together?"

"Well?" he demanded.

"Gonzalo, you're talking nonsense. I have neither a boyfriend nor a paramour. Look at my engagement calendar, where would I fit it in? As for Iluminado himself, you know I think he's a personable young man, you've heard me say that more than once. I could name you a half dozen ladies, and good friends of mine too, who would be delighted to take him into their bed on a moment's notice. I think we were right to sponsor him. We owe it to that generation. But as for any romance between us, don't you see how absurd that is?"

This was hard to say (because yes, it *was* a little absurd) but she said it with total sincerity. He would have to believe it, she thought, after letting it marinate for an hour or so.

"Now I shall tell you something else," she said, "about the nature of your wound or rather the location. Ana says people are smirking. Stop gritting your teeth, you know what the dentist told you. It may not be as bad as it seems."

But they both knew it was bad. In a macho country, a chief of state must expect to be shot at occasionally. If the bullet kills him, bad luck, but he will take his place alongside some of the most famous rulers in history. But to be shot in the fleshy bottom in a sordid crossfire between two groups of gamblers— that hurt. It not only hurt physically, politically it was a disaster.

"Now I must know," Gabriella said. "How were you maneuvered into being in that exact spot at that exact moment?"

"It was suggested to me—"

"By Vega."

"By Vega, yes. Oh, he gave me a pretext of sorts but it was obvious that he knew you were meeting this boy for one farewell cuddle—"

She interrupted. "Darling, Hernán Vega himself is the source of these rumors, don't you realize that? Yes, he had information, but not about Iluminado and me. He knew that guerrillas had scheduled an attack on the casino."

"Guerrillas?" he said hopefully after a moment. "Everybody is telling me it was some little thing with the lottery ticket people."

"Bombs and machine guns? A can of spray paint is more their style. Who do you think shot you?"

45

"One of our own, I fear. They are mostly recruits and this was their first experience with live ammunition."

"Listen to a theory of mine before you implicate innocent people. That slimy Luis García, from the good old days in the mountains, was he with you?"

"Not at my elbow. Mingling with the crowd, watching for anything unusual."

"You didn't choose to believe me when I told you I was certain he was a creature of Vega. Very well. Probably you haven't heard. Somebody set him on fire and threw him out of a high-up window. Isn't that often the fate of a hired assassin, to prevent him from talking?"

Gonzalo had gone, if possible, a shade more pale. "Are you serious? You think García shot me?"

"I think it's quite possible. On orders from at least one of your colleagues, possibly both. And in the confusion someone jostled his arm. Or perhaps they have even more subtlety than I give them credit for, and his orders were not to kill you but to make you a laughingstock by shooting you where in fact you were actually shot."

Unpleasant reflections were churning about in his head. "How can you say with such confidence that it was an attack by guerrillas? I understand no prisoners were taken."

"Now lie back, my dear." (For the hard part was coming.) "Try not to grind your teeth. This will take more than a moment."

She drew a deep breath and offered up a hurried prayer to Our Lady, who had a special compassion, Gabriella believed, for erring members of her own sex.

"I had a phone message. It wasn't a voice I recognized. That your plans had changed and I should meet you at the Bolívar. Ana had never seen the casino so I took her along. And I had a gift for our protégé. I told you about it, I think—a new uniform, so he would make a better impression in Washington. They already think we're a second-rate country, and why make it worse? As we drove into the casino garage an appalling thing happened. We were blocked by a car. Three young men came at us. I don't even remember if they were carrying guns, I was so frightened."

At least she had his attention. She hastened on.

"Ana they didn't bother about. They made me get into the back. They were quite polite, I should say, but with that dangerous politeness, do you know, and I kept my head down as they told me. It was a short trip, only a few blocks. When we stopped they put a garbage bag over my head and hustled me into a building, up in an elevator, into an apartment where they took off the bag. Ordinary bourgeois furniture, a South of France poster. Other people were there, a striking young woman, an older man, powerfully built, with a cigar."

She thought for a moment. "I had the feeling, somehow, that he might be a Cuban. They made me scribble a note to Iluminado, I suppose to get him out of the way before the attack. The woman went off with the note and they put me in a closet."

"How horrible for you." But she could see that he didn't believe her yet.

"I screamed and I screamed. I must still sound a bit hoarse. Nobody paid the slightest attention. I heard people coming and going. Then far-off explosions, shooting. I was frantic."

She helped herself to water from his bedside carafe.

"All of a sudden, the noise of furniture falling over! Pistol shots, commands. The door of the closet flew open and there stood Iluminado! Looking like the god of warfare, knife in one hand, pistol in the other, unconscious bodies strewn about the room. He had to half-carry me to the elevator, down to the street. And there, outside a café, like a fairy tale, with its wheels on the sidewalk, a car, ready to go. He drove like a madman, wanting to get to his precious casino and find out what was happening. But somebody else was in an equal hurry, going in the opposite direction."

Caught up in her story—fairy tale was the word for it—Gonzalo had forgotten his wound. He shifted position. The pain brought him back to uncomfortable reality.

"Why was he wearing another man's pants?"

She had hoped he hadn't been told. "What are you saying?"

47

"The TV reporter, the cameraman saw it. Slacks, not the usual uniform of a Colombian officer, many sizes too big."

"Ah! An explanation at last of the names you are calling me. Don't I detect Hernán Vega in this, yet again? I suppose I should thank you for not mentioning that I was wearing no underwear, which happens to be impossible in that particular dress. Yes, I noticed those pants."

She sent up another quick supplication; she would need some heavy assistance with this.

"I don't intend to ask him, knowing how prickly he is. But he was one against four, and it was clear to me that those people were serious fighters. How did he prevail? By subterfuge, I expect. I think what happened, it was the woman who was guarding him in the bedroom, and he must have persuaded her, or perhaps it was the other way round, that they should make love while they waited. When they were partially undressed he managed to get her weapon and lock her into the room. Confusion. No pants. What had happened to the key? Have to hurry. Yes, I think I remember that the commander was wearing black slacks. A much bigger man than Iluminado, certainly. When we tell people about it, why don't we omit this whole angle? For to be practical, darling! Put these suspicions of yours to one side for the moment. Hernán Vega, I'm quite sure, has left word that you are not to be bothered by reporters. By morning, unless we do something to counteract his distortions, you'll be the subject of crude jokes from one end of the country to the other."

"I fear so," he said heavily. "But I know that gleam in your eye. You have a suggestion to offer."

Indeed she did, and she no longer needed help from the sky.

"A news conference in one hour's time. We must get you a pain-killer so you can sit up normally, wearing your uniform. A little blush for your cheeks—"

"No makeup!"

"A touch merely, no one will notice. And we'll have to embellish the truth slightly, darling. Something like this. During the violent years you came to know the guerrilla mentality. You had an instinctive feeling, flying up yesterday evening, that something was about to explode in Cartagena. Your minister of public safety, usually so good at these things, somehow missed it completely. Not that you lacked confidence in the garrison commander but he has had no combat experience. You diverted your flight to take charge of the defenses yourself. Your men fought with inspiring courage et cetera and the attack was repulsed. There is no way to know for certain, but to you the operation had the earmarks of the old Fifth of May grouping. Casualties still being tabulated. One member of your security detail tragically killed, for example, you yourself grazed by a ricochet. Then my kidnapping and rescue. They'll want to talk to Iluminado, but to be frank, my dear, between the two of us, though that exploit of his was truly extraordinary, it was merely the sideshow. Let's keep the spotlight where it belongs. I'll see to it that Iluminado stays on the critical list. Happily, he leaves for Washington in the morning."

"He wants not to go."

"Oh, does he!" she said scornfully. "Then I'll say plainly, who cares what he wants? We've done quite enough for this son of your old friend."

She watched him compare possible headlines, one if he followed his wife's advice, the other if Hernán Vega remained in control of the story. Yes, it was beginning to seem obvious, in retrospect, that he had, in fact, been wounded by guerrillas.

"I hate these reporters," he said. "They're always so disrespectful. Couldn't I just issue a statement?"

"No, they must see with their own eyes that you aren't seriously hurt. I'll have a doctor standing by to cut off the questions whenever I give the signal."

So it was settled. She ran off to wake up Gonzalo's dresser and press secretary. The corridors were empty and quiet. The gunshot wounds had been treated, the tear gas victims had been sent home, the dead, including a sprinkling of unlucky civilians, were making no trouble.

Gabriella's story had been excellent as far as it went, considering that she had been making it up as she went along, but she needed some evidence to back it up.

An old Indian woman was mopping the emergency room. Gabriella gave her a pleasant good evening and picked a liter bottle off the IV rack.

"Needed in surgery."

Needed in surgery! The surgeons had sent a lady in high heels and diamonds down to pick up blood for the operating room? But even stranger things had happened tonight, and without changing expression the cleaning woman came back onto the wet floor to wipe out Gabriella's departing footprints.

Ana, in the room where she had been told to wait, was twittering with excitement.

"Tell me at once. Did he believe you?"

"Perhaps not entirely. Ana, you have to help me. I'd do it myself but there's too much to take care of here. Do you know the apartments called the Tuscany?"

"Everybody knows the Tuscany. Studios and single bedrooms, very expensive."

Gabriella fished out two keys on a gold chain. "It's 8-D. Everything has to be cleaned out, Ana, I mean every last thing down to toothbrushes. If *one object* belonging to me is found there, the best I can hope for is a very nasty divorce."

She tore a page out of a notebook and scrawled: "Iluminado, I need you, come at once.—Gabriella A."

She crumpled the sheet. "Drop this in a wastebasket. Then break things, turn over furniture. Here."

She held out the bottle. Ana put her hands behind her.

"It's nothing to be scared of," Gabriella said, "just blood."

"Did I hear you correctly? Just blood! If I prick a finger I faint."

"Do this for me and you can have my little gray Porsche, and that's on top of the bracelet I already promised you."

Ana said reluctantly, "I suppose if I close my eyes and pretend it's a Pepsi—"

"Splash it around where they'll be sure to see it. Then I want you to get seven or eight good Cuban cigars. Let them burn down and put them out in the ashtrays. One other thing. That cartoonist you brought to my cocktail party. Does he still subscribe to the Havana Communist Newspaper? If he does, borrow the latest copy, wrap a steak in it and leave it in the kitchen."

"A steak?"

"Or some fish, it doesn't matter. There's no time to explain. Now you must hurry."

Five

*O*nce upon a time the U.S. Joint Chiefs of Staff included some pretty frightening characters. All through their slow rise they had to watch themselves carefully, and now, all at once, there was no one to speak of above them, merely the commander in chief, a civilian. They could let their eccentricities out of the cage. They could come to work naked if they felt like it!

It was a bellicose group, by definition. The original function of the JCS system was to provide an arena where the service heads could mix it up privately without being evaluated and second-guessed by the press. Most of the time the warfare was verbal, but on at least two famous occasions real blows were exchanged. In the early sixties, during a disorderly debate about the future of naval aviation, the Air Force man punched the Navy man and knocked out a tooth, and then refused to apologize. After an interminable series of hearings and counter-charges, he was made to resign, but he is still one of the great Air Force heroes.

That is all in the past. These days the hard chargers, the brainiest and most aggressive competitors, try hard to stay off the Chiefs. Career goals have changed. Few corporations are willing to consider an ex-chief or ex-defense sec. for jobs that pay the really top money. They have been too visible. They may have become identified with doctrines that have gone out of fashion. Whenever they appoint somebody they make an enemy of everybody who wanted the job and didn't get it. For obvious reasons, procurement companies want to be liked by *everybody*. So when they headhunt in the Pentagon, which they do constantly, they look two or three levels below the apex, where the power and popularity curves intersect.

And that may explain why in recent years the Chiefs have seemed, somehow, so humdrum. Only real groupies can remember their names or recognize their faces. They no longer have nicknames—no more "Bulls" or "Haps" or "Chestys." Look at the annual group portrait—they don't even photograph well.

Because of the small-mesh selection process, each new generation of Chiefs tends to look somewhat alike. They are approximately the same age—three years apart at the most. They have been eating the same kind of food and taking the same amount of exercise. Consider the tens of thousands of unreadable reports they have had to read over the years and it is no wonder that four-fifths wear glasses. Naturally they are all white, with forebears from the same rather small part of the world now known as NATO.

Like firemen, like nursing mothers, they are on twenty-four-hour call, for there isn't a time zone in the world without a U.S. occupying force or naval flotilla. The night of the Cartagena disturbances, the officer at the crisis consoles was a neat young colonel named Peter Wheat. As the decoder spat out the bulletins, Wheat's face became even more grave and thoughtful. The computers surrounding him gave off a soft continuous hum, to show they were on line and ready for questions, but this was that rare decision that had to be made by the circuitry inside one human brain.

How did an attack on a distant gambling casino impact on U.S. interests—more specifically, on the voting patterns in the United States Senate? The tie-in was there, but Wheat didn't want to be accused of jumping to a too-fast conclusion. He

53

thought hard for more than a moment. All right. Bring them in an hour and a half early, he decided, so if they wanted to break it big they could get top play on the seven o'clock news.

He pressed a button and the below-ground emergency rooms came alive.

McArdle—General Dennis McArdle of the Army, this year's chairman—was a hard man to rouse, so Wheat made that call himself, staying on the phone until he was convinced that the general was actually out of bed and unbuttoning his pajamas. He lived in a far suburb to be near the golf course, and he was the last to arrive. Fully dressed but still far from fully awake, he lowered his face into the fumes rising from a cup of coffee as Wheat stepped to the briefing easel.

A West Pointer, a recent honors graduate of the Crisis Containment school at Fort Leavenworth, Wheat was considered one of the most brilliant briefers of the post-Vietnam era. Few people gave briefings willingly, so this wasn't a skill that made him unpopular. He worked to a nearly Homeric beat, clicking off points as though doing sums on an abacus. He was specially careful this morning, knowing that every officer in the room, down to the captains who had been brought along to carry the dispatch cases, kept a CYOA diary. CYOA—Cover Your Own Ass. And that was what Wheat himself was doing, for he was planning an early move to Hawk-Sisley, the grab-bag multinational. If there were repercussions from this, he didn't want his name to be mentioned, or even remembered. He was merely the duty officer, what's his name, who unscrambled the TWXs and conducted the briefing.

Each chief had his own keyboard and video display. Lights flashed continually, like fireflies looking for a sexual outlet. Ten or a dozen staff people—all males, which probably goes without saying—occupied a wedge-shaped section of amphitheater behind him. This early in the morning, it was hard to stay alert because of the vibration from the banks of computers, gossiping happily with their counterparts in far corners of the globe. From time to time discreet buzzers were heard, little high-tech gurgles and clicks. Dozens of hanging terminals had been added since the first installations. The messages flickered in a murky green glow, as though they had come a long way through water. It was all very expensive and marvelous, a command-control-communications system like nothing on earth, but its true purpose, some people believed, was psychological, to convince the chiefs that in spite of the discouraging news that sometimes arrived from the battle zones, in the long run *they couldn't possibly lose.*

Wheat was working in front of the big electronic map. Desperately needed for years, it had finally been funded and built, and now they couldn't imagine how they had managed without it. It was programmed this morning for fifteen degrees of latitude, showing most of Colombia, a small slice of Venezuela, three-quarters of Panama. Towns, countries, whole regions had a mysterious ability to change color to coincide with the changing political views of their populations. Oil workers were striking in Maracaibo. That part of the map, usually a neutral beige, had reddened as though with shame and embarrassment. As for Cartagena, where an American-owned casino had been overrun and looted by left-wing guerrillas, it was *livid,* a dangerous inflammation on the Caribbean coast, with nothing but open water between itself and New Orleans.

"General McArdle," Wheat said, "a question?"

"Give me the size of that strike force again."

"Between seventy-five and one hundred, sir, a small-unit action. But there has been no intelligence—I repeat, no intelligence of any kind—to lead us to anticipate any insurgency in the area. It opens a new zone of hostilities, at a high level of combat sophistication. Complete tactical surprise."

"Casualties?"

Wheat consulted the printout. "Six killed, sir, including both American advisers, unhappily. Eight wounded, eleven MIA."

The Air Force chief, General Tom Thorkill, asked to be recognized.

"I'll remind you, gentlemen, that we've been led down the garden path a time or two, intelligence-wise, in that part of the world—"

The CIA liaison, on the other side of the horseshoe, was given a meaningful look. Because of the extreme bushiness of

Thorkill's eyebrows, his looks were often more meaningful than other people's.

"Not looking to scratch any old itches," he continued, "but how much of this can we really believe? Playing devil's advocate now. What if we aren't talking guerrillas, Wheat, but run-of-the-mill thieves? A caper, to use the language of the street. A cool one point two million is quite a payday."

"Can we take it that figure's authentic?" McArdle wanted to know. "Because sometimes your robbery victim is going to exaggerate, to stick the insurance company."

Wheat looked at the CIA man, who responded quietly, "That wouldn't be a good idea in this case, General. Casinos don't insure with ordinary carriers, they lay off with fellow professionals. Bang, bang," he explained further.

Thorkill was in no hurry to let go of the idea. "Still playing devil's advocate, we don't want to fall into one of those credibility gaps, do we, where we tell it one way and the client comes out with a totally different version, which has happened too often. Didn't I read that Colombia just had a changeover? The new government's going to look pretty stupid if they're getting guerrillas already. Given a choice, wouldn't they opt for the caper?"

Wheat punched in Insurgency Suppression Command. The curt reply appeared simultaneously on all the screens.

"Negative."

Wheat elaborated. "The senior man in the new junta took a wound in the action. Shot in the left buttock, to be specific."

Smiles appeared.

"Exactly. Medically it makes no difference whether the wound was incurred during a firefight with guerrillas or"—he forced himself to use Thorkill's distasteful expression—" a caper. Politically, the difference is enormous."

Thorkill was nodding. "Point is well taken. I withdraw the objection."

Thorkill's console was blinking. The instrumentation was designed so he could take the call without interrupting the briefing. Nevertheless, Wheat waited, for he wanted them all to hear this.

"Awards and Citations need more detail on the Air Force major," Thorkill said. "Combat situation, unusual circumstances, so forth."

Wheat glanced at his notes. "Major Jack Grimes. Twenty-five years' service, less thirteen days. Seventy B-52 missions, Silver Star, DFC with cluster. Judged correctly that the raiders were after the money. Found in the casino count-room with empty thirty-eight in his hand. Posthumous Legion of Merit might be in order."

"Why not the Congressional?" Thorkill wanted to know. "Fact of the matter is, I believe it's our turn."

"No eyewitnesses, General. With Major Sadowski we have a very good statement from his interpreter, who was only a few feet away when it happened. Shot during hand-to-hand combat in the underground garage. Killed three."

General McArdle: "Twenty minutes from first shot to last. Took their dead and wounded with them. What it puts me in mind of—"

He didn't have to finish. The nation at large might have forgotten the Vietcong, but not these men. Those were the formative years.

Admiral Ira Brown—or was his name Green, even Wheat had trouble recalling—was busy at his console. Wheat hoped that some bright bulb in the back rows was beginning to wonder why it had been necessary to fall the Chiefs out at this early hour to be told about a small-scale guerrilla action in a, let's face it, fairly unimportant part of the world.

"Wheat, where are these fellows based?"

Finally.

"Can't give you an answer to that, sir. The chance of an operation of this size being mounted locally is considered to carry a very low order of probability. Possible foci"—he went to the flash intelligence summary—"Cordillera Oriental, Corrales-Sagamosa sector, Department Chocó between Atrato River and Golfe de Urabá—"

As he mentioned each location, a new source of shame flared on the map.

"Considering the level of defensive fire," he continued, "enemy casualties were undoubtedly heavy. Eighty-seven M-16 rifles are reported missing, twenty thousand rounds of ammo. The C-3 transport estimate is a minimum of fourteen vehicles. Checkpoints on roads leading east and south out of Cartagena were alerted within minutes. Here. Here. No reports of unusual traffic. A thirty-helicopter sweep from Barranquilla airport, on a fifty-kilometer arc, from here to here. Negative. Every vessel in the fishing fleet has been boarded and searched. Negative."

He was flourishing his ivory-tipped swagger like a baton, using Leavenworth technique. As he canceled out each source of possible contamination, that spot returned to beige. Finally only one remained, in the Darien Gap on the northwest frontier.

"You know that's not too far from the Zone," General McArdle observed.

So the first mention of the Panama Canal, in a symbolic sense the U.S.A.'s southernmost border, was made not by Colonel Peter Wheat, who wanted to survive unremarked until he could change into a three-piece suit and go to his reward in the private sector, but (somewhat inadvertently) by the chairman himself. All eyes were fixed on the map. The infection at the base of the Isthmus continued to burn, to burn, in an area hostile to wheeled vehicles, under an impenetrable canopy. The boonies! Is this America's destiny, then, always to fight with people who won't stay out in the open but run off and hide in the jungle?

"Can you tell us something about the political coloration of these people?" McArdle asked. "Just how anti-American are they?"

Wheat touched a button and a woman's face flashed onto the screens. She looked a little like the actress Liza Minelli in her very best years, not beautiful exactly, but stylish as hell and clearly intelligent.

"Señora Alvarez Blanco, wife of the top colonel. She was abducted and taken to an apartment which was apparently a combination safe house and CP. She managed to escape with the help of the garrison commander. And speaking of capers, General Thorkill—"

Another push on the button, and the woman was replaced by a dark youth in a hospital bed, heavily bandaged. His eyes blazed at the camera, warning the photographer not to do that again.

The chiefs smiled as Wheat recounted the story. This wasn't ordinary briefing material, but he had known they would like it. In this day of computerized warfare, it was nice to hear that such soldierly feats were still possible, somewhere in the world.

"You'll find a transcript of Señora Alvarez's statement in the salmon folder. Pertinent passages are underlined. The guerrilla commander was an older man who drank tea out of a glass and smoked Havana cigars. When the apartment was searched later, one of the things that turned up, the smoking pistol, if you will, was a bloodstained copy of *Granma*."

Copy of what? They didn't get it.

"*Granma*," Wheat said. "The official Cuban Communist newspaper."

An emotional barometer, planted among the state-of-the-art electronic devices, would have registered an immediate swing in the direction of euphoria. The commander in chief, a notorious smiler, was looking down from one wall, and the smile now seemed at least semi-sincere. The Pentagon's number one problem has always been the reluctance of congressmen to project their imaginations into the future. The lead time between the authorization and deployment of a new weapons system is now approximately nine years. If you have any concern for your nation's security, you can't settle for defenses that are adequate *today*. You have to be ready to counter all the murderous ideas the enemy will have come up with during the next decade. How can you even be sure who the enemy will *be* when the new systems are ready? That Chinese submarine that used to be sighted off San Diego each year just before the Pentagon sent up the budget—where has it gone?

The Angolans, Qadaffi, the Pathet Lao, the Ayatollah Khomeini, fanatical Islam—none of them ever really caught on as a credible menace. The Russians, of course, are always with us, but you have to be a little careful with them because of those warheads. So what does that leave? Nicaragua, Cuba, Grenada—no, we can scratch Grenada. Little countries, but don't forget that you don't need expensive equipment to deliver a modern nuke. The small version can be carried in a knapsack by one man . And if a hundred-man force, within walking distance of the Canal, was officered by a man who drank tea in the Russian manner, out of a glass, and read a Havana newspaper—

General McArdle, the only Catholic among the Chiefs, sketched a design in the air, possibly a cross. After a long stretch of what could only be called benign neglect, the Almighty seemed to be taking an interest in United States foreign policy at last.

Six

In the great casino sign—BOLIVAR without the accent, for accents are difficult to do in neon—innumerable flecks of silver had darted about incessantly amid the purple, like fish in wine. When Iluminado's grenade gave the trapped gas its freedom, these silver fish had rushed together to form the eye of the fireball. Some hours later, awakening in a hospital bed, he saw it again, but now it was a photographer's flashbulb. The man ducked out when Iluminado threw the telephone at him.

Now what had he done, he wondered, to deserve a photographer's attention? And suddenly the evening's events came flooding back, to set off a new explosion. Gabriella's unexpected visit, the fancied attack by lottery ticket salesmen, the constabulary sergeant's terror as Iluminado came at him through the smoke, the borrowed Jaguar, the collision. He groaned heavily. They had been in too great a hurry for seat belts. Various parts of his body had encountered various parts of the Jag's interior. Some of the pains he was feeling were familiar from his motorcycle wipeouts. He did a rapid checklist: right leg, left leg, right arm, left arm. They had put him into a head bandage. His ribs were sore and he was afraid one finger was broken.

Time passed, and he managed to press a button. Almost at once—in his other hospital experiences there had always been a long wait before someone came—he heard hurrying footsteps. A young nurse burst in, her hands clasped at her breast.

"Captain, thank heavens you're conscious. How ironic, an ordinary car crash after all your adventures—"

"The señora?"

"God's mercy, barely a scratch."

"Can I see her?"

"Not now, the doctor has ordered no visitors. That miserable photographer sneaked past somehow but they bloodied his nose for him and put him in handcuffs, I'm happy to say."

"Soldiers did that?"

"Riot police from Barranquilla."

"What name are you called?"

"Rosa."

"I had a pistol in the car, Rosa. Would you get it for me, please?"

She took a step backward, looking frightened. "Why do you want a pistol? The police and soldiers are everywhere."

"I need it to sleep."

She hesitated. "I'm the same way, I have to have my soft bear."

She whisked off, and returned presently with the Colt wrapped in a hand towel. He instructed her to crank him up and swing the bed so it faced the door. Then she had a surprising request, she wanted his autograph.

He was too weak to puzzle it out. He had known the great sign was disliked, even hated, but how did she know it was Iluminado who tossed the grenade?

"You were so—" she whispered after he signed. "So—"

Her lips came down, to give him a cool lingering kiss.

"You were just so—"

He wondered about it after she left, but thinking was becoming more difficult. Well, they had come close, Gabriella and he, and if it hadn't been for the untimely meeting with the television van— If, if. If he hadn't accepted a second gin and tonic that afternoon in Bogotá and gone into her bedroom—but then he wouldn't have been given command of a garrison, he wouldn't have had this love affair with an elegant and mysterious woman.

The pistol was a comforting presence. His fist tightened on the knurled grip.

Riot police from Barranquilla? They came under Hernán Vega's portfolio, and if riot police had been called in, obviously all was known. Major Sadowski must have told them that Iluminado had gone to his room with an assortment of lethal devices, along with instructions on how to use them. Vega wouldn't quickly forgive García's fiery death, or the damage to the luxury cars in the garage. And as for Gonzalo, the cuckolded husband—

They knew where to find him. Should he bring the pistol out in the open, or would it be equally honorable to fire through the sheet?

The door opened abruptly.

It was Colonel Hernán Vega González himself who entered, and he came within a microsecond of taking a .45 slug in the chest. Iluminado brought his head off the pillow.

"Sir!"

"At ease," Vega said pleasantly. "Get dressed, Captain, we need your help. The trail will go cold very quickly."

"Yes, sir!" Iluminado said smartly, rising on his elbows. Something else must have happened while he lay here unconscious. His head wobbled and fell back. "Though I fear—"

Vega was attempting urbanity. "My dear fellow, we will wheel you if necessary. We need the location of the building, an apartment number if possible."

Iluminado used his headache like a machete.

"Colonel! I would like to assist you but you are asking the wrong man. We did a hard march on the beach yesterday in full field equipment with BARs. At fifteen kilometers the sun went yellow and I saw the sand rising to meet me. That is the last I remember until I woke up here with my head in this bandage. There was an automobile accident, I am told, and I remember nothing about it whatever! I was thrown into the windshield, apparently. The doctor tells me there is often memory loss after a blow of this sort."

"Señora Alvarez Blanco was beside you. That you surely remember."

"I don't understand this at all," Iluminado said, frowning. "Who was driving?"

"You were, and the car had been stolen."

Iluminado frowned more intently. "It frightens me, sir, that I can't remember a thing."

"A sergeant in her husband's security detail fell, or was pushed, from a seventh-floor window in the casino-hotel. Your floor, I believe. His clothes were on fire. There were burn marks, fragments of white phosphorous on the hall carpet outside your room. Still you remember nothing?"

Iluminado went on pretending to try. "I think—did the Bolívar sign fall down? Or perhaps I dreamed it?"

Vega had a riding crop tucked under one arm, and for a moment it seemed that he was about to use it on the helpless invalid in the bed. Iluminado's finger caressed the trigger.

A long hard look passed between them.

Finally Vega snapped, "Get some sleep. Perhaps when you wake up you can help us fill in those missing hours."

The phone tinkled, a furtive and somehow dangerous sound. Iluminado snatched it up and heard his mistress's voice.

"I've been waiting!" he said. "They tell me you're not hurt?"

"A few bruises and bumps. I must say this quickly, darling, for Colonel Vega is coming to talk to you."

"He has been here and gone. I must see you at once. The last thing you said before the collision, that we have to agree on a story—"

"I tried to come to you, but no one is permitted into your corridor without a pass from this same colonel. What did you tell him?"

"That I collapsed from the heat at two in the afternoon, and can remember nothing since. I don't think he believed me."

64

"He's in a rage about the death of García. How lucky for us that you're leaving for Washington."

"Washington," Iluminado repeated. "That I had truly forgotten. My skull may be fractured, you know, how can I go up in an airplane?"

"I talked to the doctor and you'll be all right, they did X rays. It's merely a small concussion. Ordinarily they would keep you for observation, but this time you must do the observing yourself, or Vega will send someone to fracture your skull in earnest. I've just come from Gonzalo. Unlike you I couldn't pretend I had heat stroke. I gave him a fancy story, and he's calmer now. I think I can manage him, I always have, but I need time, darling, which is why you must be out of the country."

"It seems—not quite honorable. But if you say I must, I suppose I must. I've been given my side arm. Do I have your permission to shoot my way out of the hospital?"

"*Certainly not.* Your travel orders are still in effect. I'll pack a suitcase for you and bring it in a taxi to the service entrance. I'll think of some way to make a commotion and draw off the guards so you can slip away."

"There is a note in your voice," he said slowly. "Isn't there something you haven't told me?"

"A very great deal! But I shouldn't be talking even this long." In a softer voice: "My darling, you know that I'll miss you desperately."

She started missing him before she hung up the phone. Pictures came to her, the way he lit a cigar when he thought they were about to be discovered, the seriousness of his face as he leaned out the window to throw the grenade. But himself a grenade as well, a danger to everybody. Not quite honorable! Duty, honor, country, surely they had no time for that sort of thing in Washington. But she wondered, sitting there making a clatter against the phone with her fingernails, was she leaving too much to chance? What if he merely studied and went to museums and movies and so on, and came back unchanged? She would have deprived herself for nothing.

There was a way to make sure. If she could contrive things so the norteamericanos thought he had been sent to collect the under-the-table money for the airplanes— She found her address book and with a wicked little smile looked up a number.

Iluminado's father, in Bogotá, was removing MADE IN TAIWAN and MADE IN HONG KONG labels from the native Colombian handicrafts he was taking as presents to his Washington friends. The evening before, a new Art Deco nightclub had opened on the Avenue Edward VII and he had felt he ought to be there to do his *despedida*, his departure party. People kept asking him to drink one more glass of wine for the airplane. Now he was suffering from stomach upset, blurred vision and the usual twelve-hour remorse.

But when the phone interrupted his packing he managed to say gaily, "Gabriella! I watched you on television. How anyone so enchanting can have that much courage—"

"Oh, I don't think there was ever any real danger. But your son and namesake! If you could have seen him!"

"It doesn't surprise me," the father said with little enthusiasm. "When he was five years old, one of his idiot aunts gave him a Superman costume and he tried to fly from an upstairs window. The hospital tells me that he isn't seriously hurt?"

"They call it a concussion, but to me it seems more like a simple case of exhaustion. A grotesque North American adviser has had them out doing marches at two in the afternoon, when all sensible people are sleeping."

"And Nado, of course, would feel he must march faster and farther than anybody. I was the same at his age. Later, I'm thankful to say, I learned to relax. But I should ask about Gonzalo?"

"A flesh wound, in a part of the body where he presents a considerable target. I've barely been permitted to see him. It's been a continual circus! Television crews, counterinsurgency teams as they term themselves, intelligence specialists all the way up to the main man, Hernán Vega himself. Everybody asking the same foolish questions. One *extremely* disagreeable

Yankee wanted me to submit to a lie detector! If I have to rehearse that story one more time I believe I'll go out of my mind. I wonder, could I ask you a favor?"

"Gabby," he said reproachfully. "You know I consider you the sexiest woman in Colombia, I couldn't refuse you anything."

"What I'm tempted to do is run off without saying a word to anyone and come up to Bogotá. I have something to speak to you about. If I can beg a ride in somebody's airplane, would you give me dinner?"

He said cautiously, "Nothing would give me greater pleasure. However—"

"I know, you are leaving for Washington. And it was I, by the by, who suggested you for the mission. I have been reading in *Time* about this Mr. Sam Green, who would like to sell us his airplanes. He has all the old Yankee prejudices against Latin Americans. Perhaps he's been taking us too much for granted?"

"But my role, you know, is merely to—"

"To collect the questionable payments, as they seem to call them these days. I don't know why they don't come out honestly and say campaign contributions. If we have to have an election—and of course we must, as the State Department insists—how are we to pay for it?"

Castillo was laughing. "Gabriella, I always find your candor refreshing."

"De Santamaría made unrealistic demands, and we have seen what happened to De Santamaría. It is a time for lightness, for flexibility. Some cold-eyed professional bargainer, insisting on such and such a sum or good-bye, would only rub them the wrong way. The Indian village on the Río de Oro—you handled the payments so cleverly there, so *gaily* let me say, everybody was singing your praises."

"That was a delight all the way. Some marvelous all-night parties after the fertility rites. Did I ever happen to mention that that silly witch doctor cured me of headaches? Truly. Gave me such a whack with his bone, I saw Halley's comet several years early. I haven't had a headache since."

"Should I tell you, though," Gabriella said, continuing, "that Vega, for one, considered you a trifle unserious for the Washington journey? 'Playboy' I think was his word. But Gonzalo's point—*our* point, actually, he was consulting with me throughout—was that this playful image of yours provides an excellent cover. For we mustn't forget that these questionable payments are against the law now in the United States. But who would suspect the lighthearted Iluminado Castillo of any such weighty purpose?"

"A backhanded compliment!" he said, again with a laugh.

He still couldn't understand why she wanted to go over this ground again. He had been briefed and rebriefed until he could recite the numbers dead drunk or asleep. This had to be one of the most boring political cabals in Latin American history. He was to come back with a minimum of sixty-five million pesos. One and a half million dollars, U.S. Divided in three, one-half million to each junta member. The Yankee will ask, And how much is this going to cost me? A shrug from Castillo. "Three million dollars will be quite acceptable. Some of the Arabs have been getting much more." But carelessly! For there are other airplanes as good as Mr. Sam Green's Piranha. And the next day, over a bottle of wine or so, they would go up a few dollars, Castillo would come down a few, to compromise in the end at the one and a half million that had been his target to begin with.

Gabriella was saying, "I think you should simply let them worry about you for twenty-four hours. Don't even send them a cable."

"Ye-es," Castillo said doubtfully. "But I have promised to fly up with Nado, you know. He tries not to show it, but he is a little uneasy, he wonders how he will measure up against the other young bucks at the school. Which of course is ridiculous—here a father is speaking—but I should be there his first day, to provide psychological support."

"Oh, I doubt if Hernán and the rest will let him leave today, anyway. But I'm glad you'll be with him. I've worried about that dangerous innocence of his. There isn't a World War Two myth he doesn't believe. His promotion to captain was a little too rapid perhaps, and I feel partially responsible for that. He needs to know what you can teach him—another thing we can talk over tonight."

But something was queer about this, Castillo was thinking. There was an edge to her voice that told him it would be wise to do as she asked. And why was it so important, please? She couldn't have any new ideas about the Washington negotiations. As for the Nado matter, the boy was naive, yes; and if he stayed that way he couldn't expect much of a career, but he needed experience, not sermons from a father who hadn't paid much attention to him while he was growing up. No, there had to be more to it than that. Could it be possible—

Once or twice, in fact as recently as last week at the Chilean embassy, he had patted this handsome lady in the same general area where her husband had now been wounded. She had chosen not to respond. That was all right with Castillo! The truth was, he was losing some of his old eagerness for this sort of adventure. The diversionary moves, the flattery, the half-lies and protests—why couldn't the damn woman just walk into the bedroom under her own steam, and step out of her panty hose? But in a backward, priest-ridden country like Colombia, that is not the way the game has to be played.

There was a crackle on the line, lightning, probably, and his question was answered. What was the difference between today and last week at the Chileans, when she had so pointedly turned away? Today her husband was confined to a hospital bed!

It was a temptation, certainly. Delaying his trip would be a gamble, for this Mr. Sam Green was said to keep his temper on a very short leash. But how sweet, how exquisitely satisfying, to pay back Gonzalo, his stuffy comrade-in-arms, who had helped Castillo out of various small bits of trouble, always accompanying the help with a string of the most tiresome clichés—when will you start being more responsible, you must drink less and give up this obsessive pursuit of long-legged women, and show some respect for the cretins in power. Be more like *him*, in short.

There was another consideration, and in the end it was the determining one. Unless he fell in with Gabriella's suggestion he would have to admit that he hadn't meant those little pats on the ass, that his Don Juan pose was a fraud, he was a harmless middle-aged gentleman trying unsuccessfully to recapture his youth.

Which was why, when his son boarded the Bogotá–Washington plane at Barranquilla some hours later, the older Castillo was not on it.

Captain Hector Duffy, late of the U.S. Navy, was able to stay in the competitive mode only by giving himself orders, as though admonishing a slightly moronic ordinary seaman. At the bathroom mirror in the mornings, he would threaten his lathered reflection and cry, "Retaliate!" It had made him feel sheepish at first, but it definitely helped.

The phone rang. Nobody likes to be interrupted shaving, but who could it be at this hour but Duffy's employer Sam Green, Mr. G of Hawk-Sisley, known to the sensational financial press as the unfriendly-takeover king? He feared germs more than Communism (which he feared a great deal), and he always squirted the telephone mouthpiece with peppermint disinfectant before putting it to his lips. His phone voice was a whisper.

"Hector. Wanted to remind you that the spic gets in at seven tonight. His name is Iluminado Castillo. Iluminado. Castillo. I sent you a memo on it, but I haven't had a heck of a lot of success getting people to read my memos lately."

"Now, Mr. G," Duffy said, "that was an oversight, and the girl who was responsible for it is no longer with me."

But Mr. G had a negative attention span for a poor man's excuses.

"That old-fashion pride in doing things well, Hector, somewheres along the line we pissed it away. Now you understand this Castillo is strictly the umbrella man. Are you acquainted with that old-fashion expression?"

He only used it two or three times a week, but Duffy didn't want to embarrass him by telling him so.

"Out West in the wide-open days," Mr. G said, "when the collector went through the red-light part of town, he carried

70

an umbrella hooked on his arm and the madams dropped their contributions in the umbrella. And that's why they gave him the name umbrella man. All you talk about this time, Hector, is the size of the gratuity. What was his name down there, you know who I mean, Thing-a-majig—"

"De Santamaría?" Duffy guessed.

"That sounds a lot like it. He was asking ten million. I want to pick up these new clowns for one. I'll spell it out for you. That's one million for the three of them, total, not one million apiece, and if you can get them for less, I'll like you for it, Hector. They can take it in cash, or if they want it deposited someplace, that's O.K. to talk about. Offer a half million first and go up in ten thousand increments. Have you got that?"

"Got it, Mr. G."

"Now the scouting report on this guy. Don't take him to art museums, take him to jazz spots. He likes to party. It's all there in the memo. I want you to keep your thumb up his ass every minute he's here, give him twenty-four-hour hosting, because American Texas has been making noises about going after the business, and we can't let this fuck off into an auction."

"I thought we had this junta in our pocket, Mr. G."

Though he knew better, he pronounced the word with a *j*. Mr. G pronounced it with a *j*.

"They're sheepherders, Hector," Mr. G said simply. "I learned one thing long ago—never turn your back on a sheepherder."

The lather was losing some of its charge; unless Duffy could get back to the washbasin he would feel chapped all day. But if you hoped to go on working for Mr. G you didn't interrupt when he wanted to reminisce about his hard youth on the ranch, before coal was discovered on the property. Luckily he was phoning from his airplane, which came in for a landing before he could move on to the budget deficit, his other main topic.

Back at the mirror, Duffy lathered up and started over.

"Retaliate!"

But his heart wasn't in it this morning. American Texas! Those people made their own rules.

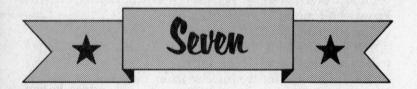

Seven

I luminado walked through the airplane, up and down aisles, looking into a galley, a splendid stainless-steel lavatory, and concluded at last that his father, for undoubtedly discreditable reasons, had missed the departure.

His face was stiff from the effort to hide his feelings. He had been counting on an experienced person's advice during the first difficult moments. The Pentagon! Fellow officers who had been there, to this or that school, had tried to alarm him with tales of bizarre occurrences in those mazey corridors, behind the thousands of doors. His orders told him (and told him *emphatically*, in the military fashion) to report to the Counter Coup orientation officer at such and such an office at 0900 hours. He could probably find it, by asking directions at every turn. But everything was computerized there, whereas here in Colombia it was all murk and muddle. What if the notification had never been sent, or had gone to the wrong address?

He wished he had been given time to read a guidebook, at least. He wouldn't know how much to tip, or which buses went where. The others would sneer at his ignorance. Should he push himself forward or try not to be noticed?

Since his orders were cut he had been practicing what he thought of as his North American look. He stiffened his neck very slowly and closed down his eyes. "Take care," this look said. "I will fight at the first slighting word." But if the others got wind of his junta connections, if, God forbid, Colonel Vega had planted a whisper about the Gabriella affair—

If he could believe Gabriella, the doctors had assured her he was able to travel. But he didn't *feel* able to travel. His skull felt as thin as an eggshell, as though it could be shattered by a harsh or unpleasant thought. Walking on a flat surface, he had to fight a tilt to the right. Even through dark glasses, each overhead light had its own halo.

A uniformed young woman smiled him to his seat. He prepared a cigar, which a sign in Spanish and English forbade him to light, at the same time ordering him to fasten his seat belt. Something was wrong; the two halves of the belt couldn't be persuaded to mate. The flight attendant noticed his difficulty and did it for him—a surprisingly intimate moment.

The engines were whining. Given permission to fly, the plane climbed steeply and broke through the fleecey ceiling. The young woman offered to fetch him a complimentary cocktail. He shook his head without looking up. He was focusing his energies, as runners do at the start of a race, with the help of a biography of George S. Patton, Jr., which his dear Gabriella had thoughtfully included in his suitcase. The battles Patton enjoyed most—though he enjoyed them all, really—were fought in the clean air of the desert, where tanks could maneuver freely and the opposing general could be counted on to accept defeat like a gentlemen. As for the Counter Coup school, it seemed precisely the opposite. It had a slightly sinister reputation. People who had been there couldn't be persuaded to say much about it.

The flight attendant was offering magazines. "Have you seen the new *Norte*? We all think it's pretty terrific."

The magazine she was recommending had a startling photograph on its cover. It showed a sordid domestic interior: a black woman in a torn slip injecting herself while a black man, beside her, put bullets into a cheap-looking revolver. A crying baby, unattended, was being watched from the corner by something small and evil.

A page number was given. Revolted, Iluminado turned there at once.

This unholy family was not, it seemed, exceptional in North American ghettos. Drug addicts roamed the sidewalks, mugging the passersby to get money for their fabulous medicine. No part of a town was safe. The parks least of all—muggers lay in wait behind every rock and tree.

This was strong stuff for someone so recently concussed. Iluminado flipped back to the frontispiece, and there, sure enough, were the clean-cut, clean-shaven jaws of the U.S. secretary of state. *Norte*, in fact, was an official State Department publication.

The smiling young woman was passing. Iluminado told her that, after all, he had decided to accept a complimentary cocktail. She suggested her country's national drink, very cold, very dry.

"On the rocks, or straight up?"

"Up," he said, but it was only a guess.

He returned to the magazine. The State Department would have no reason to lie. The warnings were true, then; he should be careful walking the streets, and be on guard at all times against pounces from behind.

Someone had taken a census of handguns. There were over three hundred million in the country he was approaching so rapidly. One and a half guns per person! The average middle-aged Yankee has watched sixty-three hours of television each week since childhood. Inasmuch as an astonishing thirty-seven percent of all TV shows celebrate violence, it was small wonder that in this gun-mad, violence-prone nation, real people are frequently shot down on little or no provocation. And the police, whose duty it is to keep the peace, watch as much television as anybody, and their guns have a tendency to leap into their hands. Foreign visitors, therefore, were advised to be deferential when asking a policeman for directions. During muggings, remember that the loss is, after all, an allowable income tax deduction and say nothing to hurt the mugger's feelings, for he is feeling guilty enough already.

But this, surely, was advice for the infirm and the elderly. Iluminado's hand slipped down his leg to touch the knife in his boot. More sophisticated airports have metal detectors, but not Barranquilla, in underdeveloped Colombia. Muggers, take warning yourselves: this is Iluminado Castillo, descended from *conquistadores,* and he does not fear to die.

The huge airplane was flying nearly empty. Seated across the aisle, a bearded fellow kept stealing looks at Iluminado, then looking at something in the palm of his hand.

Iluminado kept turning pages.

"Did the Ancients Have a Cure for Herpes? Papyrus Secrets Deciphered." "New Bermuda Triangle, I-80's Death Stretch." "Is America's Air Becoming Unbreathable?"

A two-page photograph showed a New York intersection so choked with traffic that only one solution seemed practical: tip the island and spill the whole business into the river. A small square of sandpaper was glued to the page. "Scratch 'n' Sniff," Iluminado was ordered.

He scratched.

"Mother of God!" he exclaimed, getting a whiff of New York air collected at the corner of Sixth Avenue and Thirty-fourth Street at five o'clock on an August afternoon.

The radiant flight attendant found him with tears in his eyes.

"I know," she said, instantly sympathetic. "We were put on this little old world to be happy, and what a mess we've made of it, after all."

He turned blindly and took the tissue she offered. As the magazine closed, the smell of advanced civilization retreated into the sandpaper.

"The point to remember," she went on, "is that we've pinpointed the problem and we're beginning to do something about it. Throw the rascals out! That's the American system, and we're proud of it. Here, try *Selecciones.* That's *Reader's Digest* in Spanish. They look on the bright side, more."

"Thank you, you're very kind."

He tasted the cocktail, wondering how they could call it dry. An olive lurched about sluggishly on the bottom. He put the smaller magazine to one side and went back to *Norte*. Wasn't it his duty to find out?

"Gays, Out of the Closet at Last," was the next topic. He consulted his two-way dictionary. Cheerful? In a *closet*?

Ah! Homosexuality. Until recently confined to the seaboards, the gay revolution, Iluminado was informed, was spreading rapidly to the interior. The gay people themselves had become more self-confident, even aggressive. Another photograph showed a group of angry young men fighting the police. To Iluminado both groups looked equally abnormal. Any reasonably attractive visitor, declared *Norte*, should be prepared to receive the occasional homosexual proposition. No problem, he was advised. But don't be judgmental, for gays are no less thin-skinned than other Americans.

For some time, his bearded fellow-traveler had been trying to catch his eye. Failing at this, he crossed the aisle and dropped into an empty seat. Alerted by *Norte*, Iluminado noticed details: too many rings, a handkerchief spilling out of the breast pocket of a pale cream jacket. He steeled himself for a suggestion that they retire together to the lavatory.

"Didn't I hear you talking English?"

"I speak a little English," Iluminado admitted.

"My name's Quimby. I don't know about your country. I doubt if any studies have been done on it yet, but in the States some fifty percent of all social intercourse consists of questions and answers. So do you mind if I ask you some questions? Do you come to the U.S. often?"

"No, this is the first occasion."

"Do you know, I guessed that. I noticed you reading *Norte*. How did it strike you? I'd like your candid opinion."

In Iluminado's candid opinion, it was fantastic that any government would put out an official publication of this sort. He said only, "In Colombia, our Tourist Bureau speaks only about the mountains and the agreeable climate and shows pictures of Indian villages and young women in very small bathing suits."

"Very small bathing suits, I love it."

He laid his hand on Iluminado's sleeve. It was the lightest possible touch, but a warm, somehow perverse pulse of energy passed into Iluminado's forearm.

"Now I'd like to ask you to do something for me. There's a small check in it for you."

"I'm afraid that would be impossible."

The eyebrows went up. "You haven't heard what it is yet."

"I don't want to hear. I don't believe in it, in the first place." Judge not, had been the magazine's advice, but this was a subject Iluminado felt strongly about. "The truth is, I find it disgusting."

Disbelief and amazement met this announcement. "You may not be familiar with the concept, but disgusting? That I don't see. There's nothing more boring than airplane travel. What the hell, it passes the time."

Iluminado lifted his knife into view. "And I find *you* disgusting. Return to your seat."

The rings were flying, a gold identification bracelet.

"There has to be some kind of communication glitch here."

"You are 'gay,' are you not?"

"What does that have to do—" After a moment: "I get it, you think— No, no. Hey, all I'm doing here is running a little attitude study. Takes about ten minutes and you'll hopefully enjoy it."

If anyone had any doubts about Iluminado's attitude on the subject of sex between males, he was willing to set them straight. His eyes began to close down, and Quimby said hastily, "Start with the cover story, the delights and perils of heroin. I want an impact evaluation, off the top of your head. How would you characterize your reaction? One, negligible, I don't expect to meet any heroin addicts. Two, sensationalized—things can't be that *bad*. Three, what else is new? Four, packed a real wallop. Put that knife back in your boot, Captain. It's making me talkative."

After a moment's thought Iluminado slipped the knife in its sheath, but his hand hovered nearby, in case the homosexual tried to finger his forearm again.

"An attitude study. What is that?"

Leaning far forward, ready to take flight at the first threatening movement, Quimby explained. Most Americans have reluctantly concluded that the Virgin Birth, to mention one of the best-known traditional constructs, has little to say to modern man. But everybody needs something to believe in, and they have replaced received religion with a faith in the random sample. Say somebody wants to find out how many people watch a certain television program. Eighty million households in the United States have TV receivers. You can't ask everybody, so you ask nine hundred and eighteen. Not nine hundred and eighteen thousand, nine hundred and eighteen individual people. That, basically, was what they were up to here. State had decided to modernize their public-information effort, and now they needed some feedback. O.K.—Iluminado had spent twenty-six minutes on the magazine, distributed thematically as follows: social problems, six minutes; general political and industrial, three; crime and culture, five; sex, twelve. Now. In what way did this exposure alter his prior image of the United States? Was he looking forward to his stay less or more, or about the same?

Somewhat against his will, Iluminado found himself answering. At the end, Quimby handed him a check made out to Bearer, for $2.50.

"Thank you, Captain." He was sitting back now, imagining the danger to be over. "And you're absolutely right about most government information. No literate person has paid any attention to it in years. You looked at a few picture captions and turned back to make sure that what you were reading was really a State Department publication. One minute, four seconds. We consider anything under a minute and a half remarkably fast."

"I still don't see—"

"It's a question of expectations," Quimby explained. "You brought up the matter of bathing suits. Any model agency can supply girls who look great in a couple of strings. But go to a public beach on a Sunday afternoon and how many actual human females do you see who are built like that? Not one. I mean, not one single one. Do you see the point I'm trying to make? *Norte* used to carry nothing but Kodachrome shots of

78

maple syruping in Vermont, Sunday-night church suppers in Iowa. Everybody white, everybody smiling. And then the poor tourist hits customs, immigration. Where are the smiles? If you're lucky you manage to get a cab. There's puke on the floor, the meter's busted and the driver's an obvious maniac. You look at America and *nothing's in Kodachrome!* And you remember those pretty pictures in *Norte* and what are you going to conclude? That we're even phonier than we actually are."

"So your idea—"

Quimby looked at his stopwatch. "Thirty-two seconds. Very good."

Hampered by the gin and vermouth, perhaps also by the olive, Iluminado was striving to understand. The magazine on his lap was becoming heavier by the minute.

"Then nothing I read in this magazine is true?"

"Truth has nothing to do with it," Quimby said impatiently. "I'm talking about how much tourist goodwill we can buy with our publication dollar. If we convince you that you can't walk down a big-city street without being mugged, and then nobody mugs you in the first twenty-four hours, the overall effect is going to be positive. That's the rationale behind it."

One of the characteristics of General George S. Patton, Jr., according to his biographer, was that he never let anybody take him for a fool. Iluminado rolled *Norte* into a bludgeon and disturbed the air not far from Quimby's ear.

"Now I will repeat my request. Go back to your seat."

"It's beyond me!" Quimby said, laughing.

"After all, nothing but lies! The pollution, the sexual freedom—"

"Has anybody ever told you," Quimby said from the safety of the other side of the aisle, "how good-looking you are when you're angry?"

Iluminado tried to get out of his seat. Luckily for the other he was still buckled in.

The pleasant flight attendant offered to get him another martini. Iluminado said no; he was confused enough as it was.

"Is anyone meeting you?"

"I believe so."

But this was by no means certain. Now more than ever, having been hoodwinked by the bearded homosexual and his odious magazine, Iluminado was aware of how little he knew about the world he was about to enter. He peered out the narrow window, over a trembling wing with many rivet heads missing.

And there it was: the diagonals, the right angles, the circles and straight lines. Before being built, Washington had been laid out on graph paper, and it all seemed so orderly, above all so *rational*, that Iluminado decided, once and for all, that the magazine had been lying.

A mugger in every doorway? Cruising homosexual gangs in the subway? More than unlikely, impossible.

And then they were down, and he couldn't persuade the damn belt to release him. The flight attendant had to show him again, with a light touch that sent his thoughts flying back to Colombia, to Gabriella. Quimby, a folded raincoat thrown carelessly over one shoulder, was idling about at the top of the cabin.

"Still mad?"

The pilot was there also, to thank Iluminado for flying this airline, and to urge him to have a good evening. Was a tip expected? Iluminado had only Colombian money. No, he remembered after a step. Turning back, he handed the man Quimby's check for $2.50.

His attention was taken immediately by a mountain of rusted scrap beyond the perimeter fence. A closer look showed it to be composed of hundreds of flattened airplanes.

Quimby was one step behind him. "Want a chance to earn another small check, Captain?"

"Keep away."

But after a few more steps, he said cautiously, "What do you wish to ask?"

"You've just left a Seven Four Seven flying eighty percent empty, and the first thing that hits your eye is a pile of perfectly

80

good airplanes which had to be scrapped because they could only carry half as many passengers as a Seven Four Seven. Off the top of your head."

"How rich you must be in this country."

"The gentleman wins a cigar," Quimby exclaimed happily. "The ecology nuts have been agitating to put plank fences around all the junkyards, but that's dumb. People from the developing countries, who are the ones we're trying to impress, look at that scrap pile and they want one just like it."

Encouraged, he had come alongside. Iluminado warned him to keep his distance.

"Your lying magazine tells me to be polite to homosexuals. I have no such intention."

"Kid, you'll have to stop being so ticklish if you're going to spend any time in the Pentagon."

Iluminado stopped. He needed all the advice he could get, even from a source as tainted as this.

"Are you trying to tell me there is *homosexuality* there?"

"It's buried, and that's the most dangerous kind. If you get all hysterical every time somebody brushes against you, they'll think you're criticizing."

"But I don't believe you, you see," Iluminado said a bit nervously.

"You'd better believe me. There's a new doctrine now—you don't fight for your country, you fight for your buddy. It goes back to the Spartans. Look at a drag queen like Patton, with those swishy pearl-handled revolvers—"

Hearing this imputation, the fiery general would have beaten the fellow insensible with the riding crop he carried for just such emergencies. Iluminado merely threatened him with a look and strode away.

Patton was in his mind, Patton's somewhat peculiar conviction that in an earlier existence he had served with Odysseus at Troy, with Marc Antony in Egypt. Suddenly, in much the same way, Iluminado found himself transported into one of the Gustave Doré illustrations for Dante's *Inferno*. The enormous crowd in the arrivals building had defeated the air conditioning. They were young people, mostly, and many of them clearly intended to spend the night. Disembodied voices filled the air with incomprehensible cries.

Having been fastened to his seat so he was unable to use the excellent stainless-steel facilities on the plane, Iluminado needed a bathroom. He looked around for a sign, but he was distracted by the announcements on the young women's T-shirts: SQUEEZE THEM, THEY'RE REAL. I MAY NOT BE PERFECT, BUT PARTS OF ME ARE VERY GOOD. ORAL HYGIENISTS MAKE THE BEST LOVERS. LET'S DO IT IN MY PICKUP.

A flashbulb went off in his face. Again he saw the fireball, the exploding sign: BOLIVAR, it said, then the fisheye, the slow drift of glass. An individual with luxuriant sideburns and a helmet of hair demanded to know if his flight had originated in Colombia. The face, with a fleshy nose and greatly enlarged pores, wore light chocolate makeup. A TV personage, then? Yes, now that Iluminado knew what to look for, he saw the camera, a small technical party.

He remained silent. Had someone from the enemy camp told them of his escape from the hospital?

"I wanted someone who speaks English," the man said impatiently.

Iluminado's flight attendant was there at his elbow, smiling as always.

"He speaks very good English. They won't bite, Captain. They just want to ask a few questions about what happened down there."

"I am not the person to speak to. I am merely a soldier."

"From Cartagena," the man said, holding out the microphone.

"That is true."

"How do you pronounce that, incidentally?"

"Cartagena."

"It must've been pretty rugged there for a while."

The microphone came back. What must have been pretty rugged, the flight? "No, it was quite uneventful."

"Guerrillas took over the town, didn't they, and held it for three hours?"

82

"While I've been traveling?" Iluminado exclaimed.

"Into the mike, if you will. When something like this happens, you've got to wonder. Is another small country going the way of Afghanistan, Nicaragua?"

"Cartagena is in Colombia," Iluminado explained. "Perhaps you are thinking of some other part of the world. Oh, there are demonstrations in the capital from time to time, students running around, but in our part, in the north, we have had no resistance activity for many years now. Total eradication, by forces led by our present chief of government, Colonel Alvarez Blanco."

It is a common experience at international airports. Biological clocks tend to malfunction when they are lifted six miles in the air and carried from one continent to another at a speed faster than sound. Less than twenty hours ago, Iluminado had blown up a spectacular sign and thrown a grenade or two. It would be another day before he perceived a connection between these rather minor events and the questions the interviewer was asking him now.

"Guerrillas in sleepy Cartagena?" Iluminado went on. "I was there as recently as this morning, and I can assure you that the new government has the complete support of the people. If anyone has been circulating rumors—"

But the interviewer wouldn't have lasted a week in his demanding profession if he had listened to what people were telling him.

"You counterattacked and drove them back into the jungle. That's got to be one of your greatest thrills."

The man's eyes had a curious flat sheen in the smoky light. It occurred to Iluminado that he might be a user of drugs.

The mike came at him again. "Would you repeat the question?"

"You were sitting around having a glass of wine. What thoughts went through your mind—"

This time he misjudged the distance, or he may have been jostled. The microphone struck Iluminado on the bridge of the nose. Noticing that his victim seemed unwilling to answer— that is the way with some people, show them a live mike and they go into rigor—the interviewer decided to try getting nasty, which will sometimes shock them back into the conversation.

"You've come up to get dollar assistance, is that a fair statement?"

Standing there mute, like some slow-witted, back-country peasant, Iluminado was afraid he was giving U.S. television watchers a poor impression of his country's army.

"May I hold that a moment?"

But the mike was the source of the interviewer's power, and he was unwilling to give it up. Wrapping the wire around his fist, Iluminado reeled in. As soon as it stopped coming, he gave it a hard yank.

A voice said in Spanish, "I believe I can help you."

Iluminado had been in the United States for less than a half hour, and he was already tiring of the din of English. A slim young man had come up to him, his own age or younger, in a glittering Liberace-for-President T-shirt. His eyes were concealed behind enormous dark mirrors which reflected the whole crowded scene, primarily, of course, Iluminado himself.

"I'll find your luggage for you, God willing," this strange person said, "and get you a taxicab. The price for that will be three U.S. dollars. I accept foreign currency."

"I need to go to the toilet."

"Please, let me direct you."

The interviewer was blowing into his mike, to see if it still lived.

"Can I simply walk away from this man?" Iluminado asked.

"Certainly. He is a small fish, from a local station."

Iluminado's own name cut through the hubbub. He turned gratefully. After all, they had sent someone to meet him.

It was a tall woman, with skin like expensive leather. Bony and stylishly dressed, carrying a gold-handled umbrella, she couldn't have come from Counter Coup. She must want Iluminado's father.

"I'm Isobel Clancy," she continued, addressing Iluminado's flight attendant, and it was clear from her tone that she expected any reasonably well-informed person to recognize the name.

"I'm sure he came in on your flight. Somehow I've managed to miss him."

It takes a minimum of three generations, whether in Colombia or the District of Columbia, to breed such a woman. Doña Gabriella had friends of this sort, and something warned Iluminado that if he identified himself, she would console herself for the father's absence by insisting on taking the son to dinner and offering to show him Washington after dark. Whereas all Iluminado wanted was to find his hotel, eat a sandwich or omelet, fall into bed and *sleep*, to arrive fresh at the Pentagon in the morning.

So he drifted backward and was lost in the crowd before the flight attendant could reply that indeed she had flown with Iluminado Castillo, it was a name that stayed in the mind, and he had been standing right here a moment ago, but where—?

"There is a long wait for toilets in this building," his guide told him, "but I can take you to one few people know about."

They entered a low corridor paved with some unforgiving material that sent the sound of their heel taps back and forth between floor and ceiling. They turned, turned again, and found themselves in a dim cul-de-sac where, without beating around the bush any further, his companion gave him a hard jab in the liver with a pointed object that proved to be a pistol.

"Give me your money and passport."

The glasses hiding his eyes gave back Iluminado's reflection and little else: twin Colombian officers in beautiful uniforms. It seemed wrong to be speaking in Spanish, a passionate language, not flat and angular like English.

"You are a mugger, then?"

"Not at all. Mugging is robbery with violence. There will be no need for that, probably."

Iluminado remembered *Norte*'s clear-cut instructions. Don't bargain with street thieves, but comply with their demands, comply at once, with grateful enthusiasm. Even the legendary General Robert E. Lee gave up his sword. Bolívar, too, lost occasional battles. When General Douglas MacArthur fled in panic from the Philippines, it established his reputation.

The robber accepted his wallet. "Traveler's checks. I will ask you to sign these for me."

"Do you think it is safe to take the time?"

"I believe so. I use this out-of-the-way place for that reason."

He provided the pen. Each signature made Iluminado more angry.

"Take off the uniform," he was ordered. "I can get a good price for it. Homosexuals like to wear them to parties."

Iluminado caught the sneer with a measure of relief. Was his country's uniform (slightly modified, it was true, by Gabriella's society tailor) to be flaunted by some "gay" creature in lipstick and an overabundance of jewelry?

To get out of the pants, first he would have to take off the boots. He stooped toward the knife. But if the thief was a heroin addict, which any reader of *Norte* would not find it hard to believe, the drug had a double effect. It made him suspicious and shortened his reaction time. Iluminado plucked out the knife, but before he could bring it up he was forced to accept a knee to the side of the head, and he was back in concussion country.

He was dimly aware of being handled. He wished to resist, but he lay as though crushed beneath tons of water. At the same time he was an iron bar being heated toward white, and if they pounded him long enough they would find that he had turned into something else, like a sword.

When he floated dreamily to the surface, the mugger was gone, and Iluminado was without money and uniform, the Order of the White Rose, the beautiful watch Gabriella had strapped tenderly on his wrist on his twenty-first birthday, all the things he needed to prove his identity.

He lay among gum wrappers and dead cigarettes, beneath a sign saying: THANK YOU FOR NOT LITTERING. And because no one was nearby to hear, he permitted himself a kind of dry sob. Someone would pay for this. Though not right away, probably.

The click of heels sounded like gunshots. He pulled himself up with the help of a doorknob.

One of the spectacular Washington women, nearly as spectacular as the monuments he had seen from the air, glanced into the hallway, and stopped with a gasp of surprise. High heels added to her natural length at one end, a great stack of reddish hair at the other. In between, she was wearing pin-striped flannel. She was clearly in magnificent health. It was easy to imagine her on the tennis court, unleashing ace after ace.

Iluminado struck at the gnat swarm in front of his eyes.

"I have been mugged," he said, remembering in time to speak English.

As he swayed toward her, wearing only socks and the baggy olive-drab shorts, she brought her hand out of her bag wearing additional knuckles.

"One more step and I'll smash your jaw."

But after a closer look, which told her that he was no rapist or sex freak, she produced a transparent plastic raincoat and helped him into the sleeves.

"I guess that's not much of an improvement," she said, looking him over.

On the contrary, Iluminado considered it an enormous improvement. At least it symbolized clothes.

"I am a captain in the Colombian Army. I must tell the police that a mugging has taken place."

"Well, the cops," she said doubtfully. "We've got a rule in this country—don't bother the cops unless there's no other way. Much better you call somebody."

"I know no one in Washington."

"Somebody's probably taking calls at your embassy."

But Gabriella had warned him to stay away from the embassy, it was still infested with Santamarístas. The name of the leathery-looking lady who had asked for his father swam in through the gnats.

"Isobel Clancy, sure," his new friend said, "who gives all those dinner parties. I'll buzz her. But you better not stand around without any clothes on or they'll bust you for that. There's a men's room around the corner."

"I would appreciate that."

It took courage to leave the semiobscurity of the passageway.

For the second time in twenty-four hours, he was appearing in public in unbecoming underwear, the most common of nightmares. To his surprise, no one seemed to notice.

She left him at a door marked MEN, CABALLEROS. Inside a cubicle, he treated himself to a long, rewarding urination.

Amid the erotic scribbles on the wall, someone had put up a patriotic sticker: U.S.A.—LOVE IT OR LEAVE IT. Iluminado didn't love it so far, and he would have left it with pleasure.

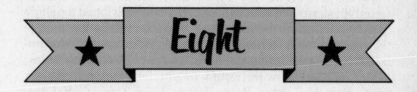

Eight

Hal Amsterdam, the well-known news personality, stumbled on his ironic twitch entirely by accident one evening. In midsentence, the lights brightened suddenly and came rushing toward him. He lost the power of speech. When he was able to locate the monitor, the words had disappeared in the glare.

A few seconds passed. In this medium a few seconds of silence can seem as long as an afternoon. That very day, Amsterdam had been signed to a magnificent new contract. He would have to pay back the money. People would come to repossess the new condo, the new wife. Flooded by a deep sense of the irony of the situation, he flexed a nameless muscle, part of the smiling complex.

The primary season was about to begin, and he had been comparing the merits of those who wanted to be president. He claimed later that he hadn't been listening to what he was saying, but it seemed to his viewers that the bland flow of newsdesk banalities had been interrupted by a rush of genuine feeling. A country with a population of 235 million, and *these* guys were the best we could do?

So irony became Amsterdam's trademark. Knowing the perils of overexposure, he released the twitch only once every three or four shows, sometimes coupling the movement with a nearly imperceptible lift of an eyebrow, an effect that many women found mysteriously sexy. His network commissioned a polling organization to do a comparison rating on all the top men in the warring news units. The questions were carefully formulated, to conceal what the pollsters really wanted to know: Which of the following would you prefer to have kinky sex with—Dan, Hal, Peter, Roger, Harry, Mike, Tom. . . . Hal Amsterdam, with his twitch, came in third overall. In the psycho-demographics he was an easy first among women between twenty-seven and thirty-seven, and they happen to be the women with the most spendable cash.

Amsterdam and his principal advisers spent most of the day trying to decide how to handle the Casino Bolívar story. Everybody else was using the obvious linkage, the W-3 vote in the Senate. Twelve senators still claimed to be undecided, and the remaining eighty-eight were split down the middle. If you believed the polls—and Amsterdam had to believe the polls, they were a big part of his business—only sixteen percent of the viewing public would really know what he was talking about when he referred to W-3. And that would hurt in the ratings; sets would be switched to one of the happier channels, where the newspeople rally each other about their hairstyles and take nothing seriously, not even hurricanes.

But Amsterdam wasn't satisfied to be merely an entertainer. If the electorate knew the facts, it would do the right thing; this was his deepest belief. The W-3 concept was just too complex to be explained in the usual minute and a half news segment. He had persuaded the network, by throwing a series of orchestrated tantrums and threatening to jump to the competition, to give him an hour special.

He used animated graphics and interviews with experts, on-the-spot pickups, stock footage from previous wars. He twitched twice. All to no purpose. The polls continued to identify that same hard-core sixteen percent, and Amsterdam was beginning to have a horrible suspicion that it might be the same sixteen percent that reads newspapers.

For those who were watching the football game that Sunday afternoon and missed the Amsterdam special, the situation was as follows:

Ever since our boys were pulled out of Southeast Asia, the long-range planners had been staying up late twirling the globe. There had to be someplace! Europe had been picked over, Africa wasn't quite ready. The Persian Gulf was just too God damn *odd*. More and more people were beginning to mention Latin America. Questioned, most of the military juntas down there were willing to admit to a tilt toward democracy, which made them eligible for military and economic assistance. But before the money could be sent, the appropriations had to be approved. Irrational prejudices against Spanish speakers are still strong in certain key states, first of all Texas and California. Many of the Texans and Californians, great friends of the Pentagon as a rule, hated to vote tax dollars to fatten some spic generalissimo. A venerable senator from Texas came to his feet, and while his colleagues sat stupefied (but then so many always sat stupefied), asked, "*Why?*"

The answer should have been obvious. No modern nation can feel secure and important without a prosperous armaments industry. One of the airplane firms had just announced that it would be forced to go belly-up unless it was given an immediate infusion of cash. Its officers had done a terrific marketing job, selling the whole line to their old Pentagon comrades at an excellent price, but the airplanes themselves were having difficulty leaving the ground. Nevertheless the check was put in the mail, out of respect for the domino theory—if one company went, they would all go. Still, everybody felt that there had to be some better way.

Michael Mirabile, who had thought up more than one major initiative of the sixties and seventies, was asked to suggest something. Stop thinking in nickels and dimes, he told them, a few planes here and there, a few missiles. Kindle the Senate's imagination with a glamorous new weapons system carrying a price tag in the billions.

Could he be a little more specific?

Well, why not—here he paused to tap out his pipe while the Chiefs curled their toes, not knowing what startling proposal was about to emerge—why not a *wall*?

Much like the one they had once talked about throwing across the narrow waist of Vietnam along the 17th parallel. By wall, he didn't mean actual masonry. He meant more like a *belt*, a *zone*, twenty k's deep, crammed with a mix of weaponry so eclectic that the enemy, one hoped, would be totally bewildered and would turn around and go home. Some unbelievable sci-fi stuff was coming out of the labs: target-acquisition gear that could sniff out an enemy by the way he voted in the last presidential election, practically, high IQ missiles and rockets which could change course in midair, microwave fields, ionized lasers.

The Chiefs liked the sound of it. Wall. It said private property. It said no trespassing, keep out, this means you.

Now where should they put this wall?

Mirabile ordered a series of polls to see what had happened to the traditional stimuli. Only one, he discovered, had kept some of its old magic, the Panama Canal. If the Canal, please God it won't happen, ever fell into unfriendly hands, an astonishing seventy-seven percent of the sample said they would feel personally threatened—diminished, somehow. Not only that, an equally astonishing eighty-five percent knew where it was, approximately.

So it was decided: the wall would protect the Canal. Everything north of the wall, in a much more real sense than at present, would be *ours*.

Next, a name.

The first generation of names—Nike, Thor, Poseidon, Zeus and the like—had been intended to frighten. The bad thing about them, they frightened Americans almost as much as they frightened the enemy. In the emotionally neutral Sentinel-Safeguard category, the likeliest possibilities had already been preempted by hair sprays and deodorants. Then came the era of acronyms. SAM was an early Mirabile triumph, closely followed by MIRV. Panty-waist senators might hesitate before voting funds for nuclear-tipped Surface-to-Air Missiles or Multiple Independently Targeted Reentry Vehicles, multiple meaning ten or a dozen warheads, each powerful enough to destroy a medium-sized city. But SAM? Or MIRV? Who could be concerned about a weapons system named for a talk-show host? Or the cruise missile, suggesting not terrible death by radiation and fire but soft tropical nights, dancing under the stars? And that cute little chap Midgetman?

As for the new wall, let's, Mirabile suggested, call it simply the Wall.

Well, the Chiefs didn't like it. They didn't think it came off.

Then how about W-3? It sounded vaguely high-tech, late twentieth century. *W*, for wall. Three, to denote that the idea had an honorable ancestry. At this late date, let's not apologize for the prototype, which might have made all the difference if the sneaks hadn't gone around through Cambodia. Wall number two, a scaled-down version, had kept the Egyptians and Israelis at arm's length in the Sinai until they had time to make friends. Continuity was implied; it was new, but not all that new.

Nods all around.

The estimated price would be $37 billion, a lot of money, true, but thirty-seven would take care of everything, all the kickbacks and incidentals. Mr. Sam Green's Hawk-Sisley would be the principal beneficiary, but so many different ingredients had been thrown into the mix that the subcontracts could be scattered through all the swing states. It would have sailed through the Senate like a fire ship, one hundred to zero, except for one factor. A senator named Hughie Shanahan wanted to be president.

Shanahan's planners had decided that it was this year or never. He had unlimited funds, toughness, an outstanding track record, a masterly TV delivery, a great-looking wife and kids, an organization studded with veterans of winning campaigns, friendships with top media people. But motivational research had told him that all this wasn't enough, he needed an issue. Not just any old issue but a *gut* issue (which was how they were talking that year). In the early primaries, he had to be seen as an underdog, so the voters would overlook his immense personal fortune. At the same time there had to be poll results showing that he had a better than fifty percent chance of winning, because there is nothing the American voter despises more than a loser.

After a long and at times acrimonious debate, the strategists suggested that he take on the Wall. They had heard about those Mirabile polls, but their own work in the field had established that though most people *approved* of the Panama Canal, and were glad to know it was there, they didn't think about it from one month to the next. Did we even *own* the damn thing anymore? Hadn't we signed some kind of treaty?

Another poll asked: How do you rate the Department of Defense? Doing a splendid job! said sixty-five percent. But they're spending too much of our money, added eighty-four percent. All right, the question was asked: How much could the Pentagon budget be slashed without endangering national security? (Agreed, no lay person can know all the ins and outs, but come on, how much do you *think*?) And the median response was eleven percent.

Shanahan's campaign was beginning to take shape.

Now how did the polled public regard the senator himself? If they didn't feel they could trust him—and they didn't, apparently—why in heaven's name not? The percentage of don't-cares would have discouraged a less driven man. A clear majority of those who were willing to express an opinion said they couldn't vote for him because he was (A) too ambitious; and (B) too negative. They knew what he was against, but what was he *for*? There was little Shanahan could do about (A). He had said again and again that all he wanted was to continue his work in the Senate and have more time to spend with his family, and if people didn't believe him they could fuck themselves (he added privately). As for (B), that finding told him that it wasn't enough to vote nay on W-3, to ridicule it and organize the opposition against it. He had to put forward an equally effective but less costly alternative. Not to be tedious about it, eleven percent less costly.

An appointment was set up for him with Admiral Wilford Marx.

Marx was not popular outside his own little fiefdom, but Shanahan had always been tickled by the little son of a bitch. Whenever the Personnel Board passed Marx over for promotion—not because he was Jewish, they insisted, but because of his abrasiveness, his difficult personality—Shanahan would call in the top admirals and take off their skin in strips. Rookie senators lined up in the back of the Caucus Room to watch him work. And Marx would not only end up with the promotion, the exemption from compulsory retirement, he would get an enlarged budget line for his specialty. He was a submariner. He felt seasick whenever he looked at an aircraft carrier. He wanted to sink them all, along with how many careers.

Various ideas had been floating around for years. Marx and Shanahan's thinkers threw them all in the pot and cooked up Circe, a self-recycling, sea-bottom missile delivery system, promising much more protection for only $33 billion. Eleven percent less than the projected cost of W-3! With Circe, there would be no culture-gap problem, no need to pay off an indigenous population. Two thousand feet down, as silent and mobile as a jellyfish; the enemy might know it was *somewhere*, but wouldn't be able to pinpoint it. The main components would be manufactured by American Texas, the Shanahan family's own multinational—one of Shanahan's most engaging qualities was that he had never claimed to be much of an idealist.

So war was declared, not a cold war but a real one involving tons of money, tens of thousands of jobs, political futures, the survival of great corporations: Circe vs W-3, Sea Bottom vs the Wall.

Some of Mirabile's pragmatic memos were leaked to *The New York Times*. Mirabile considered himself a linear descendant of Niccolò Machiavelli. The Chiefs loved him for his lack of sentimentality, about civilian casualties in a nuclear exchange, for example, and why pretend that all races of people are precisely alike? But in the *Times*—ouch.

At small Georgetown dinners presided over by Shanahan's razor-thin wife, the Circe forces patched up an ad hoc coalition. Shanahan called in his IOUs. He couldn't be bluffing, the other senators reasoned. Not wanting to be left waving on the dock, they thronged aboard. It began to seem that the Pentagon was headed for its first major domestic disaster. And the amazing thing to the Chiefs was how *gleeful* everyone was. The spitefulness, the innuendo.

But the DOD is richer than the richest family in the land. The hydrants were opened. Arms were twisted all over the Senate Office Building; Art Buchwald, the columnist, reported hearing cries of pain as he walked down the hall.

The question was, had this counteroffensive been delayed too long? Shanahan had the desire. During the easy years, the Pentagon had put on weight around the middle, becoming short-winded, slower afoot, perceptibly less mean.

And then a little band of Colombian guerrillas, bless their eyes, came in out of nowhere, assaulted the Cartagena casino, slew two American majors, and made off with $1.2 million in cash and an arsenal of modern automatic weapons. Castro, people were reminded, started with a great deal less.

In one of Shanahan's early TV spots, he had demanded to know more about this hypothetical enemy which was threatening our Canal. Had the thing been allowed to get a little out of proportion? Thirty-seven billion for a lot of highly sophisticated stuff, to protect against bolt-action rifles and machetes? The news shows had been replaying this spot all day. It had been taped weeks ago, but somehow Shanahan managed to look less trustworthy with each repetition, and not only that, jowlier. Events had answered his sarcastic question. Who threatened the Canal? Cuban-led fanatics, using cowardly terrorist tactics, that was who.

And yet to Hal Amsterdam, a half hour before airtime, it all seemed a little too, how should he put it, a little too—

He reran the raw footage. Colonel Alvarez Blanco, chairman of the Council of Ministers, had been photographed in his hospital bed. Forgetting an important military precept, he had neglected to cover his own ass. Reporters had been pursuing

Señora Alvarez all day, to ask her what thoughts went through her mind while she was being kidnapped. She was under sedation, they were told.

The Pentagon press spokesman was referring to sensitive top-secret material, certain captured enemy documents. A defector was promised. One of the casino officials, Alvin ("Big K") Kraus, had agreed to be interviewed, although up to now he had been careful not to take sides in the politics of the host country. But this was too bleeping much, and he hoped that the rats who had ended the lives of those fine American officers Jack Grimes and Chester Sadowski would be hunted down and bleeping exterminated, like the rats they were. Sadowski's father, interviewed in Peoria, Illinois, recalled his son's glory days in high-school football, and wept on camera.

All marvelous stuff, but Amsterdam found himself stroking his cheek. Shanahan was promising, if elected, to cut the military budget by eleven percent. And the Chiefs didn't want to be cut, they wanted more. But did they want it badly enough to stage a mock raid, sacrificing two American majors? In a games situation, no spiritual descendant of Machiavelli would hesitate for an instant. But in real life, where everything eventually appears uncondensed in the *Times*?

Amsterdam distrusted coincidences, but he knew they do happen. And no doubt that was all this was, a happy coincidence—happy for W-3 and the Pentagon. Why, then, didn't his ironic muscle want to hold still?

Nine

L OVE IT OR LEAVE IT.

Iluminado continued to ponder the red, white and blue sticker pasted amid phone numbers and offers of blow jobs, whatever *they* were. What did it mean, that they didn't want you to stay unless you were *enthusiastic*?

Hearing knocks, he opened the cubicle door and looked out carefully. Two young men with shaved heads had lifted their saffron robes. They dropped the robes guiltily, perhaps ashamed to be caught urinating, and tried to put a flag in Iluminado's buttonhole. This was impossible, as the raincoat didn't have one.

His redheaded Samaritan was outside, and she had bought him a T-shirt.

"It's the last one they had," she said. "I warn you, it's pretty gruesome."

HOME OF THE WHOPPER, the message declared. A large arrow pointed downward. This meant, Iluminado supposed, that the T-shirt wearer would be laying claim to a champion's penis, like their government's boasts about the number of bombs in the stockpile.

"All I could get was Mrs. Clancy's machine," she told him. "Like leave a message after the beep? What were you going to do anyway, go to a hotel?"

Yes, the St. Albans, his father had made the arrangements, but—

"But is right," she agreed. "They're stuffy at that hotel, they don't let people in without pants on. Let's get out of here, number one. I've got sort of a boyfriend who's about your size and he's an altruist. I think he'd lend you some stuff. I'll call him from my place."

"I would be grateful."

"What can I tell you? It's dog eat dog in this town usually, and it's nice to have a chance to do something human for a God damn change. My name's Doris," she added.

"I am happy to meet you, Doris."

Her red hair was like the flashing light on an ambulance; people moved out of their way. In addition to socks and shorts, the transparent raincoat and the T-shirt, Iluminado was wearing his fiercest expression, to discourage remarks. But it was a strange race of people, norteamericanos. At home his odd costume would already have made him the center of a curious crowd. "What's happening, *hombre*, advertising something or what?" Here he was the next thing to invisible. They had their own worries, he guessed. Only the taxi driver seemed about to say something. Luckily for him he kept it to himself, for Iluminado's fingers were itching to fasten themselves around somebody's throat.

Traffic was stop and go. The air was better than on the Scratch 'n' Sniff patch in *Norte*, but not by an enormous amount. Doris was telling him about some kind of march or protest, but she felt no compulsion to finish her sentences, and he didn't understand much.

She lived in a one-room apartment in a narrow glass building. She was reading six books at once, all of them open on the living room rug amid a scatter of newspapers and magazines. The bed was almost as untidy as her hair. The rumpled sheets looked extremely inviting to Iluminado; they wanted him to get in.

"You need a shower, to start with," Doris said, turning on lights.

Yes, after rolling around on the floor of an international airport, Iluminado did need a shower. She brought him a green dragon robe. Like the T-shirts, it carried a message, but it was written in Chinese. The dragon was breathing fire; Iluminado also. The water ran hot, then cold, like the country itself. First a mugger, then a hospitable red-haired woman.

It was the tiniest of bathrooms. After drying himself he had to peer sideways over his shoulder to get a sense of the robe. The silk slid pleasantly over his skin, but did he look "gay" in it? He adjusted the sash and readjusted his expression, and went out.

While he was occupied in the shower, the bed had transformed itself into a sofa. Newspapers had been gathered, the books had been closed and stacked. Doris was at the phone.

"Wow," she said, seeing him in the doorway. Then quickly, for she had known him less than an hour, too soon for a compliment: "My friend's not home yet. Hungry?"

Very, he told her. He had been offered canapés on the airplane, but he hadn't thought he could trust them.

"Campari?" she suggested.

Campari, he said, would be fine. She added gin, turning the drink from garnet to rose, and because he was probably still tense after the mugging, she brought him a homemade cigarette, imported, like Iluminado himself, from Colombia. As a matter of fact, there were fine marijuana plantations only a few kilometers from his mother's finca. His mother had a strong prejudice on the subject, he told Doris, breathing in deeply, and he could be sure of a major fire-storm whenever she noticed the smell in his clothes. It wasn't too long ago that he used to ride out on his Japanese bike and smoke with some crazy Yankees who were building a highway. Somebody told his mother, and the next thing he knew he found himself in the army.

The languorous combination, gin, Campari and smoke, had made its way to his brain. Cracks were beginning to show in his English. He was getting the Alice in Wonderland shift: Doris's legs lengthened, while other objects in his range of vision drew off to the middle distance and diminished in size. The young woman on the airplane, too, had been conspicuous for the length of her legs. Iluminado's father had spoken with awe of the towering gringo women, but then all his women, whether at home or abroad, tended to be tall. Three or four years earlier, he had conducted a semipublic intrigue with the U.S. ambassador's wife, and that one, Iluminado had no trouble remembering, had been a real pillar of fire.

Doris wanted to know about Cartagena. A shabby city, Iluminado said, a place of great poverty, a very few modern buildings, one casino, narrow streets unsuitable for automobiles. TV vans, for example, had trouble getting about. Marlon Brando once made a film there, and people still talked about that. *Burn*, it was called. In the capital, life was more various. An occasional soccer riot, touring rock groups, things to do in the evenings. But in Cartagena, unless you liked to play slot machines, there was little excitement.

"Though last night," he said with a laugh, "well, last night was a considerable exception."

She asked in what way.

Where to begin? From the first afternoon, Gabriella had been an astonishment to him. Her beauty, her tenderness. He would lie awake at night imagining her touch. But a woman the age of his mother—would a stranger be able to understand? And did he want to admit to the dirty trick he had played on poor Major Sadowski? Dirty tricks are an inescapable part of warfare; still, he wasn't too eager to talk about it.

"Here it's undoubtedly different," he said, "but in my country it's the old story still. The husband who returns home unexpectedly, the wife's lover under the bed—"

But that was wrong, too. It wasn't a laughing matter. He lifted a hand.

"Actually I don't know why I spoke of it."

So much for Iluminado, and now what about Doris?

Her father, a college professor, had come to Washington to work for a president. When he arrived home after a day at the White House, he was always in a great state of excitement.

Then his president was assassinated and he had to go back to the lecture hall. He had hated that.

Doris attended one of the famous colleges which had recently, with enormous reluctance, agreed to educate women. She had managed to raise a few eyebrows there, she believed. She was an athlete, as Iluminado had guessed. She had been able to triple-jump farther than any other woman in the Ivy League. After graduation, recalling her father's White House excitements, she had decided on Washington. And she hadn't been disappointed. When the men put on their white ties and the women bared their shoulders for an opening at Kennedy Center, people as far away as Baltimore could see the glow on the horizon. Money in unimaginable amounts. Any sum less than a billion was hardly worth mentioning. Park at a shopping mall, and out of the next car might come a senator's wife. Or Nancy Kissinger! Or the White House staffer in charge of authorized leaks!

There was only one negative: the creep she worked for. She kept feeding him fantastic ideas, and it was like dropping stones down a well. Really and truly, a world-class chauvinist asshole.

She tried her friend's number again. Still no answer.

"Don't panic," she said. "If he doesn't come home maybe we can buy your uniform back in the morning. There's only a certain number of thrift shops."

In the morning? Was this, Iluminado wondered, an invitation to spend the night?

"I'm beginning to change my mind about the United States," he said. "A magazine I read on the airplane told me to expect only coldness, hostility."

"That would be me usually, but you're pretty neat-looking, you know, this makes a difference. Didn't I say something about dinner? I'll faint with hunger unless I can get up this minute. Right away," she told herself. "*Up!*"

His eyes were closing. Not blinking but closing, in the first stages of sleep.

"I, too," he thought he was able to say.

The recent knock on the head seemed to have scrambled some of his old ideas. Why shouldn't a woman, if she was

102

attracted to someone— The things Gabriella had been trying to tell him about the insatiability of North American women—

He woke up when Doris appeared with two trays.

It wasn't dinner as the word is understood in Colombia. Doris explained that the reason the orange juice was that sickly color was that she had laced it with Spirolina, in other words algae, to bring out its nutritive quality. The sautéed kelp needed no explanation. As for the seal blubber, it was wonderful for the complexion. Eskimos had had beautiful skin until we came along with our hamburgers.

He was trying to listen. What did *Eskimos* have to do with it?

"Poor baby, you're half asleep. Dessert?"

Dessert was an apricot, served on a saucer. For apricots, Iluminado learned, are practically pure vitamin G, and G, as most people know, is the sex vitamin. As she imparted this new information, she gave him a flickering glance, which started the age-old reaction. A moment later, God knew how because he had little control over his arms and legs, they were kissing.

Gabriella had been right: a sexual revolution was sweeping the United States. Doris knew nothing about him whatever, but it didn't appear to matter. A well-placed kick and a tug turned the sofa back to a bed. There continued to be a mingling of tongues. Hers tasted of vitamin G, or was it H? He would have to remember to ask her at breakfast, over coffee, though it wouldn't be real coffee, he knew—not in this house.

Probably marijuana had been a mistake. Airplane lag isn't supposed to operate when traveling south to north, but Iluminado's head was going around like the roulette wheel at the Bolívar, with similar clicks. Time ran swiftly at first, then slowed down and stabilized at approximately one hundred and twenty seconds a minute. He heard himself laughing. This was undoubtedly good for him. Gabriella had been telling him not to take himself so seriously.

Remembering other lessons, he began to participate more actively. With this magnificent woman, there was a great deal of terrain to cover.

And the buzzer sounded.

Doorbells in Colombia are less harsh and demanding, and Iluminado didn't associate the sound at first with the door. But it went on insisting, and Doris sighed, finally, and left him.

A tiny peephole had been cut into the door at eye level. She clicked it open.

He heard from outside: "Police officer. Open up—"

She came back for the Chinese robe. "You're being rescued, it seems, isn't that depressing?"

Rescued?

It was necessary to throw several bolts in order for the door to be opened. A man entered with drawn pistol. Iluminado's first thought was that Hernán Vega had sent someone. A second man followed, pink-cheeked and white-haired, innocent enough in appearance.

"Isn't that my young man you've got there?"

"Duffy, you *prick*," Doris said.

Not a Vegaite, then. Never mind, explanations could wait. Iluminado exploded upward, taking the entire room by surprise.

This was unarmed attack, as taught by the ferocious Major Sadowski. An instant later, it was Iluminado who was holding the pistol. It was a short-barreled Smith and Wesson, a weapon to be given serious attention. He had retained his erection, and he threatened them with that as well.

"My dear Iluminado," Doris said faintly.

"Not loaded, I'm happy to say," the policeman told him. "This was supposed to be one of those deals where you show people the gun and everybody cooperates."

But perhaps he was lying? Iluminado pointed the pistol at a photograph of John F. Kennedy, looking like the martyr he later turned out to be, and squeezed the trigger. When no bullet emerged, the pink-cheeked gentleman came out from behind the door, smoothing his hair.

"I am Captain Hector Duffy, U.S. Navy retired," he announced. "I must say, I like your spunk! You realize you've been hijacked, Captain? But we go in for happy endings in this country. We're hijacking you back and giving you a lift to the St. Albans. Somebody stole your uniform, I think."

He stepped outside. Iluminado lowered the gun slowly. His erection, too, was beginning to tick downward. Looking at Doris for guidance, he noticed that either anger or the green of the robe had brought out freckles on her forearms and across the bridge of her nose, a pretty effect.

She shrugged. "He's just going to give you some money. This is the boss I was telling you about."

"You mean the chauvinist asshole?"

She laughed. "That describes him. Though I may not be working for him very much longer."

Duffy came in, carrying Iluminado's suitcase and everything the mugger had stolen.

"I heard that. I'll say you won't be working for me. You're on unemployment, as of now."

"I've been thinking about leaving anyway. That's why I've been slaving away at the Xerox lately. Just don't say yes too fast," she advised Iluminado. "Get some bidding going and watch the numbers go through the roof."

"That will be just about enough," Duffy said. "As soon as the captain gets dressed we'll be saying goodnight to you, Doris, a.k.a. Benedict Arnold."

Iluminado was feeling his nakedness. But to dress in front of these strangers would give them an unfair advantage, he felt, so he took his clothes to the bathroom. Question marks, dragging their long tails, hooked and tangled. He understood nothing! But the excellent English cloth, the knife in his boot, restored him to George S. Patton, Jr.'s, profession. His period of helplessness was over.

Doris and her former employer were nose to nose, exchanging remarks which were probably not compliments. It was all too splintered for Iluminado to follow. The policeman had helped himself to some gin, and now he took a handful of bean sprouts, which he spat out immediately.

"Can I kiss him good-bye?" Doris asked Duffy.

"You definitely cannot kiss him good-bye."

But she was on her way. It was a less than serious kiss, with a scarcely perceptible movement of the lips. She slipped him a plastic circle she had snapped out of her telephone.

"I thought that was really nice, a minute ago. Maybe we can finish it sometime."

"You stay away from Captain Castillo or we'll have you enjoined," Duffy said sharply. "And that's the minimum that can happen. Mr. G generally goes for the maximum."

They were ready. Doris tossed Iluminado the uneaten apricot.

"Don't let them screw you."

Downstairs there was another delay. The policeman wanted to be paid.

"To keep the game honest, you know?"

Duffy offered to write him a check. He took a step backward. "Cash! Cash!"

In the end they stopped at a sort of outdoor slot machine, into which Duffy inserted a card. The machine responded only after being sworn at and slapped. Then the money began to come—twenty-dollar bill after twenty-dollar bill.

"Jackpot!" Duffy said merrily.

He and Iluminado rode in back, behind wire. The inside door handles had been removed, adding to Iluminado's feeling that he had little control over what was happening. Every small irregularity in the pavement sent a shock wave rippling up to the pain centers, which were overloaded already. He was glad to have his uniform back, he supposed, glad to be driven to his hotel. At the same time, he missed Doris's untidy sheets.

All in all, a baffling half hour. *"Isn't that my young man you've got there?" "Going to give you some money." "Don't say yes too fast."* What did it all mean?

"How—" he began, but was too tired to finish.

"How did I find you? My secret, Captain! No, you'd better know what kind of person you've been dealing with. Did you catch that remark about Xeroxes?"

"The word hardly sounds English."

"It means she's been stealing my lists. Home addresses, unlisted phone numbers. All kinds of valuable information. If a man pulled something like that, the word would be larceny. But she's a woman, as you may have noticed. Their excuse is, they have to play catch-up." He made an expansive gesture.

"There are hundreds of thousands out there, and they're restless, Captain. If they ever get organized, God help us. Maybe you wondered why I wasn't at the airport to meet you. What the bitch did, she faked a message from my client Mr. Sam Green, to meet him right away at the lawyer's office in Silver Spring. Mr. G's famous for pulling that kind of last-minute switch. And he wasn't there. Wasn't even expected."

Iluminado was trying to listen, but he had caught a glimpse of the Pentagon on the far side of the river, and the lights were all on. Being newly arrived in a cynical country, he had his first cynical thought. Were the windows lighted because everybody was staying late to deal with some crisis, or because they wanted the public to believe they were getting their money's worth?

Duffy's explanation continued. "A piece of incredible luck, but Mr. Sam Green has to be one of the luckiest men in the United States, and some of that is bound to rub off on the people who work for him. I was running into International Arrivals, twenty minutes past plane time through no fault of my own, and who do I bump into but a Latino I happen to recognize. In fact, he does messenger work for me. About five-ten, aviator shades, a T-shirt that had Somebody for President on it. Any of this ring a bell? And he was carrying a pair of boots, the same boots you're wearing right now, a uniform over his arm. From some foreign army, with captain's bars! Are you beginning to get the picture?"

Iluminado had a picture of sorts, but he couldn't give the matter his full attention. For parts of downtown Washington, he was discovering, were as crowded as the *tugerios* on the slopes above Bogotá. Hundreds of shabbily dressed young people with mystifying signs, perhaps declaring that they had no place to sleep, congregated in groups on the sidewalks, on the steps of government buildings. Some plucked at guitars. Their songs were mournful. Iluminado marveled again at the power of North American propaganda. Not a word of this had been allowed to appear in the Colombian press.

The sidewalk in front of his hotel and the lobby inside were also crowded, but with middle-aged or elderly women wearing pastel pants-suits, pale yellow, pale violet, pale pink, and large labels in the shape of American flags. "Hi! I'm Edna, from Baton Rouge." "Hi! I'm Molly, from Tacoma."

"Couldn't get you the suite I wanted," Duffy said. "When the Revolutionary Dames are in town the rest of us have to move over."

He introduced Iluminado to a hotel official, who waived the red tape and summoned a bellhop.

"Ride up with you, if I may," Duffy said.

"That's very nice of you, Captain Duffy, but I think—"

"I know! You must be exhausted. And I'm sleepy as hell myself, frankly. Mr. G gets along on three hours sleep, and he doesn't take into consideration that other people may have a different metabolism. But I'm more than a trifle concerned, to be frank with you, Captain. Doris didn't pull that stunt on her own. Somebody put her up to it. I think I know who, and those Am Tex people don't quit, they keep coming at you. So why don't we do it like this? We'll have our little chat, just the two of us, and I'll leave Sergeant Rafferty on guard, to make sure you get a good night's sleep. No telling what that female will try next."

They followed the bellhop through a happy babble. The women around them were hooting, exchanging little make-believe blows, in a faint aroma of the sweeter liqueurs. They rode up with Edna, from Birmingham, and Gloria, from Boston. With the lingering marijuana fumes still in his brain, Iluminado couldn't decide how to get rid of Duffy short of using karate, and he was too tired for that.

The policeman stayed in the hall. The bellman whisked about checking light switches and window shades until Duffy paid him to leave them alone. It was a marvelous bedroom, like the setting for a television movie about the empty life of a perfume-company executive: a great bed with a canopy, lilies in a porcelain bowl, a box of chocolates, a wedge of Brie and crackers, a bottle of Campari, a bottle of gin. Iluminado hadn't realized that Campari-gin was such a popular North American drink.

Duffy bartended.

"Have a cigar?"

"Please."

The cigars came in silvery tubes. When they were ready for smoking, Duffy lit them with a gold lighter, snapped it shut and sent it spinning to Iluminado.

"To make up for your embarrassment at the airport."

Iluminado was still gripping Doris's apricot. Though loaded with sex vitamins, it was a little wrinkled and unattractive by now. Nevertheless he found himself eating it.

"She was kind to me after I was mugged."

"Kind!" Duffy stared at him. "Don't you realize yet, Captain, that what happened out there didn't just happen to happen? She choreographed the whole thing. Faked me out of the way and set up the mugging, so she could come clicking along and be *muy simpático.* 'Oh, dear me, you're hurt. Come home with me and I'll make it all well.'"

Yes, Iluminado thought, putting pieces together, it could have happened that way.

"But I still don't understand *why.*"

"Well, the gals are always whining about how hard it is to meet men in this town."

His manner shifted abruptly, as though he had given himself new instructions.

"We got off to a shaky start, Captain, but I want you to look back on the next few days as the most enjoyable of your life. Washington used to be a pretty dull town, but not anymore. We have as much X-rated entertainment as any city in America."

"I read about that on the plane. I couldn't be sure how much of it was true."

"Let's find out, shall we!" He added hopefully, "But you don't want to go anywhere tonight, do you?"

Iluminado looked toward the bed, which had been turned down for the night.

"Thank you, no, under the circumstances."

Duffy crossed his legs, making no move to leave. His socks lay on his ankles without a wrinkle. What struck Iluminado most strongly about him was that he seemed excessively *clean.* Such rosiness could only have been achieved by frequent scrubbings with a rough cloth. And a word jumped into his mind.

"Gay?" It would explain a great deal. When Iluminado burst out of Doris's bed, Duffy had cried, "I like your spunk!" Could that be gringo slang for penis?

"Don't let them screw you," Doris had said.

He went to the phone, and managed to break the code that would permit him to reach the operator. When a feminine voice asked how she could help him, he explained that this was his first night in the United States and friends were making fun of him because he didn't understand colloquial expressions.

"What does screw mean?"

Two seconds of silence. "Get off the line, crumbbum, or I'm transferring this call to Security."

"That's what I thought." He turned back to Duffy. "I'm told that it's O.K. in your country to ask people personal questions. What do you do for a living?"

"For a living." Duffy coughed out a mouthful of smoke. "I call myself a facilitator. Party of the first part, party of the second part, they're having trouble coming to a meeting of the minds. I use the analogy of a stuck bolt. It's rusted up, you can't get it to move. Squirt on some WD-40. Give it a minute, and everything sl-l-lides"—he demonstrated— "smooth as silk. Speaking of which, isn't it time to get down to business? I like to think of money when I'm falling asleep, don't you? I know you're wondering how high we're ready to go."

We? Was the mysterious Mr. G the homosexual then, Duffy only the facilitator?

"But first, you know," Iluminado said gently, "shouldn't you find out if I want to 'get down to business,' as you call it?"

Some of Duffy's drink went into his lap.

"Did that double-crossing bitch make you an offer?"

As a matter of fact, besides promising to call the secondhand shops, Doris had offered him a small loan until he could arrange for a transfer of funds.

"She mentioned something."

Duffy was more and more agitated.

"She may have tried to give the impression that she has a solid deal lined up, but that's hogwash, Captain. *Im*possible. She was just trying to get you feeling indebted. You're too intelligent to fall for that siren song. Mr. G may have his quirks, but financially speaking he's top-quality prime. Personal fortune in the high nine figures. Promises? Anybody can make promises. Whereas when I talk money, I'm talking *money*. In the sense of one-hundred-dollar bills in a TWA flight bag."

"No amount of money," Iluminado said, "could persuade me to do something I believe is immoral."

Much of the rosiness had left Duffy's cheeks.

"Immoral. Well, technically, yeah, there's a statute against it, but that's the way it is in this business, everybody does it—"

"Not everybody surely?"

"Ah!" Duffy exclaimed, slapping his forehead. "How dumb can I get? You think this is some kind of Abscam."

He unbuttoned his jacket and spread his arms. "Don't take my word for it. Frisk me."

"You will have to excuse me." Did the man actually think Iluminado was going to embrace him? "I am ordered to be at the Pentagon at oh nine hundred hours. I suppose when you were in the Navy you went to bed early?"

"With the sea gulls! At the Pentagon, you say? Can I help you with anything there?"

"I'm attending Counter Coup school. But I can find it, I think."

"Counter Coup, excellent cover. Here's a suggestion. Why don't I pick you up at oh seven hundred and we'll thrash it all out over breakfast? I get the feeling that we aren't understanding each other completely."

As it seemed to be the only way to get him out of the bedroom, Iluminado agreed to be taken to breakfast and let Duffy show him the way to the appropriate Pentagon office. Fussily, Duffy gathered himself to go. Naval captains, Iluminado knew, are higher than army captains, and if Doris had been even partially right, how did he get those promotions?

"Did you have your own command?"

Duffy peered at him suspiciously. "Told you about that, did she? Did she also tell you I was completely exonerated?"

They were talking at right angles again.

"Well," Duffy said. He looked down at the high shine on his shoes and said modestly, "Will you want a woman?"

"I beg your pardon."

"We barged in at a bad time, and that can be very unsettling, physiologically speaking. It's on us, of course."

He bluffed toward the phone.

"I believe not," Iluminado told him.

"Then let me have somebody drop by to wake you. That's so much pleasanter than the impersonal phone call." He held up a hand. "Don't thank me, it's our pleasure. Dream of dollar signs, Captain! Starting tomorrow at seven, it's a whole nother ball game."

And at last he was gone.

Along with the flowers, the chocolates and the rest, the hotel offered each guest the luxury of a generous full-length mirror. Iluminado faced his reflection, frowning. "Gay" people are to be found in all countries, but Colombian homosexuals had always been able to tell at a glance that Iluminado was a young man whose inclination was toward girls. What had happened, all of a sudden? What did they all *see*?

Iluminado himself saw only the face he was used to, a little confused, the pupils still somewhat altered from marijuana.

He broke open the chocolates, which he hadn't wanted to do while Duffy was here. For who knows, biting into a chocolate in another man's presence might be considered a sexual invitation!

Doris had been accused by Duffy of a number of things, and Iluminado thought she deserved a chance to explain. He dialed the number on the little plastic circle she had slipped him. With the apricot pit to remind him of her long athlete's legs, he listened to the phone ringing in an apparently empty apartment. Not at home—conferring with her principals, no doubt, he thought bitterly.

He looked for Isobel Clancy's number but it was not in the phone book. He dialed Directory Assistance and learned, a moment later, that the leathery woman, along with other particular people, had ordered the phone company not to release this information.

So Doris had been lying again when she said she spoke to Isobel Clancy's machine.

And an idea came to him—a little late, true, but there were good reasons for that. His brain fogged and cleared, fogged again, cleared. Isobel Clancy had come to the airport to meet Iluminado's father, and *so had Doris*! And the mugger as well!

He selected another chocolate. Standing in front of the tall mirror, he watched himself chew and swallow. Well, there was an easy way to find out. He was penniless in American money, but the hotel, he found, was willing to put it on the bill. Minutes later, the phone was picked up in Bogotá.

His father was delighted to hear who was calling.

"Nado!" From the slight huskiness, Iluminado was able to deduce that his father had been drinking champagne. "Splendid! From Washington? I was right, wasn't I—a magnificent city?"

Music was playing in the faraway room. ". . . *if* I took even one *sniff* it would bore me terr*if*—"

"I'm sorry I couldn't fly up with you," the voice continued. "Unexpected emergency. Wait one moment till I turn down the Cole Porter."

A woman laughed. The laugh sounded somehow familiar. Could it be Gabriella? Iluminado dismissed the idea. With her husband in the hospital, she wouldn't leave Cartagena. Something fell over, and the phone clicked in his ear like the hammer of an unloaded pistol.

The operator did her best, but she couldn't restore the connection. The mirrored reflection was watching again. Iluminado forced the panic out of his face. Tomorrow, as they said in North America—a whole nother ball game.

113

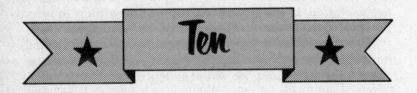

Ten

Although a third-generation Texan, Senator Hugh Shanahan did the act in the modern style. He hardly ever wore the big hat. The accent was nearly gone, returning only for those few months every six years when he had to go home to campaign.

He was no longer looked on as much of a bigot—a bit of an elitist, perhaps. He rowed in all weathers, climbed difficult mountains and played a murderous game of handball. His face would have been thought too good to be true except for deep parentheses bracketing his mouth. These scored lines said that he had seen trouble, he had suffered as much as poor people, he had just as much right to sing the blues.

He had a bad memory for names, an unusual thing in a politician. He called all his assistants Steve, which was hard on outsiders because they already resembled each other in too many ways. When Shanahan and three or four Steves came down a Capitol corridor, wearing the same suit, the same haircut, all in top shape, senators with less seniority and no inherited wealth stepped to the wall, feeling like also-rans.

He was most often seen smiling, but his face was grim at

this moment, as no one present was not on his payroll. The office lighting had been designed by a Broadway professional. Shanahan's dark curls were backlit, so it would seem to his more pious constituents, visiting him here for the first time, that he might be wearing a nimbus. Even now, in deep political rouble, he gave off a glitter of excitement, of menace.

He sat under the big flag, tooled anteater boots on the table, testing his ability to lay a wooden ball into an eggcup while his advisers bickered. One of the discouraging things about American public opinion, as measured by polls, is how quickly it can change, like a sudden tropical sunset: one minute it is full afternoon, the next minute night. In the last nose-count in the Senate, it had seemed that Shanahan, opposing the Pentagon's silly Central American Wall (silly according to Shanahan), would carry the day by six, a stunning upset that would bring him into the Iowa caucuses smelling like a winner. Then the Darien Gap insurgency, the existence of which had never been suspected by any intelligence agency, had materialized from the steam and drip of the rain forest, and Shanahan's allies threw down their weapons and ran.

It was four in the morning. They would have liked to sit back and do simulations, order more polls, but they had to reach a decision by the time the Senate convened. They had used up their time-outs. One faction at the table wanted to try what conciliation would do. Sit down with the Chiefs, throw them some table scraps, and maybe they'd be willing to make the vote close, so Shanahan would at least come out looking courageous. Not in the cards, others maintained; the Chiefs had been frightened so badly that they would settle for nothing less than unconditional surrender.

Results of the previous afternoon's preliminaries were beginning to come in. Nearly twenty percent of the sample was questioning the senator's patriotism! What could he say in rebuttal? "I'm a loyal American, all the way through! Right or wrong! Believe me." That had been tried by others, especially in the McCarthy years, and it had never worked.

Social psychology teaches the importance of moving fast, before a new attitude has time to harden. Kagoulian, the one

Shanahan aide who was actually named Steve, suggested an option. What if the boss hopped into the airplane and flew down to Cartagena, to announce his conversion to W-3 at a media conference in the gutted casino? Shanahan—the one candidate with the strength, the secure ego, to be able to admit a mistake.

Shanahan listened to the clash of opinions, saying little. His hand remained steady. The ball continued to plop into the eggcup. It was only a game, but games were important to Shanahan. He had nineteen completions in a row. From time to time the Steves sent him sidelong glances. Even God Almighty has been known to drop an occasional decision. And when that happened to Shanahan, in spite of everything his staff could do to prevent it, he had been known to give them a taste of the famous family wrath, shouting unforgivable insults for which they nonetheless eventually had to forgive him. People who build in a swamp, as the saying goes, shouldn't complain of wet basements.

The senior senator from New Hampshire, Jerry Ziegler, who had been given the nickname Zigzag because of his frequent 180-degree reversals, showed up radiating terror, with no program except to throw themselves on the Chiefs' mercy. And mercy, as everyone knows, is not part of the curriculum at any service academy. They didn't let him in to infect Shanahan. Eileen, the mother of Shanahan's seven difficult children, ordered coffee, insisted that he take a dollop of brandy in lieu of sugar and cream, laid her ornamented fingers on his wrist to italicize a point, and sent him home feeling that his career was far from over.

While this was going on in one office, a tall red-haired young woman in pinstriped flannel was being questioned in another. Less than three minutes into the interview, the chief Steve, Kagoulian, a cold fish as a rule, did an out-of-character thing. He came around the table and hugged her.

"Doris, I'm going to have somebody verify this, and then I want you to come in and repeat it to the senator. And if it hits him the way it hits me, I think he's going to give you three wishes."

Smiling for the first time in almost twenty-two hours, he

took her into the big office. The smile by itself was enough to stop the discussion. They all looked at Doris. The pinstripes fitted her the way a zebra skin fits a zebra. If Senator Shanahan had a weakness, it was for flamboyant women, and the little ball bounced from the lip of the cup, ending his streak at twenty-seven, a personal best.

"All those Hail Marys we've been saying have got us some action," Kagoulian announced. "Doris, you have the floor."

These were nervous people, up long after their bedtime. Doris waited till the fidgeting stopped.

"Seven P.M. last night," she said, going straight to the point. "Pan Am flight from Bogotá-Barranquilla. Channel Twelve checked the flight list for somebody from Cartagena who could give them an update. And sure enough, a captain in the Colombian Army, handsome as sin, like squeezy and fierce at the same time. They stuck a mike in his face. What about the guerrilla attack? And a complete blank, Senator. *'Guerrillas in Cartagena, you've got to be kidding.'* "

"*You've* got to be kidding," Shanahan said, laying cup and ball on the table. "Into a live mike?"

"Absolutely. I was about three feet away. The reason I was there—I work for a contact firm, I don't know if you've heard of it. Correction. Past tense, I just resigned. Hector Duffy Associates? His big account—his only account, really—is Hawk-Sisley, and you know how they stand with the Colombian junta."

"Fill us in, Steve," Shanahan said.

His Latin American staff man answered.

"Forty Piranha fighters, Hughie. Twenty million a copy. But there was a hassle about the vigorish. De Santamaría wanted too big an increase and Mr. G dumped him. I don't know if the new people inherit the deal."

"Oh, yes," Doris said. "My captain's here to negotiate the under-the-table. And something hit me all of a sudden. The Piranha's been having its troubles, and wouldn't the Colombians feel safer in some different airplane? The John Wayne, for example?"

An invisible string ensemble began playing Brahms. The John Wayne, of course, was the hot new fighter manufactured by American Texas, the Shanahan family firm. Although an excellent airplane, according to company officials, it was still one hundred and ten units short of break-even.

Shanahan showed his most boyish smile.

"Doris" (remembering her name, which showed the impression she had made on him), "I think you and I are going to be friends."

"I hope so, Senator, because I'm thinking about going into business for myself and I need to know a few committee chairmen by their first names."

"I'm a committee chairman," he told her, "and my first name is Hughie. Tell me more about this captain from Cartagena, where I'm glad to hear they don't have guerrillas."

"The scouting report on him is that he's fun-loving, and a friend of the free enterprise system. He was here last year. He went to parties a lot and soaked up a lot of gin and Campari. Isobel Clancy took him on a tour of the Civil War battlefields, and she told people afterward that they didn't spend much time on the battlefields. When he wasn't with Isobel he used call girls, which surprises me now that I've met him. He always asked the booker to send somebody tall, redheaded if possible, and that's what gave me my basic idea. Because I'm redheaded, as you see, and I'm not exactly chopped off at the ankles."

Another Steve, sent by Kagoulian to check with Channel Twelve, came in looking pleased.

"They didn't use it on the eleven o'clock, Hughie. It seems the guy got irritated and pulled out the mike wire. So they decided, why give him publicity? But they confirm some of the quotes." He read from a yellow pad. " *'Guerrillas took over the town, didn't they.' 'You must be thinking of some different country. Guerrillas in sleepy Cartagena? Complete eradication for many years now. If someone has been circulating rumors—'* "

Still another Steve bounced a paper clip off the table.

"Now wait," Kagoulian commanded, "before we start throwing paper clips. No way this thing's a complete hoax. Maybe he didn't understand the question, too many Negronis on the airplane. Or how about this as a possibility? He went to bed early and slept through the fireworks. Then he left for the airport in the morning before anybody could tell him what happened."

They looked back at Doris.

She had never picked up the tar-and-nicotine habit, but needing something to do with her hands, for she was as nervous as they were, she lit a coltsfoot-and-raspberry cigarette. Seeing no ashtrays—Shanahan didn't smoke, so his staff didn't smoke—she dropped the match on the carpet.

"Is everybody's seat belt fastened? The name of this sex object is *Iluminado Castillo.*"

She got nothing but blank looks.

"Iluminado Castillo," she repeated. "Tea in a glass, Havana newspaper. The one-man rescue."

"Yeah!" Kagoulian said fervently. "I hear you."

"One against four, right? I've seen him move, and that part I believe. I had him to myself for three or four hours, and I was making pretty good headway. But my boss broke it up before I could start talking airplanes. All right, you can't win them all. I didn't have time yesterday to read anything but headlines. But I don't like to let the papers get ahead of me, so after we all said goodnight I made myself comfortable and put on my glasses, and wham! There couldn't be two captains from Cartagena named Iluminado Castillo. And how come he didn't say something about it? I've been trying to remember what he did say, but we were on our third joint by then, so don't expect a verbatim transcript. Cartagena, a dull town usually—I know this is going to sound crazy—but not last night, he said, and then there was something about a husband coming home early and a lover under the bed. 'Nothing important, don't know why I mentioned it.' Well, *something* happened, some kind of commotion, but maybe somebody's exaggerating, to get us excited. I did a paper in college on Lyndon Johnson and how we got into Vietnam, and I can't stop thinking about those silly torpedo boats, do you remember, in the Tonkin Gulf?"

It landed in the middle of the table and went off like a three-stage skyrocket. Pink blossoms. Blue blossoms. White blossoms. *Bang.* Shanahan himself had voted for that resolution, and had been apologizing ever since.

119

"Holy shit," Kagoulian said.

The senator came out of his chair and made a slow circuit of the room.

"Where do we find this guy?"

Doris smiled like a pregnant Madonna and blew a long plume of raspberry-smelling smoke.

"Doris, don't you trust us?"

"I guess I have to. I'd just like to hear a sum mentioned."

Shanahan mentioned a sum, and she said promptly, "He's staying at the St. Albans. He's supposed to report to the Pentagon at nine, which gives us what, four and a half hours? What do you think, a subpoena?"

Kagoulian called the gathering back to order, and went around taking opinions. The media man—every staff needs a pessimist—wondered if the whole affair hadn't been concocted by Pentagon gamesmen, to trick Shanahan into making false charges.

"Wouldn't that be a little baroque, even for them?" the senator said. "But you're right, let's be sure of our facts before we call any press conferences."

"Alternatively," the next Steve said, "say we get our hands on this kid before they can program him. Once more, the big bad Pentagon. Two fine American officers shot down to stampede the Senate into voting for a weapons program nobody needs. That's going to shake public confidence in the divinity of the Joint Chiefs, and do we really want that?"

But the chances were, the others thought, coming back to the Tonkin Gulf, that there had been some kind of minor shootout which the media—the media, not the Pentagon—had pumped into a two-day sensation.

One of the Steves left for the airport, hoping to reach Cartagena before the cover-up was completely in place. Another began drafting a summons, commanding Iluminado's appearance before the Armed Services Corrupt Practices Oversight Subcommittee, Shanahan's principal vehicle for exposing the subterfuges and intrigues of his political opponents.

There was one black Steve at the table. He wore the suit, the necktie and haircut, but he didn't really belong. He would

120

be instantly terminated, he knew, if the senator faltered in the early primaries. The author of the standard monograph on inner-city voting patterns, he had left the inner city behind, he hoped for good.

Throughout the discussion, he had been drinking cup after cup of strong coffee. It had its predictable effect, and he had to go to the bathroom. Alone in a closed stall, he brought out a tiny one-channel radiotelephone, and activated a recessed switch.

He was calling Shin Bet, Israeli intelligence. All Texas politicians have oil in their background somewhere. In spite of Shanahan's public pleasantries, the Israelis feared that when money was on the table he might tilt toward the Arabs. They had no direct interest in what the black Steve was telling them, but they had a reciprocal deal with various U. S. agencies, trading favor for favor. The Navy should get this, they decided. The Washington agent-in-place roused a lieutenant commander on the hoot-owl watch in Flag Plot, below ground at the Pentagon.

The peacetime Navy is so barnacle-encrusted that some of its harsher critics, Admiral Wilford Marx first and foremost, think it can be made competitive only by being careened and scraped. Nevertheless it can move fast when it has to. An hour and ten minutes later, two professional holdup men entered the offices of Channel Twelve News.

Three people were present. The visitors relieved them of money and jewelry, herded them into a soundproof studio and locked the door from the outside.

Now the real operation commenced.

A signals technician was waiting outside. He found the outtakes from the previous night's shooting. Running them through a sound reader, he located the airport footage. He had brought two Nagra recorders. On Nagra I he recorded three minutes of generalized crowd noise. Transferring the film to a preview projector, he ran it again, mixing the Nagra I tape with the film sound, and recording the new mixture on Nagra II.

He kept playing with the volume. He let the interviewer's questions through, but brought up the background babble to

121

blot out Iluminado's answers. As a final step, he fed the doctored tape back into the projector. Functioning as a recording instrument, it erased the old sound line and laid down the new.

"Sleepy Cartagena—" *"If someone has been spreading rumors—"* It was all gone now, and no electronic magic could call it back.

Eleven

The off-duty cop Duffy had used earlier could be seen dozing on a folding chair outside Iluminado's door. Doris had come with Kagoulian to explain that their intentions were wholly benevolent. All they wanted to do was sell airplanes and make everybody rich and happy. She had come down a notch from the excitement of meeting a senator, but the sight of the snoozing cop set the synapses sparking again. She returned to the elevator while Kagoulian went ahead to see if the cop was impressed with his ID. Not at all, Kagoulian reported a moment or two later. An administrative assistant? To the D.C. police, that was only a small step higher than nobody.

He hurried off to get a court order and a federal marshal. While she waited, Doris had an idea. Finding a pay phone, she dialed a number she had had occasion to use when she was working for Duffy.

The listing was Womanpower Unlimited. Girls dispatched from this agency all had college degrees, or so the agency claimed, perhaps to justify the hourly rates.

"This is Doris, from the Hector Duffy office?"

"Doris, hey. Working nights now?"

"No, this is above and beyond. I just sat up out of a sound sleep with a horrible suspicion. Did Duffy remember to call you?"

"Wait a minute, look at the book. Room 1228, Saint A., a six o'clock wake-up. Tall, docile redhead. But I'm glad you called, Doris, because what's this about a guard on the door?"

"What are you talking about, guard on the door?"

"He said the guy's been getting crank calls so they gave him protection. I don't like the sound of it, frankly. We tend to forget that what we're doing here, there are ordinances against it."

"Jesus!" Doris exclaimed. "You can't trust old Duff to do the simplest thing. He said tall? That must be the little jockey-size guy from Seattle, at the Ambassador. This is somebody else entirely, a monsignor, from the Vatican I think. What a thing *that* would be. Needless to say, cancel."

"We'll have to bill you, Doris. I didn't have a redhead so Lily dyed her hair special."

"Bill us the full amount, naturally."

It was five thirty, and though Doris had been to bed briefly with Iluminado, briefly again while she looked at the newspapers, she still hadn't had any sleep. Both she and her flannel, no doubt, looked a little shopworn and seedy. She did what she could with what she had, poked at her hair, swallowed two hundred milligrams of B-12, ate a dried apricot and came out of the elevator snapping her fingers and humming.

She prodded the cop with a sharp toe. In high heels, dark glasses and lipstick, she was sure she bore little resemblance to the tousled, barefooted redhead he had seen earlier, wearing a green Chinese robe.

He felt for the room key. "Is it six already?"

"Come on. He won't complain about getting an extra half hour."

"What did you say your name was?"

"I keep trying pseudonyms," Doris said wearily, "but tonight I'm told the password is Lily. Will you hurry it up, please? These shoes are killing me."

He unlocked the door and let her in.

124

Iluminado had thrown off the sheet, and again she saw him in full erection. Young men in the morning! His eyelids quivered. Rapid eye movement sleep—she hoped he was dreaming about her.

She saw a half-eaten box of chocolates on the bedside table. Because he was a naive foreigner who undoubtedly didn't know chocolates were bad for him, she emptied the box into the wastebasket.

Isobel Clancy and the tour of the battlefields, referrals from Womanpower Unlimited—it didn't make sense. He had been a year younger then, shyer, perhaps.

"Iluminado," she whispered, "you are the *loveliest* man."

When she touched his cheek he murmured something in Spanish.

"Crawl in bed with you? Sure," Doris said, and began taking off clothes.

Iluminado couldn't remember what they called this in gringo-land, but it was amazingly pleasant. He was poised at the edge of a cliff and it was nearly time to hurl himself over. But it wasn't courteous, he knew, to think only of his own pleasure. The woman, too, had to be considered.

He opened his eyes. The first thing he recognized was the hair. It was not, as he had imagined, Gabriella. The bedsprings ejected him.

"You," he said, pointing. His finger was trembling. "You hired the mugger." He remembered Duffy's phrase. "That didn't happen to happen. You arranged it, the whole thing. When I turn my head suddenly, I can still feel his blow."

Some of her lipstick had rubbed off but she still looked magnificently healthy. No doubt he should order her to put on her clothes and get out, but this was a clever girl, a university graduate, and he would be interested to hear what she had to say to the accusation.

"I'll be glad to explain," she said, "but first why don't we—"

"Not yet. First you must assure me that Captain Duffy was lying, then I must pretend to believe you."

"All right! I hired the guy. Stealing your uniform was his own stupid idea. And I didn't tell him to slug you. You were supposed to have sense enough to hold still."

"And why did you go to such lengths, please tell me? Because you needed a companion in bed? That was Captain Duffy's suggestion, but I thought he was being, what is the word, sarcasm."

"Iluminado, damn it. I'm sorry about the way it worked out, but there's this deal I want you to listen to, and I knew I couldn't just throw it at you, I had to get you in the mood first."

"By doing sex with me, after marijuana and Campari-gins."

"Put it that way and I guess it does sound pretty cruddy. We both stand to benefit, don't you see? You've heard of the military-industrial complex? It's everywhere and Iluminado, it's awesome. All those connections were like established before we were born. People have beaten it, beaten it for real dough, but not by playing Mr. Nice Guy, believe me."

"Remember I am one day out of the jungle. Say it in beginner's English."

"How often do you get an opportunity like this? It's once in a lifetime! You've got something two people want, and they're two people who hate each other. Let me broker it for you, is all I'm saying. No need to make up your mind right away. Just talk to Shanahan before you disappear in the Pentagon."

"Who is Shanahan?"

"Who is Shanahan. I can see I'll have to go back to year one."

He listened closely. John Wayne was mentioned, the fist-fighting American actor, then a flesh-eating South American fish. He reminded himself that she thought she was talking to his father, and he kept switching back and forth, like a message making its way through a computer. His father, himself. He understood no more than two words out of three.

When she seemed to have finished, he said, with some bitterness, "You explain things so beautifully."

"I do?" she said, pleased. "People usually tell me I throw too many knucklers."

While he was concentrating on her baffling exposition, Iluminado's erection had dwindled considerably. Now he commanded it back. The time had come to establish where his preferences lay in this confused matter. Doris wanted to know if he still had a problem, but he had made up his mind to ask these North Americans no further questions. It brought out their worst side.

He knew one thing. Given his father's views about tall and redheaded women, if he had been here instead of the son, they wouldn't be discussing any military-industrial complex! With a look and a small wave, he issued an invitation. Why didn't she stop talking now and lay her head on the pillow?

"Sure," she said. "The only thing, Duffy is going to be showing up in a minute, and we still haven't talked percentages—Iluminado, remember the female juices. Ouch."

And he was in.

There was a new light in her eye. With Doris, not at all like Gabriella, it seemed that sex was a battlefield, on which she meant to prevail. They were the same age, approximately, but she hadn't wasted any of those years with the Jesuits. She established the tempo—not *largo*, which Gabriella had told him was by far the most civilized, not *presto*, either. *Allegro*, perhaps.

"Honeybunch," she whispered intensely, "you and I are going to take these people for *bundles* of cash."

But as usual she didn't say how. He was back on the edge of the precipice. No, her body commanded him—wait.

And again they were interrupted, this time by a key being tapped on the door.

"Hate to bother you, Captain, but Senator Hemlock—"

A new voice: "On our way to the Pentagon. Give you a lift?"

"This is some kind of hoodoo," Doris said.

She scooped up her clothes and shoveled them into the bathroom, dragged Iluminado in after her and locked the door.

"Now, God damn it—" she said.

In another moment he had her well forked. But his brain was spinning again and he had lost some of his competitive fever. She tried, they both tried, but they soon saw that it would no longer be possible.

"Give you a rain check," she said, and they separated with regret. "Hemlock is heavy duty, so look out. Talk to Shanahan before you commit yourself, work out the parameters."

The voices were now in the bedroom. She turned on the shower.

"Don't say one word about Cartagena. Act dumb."

"Act dumb," he repeated in despair.

"Just, you don't know what they're talking about. One hundred percent memory loss until you meet with Shanahan."

"And what do you mainly want me to forget?"

"The whole last day and a half! Put on that dopey look. They think Latins are morons anyway."

There was more, but he was losing it in the roar from the shower. She wrote $300 on the steamed-over mirror, following this with a comma and three zeros. All right, he understood that: three hundred thousand dollars.

"That's for you personally," she said, "minus fifteen percent for postage and handling. An even one and a half mil for the junta, a half million apiece."

She wrote fifteen percent in the steam and did the arithmetic, making a mistake in her own favor so she ended with $55,000. Satisfied that she had bought his loyalty with all these zeros and dollar signs, she gave him a quick hard kiss and shut herself in the shower stall.

Twelve

If it hadn't been for Parker Hemlock over the years, the United States, as a military menace, would be about on the level of the Grand Duchy of Luxembourg. This was accepted by everybody.

Diz, as his media advisers liked him to be called, in the belief that it might make him seem a little more human, was the Pentagon's main man in the Senate. Consistency had earned him a nickname—"Another Eight Billion." After the pros and the antis had talked themselves hoarse, Hemlock would sit back and calmly announce, "We can't penny-pinch when our country's security is at stake. Let's give them another eight billion." And another eight billion was what they generally got.

In his home state, numerous installations had been named after him, compensating for the fact that he had never had children of his own: an airfield, an army post, a Fleet Ballistics Missile Submarine base, the great handicraft center where the Piranha fighters were painstakingly put together. Sam Green of Hawk-Sisley had bankrolled him through the fat years and the lean. Uninformed critics sometimes tried to make something of this—the contributions closely followed by the contracts—but nobody took them too seriously. What other political system worked half as well?

An aide had come with him, a major in beret and beautifully tailored jungle fatigues, which very obviously had never been worn in a jungle. This officer checked the salute he had started when Iluminado came out of the bathroom. You don't salute when the other person is wearing only a towel.

"Colombia," the senator was already saying, having seized Iluminado's hand. "We toured your great country when the highway was opened, and wherever we went, peasants lined the roadsides waving their little American flags. I won't forget that sight as long as I live. The gratitude in those faces, the children's especially."

Reluctantly he allowed the handshake to end.

"An ungodly hour, Captain, but I've been getting up early all my life. Had to, you know, to water my granddaddy's hens. Big day ahead! Your first day at the Pentagon! Mr. Sam Green asked me to carry you—you might have a hard time getting there otherwise. We're going to hopscotch right over them in the Meadow Lark."

"I have an appointment for breakfast with Captain Hector Duffy," Iluminado said politely, "And he has promised to drive me."

"Nobody's driving anybody anywhere this morning. Have you looked out the window?"

The dappled major pulled the drapes and let daylight enter.

Iluminado looked down. Modern hotels are sealed against weather and noise, but he was able to distinguish faint cries and the clamor of sirens. People were running, in a swirl of placards.

"I don't understand this whole generation," the senator said sorrowfully.

A maid was working the corridor, placing a folded newspaper outside each door. There were large headlines, which must explain what was happening outside, but when Iluminado helped

130

himself to a newspaper from her pile, Senator Hemlock snatched it away.

"I don't allow *anybody*"—he said this with make-believe ferocity—"to read that filthy scandal sheet in my presence. They only do two things, print leaks and criticize. It's lucky for them we've got a First Amendment in this country."

They descended all the way to the basement while Hemlock, back on the subject of how early he had had to leave his bed as a boy, told Iluminado how he had pedaled or walked five miles to school in all weathers. He had hated it then, but he could honestly say now that he was the better for it. If these young people in the streets had been given the benefit of some old-fashioned discipline—

There was a white-painted tunnel, a quaint little subway car. As they rode, the flow of reminiscence continued, with the major dropping in appropriate words whenever the senator paused for breath. The car stopped after a time, they rose to the surface and came out on the back lawn of the rather large house where their president lived; Iluminado saw a mechanical exercise bull, not being used at the moment, in a garden protected by a thicket of tank traps and barbed wire. A helicopter waited. It belonged to the Air Force, and Meadow Lark was its name. Whatever primitive forms of transport Hemlock had used as a boy, it would be unthinkable for the chairman of Military Affairs to be tied up in traffic, like any ordinary person. The pilot was a female warrant officer named Brady.

"Miss me, *mama-san*?" Hemlock said as he climbed in. He kept his hand on her shoulder while he did the introductions. And now at last Iluminado was meeting a North American woman of ordinary height. She gave him a guarded look. Once more he wished that women would say what they had to say instead of trying to do it with looks. Her skin was exceptionally fair. The top halves of her glasses were smoked, like the windshields of some makes of cars.

Whining faintly, the trim little craft sprang into the air, and instantly Washington was transformed again into an orderly, rational city. The engine and rotors were amazingly quiet. Iluminado hadn't known that quiet helicopters existed; he had thought that noise was a big part of their point.

The senator was traveling with writers, bill drafters, an accountant. One or two were sipping tomato juice, perhaps with something else in it: a field bar was part of the furniture.

"Anybody who wants a drink," Hemlock said, looking especially at Iluminado, "don't let the fact that I'm not having one stop you. We have Campari, with gin or without."

Campari again—they were still mistaking him for his father, who had been known to drink Campari as a replacement for breakfast. Iluminado refused on the grounds that it was too early, and accepted a cup of something they apparently believed to be coffee.

"Never used to be too early in the morning for Diz Hemlock," Hemlock was saying. "Or too late at night, either. I am an alcoholic," he declared with the utmost gravity. "I went on the wagon before the Italians started exporting that stuff, Campari, so I don't even know how it tastes. Bitter, they tell me."

The machine went straight up, tilted and came about. Hemlock was at the window.

"We give them every advantage. Their own cars, VCRs, a good education. My pop used to strap me soundly if I used a four-letter word, and look at the filth on some of those signs. We've stopped believing in corporal punishment, and maybe that's one of the things that's wrong with this country."

Iluminado was looking down. The dispossessed, "shirtless ones" as they were known in his country—though this being the United States, most of them wore T-shirts—had taken over the streets and the spaces between the monuments. FUCK THE PENTAGON, SAVE THE STARLINGS, said some of the signs.

A sound made him turn. To his astonishment, the portly senator was pulling both ears and sticking out his tongue at the people below. They were waving and laughing.

"Freakniks! Go home to Mommy! Dupes!"

His aides gave him worried looks.

"Right," Hemlock said, collecting himself. "And that may be part of their secret agenda. Give Ol' Diz a heart attack, they'd boogie down Pennsylvania Avenue praising the Lord."

He dropped into a seat. His face, which Iluminado now had the leisure to study, was an interesting shape: closely spaced eyes like single quotation marks, cheeks in which he might be storing acorns for cold weather. A lock of hair kept falling across his forehead, and he kept prodding it back.

"I've had the honor and privilege, you know, of bending an elbow with some of the great lawmakers of this century," he said, returning to a subject that seemed to be much on his mind. "Spent many and many an afternoon in LBJ's office watching the level go down. Bourbon, he used to say, is a great lubricant of the political process. But the day arrived when it became counterproductive for me. AA gave me the insight. Alcoholics Anonymous?" He peered at Iluminado. "They're all over the world now, you probably have a chapter or two in your country. I drank because I'm basically such an uninteresting person. I am," he insisted, when the pilot, who had heard this from her left-hand seat in the cockpit, wanted to differ with him. "Sure, a senator's supposed to live such an oh-so-glamorous life. But let's face it, take away the access and the seniority and I'm as dull as a bucket of ditch water."

"No, Diz, you're not," she said.

"Yes, I am, and that's why I couldn't keep away from the bottle, I thought it made me more interesting. They give me a courtesy jet," he told Iluminado. "Air Force Three is the nickname we have for it. One of my duties as chairman is to make little unannounced forays to outlying parts of the world, to see how the weapons are working out in the field, to compile a shopping list, if you will, of the items the theater commanders feel we need if we're going to stay Number One. On this particular occasion, I was just back from a tour of Southeast Asia. In the interview at the airport, I had the misfortune to refer to the pride and the patriotic sparkle I'd seen in the eyes of our boys—*in West Germany!* A momentary slip of the tongue. I knew perfectly well that I'd just been to Asia. But I was soused, frankly, and my enemies used it against me. The chairman of the Joint Chiefs at the time, Jack Nebenzahl, Admiral 'Balling Jack' Nebenzahl he was known in the fleet, took me aside and begged me, for the good of the country we both loved, to lay off the booze. I'm not ashamed to say that I bawled like a baby. And since that moment—"

Something shot past the window. Iluminado's brain made the necessary correction. It wasn't an insect or small bird but an extremely fast airplane.

"Why, that's the Piranha!" Hemlock exclaimed. "It is *so* fast, and not only that, it flies under radar. One of the slickest aircraft Hawk-Sisley ever turned out."

Again, it was there. *Zzt!* It was gone.

"The Piranha," Iluminado said, making one connection at last. "Mr. Sam Green. Hundred-dollar-bills in a flight bag."

But the senator hadn't heard that; he was getting a feedback on his hearing aid.

"And there she is!" Hemlock said as the Pentagon swam into view. "Now there is a building that makes a statement. It proclaims to the world—Here I sit, nothing fancy about me, no frills or furbelows. But offend me at your peril! It's a new generation of soldiers now, but they all know who got them their original three hundred and sixteen million. I was only a lower house freshman at the time but I wheeled and I dealed, and I haggled and cajoled, and I didn't give up. I think I can say without bragging that I've accomplished one or two things since, but it's that first three hundred and sixteen I want on my tombstone."

The helicopter flared and changed course. Iluminado felt that it would be correct to seem unimpressed, but how impressive the place was, after all. He had read the statistics. More computers and document multipliers than in all other government buildings combined. Straightened and joined, the corridors would reach to Fairfax, Virginia. Five sides, five floors, five rings—the building was just too big to be under anybody's complete control. Babies had been born there. Some offices were never unlocked; it was supposed that they contained classified papers but who really knew?

The deep shelters below the building were designed to withstand a direct hit by the most powerful bomb in existence at the time. It was 1942, the bombs were comparatively small then, but luckily this design feature had never been put to the test. The general contractor, a gregarious Bostonian named McSorley, was sent to jail later for putting too much sand in his concrete on another government project, and had the same thing happened at the Pentagon? The Bureau of Standards did a stress study but the results are still classified. This may merely reflect the security paranoia that is general in the building.

To this day, however, the shelters are combat-ready, with fourteen thousand antiquated mimeograph machines, even more manual typewriters, great vats of distilled water which is probably a little putrid by now, thousands of crates of survival crackers. The poorly lit caverns are patrolled by career soldiers from Internal Security, picked blacks who have to stand at least six feet one. Passing the time is a problem in any peacetime army. Not having much else to do, these soldiers hunt rats. Before the Pentagon preempted the site, this section was known as Hell's Bottom, its main feature being a vast open dump. Not all the rats who lived there were willing to relocate.

Senator Hemlock had a poor head for figures. He wasn't interested in the size of an appropriation, he often said, but in the *signal* it sent to the enemy. That $316 million for construction outlays had been his first legislative success, however, and he recalled it correctly. It was a more candid year, and the client was still known as the War Department. In that Congress, there were no penny pinchers. The big thing, the only thing that mattered, was to clobber the Axis, which was the enemy's name at the time. As soon as the Axis surrendered, everybody expected the army to shrink back to its peacetime numbers, and the immense construction could be torn down and replaced by—oh, a stadium, say. In that way, the parking lots could be used. So who cared that the windows were carelessly hung, or that some of the nails were too short?

Many of the later difficulties could have been avoided if McSorley had been told to deliver a building that would still be standing fifty years later. But new enemies had appeared, causing the budget to rise by another eight billion, then another eight billion, eight billion on top of that. There was no longer talk of razing the Pentagon. Instead, people were beginning to think they should put in elevators and add more floors.

So many cornices dropped off during the early fifties that two of the five entrances had to be bricked up. The Pentagon had an unlucky reputation from the start. Seventeen workers were killed during its hasty construction. At the opening ceremonies, a section of bleachers collapsed, killing three, including the Belgian ambassador. A few months later, forty-seven persons in one of the restaurants were felled by ptomaine from eating tainted butterscotch pie; not all survived.

The sun was all the way up as the Meadow Lark slanted in from the river. The thousands of windows on the building's northeastern face were a uniform muddy orange. Washing these windows has been a perennial problem. Hooks set in McSorley's cement pulled loose so often that eventually no civilian window-washing firm in the District would look at the contract. Windows along the Brass Ring, where the high brass have the outside offices, were replaced by the swiveling kind that can be washed from inside. As for the others, they were last touched in the early seventies, and since then, of course, they have been badly spattered by the birds.

Other helicopters were ahead of them. Unable to land, the Meadow Lark completed a first circuit and started around again.

Iluminado was trying to understand the geometry of the access roads. As far as he could tell with the helicopter tilting and twisting, the building could only be entered from one direction, the cemetery.

Flatbeds carrying great rolls of paper competed for space at an unloading dock. From other docks, rubble and garbage were being carted away. Iluminado had read that every last piece of paper had to be shredded, before being buried in tamper-proof canisters to prevent enemy agents from putting it back together. But what a waste of God's bounty. An R and D firm in Hemlock's home state—this wasn't much of a contract, but Hemlock liked to say that he worked as hard for the little fellow as for Mr. Sam Green—was trying to find a way to reprocess the cellulose into a sort of paté that could be eaten by troops in the field. The problem, apparently, was finding a more digestible ink.

Every career officer, whatever his specialty, is required to

136

serve time at the Pentagon. The personnel totals, as the Meadow Lark made another tentative pass at the landing pad, were 21,076 civilians, 24,543 officers, 16,789 enlisted men, close to the population of Cartagena. Inside one building!

For senior officers, it is a period of extraordinary tension. They have completed their compulsory year in a combat-related environment. They have emerged with their faculties reasonably intact from Command and General Staff College or the new FAB (Fully Automated Battlefield) School at Fort Hood. They have taught at a service academy, commanded a brigade or wing or flotilla, and now they have come to Washington to have their office performance evaluated at point-blank range.

As in every profession, a rabbi is needed, a protector. Whenever a protégé earns a good efficiency rating, his protector is given some of the credit. And the opposite is also true: a mistake can damage them both. Outside Washington, the blame can often be shifted. The ARVN, for example—who remembers the ARVN?—managed to do nothing right during the entire length of that war. In Washington, blunders are committed in the full glare of publicity. Consequently caution has replaced élan as the premier military virtue. (And yet sometimes the rashest of ventures, certain bombings, for instance, even invasions, have been undertaken out of an excess of caution, for fear of being blamed for a reluctance to bomb or invade.) Small wonder that Pentagon pharmacies dispense such vast quantities of tranquilizers, analgesics, laxatives—167 tons in one recent year.

Any unmarried officer is looked at with deep suspicion. Not since the 1940s has there been an unmarried chief of staff. The wives hate it in Washington. Rents are impossibly high. On foreign assignment, little armies of highly qualified people, who can be paid in some bush-league currency, queue up for the privilege of cooking and looking after the children. In one Psyops survey, fifty-seven percent of all Pentagon officers reported that their wives were more bitchy in Washington, and made love less often. This was considered a significant finding, for male self-esteem, which correlates with sexual success, has also always had a close correlation with combat efficiency.

Michael Mirabile was asked for suggestions.

Mirabile had been getting his best ideas lately under sensory deprivation. Operations like his are sometimes referred to jokingly as think tanks. He himself never used the expression, considering it an anti-intellectual gibe. On one of his California excursions he discovered the pleasures of the actual zero-gravity tank, and he had one installed in his Pentagon office. Floating in that absolute silence, absolute blackness, he found that his mind could run free.

What about the coldness of all these Washington wives? Mirabile studied the Psyops report, undressed and climbed in. Fifty minutes later, mushroom-pale, more than a little crinkled, he emerged with a typically Mirabile solution.

A Rest and Recreation Syndicate, consisting of three sergeant majors, an Air Force major general and a civilian from Procurement (Mirabile himself was in for a tenth) established a field brothel in the innermost ring. Fees were kept low, supplemented by a covert grant from intelligence funds. The effect on morale was spectacular. Here was evidence, finally, that the Army was not cold and unfeeling, as its critics kept saying. It cared.

But a reporter for a well-known scandalmongering columnist was nosing around, on the scent of a story about a Pentagon gambling ring, and he stumbled into one of the document-storage rooms during a period of intense recreational activity. So much for that noble experiment.

As for the gambling ring, assemble that many people in one place and give them too little to do, and some enterprising soul is bound to start making book. Again on Mirabile's recommendation, the Chiefs decided to beat the detestable snoop to the exposé. At a hastily summoned news conference, the spokesman announced the formation of an in-house OTB, which would accept all kinds of sports action as well as running body-count lotteries and foreign affairs crisis pools. Senator Hemlock, for one, had serious doubts about the morality of this, but the seventeen percent takeout not only repaid the syndicate but enabled the DOD to purchase two extra F-16s in the first year without having to go hat in hand to Congress.

The Meadow Lark spun back and around, and Iluminado

looked into the desolate courtyard, where Pentagon secretaries had eaten their sandwiches in the early days, under the striped umbrellas.

And suddenly, so suddenly that for a moment he thought he must have returned to concussion, the whole building burst upward, exploding into hundreds of thousands of tiny beating fragments. Soldiers were running about on the roof in pairs, flapping banners. Overhead, gusting away in vast clouds which almost concealed the horizon, were more birds than Iluminado had ever seen assembled in one congregation, or than he could have imagined. They fled and surged back.

"So many," he breathed. "So many! I should think you would find them inconvenient."

"Inconvenient!" Hemlock exclaimed.

"Couldn't you—" Iluminado began.

Use weapons against them? Hemlock didn't feel competent or sufficiently rested, he said, to list all the weapons that had been hurled against this unwanted rookery. If Iluminado was interested, he could look it up in the proceedings of the various courts-martial. Previous administrations had foolishly felt they had to observe certain obsolete treaties. A window of chemical-bacteriological vulnerability had opened and these starlings had flown through it. Until recently, the birds had lived in reasonable contentment in a pine forest to the west, near an army camp. The army got rid of them there by sawing down the forest. But they couldn't very well saw down the Pentagon!

"Public opinion is a fascinating study," the senator said. "The whole thing started in a couple of New England colleges, UMass, Yale. Sort of a joke, you know. They don't care about starlings, per se. These are the crazies, the trust-the-Russians-to-do-the-right-thing people. The women involved, they say they're against the military budget but that's just the cover-up. They're basically antimen. Starlings are just a stick they can beat us with. It wouldn't have amounted to much, probably, except for the nuclear angle."

"Nuclear angle."

"Mirabile's taking the flak for it, but I'm ashamed to say that I'm the one," Hemlock said, "who happened to drop the remark.

139

What we had here, it occurred to me, was something that called for a tactical nuke. One of the clean ones, don't you know, that leave the buildings intact. After you decontaminate you can move right back in. A sequence of small, carefully controlled shots, more or less firecracker size. Well, an irresponsible New York newspaper, the *Times*, got hold of my casual remark and said it had been approved on a policy level. Whereas it hadn't even *got* to the policy level. The word nuclear is a red flag to some people, the word radiation. We denied it categorically, from the president down, but the damage was done. Add the antinukes to the kooks, that's a heck of a lot of votes. 'F. the Pentagon.' I'd like to take a strap to the lot of them."

Iluminado watched the great flock turn against the sun, and turn again—a hypnotic sight. Glancing away, he saw that the senator was down to his shorts.

"It's honorary," Hemlock said, taking a brigadier general's uniform off a hanger. "When they awarded it to me I stood there with tears running down my cheeks, unable to utter a syllable. Because I didn't earn it, you see. I didn't put my tail on the line, like you fellows. All I did was handle the appropriations."

He climbed into the pants, sucking in hard in order to close the top button.

A traffic control officer was waving them down. The beaters rushed about, trying to clear a small patch of roof. For a moment, settling, helicopter and starlings competed for the same limited airspace. The craft set down amid a whirl of feathers and small mutilated bodies, near a folding table and chairs.

An intense-looking civilian, heavily encrusted with bird droppings, sat at the table with two fingertips touching his forehead.

"It's PR, basically," Hemlock said when Iluminado looked to him for an explanation. "We've been having trouble with what you might call the nonrational sector. One of the worst mistakes the Air Force ever made, in my estimation, was that report they put out on flying saucers. All right, so most of the sightings didn't pan out. Did they have to be so *emphatic* about it? Parapsychology—that's a catchall expression for ESP and so on, telekinesis. The Russians have a big-ruble program, and we can't let them get ahead of us, can we? This guy's been working on submarine location, and somebody had the idea— see if he can help with the starlings. But I'd appreciate it if you didn't mention this to anybody, O.K.?"

The passengers, wearing plastic capes, were ready. They dismounted under heavy bombardment, onto a carpet so soft and yielding that they had to walk in slow motion, like astronauts on the moon. Above, the birds continued to squawk and scold.

They came to a door posted with notices: NO SUNBATHING ON ROOF—PEACE IS OUR PROFESSION—THIS IS YOUR BUILDING, KEEP IT CLEAN—PAY ANY PRICE, BEAR ANY BURDEN–JOHN F. KENNEDY.

The door opened, and the Pentagon sucked them in.

Thirteen

Doris swallowed a rose-hip capsule and an all-purpose complex—hold the apricots for now—dressed and went out to the corridor to find the off-duty cop Duffy had hired explaining to Steve Kagoulian, from Shanahan's staff, that in spite of the beautiful signature on his summons, it couldn't be served. Their bird had flown.

"My mother told me, if you want to get ahead in this town, don't argue with United States senators."

Doris took Kagoulian inside to confer. Shaken, he let her give him one of her coltsfoot-and-raspberry cigarettes, though if Shanahan smelled it on his clothes he might mistake it for the forbidden tobacco. You couldn't ask for a more affable boss when things were running smoothly, but Shanahan had inherited one bad character trait from his father and grandfather: he didn't believe that the law of averages applied to him. He expected to win *every time*.

A helicopter whup-whupped past the window.

"And if I had my private air force—" Doris said.

She aimed with her finger and shot the enemy out of the sky.

142

The phone began ringing. Going on her usual theory that females, starting with that disadvantage, must be ready to seize every opportunity and loophole, she picked it up. It was Isobel Clancy. Iluminado had already started his day, Doris told her. He could probably be reached at the Pentagon.

"Oh, dear," Mrs. Clancy said. "They always ask you to state your business, and I feel so silly. Are you a bird of passage, so to speak, or do you expect to see him?"

"He may call me," Doris said cautiously.

"I'm giving a gimmicky little dinner, just for Taurus people, and I want him *desperately*. Hal Amsterdam's coming, Scotty Reston. The Gerald Fords have promised to look in for a minute. We're all going to trundle out to Belknap to see W-3 in action. The army always puts on such a marvelous show."

To protect her hearing, Doris had been holding the phone away from her ear, and the invitation had escaped to Kagoulian.

"Hughie's a Taurus," he said gloomily, "and he didn't get asked. Isobel's been counting the votes."

"It's not over yet. We still have Iluminado's interview at the airport."

"We were a little slow there, I'm sorry to say. The audio's been tampered with. We've got lipreaders working on it, but the senator doesn't think it'll stand up."

"God damn it." She blew smoke at the vanishing helicopter. "They can't just *kidnap* somebody, can they? Well, of course they can, but—"

One of Hemlock's fellow senators, who had never been able to get it into his head that if you want quality, you have to pay quality prices, had developed an unhealthy obsession with the Pentagon's limousine pool. Now, in a modern, traffic-choked city, a limousine equipped with flags and a siren makes a great deal of sense. You can't beat it for practicality. General Motors knocks a percentage off the sticker price, so it isn't actually all that expensive. But this Neanderthal from Vermont—and there are probably no more than three stretch-limos in his entire

143

state—kept pounding away and pounding away, and the upshot was that the contract was put out to bid. Volkswagen won with their Rabbit. At the Pentagon! Rabbits!

The result, which a less obsessed person could have predicted, was that more people used helicopters, and that meant increased congestion at heliport security. The line inched forward. A colonel reached out to finger Iluminado's sleeve. Iluminado didn't like to be touched by strangers—he didn't like to be touched by *anybody*—and he stood perfectly still, exuding a cold wind.

"Beautiful stuff," the officer said, rolling the material between thumb and forefinger. "I go to a little Jewish man in New York, on Rivington Street, but he's been threatening to retire. When Brooks Downtown gave up their made-to-order, the flags went to half-staff around here, believe me."

Perhaps noticing that Iluminado was beginning to tremble, he removed his hand. Iluminado was called up for his photograph. He gave the camera his bullfighter's glare (another thing he disliked was having his picture taken). They photocopied his orders and recorded his fingerprints.

"I wish I had time to show you around," Hemlock said after Iluminado was issued his badge, with a coded chart of the areas he was forbidden to enter. "I appreciate the way his eyes bug out of his head when some young fellow from one of the backward countries gets his first look at the Crisis Containment room. Because who do you think got those electronics through Congress, I say modestly? But today"—he fluttered his fingers on both sides of his head—"it's busy, busy."

Bug-eyed, Iluminado was quite sure he was not. From high-beam facing the camera, they had gone down to park. What was it, after all, he told himself scornfully, but an overgrown office building?

Hemlock was hustling him toward a waiting rank of what seemed to be pedicabs. Because of the building's size, getting from point to point must be a problem, and what an ingenious, thoroughly North American solution, Iluminado thought. Most of the drivers were Asians, wearing starched and snug-fitting fatigues. One slightly built fellow signaled Hemlock by a slight flare of the nostrils. An airman, apparently, he wore three rows of ribbons, a silk scarf.

"Well now, Marshal," Hemlock said genially, "how's America been treating you?"

"Number one, Senator! Tips excellent."

"Do you think you can get us to the Meditation Room in three and a half minutes?"

"Willing to try!"

Hemlock and Iluminado climbed in. Their driver lowered a pair of goggles and pedaled off, a designer's label winking from his back pocket. He plunged down a long ramp and took the turn at the bottom with locked wheels.

"Impetuous, isn't he?" Hemlock said, checking his seatbelt. "I like it, it's in short supply around here."

Doors flashed by, each labeled in the cryptic military shorthand, DEP ASST SUBDIR MECOM FLAGFLOT, and the like. Where an occasional door stood ajar, Iluminado saw far too much furniture, two or three chairs to each desk, extra computers. Hemlock explained that sections of the building were being redecorated, and this overcrowding was temporary, not that there was much elbow room at the best of times.

An approaching pedicab carried a lounging figure Iluminado recognized at once—Quimby, from the airplane. As he went by, he saluted Iluminado with his unlighted pipe and smiled through his beard, or else did a soundless kiss.

Caution lights ahead told them to slow down.

They were coming to the Physical Fitness ring, one lane reserved for joggers, the other for roller skaters and skateboarders. Desk-bound and a bit flabby themselves, the Chiefs hated to look at flab in others, and they had decreed a half-hour's compulsory exercise for everybody in the building. Under another policy directive, exercise traffic had the right of way. Their driver, with an important passenger this morning, an honorary one-star, didn't feel constrained by this rule. A jogger stutter-stepped frantically out of their way.

Iluminado was enjoying the ride. The Meditation Room! He had hoped to see this ecumenical shrine, where so much history has been made. Patton prayed here, petitioning for a role in the big invasion, as well as his fourth star. Here the Chiefs decided that the time had come, they were finally going to stop taking shit in the Caribbean. Mutual Assured Destruction—the concept itself was worked out elsewhere, but its wonderful acronym, MAD, was coined here by an early defense secretary after a strenuous eight-hour vigil. Whenever Nixon came to the Pentagon during his final weeks, he never failed to stop off for a minute or two, to check in with a power higher than his own.

But they really ought to maintain it better, Iluminado thought when the driver slid to a stop in front of a sign with many letters missing: EDI A ON R M.

"Three minutes seventeen," Hemlock announced. "Excellent time, Marshal."

"Do our best, Senator! Appreciate U.S. democracy!"

They unbuckled. Telling the driver to wait, Hemlock worked the door open to let Iluminado pass, and entered himself. A homely little man dozed under a big hat in one of the pews.

"Mr. G? See who I've brought you—Captain Castillo."

The eyelids stayed down.

Hemlock touched a finger to his lips. "It's a good idea to let him wake up by himself. Convey my apologies et cetera, important breakfast appointment."

Iluminado's right hand began a salute, but do you salute honorary generals? Yes, he decided, and he completed a military gesture that would have given his old mentor, Major Sadowski, a great deal of pleasure.

"Thank you for the pedicab ride, sir, and the lift in the helicopter."

"My pleasure. Now I know you'll have a great time in Washington, and if there's any little thing I can do, drop in and see me. Don't worry about it, Captain," he added, drawing the wrong inference from the fact that Iluminado was still at attention. "His bark is worse than his bite."

The little man stirred, and Hemlock left hastily. The door, which was suffering from one missing hinge, nearly got away from him.

Mr. G—this would be Duffy's employer, who wanted to give Iluminado some hundred-dollar bills, and there, in fact, beside him on the pew, was a bulging TWA flight bag. But Iluminado didn't see why he should stand around fidgeting until some odd civilian decided to wake up. He had to sign into Counter Coup school. He needed breakfast. On their rapid passage through the building they had whirled past several fast-food kiosks where he could get a croissant and their version of coffee.

"Lit Up?" Mr. G said, opening one eye.

"Please?"

"Lit Up Castle is what your name comes out to in English, they tell me. Did you ever do any levitating?"

"Levitating. I'm not sure what that means, exactly."

"It's where you lift yourself off a chair by the power of will. It don't happen unless you believe in it. I believe in it but I just can't develop the knack."

He rose in the ordinary way and put out a hand. It was like grasping the thick end of a carrot.

The teeth were probably false, and so, Iluminado thought, was the smile. His quick glimpse of Quimby had brought back some of the previous day's concerns. The little man's bark is worse than his bite, Hemlock had said. Bite *what*, Iluminado wondered.

"You and me're going to set ourselves down and have a nice visit," Mr. G continued, but before he could explain further, he was interrupted by a muffled sneeze from the confessional.

He was there in two strides. He wrenched the door open to reveal a huddled priest, a tissue to his nose.

"Out," Mr. G said, using his thumb.

"Just collecting my thoughts, Mr. G, not trying to tune in on your conversation or anything—"

Mr. G proved to be wearing a pistol in a shoulder holster. He laid his hand on it, and the priest scuttled away with raised skirts.

"That there's the cocksucker," Mr. G said, coming back, "who taped Nixon's prayers. And you know Dick. Straight-ahead praying wasn't good enough. He had to bring in the barnyard language. You don't say fuck to the Almighty, not if you want to stay president."

147

He stooped to the flight bag, and pulled the zipper to show Iluminado that indeed it contained currency.

"I'm not interested, you see," Iluminado told him.

The eyes and teeth glittered. "You think there's a bug in the room, which is understandable. It's one of the main things people do anymore. I've got this little gadget here I'd like to show you."

He started to unbutton his cowboy shirt. Another thing Iluminado wasn't interested in was viewing anybody's gadget. He took a step backward. More buttons opened and wisps of chest hair came into view, then a small circular lump.

"Meant to look like a pacemaker, is the general idea. Call it a Geiger counter is close enough. Any kind of recording device within a thirty-foot radius, it gives off this flutter. Feel it yourself if you want to."

Zzt! It was that fast airplane again, this time very close. If the building had been six stories high, it would now be missing a chimney.

"The Piranha," Mr. G said. "Never mind fast, because everything's fast nowadays. But did you notice how *low*?"

He pushed his big hat off his forehead, using a thumbnail.

"What Duffy tells me he was getting from you was hostility. You and me, we've got compatible fields, I can feel it. We won't have any trouble just the two of us talking. That money is all yours, no strings attached. Count it if you want to. You'll see we've been more than fair. Now we come to the fringes."

He stumped to the stained-glass window behind the all-purpose lectern.

The artist had chosen what at the time was probably an unthreatening subject, Saint Francis preaching to a circle of birds. Unlike the flock on the Pentagon roof, these birds had been tranquilized, and seemed willing to listen. Daylight showed through the saint's stomach, where a small leaded pane was missing. Mr. G knocked out more glass with his pistol.

"Take a peek, Lit Up."

Iluminado was shy about turning his back, especially bending over, but he probably ought to find out what the little man was tempting him with. All he could see when he put his eye to the hole was part of the parking lot.

"Flap this," Mr. G suggested, offering a dirty handkerchief.

When Iluminado seemed reluctant to take it, Mr. G put it out through the hole and waved it himself.

Putting his eye to the window again, Iluminado saw movement inside a long white car, heavily chromed, parked all by itself in an access lane. Its roof peeled back slowly to reveal a hallucination in the form of another of the extraordinary Washington women.

She came out on the asphalt so he could appreciate her more fully. Bracelets slid along her arm as she swept back her tangle of reddish hair. Her dress managed to stay up without straps. The skirt was slashed from the hemline halfway up her thigh, and she was bursting out of this tight yellow garment in Iluminado's direction. All the flesh that was showing, and much was, was magnificently tanned.

She snarled at him playfully. But the birds had spotted her, and when the first spatter hit the hood she gestured humorously and retreated into the car. The roof descended.

"Name is Lily," Mr. G said, "had three years at Cornell and she's dying to meet you." He was jingling keys on a gold chain. "Car's a Mercedes. One of the great years, before they started building them short. I'm not giving it to you outright, understand, you'll be leasing it for one peso a year. If the tax liability worries you, forget it. My personal attorney wrote that paragraph in the tax bill. Here's what I'd like to suggest. I've got this hunting lodge I won with two pair in a poker game—"

Iluminado stopped him. "This is my first day at Counter Coup. I don't want to be late."

Mr. G patted his pockets and found a postdated document certifying that one Iluminado Castillo, and they had managed to spell it correctly, had attended all Counter Coup sessions and graduated with distinction.

"In your case they don't take attendance. If you'll let me finish. Why don't I get a belly-loading C-57? Then you won't even have to get out of the car. The seats lay all the way back.

Portable bar. An hour later you're on your own private island, with a live-in couple to look after the two of you. Be honest with me, wouldn't you like that?"

Iluminado happened to be closely related to one person who would like it, who would accept it with pleasure. The real target of these blandishments and flattering offers was his father, of course. Iluminado had always been careful not to think too deeply about what his father did for a living. His mother had hinted that women paid some of those bills. Iluminado sincerely hoped not, but he knew it had to be something disreputable, possibly sinister.

Now here was this misshapen gnome with his glittery leer, sure he would leap at the chance to go absent without leave with the tall, redheaded Lily. And what would Mr. G get in return? Obviously the sale of his zzt-zzt airplane to the Colombian Air Force. And hadn't Doris said something about crashes, wings falling off?

He used a schoolboy expression he hadn't thought of in years. "Why don't you just fry a banana?"

He managed to say it quietly, but it was a torch applied to a brush pile. This miserable creature was trying to bribe a Castillo! And the fact that the older Castillo would have undoubtedly taken the bribe merely added kerosene to the flames. If this spoiled his father's shady career, so be it, let him look for honest work for a change.

"I refuse your vulgar automobile. I refuse the woman, the hunting lodge. I won't take your money."

Again he saw the excellent teeth, this time in a snarl, and not a playful one like the woman's.

"Who're you trying to kid? We had you looked into! I've got a good sense of smell, and by God I'm beginning to smell Shanahan."

"The senator."

"Hughie? Shit, no. Mike Shanahan, Hughie's pa. Oh, they've got him hooked up to all kinds of machinery, he has to write his wants on a slate, but all you have to do is look in those eyes. He's thinking. Thinking up new ways to screw people."

"I have had nothing to do with either father or son."

150

"Will you get it through your head that *we are not being taped?* That so-called fighter the Shanahans are trying to un-load—why do you think nobody wants it? Because it's inferior! The whole industry knows they faked the performance stats. Did he happen to mention that the prototype blew up before they could get it out of the hangar? That man is twisted, Lit Up, corrupt. He told me once in so many words that he don't believe in the Redeemer. Never satisfied, always wants more. More companies, more market share. Reaching out, reaching out."

Mr. G, too, was reaching out, not for another company but for Iluminado.

"Don't keep backing away. I'm your best friend in this build-ing, don't you realize that? Certain people want to do something drastic about you, boy, and I've been arguing against it. The reason I did it this way, the broad, the Mercedes, I wanted to test a theory. Well, it seems I was right. I don't get into auctions. Tell me the truth—whatever the Shanahans promised you, show me something in writing and I'll give you twenty percent over and above if you'll blow the deal, go public with it. I don't just want to sell airplanes. I want to really clobber that prick."

Clobber that prick—Iluminado was getting a quick educa-tion in homosexual English. Mr. G had finally succeeded in capturing his wrist. Iluminado shuddered and threw off the hand, sending the little businessman stumbling backward.

"I won't be touched. I will not be touched."

Mr. G's boot heel snagged, and he banged into a kind of console. A tape began to revolve. This, after all, was an InterFaith Facility. A gong sounded.

"Oooooooooooom! Ommmmmmmmmm! OOOOOOMM-MMMM!"

Iluminado raised his voice, to be heard above the mystic howling. "You have no respect for your history. This room is part of an honorable tradition. P-p-atton"—he was stammering a little—"Patton prayed where you set down your money bag. You want the truth? I've been telling lies lately and living dis-honorably. It has brought me nothing but trouble. Here is a small morsel of truth. Even if you had the face of Saint Francis

151

and the shape of the Archangel Michael, I wouldn't do what you wish. But this way is easy because you're so exceedingly ugly. You're disgusting to look at."

He about-faced smartly and the spooky chant followed him out.

What had happened to the country Mr. G had known as a boy? The good old hymns just didn't seem to satisfy anymore.

He couldn't find the volume control, so he turned the thing off like the cowboy he had once wanted to be, using the butt of his .38.

He knew he was putting a strain on his vascular system, and some day the good Lord would strike him dead in the course of one of these rages. But the thought of Mike Shanahan attached to two million dollars of life-prolonging equipment always had this effect on him. He was shaking, cold.

He didn't want anyone to see him like this, so far from his usual peppery self, so he shut himself in the confessional and attempted some biofeedback, to get his blood flowing downhill again.

He had always believed that he understood spics. This old-fashioned word had kept its full range of meaning for Mr. G. They live in a hot climate and think about little but shitting and fucking. A racial swamp, everybody intermingled. Try breeding cattle that way! As a result of highly spiced food, the bullfight tradition, they're also as touchy as hell, and that was why he had been so unusually patient with Iluminado.

A great negotiator, which Mr. G considered himself to be, has to guess what the guy on the other side of the table really wants. Not what he *says* he wants, but what wakes him up at three in the morning and keeps him awake because he can't get it out of his head. And what spics want, in Mr. G's judgement, every spic he had ever had dealings with, is the U.S. standard of living and American women. No question about it, Iluminado had experienced a definite saliva-rush when he saw that tall, sulky broad, Lily—Mr. G had fucked her himself, and she was the best. All Iluminado had to do was say yes, and she

152

would be his companion on an all-expenses-paid, three-week siesta. And yet he had said no, in fact had practically knocked Mr. G down.

So now they knew where they stood.

Before messing up the tape of Iluminado's interview at the airport, the electronics guy had transcribed the answers and delivered them to the Chiefs. It was tongue-biting time. Apparently a gigantic mistake had been made. They roused Duffy, and he reported other puzzling remarks—"What makes you think I want to do business with you?" and so on. Hernán Vega González, the Colombian intelligence colonel, passed on some rumors about Iluminado's personal life and all in all, well, it didn't add up to guerrillas.

That evening in Cartagena had definitely been organized; it was too fucking perfect. Luck had been running bad for Mr. G lately but when it ran this bad he knew there had to be someone behind it. And who could it be but Shanahan? The moment he heard that the Bolívar's cage had been cleaned out during the operation, Shanahan's name had jumped into his mind. Hijack the Piranha contract, embarrass the Chiefs so they lose the Wall vote in the Senate, and on top of all that you clear enough to cover your out-of-pocket expenses, maybe make a few dollars. Yes, it had the Shanahan earmarks.

The unfriendly takeover scam is a gorgeous way to make money when you're the only one after that company. But when somebody else is going against you—Am Tex, more and more often lately—you can lose skin. One-to-ten leverage is what made this country great, but when a one-to-ten deal goes sour, it goes just ten times as sour. As for Pentagon business—it is nice, much of the time. But big as that budget is, and getting bigger, it isn't big enough to keep everybody happy.

Mr. G had had some great years, sixty-percent-return-on-equity years, and for a time it looked as though Hawk-Sisley might be the IBM of the 1980s. It didn't happen. One of his most reliable senators was videotaped accepting money from an Arab who was really a Jewish FBI man. Dumb! The Piranha, his new high-performance fighter, developed a mysterious malady. No one could diagnose it. Nothing was obviously wrong, it just didn't want to perform. Mr. G even brought in his medical dowser, who went over the plane from nose to tail with a forked twig and didn't get any reaction at all.

And all of a sudden, unless the Colombian deal held up, unless the Senate funded W-3, the whole ungainly contrivance Mr. G had built would sink like a stone. And Mr. G himself, who had cut a few corners over the years, neglecting to file all the necessary papers, would wind up in Costa Rica or some equally dingy location, to live out his declining years among spics.

At the same time, pretty much the same thing had been happening to Shanahan. Am Tex spent heavily to get the new missile-cruisers. This was untested technology. Now they were six years behind on delivery, losing $215 million a vessel. Negative cash flow would be one way to put it. In the overseas markets, the Piranha and the John Wayne had been murdering each other. In sum, Shanahan needed Circe as much as Mr. G needed the Wall.

With the Lily-Mercedes gambit, Mr. G had established to his own satisfaction that this Iluminado Castillo was Shanahan's boy from the socks up. He knew that type of back-country shit-stomper. Buy him once and he's yours for life. The loyalty to the brand, that special hair-trigger touchiness, you used to see it all the time in the tank-town cowboy saloons. Thank God the type had all but died out in this country, or Mr. G would never have made it into the *Fortune* 500.

"*I won't be touched.*" Eleanor, the only one of his wives Mr. G really remembered, had shivered away from his hand in much the same way. Though it hadn't kept her from cashing the alimony checks, had it! Hell, Mr. G knew he was ugly-looking. Why should he care that he had never been popular? Actually, the kind of static he gave off often helped in a negotiation. He was so obviously willing to run over his own grandmother, as they say—people want to get in on it.

For some reason everybody liked old Shanahan. That whole family was supposed to be so fucking *charming*. Their wives rarely divorced them.

Hoping to cleanse his head of the subject, he was endeav-

154

oring to levitate. This had happened to him just once, on a toilet seat. He was getting over a virus, with a one-degree fever. There he was, straining, his head filled with feverish shapes, and damn if he didn't rise three or four inches. He never succeeded in doing it again.

Iluminado Castillo—clearly a ticking bomb. About to start telling the truth, was he? One or two casual sentences on a national news-show would put Shanahan in the saddle and the Chiefs back in the doghouse, from which they had only lately emerged. Americans don't mind being lied to, it's part of the political process. But this particular lie was so *clumsy*. If the Chiefs, with $330 billion a year to play with, couldn't pull off a simple little sting and cover-up without ending up buried in bird shit—

What the kid didn't seem to realize—it had been easy getting into this building, but it might be a hell of a lot harder getting out. The Pentagon, after all, was corporate HQ of the biggest business in the world, and that business, without putting the usual frosting on it, that business is killing people. Every Thursday morning between nine and twelve, these guys played war games involving 100 million deaths—*minimum*. For PR reasons, they wouldn't want to be overheard discussing one single death, because that is usually thought of as murder. It had to be done with thought flashes from one to the other, a widening of the eyes, a nearly imperceptible movement of the shoulders. Thus Iluminado's sentence had been passed. If he turned down Mr. G's overture, he was a dead man.

Somebody scratched on the confessional grillwork.

"You in there, Father?"

Mr. G acknowledged his presence with a grunt.

"Father, I've sinned against God and against nature, I'm guilty of the sin of ambition. The Selection Board narrowed it down to seven, and, Father, these are all terrific guys, terrific soldiers. But I'm the one who deserves that star. The opportunity arose and I'm sorry to say I gave way to temptation. I broke into the computer and changed all their Outstandings to Excellents."

"Get out of here, creep," Mr. G growled.

After a stunned moment: "Don't you think it's a bit early in the day to start hitting the bottle, Father? I know I'm a fine one to preach, but—"

Mr. G told him to get lost or he'd give his ass an act of contrition he wouldn't forget in a hurry. Catholics! When Mr. G did something he was ashamed of, he didn't go whimpering to his pastor for absolution. He lived with it.

Being admitted to the Command and Flag Officers' Mess for the first time, civilian guests were sometimes reminded of what they had been told of the old Pullman diners—stiff linen, a single rose on each table, black waiters who know they have no chance of rising to be president of the railroad and are happy to go on waiting on table. The china was Royal Meissen, liberated from the German General Staff in '45. And there was a certain reassurance in that: we may lose an occasional skirmish, but we win all the big ones.

The Chiefs had been riding a roller coaster for twenty-four hours, gloom, euphoria, and once again gloom. They couldn't eat much. Mr. G loved this place, and he made them wait until he ate his way through a stack of the good Command and Flag Officers' flapjacks and swallowed a pint of their black campfire coffee.

He mopped up with a linen napkin the size of a hand towel. "Well, I talked to the guy, and it's just as I figured. They got him roped up real good."

Glances flew. Tiny shrugs were exchanged. The time had come for the Cat.

Fourteen

People who shine in school and college are often grievous disappointments in later life. West Point cadets seldom have this problem.

Once every two or three seasons, a young man shows up who is so remarkably gifted that the word goes out—here is a future three-star, perhaps even a CEO at Northrup or General Dynamics. And because the people who are circulating the prophecy are also the ones who can make it come true, the guy must do something spectacularly awful to miss.

George Catlett Marshall Higginson was such a phenom. Because of the way he moved on the basketball floor, his teammates shortened the first of his middle names to Cat. He jumped like a cat. Under the basket he used his claws, but only against opponents. Fencing was his second sport, and he made sword-play the fashion that year. He had nothing but friends. The faculty couldn't believe his brains.

Some years after his graduation he and others were fighting a war on the far side of the globe, and it was going badly. The magazine *Life*, looking for a soldier to put on its cover, chose the Cat. He was a lieutenant colonel by then. Their photograph showed him exhausted and dirty, with other people's blood on his forearms. It was one of the classic photos. War, it said—it is brutal and terrible. But beautiful too, and how could we get along without it?

Soon afterward, the Cat had his accident. That was how he thought of it still—like an accident on the highway, slippery pavement, the other car out of its lane. He had been given a notorious fuck-up battalion with the worst stats in the Zone. Body-count practically zero, highest VD, most officers fragmented by Claymore mines in their sleeping bags. Even the senior noncoms had given up cigarettes in favor of stronger smokes and were refusing to get up before noon. Salute an officer—no way.

A New York congressman showed up, investigating complaints from constituents about how the Cat had been failing to coddle their sons. This man was a known leader of peace marches. A delegation he had organized had even visited the enemy capital to bellyache about bomb damage. One word led to another, and the Cat shot him.

It was spur of the moment. He hadn't intended to do it. He had just clawed his way back from a fourteen-day deep penetration. Two of his best sergeants had died in his arms, screaming like women. He was *fed up* with the lack of back-home support. One minute the congressman was sitting there making treasonable statements with that shit-eating Lower East Side grin on his face, and the next minute he was stone cold dead on the floor of the hooch, and no amount of wishing, no miracle antibiotic, would put the brains back in his head.

He had been shot by VC, was the story. Stupid gooks didn't realize they were wasting one of their chief apologists. For obviously the army had to protect the man in the famous photo, which had summed up all those intangibles that distinguish the Point from Regular Army. But there were no more photo opportunities, no more command assignments.

He didn't complain or try to pull strings. Put a true wearer of the Ring in charge of the company latrine, and he'll make damn sure his toilet bowls are the most sparkling toilet bowls in the entire God damn army. In truth, he was perhaps a trifle relieved. The spotlight had been flattering and all, but it had also been a bit of a strain.

A job was created for him in ClanDes, Clandestine Destabilization, in charge of what was known as Contract Abrogation. This was light duty. Some years went by, and though he and the picked men in his unit skateboarded and jogged a lot and stayed psychologically fit, ready to go into action on an instant's notice, they had not yet been called upon to abrogate anybody. There had been times when the Cat had actually had a target in his sights, a round under the hammer, but somebody had always countermanded at the last minute.

That wouldn't happen this time. With Iluminado Castillo, there was no other way.

Contract Abrogation went into high-security mode. They had to be supercareful because of the explosive proliferation of intelligence agencies now that unaudited funds were available again. Every office in town felt that it had to have its own intelligence arm. There was even a crazy rumor that Central Intelligence itself, because of its bad press, had been divided up and regrouped. The building was still there, people still went in and out, but hadn't the *real* CIA, the dirty CIA, been superseded by a new agency so secret that it was still without name or initials? The Chiefs, who should have been the first to be told, made a serious effort to find out, but they got nothing but Mona Lisa smiles. Did that mean that the people they asked knew the answer but had been forbidden to speak, or that they didn't know either but wanted the Chiefs to think— The modern world has its difficulties.

The Cat rendezvoused with General McArdle, unattended, in a condemned enlisted men's latrine. McArdle had brought the file, and told the ClanDes man no more than he Needed to Know, which wasn't that much. The Cat saw at once that this was going to be tough. They couldn't allow the target out of the building; above all, he had to be kept away from the press. At the same time, they couldn't just walk up and shoot him. The story had to be airtight, with unimpeachable witnesses.

Here they missed Mirabile. But that thinker cared for his brain the way professional quarterbacks care for their knees. He had been kept up until long after midnight, and he needed his ten hours. The Chiefs knew from experience that there was no use waking him prematurely. He would merely mumble some banal suggestion, far below his usual standard, and a moment later his eyes would close and he would be bubbling and steaming like some not-quite-extinct volcano.

Reconnoitering, the Cat located an office awaiting repair, directly across the courtyard from the Counter Coup auditorium, where the students were being given the orientation lecture. Using East German binoculars, in their collapsed state no thicker than a cigarette case, he located his man, identifying him from a glossy blowup of the photo that had been taken when Castillo entered the building. The chairs in there were almost sinfully easy; some of the students were already nodding. Not Castillo, however. He was writing everything down.

The Cat studied him. Now that the focus was on Central America, he had been learning Spanish and reading intelligence papers on the military and political leaders (often the same man) in the region. There were small touches in the Colombian's uniform he hadn't encountered before. Order of the White Rose? The Finns were supposed to be very chintzy with that.

He used his miniaturized range finder. Thirty-seven yards, an easy dunk for the Cat, the top of his class in marksmanship as in so much else.

Now how would they say that this tragedy happened? The VC ploy was no longer available. An exchange of fire between starling lovers and Special Security? The advance guard of the demonstrators was already approaching the bridge, and the Cat's people could be instructed to get out there and mingle, let go a few rounds. But some smartass leftist reporter would be sure to check the bullet's trajectory against the Pentagon floor plan. A wild round would have to ricochet more than once and make a right-angle turn. Not very plausible.

Across the courtyard, the target was called to the rostrum. A street grid had flashed on the screen. Presumably they wanted him to explain the disposition of forces during the recent Colombian coup. To get to the aisle he had to disturb a haughty black, making him wake up and draw in his knees. A Masai? You never knew with these schools. Something was said. Castillo whirled, and the fire in his eye gave the Cat his idea.

A quarrel over some little sticking point. These high-strung, *machista* Latins. An insult, the insult returned, a knife stab to the heart.

Returning to clandestine country, he mobilized his command. To give orders and have them instantly obeyed: the Cat had nearly forgotten how pleasurable it could be. One man ran this way, another that.

When the press-liaison lieutenants were bragging about the Cat before he murdered the congressman, they had always mentioned that along with his other accomplishments—Olympic fencer, NBA offers, fourth in his class academically, which wasn't saying much as nobody has that kind of illusions about the Point but where did he find the *time*, Silver Star, Congressional Medal, blah blah blah—the son of a bitch played the flute. Under mortar attack, or during the last minutes of the countdown before some desperate foray, he would break out his flute and play the spine-chilling movement from Handel's E minor sonata. It became part of the myth.

His colleagues experienced this music now for the first time. The Handel E minor! Their first abrogation! The temperature in that part of the building dropped several degrees.

The Colombian payoffs had been badly bungled, in Hector Duffy's opinion. Hawk-Sisley's man in-country had had an attack of last-minute jitters. It was Mr. G's money he was about to pay out, and everybody who worked for Mr. G knew that he was allergic to alibis. He claimed that they stuffed up his sinuses.

161

So the emissary parted with only ten percent of the promised sum, a schoolboy's mistake. As soon as the colonels squeaked through their first twenty-four hours they were no longer a speculation. Naturally they wanted Mr. G to sweeten the deal. Oh, they had a gentleman's agreement, but there aren't too many gentlemen in politics south of the tropic of Capricorn. Or north of it either, for that matter.

Even computers occasionally err. Look at the printout on Iluminado Castillo and he didn't seem to be much of a problem. Campari-gins, introduce him to women. Nevertheless Duffy suspected that he was going to be canny and dangerous. Everybody thought Mr. G was made of money. Well, he *was*, but his bank debt was killing him. Then this unexpected Am Tex intervention. Multinats are better off faceless. The clever ones keep changing their names so no one has time to get to hate them too much. But Am Tex not only had a face, it belonged to Mr. G's old foe, Mike Shanahan, and if Shanahan got there first with Castillo, Mr. G, Duffy knew, would want Duffy's ears.

Working on strategy, trying out bits of dialogue, Duffy had trouble getting to sleep. Then the usual call from Mr. G at one in the morning. After that, more sleepless hours, frightening dreams, and he slept through the alarm.

Washing less completely than usual, he hurried to Iluminado's hotel, where he learned that the boy had given him up and left for the Pentagon.

Plenty of time. At each stoplight, an unruly mob swarmed over Duffy's car, shouting slogans and slapping their hateful stickers on his bumpers and rear window. In the end, after further indignities, he had to abandon ship on the wrong side of the river and proceed on foot. The demonstrators, having been teargassed and fire-hosed and spread-eagled, had lost much of their early-morning good humor. They were throwing bird shit packed into snowballs. The one they hit Duffy with had been built around a three-quarter-inch nut.

Pentagon PR made a big fuss over him when he arrived, videotaping his injury for the midday news. Though he had spent twenty-eight years on active duty, this was his first combat wound. Wearing a butterfly bandage, he arrived at the Counter Coup lecture hall a half hour late.

All the Pentagon schools carry a faculty overload, a teaching assignment being one of the obligatory rest stops on the road to the summit. Here at Counter Coup, most of the actual instruction was handled by guest lecturers, ex-authority figures now serving their country in the private sector. It is no secret that these new jobs pay very well, and this gives the student body something to think about, perhaps new career goals.

Asians, Africans, Latins—Duffy didn't see a spare ounce of flesh in the room. He reminded himself to eat only yoghurt for lunch. And where was his boy? There, seated well down in front, taking notes. Duffy stole down a side aisle and found a seat in that row.

Today's lecturer, an authentic celebrity, had been in charge of decision making through several ten-minutes-to-midnight confrontations. He was enunciating carefully, because some of the comprehension of German-English out there was not of the best. He had lost a step since his departure from power but he himself didn't think so. He kept coming like the hot wind off the desert.

"You gentle-men will be here twenty-one days. During that time, two coups will occur somewhere in the world, perhaps even in one of the countries represented in this room. On a yearly average, out of every two coups undertaken, one point four will succeed. We may not applaud these statistics, but we are sitting in a building, gentle-men, dedicated to the facing of facts."

After his truncated night, Duffy felt his eyelids beginning to droop.

In countries where coups are part of the heritage, the lecturer was saying, there is no hope of eliminating them completely. So why bother to try? An unsuccessful coup gives you an opportunity to identify your most ambitious opponents. Squelch a few coups in a row, and it may give you the self-confidence you need to run an election. For elections, he told them a trifle sternly, even when less democratic than an American might wish, with two parties and exit polls, are much more satisfying in the long run, as well as less embarrassing to your friends to the north who are trying to give you money.

What are the preconditions, he asked, the so-called coup climate? Economic troubles; everybody has those. A single center of power, only a minority of the populace politically active. He went to the mainframe. The coup-climate program was running. What were the chances of a successful coup d'etat in the U.S.A., for example? The computer reflected for no more than a minisecond. YOU KIDDING? was the user-friendly response. Thailand? A Thai was taking this course, as the lecturer certainly knew. COUP PROGNOSIS THAILAND, GOOD TO EXCELLENT. Colombia? TOO SOON.

Any questions? A hand was raised hesitantly.

"Please, sir. How long can a new strongman have the honey's moon?"

At home, the Counter Coup students were still on the first step of the escalator and few of them had anything to do with the awarding of contracts. Still, as the lecturer had been saying, the world is in flux, and changes are certain. So Duffy was not the only industrial rep in the auditorium. For the three weeks of the school, finders, consultants, free-lance and contract spooks would circle the students like friendly piranhas, smiling and offering gifts and advice.

And there were other outsiders. Counter Coup, with its celebrity lecturers and state-of-the-art teaching aids, was one of the Pentagon showpieces, and today, as part of the all-building W-3 effort, PR Command was hustling tour groups through in an unending stream. The visitors had been told to be quiet, but the jostling, the murmurs, would have unnerved any ordinary lecturer. This one had been through too many storms.

He reloaded the computer and called an African up to make a fool of himself. Imagine that you're in charge of your country's security, the lecturer told him. You understand that a coup is brewing. Given the authority mix, the relative force levels, the degree of foreign involvement, various loyalty-disloyalty factors, what is your first move?

The young African, dressed in a shapeless uniform left behind by the French, tried this expedient and that. Everything he did only made matters worse, and presently the computer delivered its verdict: COUP SUCCESSFUL. CHIEF OF SECURITY BEHEADED.

The student's mistakes may have cost him his head, but he didn't seem particularly downcast. Flashing a big smile, he went back to his seat.

Another party of tourists filed in. The little hairs at the nape of Duffy's neck sent him an ominous message and he looked around. These were Revolutionary Dames, part of the same infestation he had seen in Iluminado's hotel, and they had picked up a hitchhiker.

Doris!

To blend with the background, she had gone to the pantssuit uniform. But whereas the genuine Dames were in pastel, she was in green and white stripes, a peacock among pigeons. She had spotted Iluminado, and was maneuvering into position. With only minutes to go, the lecturer was playing the keyboard with both hands. Duffy himself had delivered a lecture or two in this room, so the hardware was familiar. The small control console at the right of the rostrum was not being used. He went to that station and typed quickly: TALL REDHEAD BACK OF THE HALL. WELL KNOWN NUT AND PUBLICITY SEEKER. GET HER OUT OF HERE.

Each seat had its own postcard-size video display. He selected two students: the powerfully built African who had just, so to speak, been beheaded, and a lithe-looking Japanese, a martial artist, Duffy hoped.

ALERT ALERT— The words flashed onto their screens, blinking on and off to get their attention. TALL REDHEAD—

Still elated after his duel with the computer, the African reacted at once. The Japanese had to be signaled repeatedly before he understood that the message was directed at him.

But they broke a basic coup rule, telegraphing their intention. Doris whipped off her shoe and stepped forward to meet them at the top of the aisle. The heel caught the Japanese on the temple and he went down like a felled tree.

"Iluminado!" she cried. "New offer!"

The African gathered her in. The Revolutionary Dames shrank back from the rank-smelling young officer, who had experienced his own revolution so much more recently than theirs. Duffy was on his way. Doris, kicking, was lifted clear of the floor and borne backward.

"Two million two plus seven hundred thou with escalators!"

Outside, she quieted down quickly, seeing that they had her outnumbered.

"You win, boss. I guess I'm doomed to be a secretary-receptionist the rest of my life."

This was an attitude Duffy liked to see in the young women who worked for him. He didn't trust it, however. The African turned out to know a little karate—so much for geographical stereotypes. He could have brought her along with a thumb on a pressure point. Instead, he fastened one large hand on her haunch, the other on her breast. You would expect someone from a bare-breasted country to be without that particular hang-up. Not so, it seemed.

Duffy needed to sit Iluminado down for their postponed talk about money, but the boy was now locked into the Counter Coup schedule. The next event was a visit to the Crisis Containment room. The students always came away from there with a healthy respect for American power. Dazzled, realizing that he was only an insignificant gofer from a junta of nobodies, he would put up token resistance. A Command and Flag Officers' lunch, Duffy decided; forgo the yoghurt for today. A few Camparis with gin to start, a Burgundy from the top of the list, finally champagne to celebrate Iluminado's acceptance of Mr. G's generous offer.

First, though, he had to be sure that Doris was off the premises. All the way off! Never underestimate your enemy, an old military adage.

She still hadn't quite given up.

"Duffy, the numbers they're talking about are *unreal.* I don't suppose you'd consider defecting?"

"Certainly not."

But recalling another military adage, that you can't know too much about your enemy's intentions, he asked her to expand on the suggestion. It proved to be all on spec. Whereas with Mr. G, Duffy had it in writing; not that Mr. G respected the sanctity of contracts between parties with unequal bankrolls. "Sue me," were two of his favorite words.

"You're wasting your breath," Duffy told her, and although he admired her combative spirit and was even a bit sorry that he wouldn't be seeing her again, he couldn't resist helping her down the front steps with a push from the rear.

"American women so *soft*," the African said as they went back in.

Pentagon lecturers are rated primarily on their ability to close out a class on time, and this virtuoso had never missed by more than a few seconds.

"Iluminado!" Iluminado heard. "Escalators!"

It was Doris. She was being lifted by a large Ugandan, under Duffy's direction. Iluminado felt an irrational impulse to rush to her aid, but at that moment the lecture ended, in an explosion of visuals, and the aisles were immediately jammed.

He was carried slowly up toward the exit. There in the last row, as relaxed as a snake, Quimby, who had managed to confuse him so badly on the airplane, was watching him approach with his little homosexual smile.

"Iluminado, isn't it? Any questions so far?"

Iluminado had nothing *but* questions, not that he could expect a straight answer from anyone so sexually crooked.

"But this school is all backward! When he says what a government should do to protect against coups, nobody listens. Nothing but yawns. Then when it's the other way around, the six things to remember for a coup to succeed, everybody wakes up and is scribbling away madly."

"So what's your question?"

"It should be called the Coup school, not the Counter Coup."

Quimby was chuckling thickly. "You don't think we could bring junior officers in from all over the world and teach them how to overturn their own governments, do you? Those governments are good clients of ours. But you heard the professor, face facts. There are always going to be coups. Bolivia's had twenty-seven in the last twenty-one years, some of them pretty messy. There's a right way to do things, and a wrong way. If you don't do it right the *public* can get involved, for Christ's sake. And if the coup works and the new guys got their training from us they're going to be grateful. They'll go on borrowing dollars and buying our airplanes. All pretty obvious, really."

There was much to think about here. It was clear, from the way Duffy and Doris had been trying to give him money, that his own junta was not quite as corruption-free as he had supposed as a newly commissioned lieutenant. Years from now, if somebody invited him to join a conspiracy, he would have picked up a few useful pointers this morning.

"Let's have dinner tonight," Quimby offered, "and we can discuss it in depth."

"Thank you, I think not."

The chuckle again. "You may be misunderstanding me, you know. It could be the concept that interests me. The innocent visitor from some other galaxy, how he adjusts to life on this civilized planet."

"I doubt that very much."

The exchange had delayed him, and his fellow students were gone. Off to the CCR, according to the schedule, but where and what was the CCR? While he was hesitating, the entire student body, led by an Air Force colonel, came down the corridor, swinging their arms almost to the horizontal, in the fashion of second-class armies. The colonel brought them to a halt in front of a wall map.

YOU ARE HERE, it declared.

An immense arrow pointed to an intersection of corridors. The colonel didn't see how they could possibly be there.

"That's the trouble with running tours," Quimby said. "The boy scouts keep switching the signs."

He offered himself as guide. After a short march, with many bewildering turns and shortcuts, they arrived at the CCR. Of course, Iluminado remembered, Hemlock had mentioned it—Crisis Containment room.

The Dames, minus Doris, were already there, not quite believing their luck. For what they had been invited to witness was nothing less than the making of history. One oddity about these women, Iluminado had already noticed, was that they were either too fat or too scrawny. There was nobody in between; probably something to do with the diet.

The visitors' gallery was nothing but a wide place in the corridor with a long picture window, soundproof and triple-glazed. A one-star PR general, wearing earphones, stood by a bank of switches, ready to open the outlets if there was anything he thought these uncleared outsiders could safely hear.

Iluminado squeezed between Dames, one fat and one thin, and looked down into the great hall. The War room, it used to be called, and War room was still the name used in apocalypse movies. The legendary board was still draped but the lords of the Pentagon were beginning to assemble at the great curving table. Dispatch cases were everywhere, many connected to their masters by umbilical chains. The scene smoldered with gold braid and stars. Again Iluminado had to stiffen his face and partially shut down his eyes. Where but in Washington would you see such a table? Not in Beijing, certainly. Not in Moscow.

One of the Dames pointed, with a sharply indrawn breath. A jaunty civilian had entered, through shadows, wearing a plaid suit and rueful smile. From this downward angle he seemed to have only two dimensions, as though he had been jigsawed out of plywood. It was the president himself, she informed Iluminado. Though commander in chief, and thus the superior officer of every man in the room, he was largely ignored.

The Dame kept laying her hand on Iluminado's forearm, in the U.S. style, as she pointed out other celebrities.

There was Iluminado's new friend Senator Hemlock, masquerading as a brigadier general. The vice president. The defense sec., the sort of short man who enjoys the company of very large dogs, Saint Bernards or Great Danes. Michael Mirabile, the strategic thinker, General McArdle, chairman of the

Joint Chiefs of Staff, who bore a surprising resemblance to Iluminado's dentist, back home in Pamplona. A row of senior citizens, some of them *very* senior, in wheelchairs. These were the chairmen emeriti, the elders. One had served the nation as chief of Selective Service through all the wars in his lifetime. He remained spry, as Iluminado could see, ready to be drafted again at the age of ninety-four. And why, the Dame wondered, were so few young people today prepared to follow his example?

Next to him, a rug across his old knees, was the famous bombing chief, she couldn't remember his name at the moment, who had invented the main slogan of his generation's war: "We'll bomb them into the twenty-first century." He cocked his cigar at each new group of visitors entering the gallery. One hand came off the arm of his wheelchair, index finger extended. Number one, he seemed to be saying. This is the United States of America, and we will not settle for second.

Outside the building, another octogenarian, a stand-up comic named Harry Lord, who couldn't stand up for long at a time any more, was unkinking his old bones from the Rabbit that had been sent to bring him in from the airport. A millionaire many times over, Lord honestly preferred limos. But if the Chiefs thought it was necessary to mothball the Cadillacs to propitiate certain damn fools in the Senate, Harry Lord, for one, wasn't about to say that they were taking the coward's way.

Only one thing besides the national anthem and the sight of a rippling American flag could make the moisture stand in his eyes: a great broad, like the one in the green-and-white stripes who was hurtling down the steps toward him, her hair like a haymow on fire. He had barely had time to wonder if his friends here meant her for him—if so, it would be considerate of them—when she crashed into him and they tumbled to the pavement together.

His writers stood him back on his feet. They were nearly as shaken as he was, because if anything happened to Harry Lord—

Jokes were their only vocabulary. "If you have to fall down, Harry, that's the best way."

" 'Ere, Miss, brush you off, Miss."

"If anybody's going to brush off this lovely young creature," Lord said, "I'm the one who had the collision."

She was wearing a Revolutionary Dames badge: "Hi! I'm Doris, from South Bend." And what infraction of the rules, Lord wanted to know, had caused Doris, from South Bend, to get herself tossed out of the Pentagon?

"They make me so *mad!*" she said. "The narrow minds of some people."

She turned to shake her fist at the building. Lord didn't like that, but she went on to explain: she had little seniority in her chapter, so whenever the ladies threw a potluck supper, who got to wash the pots? But Doris didn't mind, because she was so proud that she could trace her descent from one of those indomitable women who helped load the cannon and share the privations of the soldiers at Valley Forge. Now a busybody named Emma Lou Wickingham had looked this ancestor up in the archives, and claimed to have proof that she didn't exactly fight in the Revolution, load cannon and so on, she had been—you know, just sort of *along.*

"Child," Lord said.

The Dames were wonderful women in so many respects, but yeah, a little small-minded sometimes. It did seem a shame that after coming all the way from South Bend, Indiana, Doris should be deprived of the tour on a technicality. He agreed to take her under his wing.

The guard at the door had just seen her ejected, and Duffy had ordered him not to let her back in. But if Harry Lord was her sponsor, the Harry Lord who golfed with the Chiefs and would willingly fly to the moon if there were soldiers there who were homesick for one-liners—

Isobel Clancy, the city's premium hostess, had heard Lord was on his way, and was waiting at the top of the steps, wanting to invite him to a little Taurus dinner she was giving. The hairs on Doris's forearm mingled with the alpaca hairs on Lord's sweater, sending a charged invitation. This was old-fashioned sexism of the very worst sort, and Doris's feminist friends would despise her for it; but in this male-dominant environment, a girl needed a masculine protector.

He told Isobel, an old friend, not to count on him for dinner because he thought he was going to be busy.

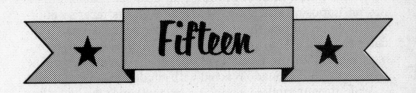

Fifteen

The drapes parted, and the great board burst into view.

From seeing the movie versions, Iluminado had expected a map of the world in the Mercator projection, with colored lights giving the location of silo fields, flight paths, nuclear subs on station, target populations. Not at all. What he saw was one hundred heads. The United States Senate! The faces were all white, ninety-eight males and two females, grouped under column headings: OURS, THEIRS, FENCE SITTERS. It was a clear representation of good and evil. OURS were studio portraits, with the marks of slyness and venery retouched away: statesmen, patriots, at the height of their mental if perhaps not their physical powers. THEIRS were unflattering newspaper snapshots: politicians of the sleaziest sort, who would tamper with their student interns and sell their mothers for a bottle of cooking sherry.

Well, their electronics were certainly impressive, Iluminado would have to admit. On one big screen and dozens of smaller ones, pictures flickered continually in an eerie silence. The big screen showed an interior which must be the Senate chamber itself. A senator was speaking to empty chairs. Two others were

173

reading their mail. Through the magic of closed-circuit television, other screens showed the cloak rooms, the steps of the Capitol, a barbershop. In a magnificent lavatory, a portly gentleman with a cascade of white hair dribbled a weak stream into an imposing marble basin. Now a giant's face, so enormously enlarged that the hairs in his nostrils looked like tropical ferns, came onto the large screen. He was talking into a stick mike with the Capitol's dome in the background. The ladies around Iluminado reacted with shudders of recognition.

"Hal," they murmured, and the scrawny Dame who had taken responsibility for Iluminado's education told him: "No one can ever take Walter's place, but what can I tell you? I feel *comfortable* with Hal. And he's miles ahead in the ratings, so the rest of the country must agree with me."

This was a network pickup, going out to the multitudes, so the PR general at the sound switch decided to let them hear it.

"—to protect the Panama Canal," the voice was saying. "Not since the MX debates can old Washington hands recall an arm-twisting campaign as ferocious as this. In the cloakrooms and corridors, on the floor of the Senate itself, the persuaders are at work. As late as last night, Capitol insiders considered the vote too close to call. But by this morning, after a series of power brunches, calls from the White House, an estimated three million identical postcards, the Pentagon bandwagon was back in the fast lane, passing every car on the road. As the debate goes into its final day, our latest projection is"—he paused for a double-check, for a network's projection is often as important as the vote itself—"*fifty-three for, thirty-one opposed*, a majority for the Pentagon's controversial Wall. And this is Hal Amsterdam, on Capitol Hill. Back to you, Albert."

From four-star general to the lowliest first lieutenant pushing the coffee-and-Danish wagon, the officers in the CCR were on their feet roaring. The signaling arm of the old bombing general in the wheelchair had gone into spasm. Number one!

"Did he say a *wall*?" Iluminado whispered.

"It has something to do with the Pentagon budget," the Dame whispered back. "I don't bother to keep up with it. When the

Joint Chiefs say we need thus and so, by glory that's good enough for me."

Changes were taking place on the board as the Amsterdam projection took effect. Three faces in the FENCE SITTER column moved over to OURS, losing their shifty grins and the bags under their eyes—instant face-lift and personality change.

Another elderly man, some kind of entertainer, stepped up on the briefing platform and began firing off a series of very quick jokes.

"Harry Lord," the Dame told Iluminado. "He's the funniest man. You'd get more out of it if you could understand English."

As well as Iluminado was able to tell, the jokes were about Senator Hemlock's drinking problem. Hemlock himself was laughing along with the rest. Judge Taylor bourbon, distilled in his district; exclusive purveyor to all Pentagon messes, when Hemlock went AA, distillery hung a wreath on the door. Wouldn't say that that whiskey was strong, but tank crew at Fort Hood ran out of gas and filled up with the Judge. First tank to fly nonstop from Texas to Germany.

An arm-twisting joke. A contortionist came out with both arms braided behind his back, croaking, "I'm for the Wall! All the way!"

A joke about a dog and the Wall, about Senator Shanahan's family, about General McArdle's terrible golf game, about limousines—but Iluminado gave up. Leaving all age groups limp from laughter on both sides of the window, Lord tottered off to happy applause.

The unattended microphone drew the commander in chief.

He still had the curious two-dimensional look. The PR general prudently cut off the sound. This president, though not as foulmouthed as some of his predecessors, had been known to do blue material in front of an all-male audience like this one. The smile came, the smile went, like a partially unscrewed lightbulb. He lost his thread once or twice but that didn't fluster him in the least; he was all right again as soon as he found the right card. Now his style changed, becoming less genial; he hammered the air with his fist, to show these fighting men that he could be as truculent as anybody. It is not unusual for an old man to want to be considered younger than he actually is, but Iluminado didn't think that was quite what he was seeing here. This was an old man pretending to be a boy who was *pretending to be grown up.*

His gestures were taken from prizefighting and football, the manly North American sports. His listeners didn't give him their full attention until he drifted back as though chasing a pass and fell off the platform.

The vice president, sitting by himself in a folding chair, leaped to his feet, hand to his lips. Aides patted the president back into shape and assisted him to his seat, where a makeup man wiped the glisten marks from his forehead.

All at once everyone in the room was up, booing and whistling. On the big screen three men were seen entering the Capitol. They looked somewhat alike. By some trick of the light, the head of the big man in the middle seemed to glow from within.

This was the enemy, Iluminado was told, Senator Shanahan and two of his slimy staffmen. For the umpteenth time, he was opposing the Pentagon for selfish political reasons.

A troop of uniformed boy scouts had joined the onlookers, and they were booing along with the rest.

"Drop dead, Shanahan! Back to Moscow!"

Below, a full colonel was up on the platform with a swagger tucked under his arm.

"I'm going to put the sound back on," the PR general announced. "I want you to hear this guy. It's Colonel Wheat, the best briefer around. But promise you won't repeat anything you hear."

They assented eagerly. The colonel's dry, unemotional voice was allowed through the outlets.

For obscure parliamentary reasons, he was saying, the W-3 vote could only be taken on a calendar Wednesday, and today, unfortunately, was Thursday. Never mind, their friend Senator Hemlock had secured the Senate's unanimous consent to *act on the assumption* that it was Wednesday. The key test, both floor leaders had agreed, would come on an amendment, or to be really pedantic about it, an *amendment* to the amendment.

They were counting on the presiding officer—here the vice president half rose and shook hands with himself—to make sure that the members had a pretty good inkling of what they were doing. In a nutshell, a nay vote on the amendment would be an aye vote for W-3.

Iluminado repeated some of this to himself. Nay on the amendment, aye for W-3. Calendar Wednesday, though today was actually Thursday.

Wheat had the army briefer's rapid-fire, no-nonsense delivery, and Iluminado could understand only scattered fragments of what he heard next. Lose on W-3 and enemy would be encouraged to squeeze here, slash there, back to bare-bones austerity. So get over there, and get their hands dirty. Like a pregnant woman, Iluminado thought he heard. (A *pregnant woman*?) Give them what they crave. If all else fails, fall back on the golden handshake. But carefully! Use PACs. Don't leave a paper trail.

The PR general hesitated, his hand on the off switch. Was some of this stuff too strong for civilians? But the scouts were too young to be interested, the Counter Coup students didn't understand English that well, and as for the Dames—

"Fight fire with fire," Iluminado's Dame said approvingly. "Those Shanahans have been throwing money around like I don't know what. I say beat the skunks at their own game."

Wheat again. Automatic one-grade promotion for every changed vote. Marketing packet, list of twenty-five major contributors for each fence sitter and Shanahan doubtful. Psychiatric profile, net worth statement on each. Favors owed. Subcontracts, the red blood cells of political action. This building never lost a major vote. Nonchalanted a few but never defeated *mano a mano*. You're going to be bloodied but you can tell your grandchildren—

Meanwhile, the screens behind and above him displayed a rapidly changing sequence of patriotic effects: advancing tanks, plane formations, flags, marines storming a beach, Abraham Lincoln, sky full of helicopters, more flags.

Finally a clergyman was brought up to pronounce benediction.

"Lord God of hosts," he prayed, in part, "bless, we beseech thee, the efforts of these thy servants—"

"Thank you-all," Wheat said when he finished. Or was it, "Thank you, Oral?"

A Third World officer, a captain like Iluminado, was walking toward them. Something about his uniform and the way he moved pulled Iluminado around. What was it about that saunter, the arms hanging straight down, thumbs out—

His cap was folded the long way and stuck through his left epaulet, the fashion in the Colombian army. As he came closer, Iluminado saw the condor stamped on his uniform buttons. A compatriot then, a Colombian. But he had pale blue eyes, as cold as the runoff from a glacier, and unnaturally perfect teeth, a combination seldom seen in the Colombian Army, even among officers.

"Yes, I thought I smelled a countryman," this man remarked lightly in Spanish, "no doubt from the regime of the plastic colonels?"

It was actor's Spanish, carefully punctuated to make sure that Iluminado caught the sneer.

"And you are of Santamaría, evidently," Iluminado replied.

"I am proud to admit it, for he put the nation back on the map of the continent, after so many blank years. Tell me, please. Is it pleasurable, licking the U.S. ambassador's backside? I think your colonels must find it so, or they wouldn't slobber so much while they do it."

He paused to await an answer. Iluminado's heartbeat was rapid and very close to the surface.

He could only say, "But unlike Santamaristas, we in the new regime draw the line at carnal connection with our mothers."

The Counter Coup students, almost without exception, came from countries where the dueling spirit survives, although the activity itself may have been outlawed. Even without a knowledge of Spanish, they could tell that these were serious insults. A ring opened around the two men.

"The Order of the White Rose," the stranger continued, flick-

178

ing the offending decoration, which Iluminado should never have allowed Gabriella to persuade him to wear. "Let me imagine the citation. For gallantry in action in the backseat of a car, with the wife of some colonel or other—"

Iluminado's heart gave a jump. If the man had been told about Gabriella, it meant he had been sent here on purpose to pick this quarrel.

"In truth," he said deliberately, "I received the order for gelding Santamarístas. And I assure you this was far from easy. There was so little to take hold of. A grape will give you the top edge of the comparison."

The pale eyes changed very slightly. The verbal preliminaries were almost complete.

"But one thing confuses me. How did you conceal from the colonel's wife that you really prefer it with boys?"

"You don't know me. But I know you by your walk, *señorita*."

The Santamarísta threw one wrist to the side; a knife had jumped into his hand. His feet opened and closed.

It was a fencer's lunge, fast and unstoppable. Iluminado reacted in the only possible direction, backward, but he had started too late. Providence intervened, in the unlikely person of the scrawny Dame who had already befriended him. Seeing the knife come out of concealment, a move hidden from Iluminado himself, she struck with her rolled souvenir program. It diverted the thrust, and the knife blade passed harmlessly through Iluminado's sleeve.

Snatching a boy scout's hat, Iluminado whipped it at his adversary's eyes and kicked upward. It was like kicking into a tree.

He caught the knife arm and tried to snap it at the elbow, a move often described, with almost sensual enjoyment, by Major Sadowski. Even off-balance, the man was a problem to hold. They went careening into a naval commander in whites, who had been giving away ball-point pens.

The pens went flying. Under the ill-fitting uniform, the Santamarísta was nothing but bone and muscle. Iluminado smelled deodorant and after-shave lotion. It was the smell of the hosts at the Bolívar, and he realized that this man, too, must be a

179

Yankee, for no Latin American has that peculiar mixture of smells. Mr. G had warned him: *"Certain people in this building want to do something drastic about you, boy—"* And it could hardly get more drastic than this. The Dames would make excellent witnesses. What had they seen? A falling-out between two hot-blooded officers of the same nationality but opposite politics, an exchange of angry remarks, culminating in the ultimate homosexual insult. Then a quick knife thrust, the killer would plunge down a ramp, and after that, try to find him.

"Help me, please," Iluminado gasped in English, holding on grimly. "This is a red Cuban, a political assassin."

But his fellow students had been together for too brief a time to develop much unit feeling. They were from nonaligned countries, and the way the man handled the knife gave them a strong incentive to stay nonaligned.

Iluminado let go with a push. The knife fighter slipped on the pens and for an instant went to one knee. Iluminado snatched at his boot top. Now he, too, was armed, hiding the knife in the boy scout hat.

"Why are you trying to kill me? I have done nothing to you."

He extended the hat clumsily, pretending to be afraid. And it was an easy thing to pretend, for he knew very little about knife fighting. He had witnessed just one such fight in his life, between two drunk mestizos at a fiesta. They had flailed away at each other, causing fountains of blood to flow, and had then mopped themselves off and continued to drink and sing. In Cartagena, Iluminado and some of the senior noncoms had practiced knife throws, aiming at cigarette packages. As often as not, Iluminado's knife would strike handle end first.

"Cool it, guys," the PR general was saying, without much conviction.

The killer prowled forward, angrier now. He faked one low move, another. Iluminado winced back and away. The third, he was guessing, would be the serious one, for three has always been a ceremonial number. He struck through the hat without waiting, a thrust toward the throat.

It fell an inch or two short. Smiling, the man let him recover.

"Say a prayer, Castillo. You are about to die."

180

Duffy wasted a full quarter hour trying to get new instructions. Mr. G wasn't in his car or his airplane, at any of his various companies or the law firm, and nobody at any of those numbers had any useful ideas.

So Duffy was on his own, as usual.

He was thinking, as he often did nowadays, of those peaceful years in the Navy. *So* uneventful, except for that single accident, and no damage was done, after all; it came down in the water. But here in the ordinary world—

His step quickened as he approached the CCR visitors' gallery. What were they watching, a crap game?

No, it was more like a cockfight. Two of the mettlesome Counter Coup students were rolling about on the floor, doing their damnedest to destroy each other. And one was the very boy Duffy was supposed to be baby-sitting!

He went into tumbling orbit. The agreement hadn't been signed! Hadn't even been initialed! Had hardly been talked about! If anything happened to Iluminado, Mr. G would refuse to return Duffy's phone calls. As his own personal corporation, Duffy wouldn't be eligible for unemployment insurance.

Without giving a thought to the usual fate of the hen who tries to break up a cockfight, he waded right in. This was eighty percent economic necessity and twenty percent because he sort of liked the young man.

Iluminado was on the bottom, his opponent bearing down on his knife arm. Light flashed from the other blade. Duffy swung his dispatch case.

The reinforced corner caught the guy on the ear. It distracted him slightly, perhaps not enough. He rolled, quick as a cat— and that was who he resembled, Duffy realized, the man on the famous *Life* cover. But Duffy, too, could be quick when his livelihood was at stake. He flung out a hand and hit the LZ button.

Instantly, a gasified tranquilizer rained down from cocks in the ceiling.

When the Chiefs decided to go the tourism route, as part of

181

their new policy of demystifying the building, they had accepted the fact that there might be security problems. The CCR gallery, for instance, would be an ideal place for a dissident group to go limp or create some other form of disturbance. Not that it couldn't be handled, but why break heads and bring in the civil liberties people, when there were easier ways?

LZ, quickly rechristened Lazy Bones, had been developed by Hawk-Sisley chemists. It was a riot-control weapon with none of the political side effects of the ordinary gases. One gulp was more than enough. Odorless, colorless, it headed straight for the switching centers, where it turned down the dimmers. Not all the way down, just enough to slow every physical process by approximately half. Pulse rate, metabolism, arm-leg movements, speech—the works.

At the same time—the wonders of chemistry—it tripped the euphoria switch. Anger and stubbornness relaxed their grip on the rioter; he could no longer remember his grievances; he was purely and simply happy to be alive on this earth.

Both fighters had risen. The knife point came in under Iluminado's arm and gave him an affectionate prod. Iluminado wheeled, bringing his own knife around. But it was a prop weapon now, cardboard and aluminum foil. The other, who had so recently been trying to kill him, lifted his chin to accept the caress. The point barely touched. The tiniest droplet of blood stood on his skin.

The Dames applauded, too limply to make any sound.

They had backup security, Duffy knew. Whenever these cocks were opened, urgent riot warnings went off in the Ring guard post. His last rational thought, before he, too, began to ride those waves of good feeling, was that armed assistance was on the way.

One glance was enough to see that Doris was a female, so she wasn't allowed into the CCR with Harry Lord. Because of their monthly bleeding and other impurities, even cleaning women were forbidden to cross that threshold, a superstition dating back to the first days of warfare.

She hailed a pedicab. Now where, she wondered, behind which of these tens of thousands of doors, would she find her neat-looking Colombian captain?

For every infantryman engaging the enemy, American military doctrine calls for a support structure of fifty-three others, to keep him fed, supplied, healthy and entertained. And so it was in the Pentagon today. The Chiefs might be orchestrating one of the fiercest lobbying efforts in American history, but in the rest of the building it was business as usual. Doris was sent from office to office. Every contract facilitator has places where they let him hang out and make phone calls, but no one had seen Duffy this morning. Maybe the gym, the sauna? Doris had already tried the gym and the sauna.

An alarm bell was clanging. On the theory that wherever the action was, was where she would find her young man, Doris ordered her driver to U-turn and pump hard toward the sound. And sure enough, Iluminado and another Third World officer, grinning like idiots, were outside the CCR gallery, doing a graceful pas de deux with knives.

The driver braked. "Watch it, lady, somebody turned on the Lazy Bones."

The two dancers did a slo-mo pirouette and gave each other another symbolic touch. A security formation in gas masks, with everything bouncing, turned a corner and double-timed toward them, ready to bust the whole scene, regardless of race, creed or color.

Doris couldn't sit there and watch it happen. She took a deep breath of uncontaminated air, darted forward and plucked Iluminado out of the dance.

He seemed happy to see her. She walked him backward and dumped him into the pedicab. The driver was shaking his head.

"No, *ma'am*. Can't get involved."

In another second or two her eyes would pop out of her head like champagne corks. She fished out a handful of money, but when the driver continued to shake his head she slipped on her metal knuckles and slugged him.

It was a real country and western haymaker, up from the

floor. He watched it come, unable to believe that a woman— It gave him the full Lazy Bones effect, without the euphoria.

Duffy wavered out from the wall. "Looooovvvely. Dorrris. You can haaavve your job back."

She leaped onto the bicycle and pedaled away, hams working like the piston rods in a dragster. To Iluminado, in his slowed-down condition, it must have seemed that they were moving faster than sound. He urged her to go even faster. She hadn't been on a bicycle in years, and while Iluminado continued to tell her to speed up, her pedaling muscles begged her *please* to slow down.

She threw a look over her shoulder. Two gas-masked security men had commandeered a pedicab, and their bicycle was being pedaled by a professional.

The ex-director of Selective Service in his battery-operated wheelchair, the luxury model with all the options, was traveling east. The ex-Air Force chief, in his, was traveling west. They slowed for the Physical Fitness Ring, and decided at the same moment that it was safe to cross.

"Lean and mean," the ex-Selective Service director said.

"Lean and mean," the ex-Air Corps chief replied. *"Look out!"*

A runaway pedicab was charging at them. The driver, a crazed woman with streaming red hair, waved them out of her way. Peaceable people really, they were perfectly willing to move out of the way, but their reflexes had slowed with the years. One turned left, the other right. A moment later, everybody was down.

A grim jogger went by. He didn't feel he could stop; he was trying to lower his lap time.

The pilings opposite the Mall entrance had been subsiding for years, giving the building a pronounced sag toward the southwest. A skater or skateboarder could enter the Fitness Ring at eleven o'clock (using the Air Force compass), and glide down to five, the 100, 200 bays, and catch a pedicab back.

A two-star general, a notable Rapid Deployment hot dog,

184

was now making the skateboard run: Sony earmuffs, crash helmet and knee bumpers, blue nylon sweats with the two stars embroidered over the pocket. He came barreling along to music that only he could hear, with considerable hip and shoulder activity. He was good on the board, and he could probably have managed to pick his way through. But Doris's bike chain had snapped, and she needed wheels. She kicked the board out from under him.

Iluminado waved languidly. "Do you know what I'd like?"

She had an idea. He'd like to have sex, in some interesting variation. But for now, the fireman's carry. He was as floppy as Raggedy Andy. Right arm between his legs. Wrist in one hand. One quarter knee-bend. *Hup!*

She stepped cautiously onto the board, which came completely around and attempted to run uphill. Overcorrecting, she made another jogger jump for his life.

Under its previous rider, if the skateboard's wheels had been chalked they would have left slalom marks, a linked sequence of fat and thin *Ss*. Its new course, under Doris, was more like an ICU cardiogram, all zigs, zags and lurches. Feeling Iluminado beginning to slide, she shrugged him back into place, and as their weight shifted, the board reared, took the next turn by itself and shot down a ramp.

Iluminado was unalarmed by the breakneck descent. His cheek fitted comfortably into the small of her back. He was laughing to himself, entertained by the muscular changes.

When they came out on the flat, the new shift threw Doris back on her heels, and again the board threatened to continue without them. Ahead, a cruising patrol had just heard the flash: be on the lookout for redheaded female civilian riding a skateboard with Colombian captain over her shoulder. Doris and Iluminado fitted this description exactly. The soldiers pointed and started to run.

Iluminado had decided to trace the green-and-white stripes upward, starting with the backs of her knees.

"Baby," she said, wriggling, "I'm trying to concentrate."

Any skateboarder knows what happens when you wriggle erotically on a moving board. The board changes direction.

They rocked into one of the spoke corridors. B Ring flashed by, C.

A robot mail wagon was beeping toward them, following a preordained path. Sensing an obstacle ahead, it came to a halt. Another collision seemed certain. Iluminado slipped a few inches, Doris corrected, the board changed course again and they whipped past the mail wagon with inches to spare.

Then they were on another downward incline and had left the pursuit far behind. A large sign warned them: BLASTING AHEAD, TURN OFF TWO-WAY RADIOS. Then: CAUTION, CORRIDOR 8 CLOSED FOR REDECORATION. TO REACH 300 BAY, USE B RING, CORRIDOR 5. To which some cynic had added, in longhand, "Or better still, write."

Doris was moving too fast to read the small print, but she knew from the debris scattered about that they had entered one of the Pentagon's problem areas. During the miserable years after the Vietnam debacle, the Chiefs hadn't been able to bring themselves to cut back on the sexy new weapons systems. Each had its constituency, Hawk-Sisley, General Dynamics, Am Tex and the rest, and they were all clamoring for the money. Each service wanted its share—had to have it, in fact. If Navy agreed to let Air Corps build the big-ticket bomber, Air Corps would agree to let Navy pull the battle wagons, those grand old ladies of the sea, out of dead storage. So what the Chiefs did in the end was what every civilian homeowner does with a similar problem. The totals stayed reasonably healthy, but the maintenance and repair line went down, down. Now they were paying the price for all the years of neglect.

It was probably time, Doris decided, to get off the skateboard and walk. But how do you get off a rapidly moving skateboard without falling down?

At Doris's level of competence, you don't. Again, Iluminado helped. Beginning to come down from his Lazy Bones high, he lifted his head to see where they were. Doris had thought that she and the board were finally beginning to develop a certain rapport, but now the damn thing fooled her completely, turning sharply and carrying them into an empty office.

Here they separated. The skateboard did solo somersaults

and Doris and her passenger went through a partially dismantled wall, ending on the floor in a welter of wood scraps and plaster.

Without waiting for the dust to settle, she started to count arms and legs. The striped ones, she knew, were hers. Nothing seemed broken.

"But how *magnificent*," Iluminado drawled. "I can tell you, a Colombian woman would have been far too bashful. Now I think it would be nice to take off some clothes."

"Not right this minute, Iluminado. Don't. I like that, but get back on Eastern Standard, will you? We've got to think, and we've got to move."

"We've got to think," he agreed, continuing to sort out the green and white stripes. "And we've got to move."

"The guy with the knife—I only got that quick glimpse, but I know I've seen him before, or his picture. What was the fight about?"

He waved with his free hand. "Nothing important. I would have killed him in one more minute. This decoration was a present from a lady, you see, it wasn't awarded officially, and somehow he guessed that. Then he said I prefer the company of boys. You know that's a lie."

"Why do you think soldiers were chasing us?"

"Were soldiers chasing us? I imagine it's illegal to fight with knives in the Pentagon."

"It's illegal to be *you*, don't you realize that?"

But she couldn't explain too fully or it would drive up his price. She began brushing off plaster dust. Iluminado helped. She must be getting some of the stale Lazy Bones fumes, for her mind was back on the skateboard, zigging and zagging. Not that she hadn't thought he was cute before, but the tranquilizer had taken off some of his *hombría* edge, and this guy was actually *likable*.

"I've been trying to think of the word to describe you," he said, "and I believe I have it. Doris, you were *splendid*."

She was glad to hear that he thought so, but she managed to pull away. She had to get him to safety before they started combing the building. They were looking for a woman with long red hair, a young man in Colombian uniform. The uniform would have to wait, but meanwhile—

She scrabbled in her shoulder bag, and brought out a pair of curved scissors.

"Doris!" Iluminado exclaimed when the first red hank hit the floor.

"Now do you understand that it's serious? I've been growing this a long time." She continued to hack away. "We've got to get from Point A to Point B without being grabbed, and we can't go together. You stay here, and I'll get you something to wear. Here's some numbers to think about. Remember the price I mentioned?"

She rattled off a sequence of categories and dollar amounts. Iluminado's own personal tip, if it could be called that, would be a million and a quarter. He shook his head, smiling.

"The hard thing about speaking a foreign language is to know when someone is joking."

"Iluminado, don't be insane! There's a top limit, and that's it."

But she couldn't stay to argue. She told him again not to move from that spot, and gave him a good-bye kiss, stepping out of his arms before they could close. Because of the Lazy Bones he was still a tick slow.

Iluminado laughed aloud. She had done a savage job with the scissors, but she was still a persuasive commercial for megavitamins, marijuana and oral sex. In the United States, it seemed, the courtship roles were reversed. Having taken a fancy to him, she didn't sit home hoping the phone would ring. She threw him over her shoulder and carried him off.

To get back some of the skateboard feeling, he did a little leap he had learned when his father was seeing the British ballerina. He floated briefly and came down with a jolt. What made him think he could trust her? Yes, she was splendid to look at, with a fine seat on a bicycle. The great female statue guarding the entrance to New York harbor, if she could be imagined wearing a green-and-white pants-suit, would probably look very much like her. She had chopped off her hair for him, she had clearly enjoyed their foreplay, as he thought it was called, and yet it was obvious that her real motivation was the money she would collect if Iluminado agreed to recommend that Colombia purchase their airplane.

He looked around. A broken-backed chair, a filing cabinet with its insides spilling out, it was like the *Norte* photograph of the abandoned sections of New York. He slapped off some of the dust, spat on his fingertips and smoothed his eyebrows and mustache. That was all he could do until he found running water.

If time had moved slowly under Lazy Bones, it was hurrying now. This was his first Counter Coup day. He had come late to the opening lecture and now he was late again. They would mark him down as a *mañana* type.

No, what was he thinking? He had boasted that he would have killed the bogus Colombian if the fight had continued. It was the other way around! *"People want to do something drastic—"* When Doris came in he announced his decision. He was going to follow the signs to the nearest exit. Change hotels, and not tell anybody where he was, not even her. Perhaps in a week's time—

She interrupted. "Step outside in that uniform and you'll get bullet holes in it. The place is on full alert. Patrols everywhere."

"Oh, yes. I believe every word you say."

"Back to normal, I see. Here, put this on."

She had brought him a one-piece garment, violently orange, with a legend in script across the left breast: FOR A CLEANER AMERICA, and under that: MYRON.

"You'd be surprised how much he made me pay for this," she said. "Shanahan's setting up something. We'll get a pneumatic any minute. Incidentally, I told him what you said and he's willing to go one and a half, but that's all the traffic will bear. Honey, cooperate?"

She actually seemed to think that he was going to walk around the Pentagon in that ludicrous costume.

"I definitely won't. You don't understand one single thing about me."

And the air-pressure message arrived. This sensible system was installed in the early years, when the Chiefs were in one of their recurring tizzies about the advances in electronic eavesdropping. At the Soviet embassy, on fishing trawlers just off our coasts, the great dish antennae were picking up every telephone call. "Tuna on rye, hold the mayo." "Subscribe now and we will send you absolutely free—" God knows what the KGB made of it all.

It was an old idea. As opposed to phone calls, the pneumatic mode was cheap, speedy and totally secure. The message was written on photosensitive paper which went blank thirty minutes after being exposed to the light, screwed into a little capsule and put in a vacuum tube. At a central station, it was rerouted mechanically. Instants later, it arrived at its destination.

The trouble was, it arrived with considerable force. That had been O.K. as long as the building was new.

Whump! A section of ceiling fell down.

Again, Iluminado found himself on the floor, not really unconscious but in no mood to argue about unimportant matters, such as what he would wear.

He let Doris put him into the odious garment. His name was now Myron, his goal was a cleaner America.

Doris was crumpling Environmental Impact statements and stuffing them into the beautiful uniform Gabriella had had made for him. When the headless dummy was complete she partially covered it with broken pieces of sheetrock.

"Who do you think that will fool?" Iluminado inquired.

"Nobody for long, probably, but all we need is about fifteen minutes."

The pneumo message was merely an office number—one digit, a letter, then three digits. Doris scratched a map in the dust. Here was Point A, their present location. The first right, up two floors, a left, Ring C to the right, all the way around. *Voilà*—Point B.

She gave him a long-handled push broom. "This will make you invisible, we hope. Now everything's going to be all right, sweetie. Just act natural."

Amazed, he asked her to repeat that, and he had heard her correctly. She actually expected him, a soldier, to act natural, pushing a broom, wearing a smelly orange disguise, thousands of miles from home.

Senator Shanahan was all over the CCR monitors, exuding confidence, as though he had two aces up and a third in the hole. When he left the Senate floor to go to the bathroom, the closed-circuit eye showed him pissing without any self-doubt whatever. The Chiefs watched in dread. A winner stood at that urinal, not a man about to suffer the most humiliating defeat of his life. What did Shanahan know that they didn't know?

All they could do was worry. This set them apart from the others, who were still revved up from Wheat's briefing. Pulverize! Cross the river and hit!

An officer from Contract Abrogation made his way toward McArdle. Even before he spoke McArdle knew from the anxiety lines on his face that he was bearing bad news. But he couldn't divulge it here. A five-way glance was exchanged. The Chiefs' hasty departure sobered the gathering and started some crazy rumors. Red Army tanks assailing the Fulda gap? Computer meltdown inside Cheyenne Mountain?

It was nearly that serious. Somehow the Colombian target had managed to survive a knife fight with the man who had taken the bronze in fencing at Mexico City. He had escaped, and was still at large somewhere in the building.

The ad hoc anti-Castillo command post was now tied into the high-security net. No one had been found who would admit to having turned on the Lazy Bones. The mysterious redheaded female who had plucked their victim out of the fight was apparently one of Harry Lord's army of girlfriends. That was a big surprise to the Chiefs because Lord was one of the most pro-Pentagon men in the country. The Cat had stood under the Lazy Bones spigot for a full thirteen minutes, and he couldn't see why they were making such a big fuss. It was almost noon, on a lovely day. Why not take crackers and cheese and a pitcher of Marys out to the riverbank and do the debriefing there?

Every housekeeping soldier in the building was mobilized for the sweep. Two redheaded women had been spotted, but both had cropped hair, whereas Harry Lord was willing to swear that the one who tricked him had sported a tawny mane down to her vaccination.

And all at once the manhunt was over.

The commander in chief, having thrown out the first ball, had to stay and watch a few innings, to show he was part of the common endeavor. Then he had to get up and leave, to show that he had business on his own side of the river, which was too important to allow him to dawdle about here. Such was the ritual. The vice president tagged along, but somebody said something rude and he let them go on ahead. If they didn't appreciate all he had done for the party, beg pardon the country, fine! Great!

While he was sulking, he noticed wheel tracks in the dust of an unused corridor. Made by a skateboard? He followed the trail in growing excitement. A controlled skid, a sharp turn, a split-second total reverse—that skateboarder was obviously world-class. Signs warned him to turn back, to shut off his radios. He persisted, and came finally into a bombed-out office. And there was the skateboard, wheels uppermost. The impact had brought down the ceiling, and a man lay crushed beneath the rubble.

The vice president was a bit squeamish about dead bodies, but he brought back proof—a condor button and a military decoration which the Cat, back to normal again, was able to identify at once as the Finnish Order of the White Rose.

"Castillo, all right. Now you'll excuse me, gentlemen. I'll step down there and give him the coup de grace."

"Negative," McArdle said, in the voice of command. This was his best time of day. It usually didn't last long, but as his aides liked to point out, some people don't even have that. "I understand why you want to be in at the death, Cat, but we're on Yellow Alert, and people are going to remember anything out of the ordinary. If they see you in that part of the building, for instance. Then what if some mouth-off in the Shanahan camp asks for an autopsy? What's this? Bullet hole in the back of the head, how did that get there? No, look. We've got the VP's statement, and you can't get better eyewitness testimony than that. He says the guy's skull was flattened. Anybody with any intelligence stays out of that area. Proceed at your own risk is what the signs say. He disregarded the warning or maybe he couldn't read English. *Tough* shit. Let's handle this as a routine case of a falling ceiling and bulldoze him out. Do you follow me?"

They seemed to.

"Terrific thinking, General."

"Textbook."

Again, the Almighty, whose name is invoked rather too frequently in the Pentagon, some people think, had given them a perfect solution. No military funerals for enemies of democracy. The rubbish contractor made twice-a-day runs through the condemned sector, trundling debris off to the chute. He didn't pick or scavenge, he just bundled everything up. Trucks waited below.

So—so long, Iluminado Castillo. *Hasta la vista*, O.K.? Better luck next time.

The Pentagon concourse was the first of the great shopping malls. Everything is given the PX discount except the stamps at the post office. It was bright there once, but as bulbs burned out they were seldom replaced—the maintenance budget again.

Doris kept looking at show windows, hoping to sort out the murky reflections. In the half-light everybody looked equally sinister.

Admiral Marx, after getting a fast update from Shanahan, was sending a vehicle for her. Feeling conspicuous out in the open, she went into Burger King and ordered an orange juice. Seeing it poured from a carton, she laced it heavily with instant ginseng and algae. The first mouthful didn't stay down. Harry Lord, a man she didn't want to see at that moment, had slipped onto the next stool.

"Doris, your hair! What happened, for God's sake?"

Her hand flew to the devastation. "The Pentagon shop is supposed to be marvelous, but I think they took off too much, don't you? Harry, where *were* you? I waited and waited."

"Aah—I kept getting waylaid. One pfc, I entertained his *grandfather*, would you believe? I've been around a long time, a very long time, Doris, and I'm happy to say I still get a good erection."

He was patting her affectionately between the shoulder blades. "I ran into Isobel Clancy again and she put on the pressure. I'm afraid I've got to go to her damn dinner. And I can't even squeeze in a matinee. Deng or Whang or whatever? The Chinese premier? I've got to play golf with him. Don't leak this, I'll deny it, but he kicks the ball if he thinks nobody's looking. I've been telling State they're crazy to trust him. Give me your home phone. I go coast to coast all the time, and it doesn't have to be nonstop."

He entered the number in a small book with gilt lettering: ASS, fondled her lightly once more and pushed off.

Colonel Wheat was waiting outside the Sixty-second Tanning Salon.

"Headline," Lord said. "Eighty-year-old loverboy can't keep his hands off luscious young broad."

Wheat was holding one of the new Japanese pulse-receivers, its sensitive needle locked on the tiny burrlike device which Lord had just planted on Doris. The needle betrayed agitation. Doris appeared, and climbed into a bicycle-powered personnel carrier.

"Navy pay-wagon," Wheat said with satisfaction. "Even money she's going to Admiral Marx. Giving aid and comfort to the enemy—that's *baaad*. If we can stick him with this, maybe we can finally excess the little son of a bitch."

Sixteen

Admiral Marx got the idea for Circe one afternoon while sitting on the bottom of Chesapeake Bay in a one-man recon sub. But he made a mistake with the name. Circe, he learned later, was the lady in the old story who turned sailors into pigs. Marx, however, was the stubbornest man in a stubborn service. Circe: it had a nice ring, he thought, so Circe she still was called.

Deterrence has been around for so long that most people have forgotten what it is. To say it again: each superpower has a stockpile of weapons that can end life in the enemy's half of the planet, and for political or religious reasons he may very well do just that unless he is stopped by the reflection that the other guy has enough stuff in concealed or protected locations so he can come back and take out the rest. Actually, it makes a certain kind of deranged sense.

Concealment is the key. Silos for land-based missiles are fixed points on a map. Bombers can be seen from those wide-open eyes on the satellites. But submarines, Marx's department, are stealthy, elusive things, and when they're on station they are out of sight most of the time. Out of sight, but not

195

out of earshot. Even the most silent sub will create some small rustle as it slips through the water. Our number one enemy (talking about the Russians now) has seeded the ocean bottoms with tens of thousands of tiny listening devices. There they are, randomly scattered about like black-eyed Susans in a meadow, listening, listening. And not being human, they never sleep.

A submarine's noise is seventy-five percent engine, twenty-five percent tie-in to the grid. What made Circe so credible was that she would be able to get along without both. Only a psychic would be able to find her (not that both sides, we are told, haven't been working on that). No propulsion system at all; she would drift with the deep-water currents. No microwave sputter. The transmitters would be activated only in conditions of the most dire emergency, like a sprung seam or the failure of one of the recycling systems, or, from the Washington end, the transmission of the terrible news that deterrence had failed, and so go ahead and cut loose the missiles.

One of the reasons the traditionalists didn't like the idea of Circe was her conformation. All previous undersea craft have been basically shark-shaped. Sharks, whatever else they may be, are definitely *machista*, and they fit the military's self-image. Circe, on the other hand, would look more like a large, gentle polyp. Like the windblown ships of the old Navy, she would be rudder-controlled, varying her depth by buoyancy changes, her speed by putting out drogues. Or she could drop a hook and come to a stop—all in absolute silence. Marx's opponents granted all that, but they kept coming back to the shape. A polyp: what kind of *statement* did it make?

Marx was proposing four Circes in all, two in each major ocean. They wouldn't come cheap, for the zirconium hull had to be able to withstand the weight of five vertical miles of water. The circular life-support systems had been tested in moon travel. By one of those fortuitous accidents, only American Texas, which needed the business, had the facilities to manufacture those pods. Thus another circle was closed. Good for Shanahan's candidacy because it was eleven percent cheaper than W-3, good for Marx's career, good for Am Tex's P and L statement, and God *damn* good for the country, which probably went without saying.

There was only one genuine drawback, and the critics fastened on that.

On Circe the crew would be isolated for extended periods of time. An ordinary submarine patrol lasts seventy days, which can seem an eternity. The same faces, the same preppy chickenshit officers, no television or newspapers, no alcohol or narcotics or women. Not much elbow room on a submarine. Nobody pretends that it's easy, but at least somebody onshore knows approximately where you are. Whenever you check in they change the pin on the map. Now and then you can come to the surface for a look around. There's nothing much to see except water, but at least it's a change. Each crew member is allowed to send and receive a weekly twenty-word radio message. In twenty words, a wife or a girlfriend can say quite a lot.

On Circe, the stats would be considerably hairier. A six-month cruise, Marx believed, would be just about right: one hundred and eighty-two days between launch date and crew change. No problem for polyps, but would human beings be able to stand it?

Marx couldn't understand why the matter even had to come up. Naturally the crews would be carefully screened. He himself would like nothing better than six months on the bottom, drifting and dreaming with a few congenial companions, the books he had never had time to read, a chessboard, above all, an opportunity to *think*. Others were less sanguine. His foes, CinCus Nav Eur, CinCus Nav Pac, the aviators, the flattoppers, the wagon masters—the whole rest of the Navy, actually—cited a classic study of isolation in snowbound New England, before television and salted highways. For every thousand persons, there were three murders (1.4 committed with axes), four suicides, seventeen reported cases of incest and bestiality, thirty-four miscellaneous breakdowns, women tearing their clothes off in church and so on. All this without the added complication of celibacy. Of course the Circenauts could and undoubtedly would masturbate, but that isn't quite the same thing, is it?

197

In more recent times, consider the difficult winter of '81 in Antarctica. A fire destroyed the Americans' main generator, so no messages could get in or out. Though the party wintering over stayed warm and continued to eat well, there were emotional storms, withdrawals, an unprovoked assault by one scientist on another with a sharpened screwdriver.

A psychiatric commission was set up to consider the problem. Two hundred thousand dollars later, the doctors reached their decision: the Circe system posed unacceptable risks. It was true that nothing might happen down there, but if it did, the armament wouldn't be axes or screwdrivers. It would be nuclear.

Marx refused to accept the decision. There was only one real way to find out—to do a controlled simulation, ask for volunteers and set them adrift. But the R and D barnacle boys gave it the thumbs down, without even bothering to say why. One word was enough, the coldest word in the English language: "Disapproved."

Then Marx had his really genius idea. Did the experiment have to take place on the actual sea bottom? Not so long as the volunteers *believed* that was where they were. And it came to Marx like a lightning flash, accompanied by high winds and thunder: would it be possible—he hardly dared put it in words— would it be possible to build the prototype *right there in the Pentagon itself*?

At any other period of history, certainly not. But so much construction was being crammed into this fiscal year that a little more hammering and clanking, the hiss of a few more torches, might not be noticed. Forklifts and minitractors pulling loads of building materials were constantly coming and going, and nobody gave them a second look.

Marx was an old man, he should have retired two decades ago, what could they do, cashier him? Damn the torpedoes! He switched funds around, created a dummy pay roster, a whole suit of phony paper, and had them start ripping out walls.

Even in ordinary times, nobody was admitted to Marx country without being invited. He had absolute control of the fourth and fifth deck 800 and 900 bays over the River Entrance, Rings D and E. The third deck below this little fiefdom was awaiting redecoration, the term they were using for tearing out everything. It wouldn't be hard to squeeze in a twenty-by-sixty-foot tank, with a cubic capacity almost one fifth that of an ordinary Poseidon-class missile boat.

A submarine, after all, is only a succession of skinny compartments strung along a longitudinal axis. In Circe's design, the compartments were separated and hung as pods from a central tower, giving the crew members five-foot-ten overheads and a measure of privacy. The tank and pods were manufactured in sections in a high-security corner of the Am Tex yard in Corpus Christi, Texas, and shipped to Washington in crates labeled Test Module NucEx Propulsion System. Marx himself supervised the assembly, introducing modifications as they went. It was finished in record time for a Pentagon project. Marx enjoyed ceremonies, and he and a group of his closest associates broke a bottle of champagne over the descent capsule after they filled the tank. Strictly speaking, water was not a necessary part of the experiment. But to make the Circenauts' captivity more enjoyable, Marx planned to encourage them to study the sea creatures around them through specially reinforced ports. Some bizarre nighttime specimens had been brought up from the deep ocean.

To a Navy man, launching any new vessel is a strongly emotional moment. Marx went down in the capsule and walked through the pods. Everything was tidy and shipshape. Well, it was beautiful, and he didn't see how it could miss.

Marx's people were fanatically loyal. This wasn't the first secret he had asked them to keep. Two months into the patrol, a minor technician got drunk and told his wife, a JCS typist, and it got to the Chiefs. They were predictably furious. But they took Michael Mirabile's advice and did nothing about it. Marx would have a hard time hushing it up if his volunteers drowned or went spectacularly mad; his friends in the Senate wouldn't be able to save him. On the other hand, if the experiment appeared to be working, they could figure out a way to abort it before the six months were up.

But Marx, an excellent chess player, was one move ahead. Queer things happen to biological clocks in the absence of natural clues like sunrise and sunset. He arranged for every timepiece in the pods to speed up ten minutes an hour. Thus they would do their six months in five. Once more, he wasn't looking for literal truth. So long as they *believed* that they had been down for six months, it would prove that the concept was viable. The little bastard was clever!

Like the first generation of astronauts, those picked for the program all came from similar small towns in farm country, each the oldest child of white, churchgoing parents who had always voted Republican. As confirmed submariners, they were used to periods of sexual abstinence. One, in fact, was a lapsed monk. They were all rather small. Marx was a small person himself, but he was taller than the tallest volunteer by a full inch and a half.

Of the original twenty-four, eight remained after three weeks of stress testing and long conversations with hostile psychologists. Their blood-pressure readings were superb. They were as tough as shoe leather, team-oriented, absolutely devoted to Admiral Wilford Marx, by the end of the testing period almost in the relation of sons. As for motivation, they would be getting $30,000 hazard pay, and Marx's own literary agent had put together a deal for the book rights, so they were motivated from the soles of their feet to the crowns of their heads, an average distance of five feet three inches.

They drank rather a lot at the bon voyage party, as even ordinarily abstemious people are likely to do during Mardi Gras. Marx kept proposing toasts, to John Paul Jones, to Admiral Bull Halsey, to the paperback contract, and by the time they were piped aboard the destroyer that was to carry them to the rendezvous, their compass needles were spinning. Without their knowledge, three hundred milligrams of Dalmane, the powerful sleeping potion, had been introduced into the final bottles of champagne. As soon as they fell asleep they were off-loaded and bused to the Pentagon. They woke up aboard Circe, with a dim recollection of clanging hatches, a long, dreamy descent.

200

All the instrumentation told them that they were off Cape Charles at twelve thousand feet, drifting southwest. Five months and a few hours later—six months by the log, if everything went according to Marx's plan, they would rise to the surface, force their way into the communications grid and announce their location. By that time they might be almost anywhere in the Western ocean.

Behind tiny apertures camouflaged to seem part of the ship's furniture, miniature cameras kept watch. For the first several weeks, Marx and his Psyops team were never far from the fifth-floor monitors. He was keeping his regular punishing schedule, and visitors not in on the secret found him abstracted at times. Was he finally beginning to show his age? He would interrupt himself in midsentence on the pretext of having to go to the head, and nip down the corridor to see how his tiny protégés were doing.

How could anyone have had any doubts? They stood their regular watches, attended lectures, looked after the hydroponic gardens and pumped iron. And drilled, God, how they drilled. Soon they could have been roused from a deep sleep and launched those Trident Ones without even waking up all the way.

"Missile stations. This is a drill, this is a drill. Two SQ. Target— northwest corner, Square of the Glorious Revolution, Kiev. Assign. Prepare. Away."

As Circe drifted—and she had to be drifting, all the instruments said so—the targeting data was constantly brought up to date. Their targets were not all in the USSR, by any means. Marx had never been able to warm up to the Italians, for example, the eye rolling, the gestures, all those Red mayors. So Rome was down for a warhead, on the chance of a takeover there.

He had instructed his designers to keep the technology simple, because that wasn't the point of the exercise. There was only one early malfunction—a few video pickups developed unexplained blockages, resulting in blind spots in some of the pods. He shrugged it off. Eighty-five percent coverage was good enough.

201

The men obeyed orders cheerfully. They played chess less often than Marx would have liked, preferring poker and craps. One of the petty officers ran an occasional séance. The ex-monk had gone back to monk's garb—sub commanders permit beards to be grown, and pretend not to notice small eccentricities of dress—and was illuminating Naval Regulations, the only available manuscript: a harmless hobby. They smiled more than people normally do except when running for political office. If they quarreled, the commander issued a round of tranquilizers and assigned them some simple competitive task. The winner would get an extra helping of sprouts or plankton for supper. They had taken a whole shelf of movies, but in the end they settled on two, *King of Hearts* and *The Rocky Horror Picture Show*, and played them in double feature night after night, turning off the sound and lip-synching the dialogue.

The Cassandras had been so sure the men would go berserk with all that quiet and solitude. Not at all.

The armored personnel carrier that had picked Doris up in the shopping mall took several precautionary detours and delivered her to Marx's office. A neat little gift-wrapped parcel behind his enormous desk, Marx was fully erect and straining upward, like one of his undersea missiles awaiting permission to fly. He was perhaps the only man left in the Pentagon, one of the few in the United States, to comb his hair from a center part.

Senator Shanahan was there, with Kagoulian. Seen in close-up, there were uncharacteristic smudge marks under his eyes. His lips moved soundlessly, as though he was counting to fifty-one, the number he would need if the entire Senate showed up for the vote. He was still stuck in the low thirties. Defeat, an end to his presidential ambitions, sneers from *Newsweek* and *Time*, rejections from women, his father's amused contempt—this all now seemed certain.

"So you're the famous Doris," Admiral Marx said. "The virtuoso of the skateboard."

She moaned. "I still don't know how I lived through it. Any sign of Iluminado?"

"Half my crew's out looking for him. There isn't much time. Hal Amsterdam ought to be here in another five minutes. We've patched in a network connection so we can send it out live."

He was bouncing slightly as his buttocks clenched and unclenched. A pencil snapped in his fingers. At tense moments, Marx was a great abuser of pencils. During the nuclear-propulsion debates of the sixties, he had destroyed several dozen a day.

"Tell me about this young man of yours. They've had him for four hours. Will he stick to his story, that nothing much happened in Cartagena?"

"He didn't want to discuss it, Admiral," Doris said. "He was feeling the Lazy Bones, and all he wanted to do was snuggle. I did mention airplanes, Hughie, and he said no again with a very strange smile."

Shanahan was stroking his nose, one of his recurring gestures. He had been called hard-nosed too often; he may have wanted to reassure himself that it was ordinary flesh and blood.

"He knows he's important, obviously. Steve, recommendations?"

Kagoulian was ready. "All the raw stuff from Colombia tends to confirm Tonkin Gulf. But we're already getting too many not-sures and can't-remembers, and in another few hours the town will be totally zipped. As the admiral says, there's the time factor. What would everybody think about packaging both things together? Why not announce Circe today?"

A pencil snapped. They waited for Marx's answer.

He said slowly, "I think the suggestion has a great deal of merit."

"Don't the little guys still have another few weeks down there?" Shanahan wanted to know.

"Week and a half," Marx said. "That's close enough. Something like this: we've decided to jump the gun because the nation's on the verge of making a tragic mistake. The Chiefs have overreacted to a rather minor event, and here is the commander of the Cartagena garrison to tell us what actually happened that night. Then segue into Circe, the cheaper and saner alternative."

He was interrupted by a loud altercation, in English and Spanish, in an outer office. The door flew open. A marine private came in backward and sat down hard.

"They found Iluminado," Doris said.

Getting to and from the Pentagon by car, difficult enough on ordinary days, today was all but impossible. Stoplights had been sabotaged by starling lovers. Wrecks had been abandoned at strategic intersections.

And there were other disruptions. A two-truck convoy loaded with demolition debris, attempting to cross the Arlington bridge, was boarded by a group of determined young women. Distracting the driver with lewd suggestions, they attempted to get at the lever that would dump the rubble into the street. One attack group succeeded.

And to everybody's surprise and dismay, out tumbled a corpse in officer's uniform. It had been savagely mutilated; it was headless, without hands or feet.

Cops came running. But apparently somebody had been trying to play a grisly practical joke. It wasn't a corpse at all, merely a paper-stuffed uniform.

Every tactical unit of the D.C. police includes an intelligence specialist, who liaises, as they say in that business, with an appropriate federal contact. Within a half hour the Joint Chiefs had the news: their enemy had not, as they supposed, been crushed beneath the falling rubble. They had been tricked once again.

Soon the JCS guards were closing in on the Marx sector from all five directions. In the Pentagon, only these elite soldiers are allowed to wear Afros and to go about without headgear. They get extra pay and special prices at the PX. Most of them suffer from elbow ailments because of the frequency and sharpness of their salutes.

"Hal Amsterdam clearing through heli security!"

Marx, already stretched to his full height, seemed to add another half inch. He wanted those JCS guards bottlenecked. Engage them in conversation, he ordered. Flatter them on their haircuts, the sheen on their leather. Sincerely, without irony.

The first step in the command process is to solicit input. Where should they stockpile Iluminado until they were ready to bring him out to be interviewed? Marx rejected each suggestion as fast as it was made.

"Idiotic."

"First place they'd look."

The solution was obvious, though no one but the chess-playing admiral had been able to see it. What was wrong with inside Circe herself?

Of course!

Disaffection and cynicism, so common elsewhere in the building, had made little headway here in Marx country. They loved their feisty admiral (and anyone who didn't, let's face it, was out on his ear with an unsatisfactory efficiency rating, for Marx ran a taut quarterdeck). Marxists poured out to clog the corridors. The checkpoints were reinforced. At the Fitness Ring intersection a barricade was quickly thrown up around a wrecked pedicab and two motorized wheelchairs.

Taking Shanahan and a little escort flotilla, Marx strode to a door with the misleading label: "NucProp DepCom NSSSC"— complete nonsense, of course, as no such person existed. He slid a punched card into a locking device. Two clicks, the rasp of metal against metal, a gurgle, and the heavy door swung open.

Inside, the decor was standard Pentagon issue. Circe's intelligence was built into the backside of what from the front looked like ordinary software storage. Marx stopped short, as though hit with a marlinespike. There was no one on watch at the console!

He snapped at an underling, who scuttled away. What Marx saw on the monitors—or what he didn't see, rather—puzzled and worried him. In the crew's mess, two floors below in Circe, the ex-monk was illuminating the initial *T* in TAKE ALL YOU WANT, BUT EAT ALL YOU TAKE. He was the only Circenaut to be seen. Where were the others?

The indicators gave readings within normal ranges, but at the extreme left of the top row of buttons and switches a little red light was on. Not blinking to call special attention to itself, merely on.

Marx couldn't be expected to remember everything—he was seventy-seven years old, after all—but wasn't that the signal that Circe's commander wanted to talk?

A pencil snapped in the OpDep's fingers.

The aide returned. "He's out with that virus that's going around, sir. I don't know how it happened, but nobody arranged for his relief."

Marx saw black flies for a moment. This was the sort of slackness he absolutely. Did. Not. Tolerate. He didn't ask much, merely perfection, and when it wasn't forthcoming he couldn't order a masthead flogging, which was no longer permitted under the regs. All he could do was banish the offender from his presence. He didn't want to set eyes on that man ever again.

Hot words rose to his lips but he choked them back for there wasn't time.

He threw a switch.

They heard nothing. But alarm bells must have sounded in Circe, for the ex-monk in the crew's mess started violently and upset his paint can. Circe's commander ran into the pod, zipping his one-piece poopie suit. He had grown a pretty fair beard since Marx stopped watching the monitors. He looked like a small, very seedy Old Testament prophet, down from the mountains to denounce the wicked carryings-on in the plains.

He looked around furtively and whispered into the microphone, "Request permission to surface. I say again. Urgent. Request permission to surface."

"Stop driveling," Marx said sharply. "Stand tall, man, you're a submariner."

Every angle of the commander's small frame showed astonishment. "*Admiral Marx?*"

"Evidently. Make your report."

The commander hunched forward. "Patrol has been compromised, sir. They have a woman aboard."

"Poppycock."

"I don't know how they did it, but remember how high they scored on the ingenuity tests."

Marx's voice dripped with disgust: "If you wanted to chicken out on me, I'm surprised you couldn't think of a better excuse, considering all the free time you've got down there. Stand by."

He consulted with Shanahan. A little creative deception was in order here, they agreed. Hal Amsterdam would find the experiment's success more impressive if he could see it in action, while the commander still believed what his instruments told him, that he was deep in cold water off the north coast of Scotland.

Marx reopened the circuit. "One of the relays has failed. It's nothing to worry about. I'm sending a microwave technician down. Now shape up, Commander. You won't have time for a haircut, but put on a decent uniform. That poopie suit's a disgrace."

The commander, starved for officer-level conversation, wanted to continue the exchange. Marx cut him off with a snarl.

Disguised as Myron, working for a cleaner America, Iluminado had been sweeping a path from Point A to Point B, becoming angrier with each push of the broom.

"Tell me," he wanted to say to the North American officers in their freshly pressed uniforms, who passed without really seeing him, "what taboo have I broken? Whom have I managed to offend? All I did was turn down a bribe offer. Yes, I have found things to criticize in your country, but from this moment on I promise to keep my opinions to myself."

Ahead, tall black soldiers, each with his own individual explosion of hair, were checking badges. Iluminado made a sudden about-face, turned at the next corridor, and in another moment was totally lost. Point B, he knew, lay somewhere to the south. But which way was south? He guessed to the left, and immediately clashed with a party of marines.

He was just the person they'd been looking for. Marines— Major Sadowski, after two or three frosted daiquiris, had frequently referred to a famous equation. One fighting Yankee leatherneck is the equal of fourteen Nips or gooks. Out of respect for Iluminado's feelings, he hadn't said how many Latinos, but it was probably a similar number.

Now it was broom handle against .45s. They disarmed Iluminado and hustled him from ring to ring, sending scouts ahead to guard against ambushes.

One of Marx's people had had an independent idea for a change. This was something the admiral approved of in theory but didn't often encourage in practice. They put Iluminado in whites and dressed a yeoman in Myron's terrible orange coveralls, adding a mustache with an overlay marker. Doris pedaled off with the decoy, and presently they had a whole pack of JCS guards after them in hot pursuit.

The real Iluminado, meanwhile, seemed suspicious, Marx thought. Surely he realized that Marx was his friend?

They needed the boy's cooperation, so Marx gave him the smile he usually reserved for senators, and said they had something they wanted to show him. Marx felt sure he would be interested—it was an entirely new kind of submarine on simulated patrol, not at sea but in a tank and guess where—in the Pentagon!

"First," Iluminado announced, "I would like to see yesterday's newspaper."

"No time for that now."

"But I disagree." He took a seat at the navigation table. "And may I have a cigar?"

Except for Iluminado himself and possibly Shanahan, no one in the room breathed for a moment. You don't contradict an admiral on his own bridge, and you don't sit down while he's standing. You don't demand a God damn cigar!

Marx felt strongly tempted to blow him out of the water,

but no, that wouldn't put him in the right frame of mind for the Amsterdam interview. When Marx breathed, everybody breathed. A moment later, Iluminado had his newspaper and cigar.

They watched him light up and read. Guerrillas—Casino Bolívar—the colonel's wife kidnapped and rescued. He followed the story into the interior. He refolded the newspaper and his eyes met the admiral's. Their temperature was absolute zero.

"You said you have something to show me."

Shanahan and Kagoulian came with them. Again Marx used his punched plastic card. The door clicked, clanked and opened.

Marx explained what they were trying to prove. Absolute silence, absolute secrecy; the totally secure deterrent. Iluminado listened closely, but as English was not his first language, particularly arms-control English, he may have missed some of the fine points.

There were more coded procedures. Iluminado took an astonished step backward as the silvery descent capsule, wet and glistening, came up out of the floor. Marx was used to the idea, having conceived it himself, but seeing that capsule now through an outsider's eyes, he realized what a truly *extraordinary* thing he and his crew had accomplished.

"We've gone to great lengths to replicate the actual sea-bottom environment. Ask them to turn on the outside lights and show you the fish. Steve, you'll go with the captain?"

"Well, you know what, Admiral," Kagoulian said nervously, "we've got a fast-breaking situation here, there's still quite a bit of staff work to be done on the interview—"

Shanahan, like Iluminado, was seeing the capsule for the first time, and he was intrigued by it. If anything went wrong with the machinery, you could be trapped inside. If the seams didn't hold, you would drown. He had been too busy lately to do any white-water canoeing, or to climb any challenging mountains. When he praised Circe on the floor of the Senate, wouldn't it be more persuasive if he had been aboard, and could speak from personal experience?

So it was settled. He would accompany Iluminado.

As soon as they satisfied the search parties that the subversive Colombian was not in this part of the building, Marx would give Amsterdam the preliminary brainwash, with graphics and visuals, and send him down with a Steadicam and a sound man. He could do the stand-up right in the Circe wardroom. That evening, CBS and ABC viewers would have to keep adjusting their color controls, for Dan and Peter, deprived of this major exclusive, would be livid with mortification, green with envy, yellow with ratings sickness.

A floor plan of Marx country was taped to a mirror in the Chiefs' command post in the abandoned latrine. General McArdle, sleeves rolled to his elbows, stood with hands on hips in the recommended position. That elusive quality called command presence—he definitely had it today.

As the front-line reports came in, they x-ed off room after room, until at last no rooms were left. The JCS guards had looked into every closet, under hundreds of desks. Somehow their slippery quarry had escaped them again.

Mirabile still slept. McArdle made a conscious effort to think in the Mirabile way.

He had watched it happen often enough. The little button-eyes would retreat into their buttonholes. The jaw would hang slack, color would rise, the features would seem to thicken. And at the exact moment when it seemed he was about to pass into absolute idiocy, he would come out with a brilliant restatement of the problem, topped off with a brilliant solution.

But there must be some secret ingredient. No matter how hard McArdle strained, nothing would come.

Castillo was not the only one who had vanished. Senator Shanahan had been seen to enter Marx's corridor and no one had seen him leave. And Hal Amsterdam—what was *he* doing there?

One of their trusted intelligence assets, a robot mail wagon carrying a tiny camouflaged camera, was beeping its way from office to office. The Robot Control officer spotted something and summoned the Chiefs.

They saw briefing easels being carried into Marx's office. Big glossy bar graphs, polyp renderings, dollar projections. They looked at each other. Marx was about to blow Circe!

No wonder they hadn't been able to locate Iluminado. He was fifteen thousand feet down, if you believed the depthometers. And Shanahan was with him, rehearsing him on what lies to tell at the press conference.

"Blow Circe," McArdle said softly, liking the way it sounded.

Why shouldn't they *really* blow Circe, in the sense of blow up, detonate?

"Yeah!"

"Oscar idea, Mac."

That one little bang would solve all their problems. They summoned the Cat. He came in with eyes down. What bothered him most about the Lazy Bones experience was not that he had enjoyed it—he knew about the euphoria effect—but the admiration, even respect, he had felt for his opponent. Well, there had been precious little respect in the looks he had been getting from the Chiefs. Why hadn't he held his breath or something?

McArdle explained his proposal, a simple underwater demolition. The Cat perked up at once, and the combat sparkle returned to his eyes. He had not only taken scuba courses, he was the scuba instructor. He was an acknowledged expert at low-yield explosions. They were aiming for zero survivors, so this time there was no need for any credulity-straining cover story. It would be perfectly clear what had happened. Circe's main pod had ruptured because of poor quality-control by the civilian contractor. And who was the civilian contractor? Am Tex, Shanahan's firm.

"Playing devil's advocate now," General Thorkill said. "The fact that a United States senator is down there with him—"

"Just where he shouldn't be," McArdle said happily, for Shanahan had said and done so many unforgivable things to them over the years.

Seventeen

Iluminado's lovely, his terrible Gabriella, to account for their presence together in the stolen Jaguar, had indeed spun a very wild story. But the casino cage looted? The two majors slain, Gonzalo himself and many others wounded in a mad firefight against phantoms? Had it really happened?

Now the tiny admiral, a contained bundle of radioactive ego, old enough to have known Patton, was insisting on showing Ilumiado some kind of submarine. In the corridor, sailors were running up and down like chickens who think they have seen the shadow of a hawk. Using punched cards to unlock a door—the technology was probably Japanese, Iluminado thought, but the idea was pure United States. Inside an ordinary-looking office, Admiral Marx delivered a brief lecture on retaliatory deterrence, the third leg of the triad, destabilizing first-strike capability—whatever these terms meant—and suddenly a tall, glistening cylinder materialized out of the floor. It was wet!

Marx invited Iluminado to climb in. He refused politely. The thing was an enlarged version of the pneumatic message capsule, and if he did as they wished, he was sure it would whoosh him away to some uncertain destination.

No, it was safe as houses, the admiral assured him (but hadn't they said the same thing about DDT and nuclear power?) and not only that, one of the civilians would be riding with him. Iluminado continued to say no until there was a loud knocking on the door, followed by a demand in a black man's voice. Unlock the door this instant or he would shoot it open.

Remembering that for whatever reasons there were people in the Pentagon who wanted to do something drastic about him, Iluminado stepped into the capsule. A big man with a smile like a lighted Christmas tree came in with him. That blaze of teeth, the overpowering North American smells—it was a sensory overload. Their bodies touched at too many points.

"Doris tells me you don't like our price?"

It was Senator Shanahan, of course. Iluminado worked an arm upward and pressed the Stop button.

"Circumstances have made me important, it seems. I understand now that you have only one measure of importance in this country, and that is money. To answer your question, no, I do not like the price. It would be a humiliation to accept it."

He stabbed Go. Shanahan had no time to comment, for although the journey had hardly started, it was already over. The jolt as they docked threw them into each other's arms.

The senator laughed. "Tight fit. I'll see if the accountants can shake out a bigger number. You'll be hearing from us."

He stepped out into a cramped docking pod, spun a wheel and lifted a circular hatch.

"After you, Captain."

Iluminado looked down into a dimly lighted interior. A heavily bearded face returned his look from the bottom of a ladder.

"My congratulations, Commander!" Shanahan boomed. "A magnificent achievement! The entire nation is grateful!"

Iluminado forced himself to descend, one hard rung at a time.

213

Eight underscale figures were crowded into a tiny compartment. They ringed Iluminado, examining him with an intensity he could feel as actual heat. The air here had been breathed too often; it was stale and unpleasant. The entire environment was in a sort of uneasy suspension, each random movement immediately establishing its own correction.

Shanahan came thundering down. The commander drew back, combing his beard with his fingers, his eyes alive with suspicion. Shanahan had to stand in a crouch to keep from scraping the overhead. The great confident voice rang from bulkhead to bulkhead.

"You and your crew have pushed back the frontiers, Commander. A feat that would only be possible under a free democratic system— You make me proud to be an American."

He asked each man where he was from. Hearing the name of his own state among the mumbled responses, he gave this man a rough hug along with the handshake.

The commander, meanwhile, was winking and making significant signs that seemed to be directed at Iluminado. Iluminado could only shrug in response. He had enough trouble understanding what these Yankees actually said, without trying to make sense of their pantomime. A hand came out. He was tugged into a little communications and maneuvering pod. He understood now that this was some kind of training exercise, like the hundred and ten ordeals of the earliest astronauts. All the controls looked authentic, but drastically miniaturized. The bulkheads were covered with illuminated graffiti—DON'T GIVE UP THE SHIP. FIRE WHEN READY, GRIDLEY. Some of the initial letters could only be guessed at, being in the form of dragons, naked long-haired women, small fauns, one with the face of the bearded commander.

The commander showed Iluminado a pale blue line traced on the deck.

"Cameras!" It was a sibilant whisper, with some loss of saliva. "Stand here and they can't see us. Who is that loudmouth with you?"

"Senator Shanahan."

"Aha! Shanahan of American Texas. They don't give a damn

about us, they just want to find out what's gone wrong with their precious baby." Abruptly, with a forward thrust of the beard: "Are you Naval Academy?"

"Not at all."

"I surmised as much. Some kind of foreign-born, aren't you? So you're not bound by the oath." He pulled Iluminado closer. "What is the madman planning? You can tell me. I don't ask you to say yes or no. Merely look in my eyes. Marx planted an agent aboard, didn't he, to watch me and report?"

Again, Iluminado could do nothing but shrug.

"I see I have guessed correctly," the commander said, nodding. "If I turn my head quickly, I can catch the murderous looks. The admiral is Jewish, you know. Karl Marx was the father of international Communism. Karl Marx, Wilford Marx—notice the similarity of names. They are trying to poison me. I eat nothing I haven't prepared with my own hands. Did he tell you he hocused the clocks? Everything had to be sterile, we were told, a totally sterile environment. They made us strip and pass through a germicide spray. I went along with that, but when they said to turn in our watches I knew they were up to something. I field-stripped mine and distributed the parts in my bodily hair. So I know what date this is! I admit I forgot to wind it five or six times but I've compensated for that. I made a pact with that devil, and I lived up to it to the letter. When six months were up, I opened the circuits. 'Circe speaking. I am alive! A little taken aback, aren't you?' And nobody answered!"

He had a convulsive grip on Iluminado's arm. In the eerie light, his pupils seemed to rotate like pinwheels.

"I was sure he was dead. Listen, that man is ancient. And what a secretive bastard. This is a covert mission, nobody authorized it. And wouldn't it be just like that crafty son of a sea cook to wink out with a heart attack without telling a soul about Circe? *So I took her up!* On my own responsibility, I gave the order to surface. I tell you I was shaking with excitement. Once again, to smell the sea-spray, to see the clouds chasing each other across God's own blue sky. And at one hundred and fifteen feet, it was like hitting an ice pack. An impenetrable

215

barrier. Now you see why I've been calling him those bad names. He sneaked in an automatic cutoff so we couldn't surface without his permission, and that had to be part of the original plans. Which means he didn't trust us from the beginning."

The pupils pinwheeled.

"And I used to worship that man. I stood at attention constantly, broke pencils. All right. So be it. I put you on notice. You think you can drop in on some spurious pretext, gig me for sloppy housekeeping and get back on board in time for your five o'clock cocktail, leaving me to these wolves. No, my fine young popinjay."

Leaning closer, his breath heavy with the smell of hydroponically-grown vegetable matter, he whispered, "You're taking me with you. There is one single escape hatch, and *I have the key!*"

The Chiefs went to the big computer, which never forgets anything. And to everyone's surprise, there in its memory was a fully worked-out and footnoted contingency plan for Circe's destruction, commissioned weeks ago by some anonymous intelligence specialist, as a possible option. Everything was assembled and ready—an oxyacetylene torch so new that the price tag was still on it ($24,476), C-4 explosive, spring-activated time-set detonators, diver's respirator, flippers.

A little flute music first, to set the mood. Mozart today, the Cat decided. He blew the descent-to-hell theme from *Don Giovanni* and improvised for a moment. That was all he had time for.

He suited up and climbed through a hole cut in the back of a fourth-floor supply closet. He squeezed out on the top of the tank, which rose to within a foot of the ceiling, pushing the torch and other equipment ahead of him. After starting the torch he fooled with the mixture until he had it the shade he wanted, a hard, deadly blue.

In less than a minute he had opened an improvised manhole. After one last recheck, he slipped into the water.

It was as black as strong coffee, for at these presumed depths,

216

to anyone peering out from inside it is invariably midnight. Weird phosphorescent creatures fled away as he slithered downward, following the beam cast by his diver's headlamp. First he circled the installation to choose a vulnerable spot. The domed pods, locked onto the central core, seemed like a dolls' dwelling. It was hard to believe that eight grown men had lived there all these months without going out of their minds. Of course they were submariners, and thus a little skewed to begin with.

Those eight, plus the two visitors from the outside world, were now taking their final breaths of the recycled air. Well, hell, the Cat thought—they should have thought twice before they incurred the displeasure of the Joint Chiefs of Staff.

It was the work of a moment to attach the C-4 and tie in the detonator. The timer was set on a six-minute delay. Six minutes, in an operation like this, can be an eternity. Rise to the surface, towel off and dress. Get rid of the gear in the nearest Dumpster, walk to a coffee shop, sit down and order. *Boom!* What was that? Somebody dumping rubble, probably.

He kicked out angrily. One foot was tangled in something.

Doubling backward and twisting, he found himself staring into the great single eye of a squid. Fucking Marx and his realism!

He snatched out his sheath knife. But water was the squid's medium, not the Cat's, and it was a slow dreamlike thrust, a little off-target. A tentacle floated up and wrapped itself around his fighting wrist.

He shifted the knife as another tentacle, coming over the top, brushed his regulator valve. The air he was getting suddenly tasted of bad clams.

Six minutes no longer seemed like much time. He reached out, hoping to turn off the timer, but the squid chose that moment to yank at his wrist and the whole lump of explosive came loose! He watched it sink slowly to the bottom of the tank. He was unable to follow, being enveloped now in the creature's multitudinous embrace. A horrible face was pressed against his. Didn't it realize that unless it released him at once, they would perish together?

Every village in the world has its idiot, including the village Iluminado grew up in. You don't argue with such people, you make the sign of the cross and pass by on the other side of the road.

Neither national interest nor personal honor seemed to be at stake here, so he pretended to fall in with the demented commander's suggestion, which was to leave Shanahan aboard while the commander took Shanahan's place in the two-man escape capsule.

"Though I'm not sure Senator Shanahan will agree."

"He will agree," the commander said grimly, and brought out a homemade firearm, little more than a short pipe, a paper clip and a rubber band. "Talk all you like about nuclear, up to a range of two and a half feet this is the ultimate weapon. I need a hostage, you see, or I won't get a court of inquiry. And do I have a story to tell. I've written it all down, the looks, the near accidents—"

Only one seaman was still in the central pod. He was doing squats at the ladder. The commander ordered him to stand clear. The man sent him an evil over-the-shoulder look from the squatting position. Iluminado, too, if he had received such a look, would have wanted to put it in writing.

"You told us to exercise more, Commander."

"Not with visitors here, imbecile. Out of our way."

"Trying to run out on us, are you? A captain's supposed to go down with his ship."

Out came the commander's homemade small arm, but before he could bring it to bear the seaman spun around and butted him hard in the stomach.

Here, finally, was one fight Iluminado thought he could stay out of. When the struggling pair rolled too close, he prodded them away with his foot.

Freeing one hand, the seaman fumbled a crumpled paper out of his pocket and ordered Iluminado to read it.

Iluminado smoothed it out.

"FLETCHER, machinist's mate," he read. "What I rite here is

the TRUTH. They all watching to see when FLETCHER will crack, SKIPPER especially, the vishus bastard. Keep stretching the time stretching the time, see how much FLETCHER can take. Been down here eight months today. Took eight months to break FLETCHER did it, nothing special about FLETCHER so six month patrol O.K. for average person. They all in it together specially those second watch cocksuckers—"

A monk wandered in, wearing the tonsure and belted robe. On the deck, the machinist's mate seemed to be winning. He had the commander by the beard and was banging his head on the plates. The monk had to step over them to reach Iluminado.

"I don't believe you've seen an example of my work, have you?"

He unfurled a scroll. The illuminated initial showed a raven-haired nymph being chased by a satyr, who again resembled Circe's commander.

The Gothic text said:

"I pretend to be crazy because that way they leave me alone. I am in grave danger. Old man has stopped eating. He thinks they put steroids in the food to fatten him up. But his system demands protein. I see him looking at me because I am the plumpest. I can't help it if I'm naturally stocky can I. He studies pork recipes in Joy of Cooking, and we have no pork in the locker only water-grown spinach and lettuce."

Still another crew member sidled in and attempted to hand Iluminado a corked vinegar bottle.

"When you get back up, drop this overboard, will you? For laughs?"

The plump monk lost his amiable look. "You wrote that about me!"

They competed for control of the bottle, which fell to the deck and smashed. Tightly rolled sheets sprang open. The monk pounced. The first few words were enough: "Mutiny on the Bounty will be child's play unless—"

"Hey, wow," the monk said. "And I thought you loved this man's Navy. Let's give old Fletch a hand."

The machinist's mate had clamped a new hold on the commander, pinning him with a leg scissors while attempting to twist off a foot. The monk armed himself with the jagged bottleneck.

"Ear to ear!" Fletcher shouted. "Blood in the scuppers!"

The shout brought in the rest of the crew. But where was Shanahan? A politician, he must have had experience handling unruly crowds.

"I resign my commission," the commander announced to the faces above him. "Take the con, men."

Iluminado realized that he had witnessed his first coup. A little unorthodox by Counter Coup standards, it nevertheless seemed to be a total success. They disarmed the commander and let him get up. They were capering about laughing and hugging, exchanging hand slaps and comradely taps on the ass.

The commander insisted on being included in the hugs. He was as mutinous as anybody, he maintained. He had vowed to avenge himself on the black-hearted admiral, the author of all their troubles.

The only question was, how?

They sobered abruptly. For the fact was that in spite of the new political atmosphere aboard Circe, they were still prevented from reaching the surface by some kind of weird electronic veto, with an escape capsule that would carry only two at a time; three, if they happened to be unusually small.

And which three, was the point. Then after they got to the surface, would Marx authorize sending the capsule back to evacuate the rest of the crew? Abort the mission? Abandon all this valuable hardware? *Marx?*

The commander now showed the advantage of an officer's training.

"It's lucky we've got something to barter. In here, men."

They flooded back to the communications pod, where the large senator was roped to a chair with a towel in his mouth, a Gulliver who had underestimated his short-statured opponents. The commander reached past him and grabbed the mike.

"Circe calling Washington. Come in Washington."

But too much else was happening on the fifth floor of the Pentagon. If they were listening up there, they didn't care to admit it.

"Come in, Admiral Marx, you superannuated pipsqueak. What are you doing, buggering your exec? Or I should say *trying* to bugger. The mess boys tell me that tiny deterrent of yours is no longer credible."

He threw the switch to Receive but there was no answering burst of vituperation. Iluminado could see how the crew had felt, calling and calling, getting nothing but static.

"The truth of the matter—" he began, but Shanahan gobbled from behind his gag, "Uuh. Ay. Unh. Op." In other words: don't say it, stop, these are dangerous men, greatly excited. The truth would only infuriate them.

The commander whirled on Iluminado and made him accept the mike. "You're the expert on microwaves. I'll give you exactly one minute."

The truth, which again Iluminado didn't think he could safely impart, was that he didn't know what microwaves *were*, let alone how to induce them to carry a message. He stared at the buttons and dials without seeing anything at his level of comprehension, such as a simple on and off switch.

"Oo uh a el oo."

Without asking for a yes or no vote, Iluminado loosened Shanahan's towel, allowing him to say, more intelligibly, "Do what they tell you."

"I would be glad to, Senator. However—"

"Marx will understand that you're doing it under duress. *Don't forget that Hal Amsterdam's coming.*"

Hal Amsterdam, the TV celebrity, Iluminado had seen him on the CCR screens. Yes, the mutineers would be delighted to air their grievances on national television. Meanwhile, Shanahan was saying, humor them before they kill somebody, pretend that you know what you're doing.

All right. To begin with, he was helpless without pliers. What was the English word? Squeezers wasn't quite right. He mimed a clutching tool and a screwdriver. One of the crew faded away and brought back a toolbox containing everything a microwave technician could conceivably need, except instructions on where to begin. They dearly loved their machinery, these Yankees. Why couldn't they be satisfied with something simple and reliable, like the old-fashioned pneumatic tube?

He unscrewed four corner screws, whereupon the front panel fell off. It was like removing an abdominal wall. The inside of the box was packed with mysterious spaghetti.

He picked a switch that looked harmless. When he closed it—or opened it, possibly—he produced an ominous sputter, as though the equipment was about to blow up. He hastily returned the switch to its earlier position.

"Someone," he said accusingly, "has been tampering with these controls."

"Me, I'm afraid," the commander admitted. "I admit I don't know the first thing about it."

Iluminado muttered something about incompetent donkeys, freed several wires and changed terminals, causing two printed circuits to pop off the board.

"No cause for alarm," he said. "Those are only for use in case of emergency."

His audience obviously thought that an emergency was what they were having. The commander had mentioned the clocks, and it did seem to Iluminado that the clock on the opposite bulkhead was behaving erratically. Was the minute hand running backward?

The commander produced his terrible pistol and put it to Shanahan's temple.

"Enough of this shilly-shallying. Get me a video circuit. I want Marx to see his pet politician with a gun to his head."

"A broken bottle at his throat?" the monk suggested. "Wouldn't that be more graphic?"

"No reason we can't do both."

"They mean it," Shanahan said hoarsely. "Iluminado, do something. Your price is now one point eight."

"Money," Iluminado said, gazing without hope at the tangle of colored wires. "The gringo solution to everything."

"Two even."

The brain is a marvelous organ. There Shanahan sat, sweat collecting in the gutters on either side of his mouth to run down and drip off his chin, and Iluminado's mind jumped to another time he had seen Shanahan's face, wearing quite a different expression. It had appeared for one moment on the big CCR display, in what was apparently a snippet from a political commercial. "And just who is threatening the Canal?" And all at once Iluminado had part of the answer. Gabriella's guerrillas! The Pentagon needed those guerrillas, and he had more or less accidentally told various people that they didn't exist. What an enormous relief to understand *something* at last.

He worked his head into a set of too-small earphones. On the dials, needles were swinging wildly. He pressed buttons at random. One of them brought back the sputter.

"Admiral Marx!" Iluminado said, with authority. "Come in, damn you!" What had the commander called him? "Pip squeak!"

Overdoing every facial expression by a factor of ten, in what he took to be the North American manner, he pretended to search through the earth's envelope for some sign of intelligent life. Hold on. He thought he heard something. But it was terribly faint.

"Washington? Is that you, Admiral? Can you see us?" He reported to the others, "He can see us. He wants an explanation of these theatricals with Senator Shanahan."

"Theatricals, we'll show him theatricals," the commander exclaimed. "Tell him we're surfacing, and if we bump into anything this time, there are only going to be ninety-nine United States senators."

"Don't wave the gun," Iluminado said, frowning. "It bothers me. Now I've lost him again."

"And a one hundred thousand dollar indemnity per man," the commander continued.

"You've got it," Shanahan said promptly. "Untie me. I'll write you a check."

"Wait!" the commander said. "What if Shanahan is no longer his friend? He feuds with everybody sooner or later."

"I had him to dinner just last week!" Shanahan protested. "I let the little bastard beat me at chess!" He added hastily, "Not using little in the pejorative sense."

"In warfare," the commander said, thinking, "you have to be prepared to take casualties. They can always replace a senator. We may be going about this the wrong way."

He jabbed a button, causing a horn to respond: "Ah-*oo*-ga. Ah-*oo*-ga."

"All hands battle stations submerged!" the commander cried. "General quarters, condition purple! This is not a drill, repeat, this is not a drill. Missilemen, retarget your missiles."

Iluminado raised his voice. "Can I have a little quiet here, please?"

But the men were already scattering. A voice called from somewhere, "Missilemen on attack stations."

"Flood tube number one," the commander ordered.

In a moment: "Tube number one flooded, sir."

"Flood tube number two."

"Tube number two flooded."

"Computermen! Scratch Moscow, scratch Managua. *Substitute Washington!* District of Colombia! That'll take some of the starch out of him," he told Iluminado. "We carry a throw weight of one hundred and seventeen megs, which is not to be sneezed at. Ground zero, the *Pentagon*. Hell, give them a double. Take care of the damn starlings while we're about it."

The answer came back almost too quickly. "Missiles ready to fly, sir. New targets plotted yesterday."

"You rascals," the commander said affectionately. "Now let's get back to the time-honored Navy way of doing things, shall we, and start obeying our commanding officer?" He looked at Iluminado. "No answer yet? I know Marx, he's sitting there with the sound off, gloating. Brother Gregory," he called, "report to 'neuvering pod on the double."

The monk scrambled in. Yes, he carried his calligraphy tools under his robe at all times. Finding a section of bulkhead that he hadn't already illuminated, he wrote to the commander's dictation:

"Stow the fancy lettering," the commander told him, and he went on in ordinary print:

TRIDENT ONES TRAINED ON PENTAGON. PERMISSION TO SURFACE OR ENTIRE CITY WILL BE HIROSHIMAED.

The commander was stamping around in the constricted space brandishing his dangerous weapon, with no thought for the delicacy of the firing mechanism. And at that moment there was a deafening explosion.

It wasn't the sound made by a pistol discharging by accident. It wasn't the premature departure of one of the missiles. For those trapped inside Circe, it was something infinitely worse.

They had taken a depth-bomb hit, the submariner's nightmare. Iluminado, pelted by small rapidly moving objects, was blown backward. The vessel was shaking violently. Light bulbs shattered. After an instant's awful blackness, green crisis lights flicked on.

Like a sudden tornado, it passed. The compartment was now at a severe sixty-degree tilt. Printed circuits were everywhere, like scattered playing cards. The horn continued to insist: "Ah-oo-ga! E-mer-gency! E-mer-gency!"

The commander, his face ghastly in the green light, said savagely, "That black-hearted scoundrel had us booby-trapped the whole time."

"Water in the missile pod!" came from the sound outlets.

The commander fought his way up. "Missilemen, man the pumps. Planesmen, check trim indicators. Blow forward buoyancy tanks."

"Assault-pod welds leaking, sir. Water in galley bilges."

"Abandon assault-pod pumps."

Shanahan, too, contributed an order. "Untie me, somebody."

Iluminado found the broken bottle, and cut him loose.

"Marx!" Shanahan shouted, positioning himself well inside the blue lines so he would have to be seen on the monitors if anybody was watching, which Iluminado now seriously doubted. "Enough!"

It was more than enough, in everybody's opinion. The flow of orders resumed.

"Rig bow planes. Blow starboard tanks. Jettison all ballast, I say again, jettison all ballast. Clear air-release vents. Stand by to close watertight doors."

For every order there was an acknowledging response. In spite of the frantic honking, the clanging of doors, the implacable rush of water, the voices betrayed little excitement, or even a great deal of interest. They might have been ordering lunch. All in all, a fine example of naval technique.

Nothing much seemed to be getting done, however. The deck stayed at the same frightening tilt and the water was rising.

The commander had worked his way to the narrow hatchway to the central tower, with its ladder up to the escape hatch and the docking pod. In midcommand, he hurled himself through and tried to slam the watertight door. Iluminado had seen it coming, and had his foot in the opening. Two seamen jumped the commander from behind, trying to pry the escape-hatch key out of his pocket.

"It'll hold three!" the commander yelled.

In a pinch, yes, but it wouldn't hold four, and a fourth crewman had now joined the struggle. By cutting the pocket off with his palette knife, the monk succeeded in getting the key but it slipped from his fingers and dropped into the black water.

The fight stopped abruptly. An extremely elegant fish swam by, giving off light.

The horn gave a final gurgle and died, which didn't mean that the emergency was over.

"Now I'm getting really pissed off," the commander announced. "Hell with it, I'm going to fire those missiles."

"*There aren't any missiles!*" Shanahan cried. "Don't you realize yet that this whole thing is a simulation?"

The commander gave him a pitying look. The civilian had cracked under strain, as civilians have an unfortunate tendency to do. He took a deep breath of the rapidly worsening air and went underwater.

New waves of combat-lobbyists were leaving the CCR to storm the Hill. The Revolutionary Dames, who ran the most effective ethnic lobby in town, had already switched two votes. The Chiefs, back at their crisis stations, had been able to make one unofficial subtraction from the Shanahan total. The senator himself, they had every reason to believe, would not be present and voting.

It was time for Hemlock to change back into civvies. Security decided to take him out by the underground passage which led to a private dock on the Potomac, where a Coast Guard launch was waiting to take him upriver. No doubt they would be bombarded by demonstrators as they passed under the bridges, but Hemlock would go on the Senate floor wearing those splotches like decorations.

A muffled explosion. Circe had had her accident! A victory look flashed from Chief to Chief, and then they were careful not to look at each other again. General McArdle, even more pleased than the others because this had been his idea, returned to his yellow pad, on which he was doodling howitzers. In another moment he would add balls to each, changing it from an artillery piece into the male genital organ. There was nothing perverted about this. It happened to be one of the few things he could draw.

A black drop appeared below a howitzer muzzle, as though it had ejaculated prematurely. He looked up. The damn ceiling seemed to be leaking.

He caught the next drop on his palm: it was some vile stuff that smelled of putrefied fish. The condition of this building! One of these fine days they had to sneak an extra billion or two into the budget, gut the whole place and pretend it was 1942 again, start over from scratch.

A black stain, in the approximate shape of the South American continent, had appeared on the ceiling plaster. Others looked up to see what the chairman was finding so fascinating.

227

Darkening, the stain sagged downward, looking more than ever like that cockamamie continent, and then damned if the whole thing didn't let go.

Tons of water poured through, bringing miscellaneous objects. A giant squid with fewer than its allotted number of tentacles! The Cat in his mask and flippers! Circe's bearded commander in his poopie suit! A monk! A dummy Trident One missile! Iluminado Castillo! Senator Shanahan! (Alive, unfortunately, so change the tally again.)

Finally, a wet-haired young woman wearing nothing but an unbuttoned housecoat. McArdle and the others hadn't been this surprised since the start of the Tet offensive.

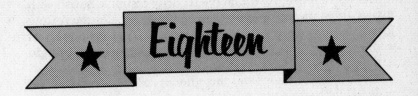

Eighteen

Michael Mirabile smiled in his sleep. He was dreaming that he was more famous than he actually was. Then he dreamed an explosion, which shook him awake. His secretary had been ordered to wake him, but he found her snoozing herself. This Iluminado Castillo thing had been hard on everybody.

An Air Force bomber was waiting to fly him to Aspen for a cross-discipline seminar on the multiple pitfalls of arms control. These weekends always drew a good crowd of women, postdocs and grad students, and sometimes Mirabile could awe one or two of them into overlooking the fact that physically he was a little repulsive.

He decided to drop in on the Chiefs, to give them his phone number in case they needed any spur-of-the-moment conceptual thinking. As he approached the CCR, he had a definite sense that something was wrong. He couldn't ask anybody, for he was Michael Mirabile. He was the one who was supposed to *answer* the questions.

The glass in the visitors' gallery had gone opaque. And there was no guard at the door! That was impossible—there were always guards at this door.

His heel slipped. He found the security vestibule awash with two or three inches of foul-smelling liquid. One of the A Ring johns had backed up again, he supposed. And wouldn't you know it would happen when he was wearing his new Giorgio Armani jeans.

He turned the knob, and the effluent rose to his ankles. He walked into a scene that might have been staged by that master of spectacular effects, the late Cecil B. DeMille. Mirabile's eyeballs, his least attractive feature, always popped slightly. Now they seemed to be straining to salute.

One of the resident senior citizens, who was still maintaining that there was no diplomatic problem that couldn't be solved by a good carpet bombing, had been picked up, wheelchair and all, and deposited on a free-standing computer. His cigar had been mashed back against his face. And he had a woman on his lap! That really took Mirabile aback, because this was the CCR, the female sex was absolutely forbidden. With the index finger of both hands, the ex-chief was proclaiming his beloved country's standing in the world. Number One! We won't settle for second!

Well, we wouldn't be number one much longer, Mirabile thought, if things like this kept happening. Circe had ruptured, apparently. When the room was constructed, it had been bug-proofed with a foil baffle under the floorboards, so it was like a bathtub without a drain. Small, bearded sailors were everywhere, shaking their heads in amazement. What sort of fairy-tale cavern had they tumbled into, here at the bottom of the sea?

The dampness was causing short circuits. On the big board, the monitors showed dazzle patterns and overlaps, the digitals had gone out of control. The probable W-3 vote was into the hundreds of thousands, and continuing to climb.

General McArdle came splashing toward him.

"Mirabile, am I glad you're awake."

230

They all had to change out of their wet clothes. They did the postmortem in a heavy-security cubicle in the Command and Flag Officers' Sauna. McArdle, wearing his towel like a toga, had the unpleasant duty of bringing Mirabile up to date.

"No," Mirabile breathed as he listened. "No, no, no." He added, "No!"

"It seemed to us—"

"I've told you time and again, General, one story is no longer enough. You need a backup, and sometimes even another backup for that. We learned that from Watergate. Seven thousand media people in this town, and they don't get promoted for believing the press releases. If they smell something they're going to keep digging and digging, and sooner or later somebody's going to dig in the right place."

He was putting it simply, because to be realistic the Chiefs weren't too comfortable with abstract ideas. Now where was everybody? Run through their cast of characters.

The principal target, Castillo, was in sick bay, sedated to the eyebrows. To cut down his mobility they had put him in traction. The Cat was one room away, unnaturally silent. The Circe crew had been issued a fifth of bourbon per man and were being treated for sprains, abrasions, shock and combat anxiety. The mysterious female who had been carried out on the flood had been taken to McLean for some strenuous debriefing. Some kind of agent, obviously, but nobody had been able to establish what service she belonged to.

Hal Amsterdam was prowling the corridors, demanding the exclusive he had been promised by Marx. Shanahan had insisted on being treated by his own doctor, so any thought of a little creative malpractice there had had to be laid aside for the time being. His supporters in the Senate were maneuvering for a one-day postponement. What did Mirabile think, go along or move for an immediate vote?

The human brain is electrically powered, scientists claim, and when Mirabile was *really* thinking, he could almost hear a low-voltage hum. This was a minor problem. It took less than a minute. Postpone, he advised. Use the delay to dispose of the Castillo matter. This time, dispose of it right.

"I don't like all this fancy stuff," the Air Force chief declared forthrightly. "I mean seriously. Sometimes you can't stop to take prisoners. You do what has to be done. The American public understands that. We've finally got our hands on this guy. I say wait till it's dark, bundle him out and *terminate* him, God damn it, no ifs, ands or buts."

Patience, Mirabile told himself. This soldierly realism, as they thought it to be, was the main thing he had to contend with, day in and day out.

"You're forgetting Hal Amsterdam, General," he pointed out. "We don't know how much they've told him. He doesn't often get a chance to do any investigative reporting, and he won't take don't know for an answer."

And there it was—the idea came to him, with none of the usual fuss. Stage it for Amsterdam! Make him an accomplice, an eye-witness. If he sees it happen with his own two eyes, how can he disbelieve it?

Counter Coup was Iluminado's cover. Now let's see.

A copy of the Counter Coup schedule arrived by pneumo a few minutes later, accompanied by the usual dry puff of starling guano. Mirabile studied the sheet while the anxious Chiefs studied *him*. They saw the beginnings of a smile.

"Lecture and demo, W-3, computer-controlled zone-interdiction, Fort Belknap, twenty hundred hours." An incurable civilian, Mirabile still had to do the arithmetic in his head: twenty minus twelve, eight P.M, why couldn't they say so?

"Gentlemen, there's our answer. *He makes the mistake of underestimating the Wall!* Do you see it?"

They almost did, perhaps.

Mirabile continued: "One good thing about all those silly spy novels, they've conditioned the public to expect at least one major death. Who can doubt now that this Latino is a top Soviet agent? Dear God, he infiltrated *Circe*. That has to be the intelligence coup of the decade. Checked out all the new targeting mechanisms and left a bomb behind when he left. Now he's pushing his luck. Using those Counter Coup credentials to try to pull the same stunt with the Wall."

He loved this moment especially, the look on their faces as they watched a Mirabile scenario take shape out of nothing but motes of dust in the air. He took his brain out of gear and freewheeled it, muttering in broken sentences.

"He photographs control bunker from inside. Gets all the plans and specs. The whole schmeer, all the secrets. Tries to get away. Will he or won't he? Make it look like a contest. Guy outwitted us once, maybe he can do it again. But he can't get through W-3. It's too much for him. God, I like this idea. Doesn't happen behind closed doors. Right out in the open in front of some of the most prominent people in America, out there watching the demo."

Hitting on something of this order of magnitude was the next best thing to a religious experience. Whenever it happened Mirabile always remembered the high spot, his career turning point. They had come to him with an intractable problem. Mirabile, help us. The enemy hides under the canopy where our gunships can't see him. What should we do? And Mirabile had clenched his teeth and turned on that *power*. A long moment later, one word.

"Defoliate!"

He continued to throw it at them.

"The guy wins the first round, and maybe the second. We've got him on a short leash all the way. Chopper sweep, flushes him out like a rabbit. We chivy him from station to station. Whole thing is carefully programmed. Live target tonight! It's primal, gentlemen. We sell it with blood. Find, fix and *annihilate*."

"Annihilate, yes," McArdle said. "Kill him, in short. Get him out of our hair. Which component are you thinking of using? Not the anti-tank lock-on. That would confetti him."

"I think Porcupine," Mirabile said judiciously, "the flechettes. Amsterdam will be right there when we search the body and find the film in his pockets. They might not believe us, but Hal Amsterdam they'll have to believe. Proving two things! That the Soviets must really be worrying about W-3, or they wouldn't send their best man. Two, that the thing really works. It really kills people, in spite of the loose talk we've been hearing from Shanahan lately."

"I still wish—" General Thorkill said. "Because isn't it a little—you know, just a little—"

The word he was fumbling for was probably baroque. Well, sure it was baroque. Mirabile, too, missed the old days, when you could make an announcement and everybody would believe you except professional leftists. But that was what the Reagan press conferences had done to the fine old craft of public relations.

Iluminado awakened in some kind of noxious puddle, on the receiving end of mouth-to-mouth resuscitation. His own tongue came out, and the tips briefly embraced. It tasted very much like Doris.

He opened his eyes. It was Quimby. Iluminado shuddered away.

The air inside Circe had become very foul at the end. Was he hallucinating again? he wondered as he looked about him. A *squid*? And what was a wheelchair doing on top of a computer?

He escaped from these difficult questions by slipping back toward unconsciousness. He felt himself being lifted and held upside down to let some of the water drain out. Then he had a dim sense of being carried along an endless echoing corridor.

"Hold it," a voice ordered.

A man with a microphone was above him. By the way everybody ducked and kowtowed, this must be some kind of potentate. A muscle jumped in his face: Hal Amsterdam.

"Tell me, Captain, what really happened in Cartagena?"

The old question again. Iluminado knew what had happened in Cartagena: the wife of a ruling colonel had come surreptitiously to his room and taken him into her mouth. More puzzling was what was happening here in the Pentagon.

Again he lost most of the picture, though he still had the heel taps and voices. There were medical smells. From every-

234

where, people converged on him with needles the size of squash rackets.

He slept, and dreamed that he was trapped in a submarine movie. It was only a special-effects submarine, so there had to be some way to get out, but Iluminado couldn't find it. The light brightened gradually and some of the mist blew away. He was in a hospital room. One of his legs seemed unusually clumsy, and no wonder—it was encased in plaster and fastened to the ceiling. A nurse's uniform was moving about the room, topped by another face he was able to recognize. This time it really was Doris, or someone who resembled her closely, down to the badly cropped hair. That she was chiefly interested in money, he knew; but nonetheless he was delighted to see her.

"I broke my leg falling out of a submarine."

"No, you didn't," she said. "They put you in a cast to slow you down. You've been making some pretty quick moves. You're supposed to be tranquilized but we gave you an antidote. Hey— you played Hughie just right. He's adding three hundred thou."

Now it was the sound he lost. Her lips continued to move, but her face floated away until it was gone in a rising swirl.

Only a few dozen people know of the big computer. Only ten have high enough clearance to appear before it in person. The printouts are read on the spot, and burned in a special high-security brazier.

Some years back, an untried administration, not used to the responsibilities of power, ordered the major domestic intelligence agencies to get rid of between twenty and thirty million individual security files, on the grounds that this wasn't what the Founding Fathers had had in mind. Civil liberties organizations were invited to send representatives to witness the shredding. It took days, for this stuff had been accumulating since 1919. The archivists seemed oddly unmoved as their lives' work went into the shredders. And there was a reason for this: during the previous weeks, copies of everything had been conveyed secretly into the Pentagon to be data-banked for use in later emergencies. Much better to have it all under one roof, anyway.

One of the intelligence community's little-known characters was brought out of retirement to serve as curator. He had used many names. He wasn't literally faceless, but the face he had now wasn't the one he started out with. Three times he had put his features under the knife. The last time, to *really* confuse the enemy, he had ordered a Slavic look; it hadn't quite worked.

This venerable gentleman knew perfectly well that Michael Mirabile was one of the cleared ten. Nevertheless he wanted to see credentials, on the off chance that the clearance had been lifted in the last twenty minutes.

"She's not too lively today," he said, removing the screen. "Water got in from someplace. The funny things dampness can do. I recall one humid day during Carter's last weeks—"

He was a great reminiscer, but you couldn't let him get started or you would have to hear about Chile, '73, the private army in Cambodia, Guatemala, '54.

Brady was the name of Hemlock's helicopter pilot; Brady, Melinda Jane. Mirabile looked up the code and punched it in.

The computer pondered, and started to print. But Mirabile's request had been misunderstood, and he was getting stale keyhole gossip about a lesbian art professor at UCLA, whose file had been opened in '76 when she signed a petition against capital punishment.

"Let me," the archivist offered.

He punched out the code again, each digit a stinging reproach. When the machine still equivocated, he gave it a hard slap, the sort that will sometimes clear up a television picture.

It shuddered and came. The archivist fed it to Mirabile one page at a time, then fetched the burning materials. Mirabile studied the smoke as it rose. He had little sympathy for overly ambitious females. What would they want to be next, chairperson of the Joint Chiefs of Staff? All Warrant Officer Brady wanted, she had confided to a girlfriend who had confided in somebody else who had confided in the computer, was to be senator. Her own senator, Hemlock, was already married, but he had promised to start divorce proceedings as soon as he was assured of another six years. It is well known that when a senator dies in office, as many manage to do, the governor of his state will frequently appoint his widow to fill out his unexpired term, and this was Brady's long-range plan.

Mirabile found her in the library with her glasses on, reading *Architectural Digest.* Her uniform had been spattered by starlings and was at the dry cleaners. One of Mirabile's hobbies (he was a bundle of contradictions) was women's fashionable clothes. The turn-back cuffs and bone toggles on her soft green leather suit told him (1) Italian, from one of the big fashion houses, and (2) expensive.

He took her into the corridor. He had never wasted any fantasy time lusting after senators' girlfriends, and the feeling was undoubtedly mutual. With somebody this good-looking he usually did it in baby talk, but having just been informed by the computer that the young woman's IQ had been tested at 158, he didn't bother to spell it all out.

The Colombian captain she had airlifted to the Pentagon that morning? Had Hemlock told her that this man had now been identified as a dangerous enemy agent? Probably not, for Hemlock was known for his absolute discretion (since he stopped drinking). Well—top spies, like top racing drivers, seldom die in bed. The Chiefs had decided there was no chance of doubling this Castillo, he had to be moved out of the way, abrogated. The order had been given, but various things had gone wrong. Never in Mirabile's Pentagon experience had so many things gone wrong, in so many ways, in so brief a time. They had found him, they had fixed him, but Mirabile was sorry to say that they hadn't been able to annihilate him.

Because he had allies. A certain weak-sister senator. An off-the-wall admiral. Certain media people.

"Trust me," Mirabile said. "If we let them question this man, W-3 will go down the drain."

W-3! He was talking about the country's security, about thousands of jobs, tens of thousands of votes, Hawk-Sisley at ninety dollars a share, Mr. G grateful and generous, Hemlock's reelection assured. Divorce and remarriage.

Trust him, he had said, but Brady didn't seem to, entirely. He was forced to allude to something else in the computer's grab bag of unevaluated data. Hemlock had been strongly attracted to her, she had told the girlfriend, who had passed it on to the computer, but whenever they were alone together all he could do was stammer and blush. So Brady had had to force the issue. The engine failure? The emergency landing and the night in the Pennsylvania motel? The next day, the computer happened to know, mechanics had found nothing wrong with the engine.

Her gray eyes met Mirabile's with a gratifying lack of repugnance. "You're a real shit, aren't you, Mirabile?"

The Circe catastrophe had generated more casualties than the Pentagon sick bay could handle. Claiming to have two years' nursing experience, Doris volunteered to help. They were glad to have her, and found her a uniform that was only a trifle too tight.

She looked in on the unconscious Iluminado, smoothed the hair away from his forehead and copied the chart at the foot of his bed. Then she hunted for Shanahan. When Shanahan's doctor arrived, he reviewed the medication Iluminado had been given and worked out a counter shot.

Doris was wearing the uniform, so she was the one who had to administer the needle. It took her four tries before she could get it all the way in.

A small bearded hobbit, more than a little drunk, was regarding her from the doorway.

"You don't fool me with that uniform. A real nurse knows how to give people a needle. Marx sent you to spy on me, didn't he? Do what I tell you, Miss Proud, or I'll denounce you to the authorities."

He wanted a light massage, and because he was a submariner and used to close quarters and constriction, he asked to be tied to the bed.

That didn't seem too unreasonable, Doris thought, and it would keep his thumb away from the call button. He might have preferred chains, but she had to do it with adhesive tape and two-inch rolled bandage.

Then he had another request.

"I've been getting the runaround, Mirabile," Amsterdam said dangerously, his twitch more conspicuous by natural light.

"Looking all over for you, Hal. Want to talk to you deep background."

He swept Amsterdam into the dispensary. Scenario—Mirabile himself had coined that misuse of the word, to describe the hypotheses and mad flights of fancy with which he had dazzled generations of Chiefs. Naturally most Mirabile scenarios ended happily, with a U.S. win. For those occasions when reality intervened, he had concocted a basic all-purpose cop-out: "Blame it on CIA."

First he debugged the phone, using a pocket imploder invented by the ever-ingenious Japanese. The gust of energy he sent into the mouthpiece would destroy any mechanical eavesdropping device. If an actual human being was monitoring the tap, he would hear bells for days. Now it went without saying (he thought he nevertheless had to say), that if Amsterdam put any of this on the air they would deny they had talked to him, but the Chiefs had reason to believe that a certain Iluminado Castillo, probably not his right name, while masquerading as a Cuban-Soviet agent, was actually high on the pay roster of—

Amsterdam broke in before he could go on.

"Mirabile, what happened in the CCR?"

In the CCR? Why, nothing, as far as Mirabile knew. Why did Amsterdam ask?

Amsterdam hadn't covered any wars personally, but he had heard bombs on many a sound track, and that loud bang a half hour ago had definitely been made by a bomb. A delegation of Moral Majority clergymen had been watching proceedings from the CCR visitors' gallery. Ordinarily Amsterdam wouldn't attach much weight to their testimony, because when those Bible thunchers felt the spirit they tended to see things that weren't there. But one of them had smuggled in a Polaroid camera, and he had shown Amsterdam a very peculiar photograph he had taken.

"It's fuzzy, because the window was already beginning to up. You know the standard Polaroid three-shot, three sub-s staring straight at the camera, the one in the middle with

"Where would I get a *feather*?" she said. "They don't sell S-M stuff at the PX."

The light changed as a starling formation wheeled past the window. Right now a shortage of feathers was not one of the Pentagon's problems.

"All right," Doris told him. "Don't make a pest of yourself while I'm gone."

The struggle for control of the roof was continuing, with the outcome still in doubt. After gathering a bouquet of feathers, Doris had to stand out of the way of a little medical procession.

Orderlies were wheeling a patient inside an oxygen tent. Two bare feet stuck out of the bottom. One leg was in a cast, and Doris's heart gave a thump. The feet looked vaguely familiar, but when she had had the chance, she hadn't given Iluminado's feet that much attention.

A Bell Medevac, an ambulance ship, was waiting. The orderlies passed it by, and slid their patient into the helicopter beside it, a greatly modified Huey. Its name was the Meadow Lark. Hadn't Doris heard that Senator Hemlock was chauffered around in a craft with that name? Hadn't she seen it that morning from Iluminado's hotel window, and wished she could shoot it down?

Hearing rumors of a structural collapse in the Pentagon, tʰ media had flooded the corridors. Their one chance of gettinʲ straight story, they all knew, was to startle it out of somebʲ during the first half hour. Rudeness is rule number one in dog-eat-dog profession. Seeing Mirabile coming, they ᶜ in on his pedicab, waving their notebooks and micropʰ Mirabile would be the first to admit that he was terriᵇ the press. He had a hard time concealing his belief tʰ were, by and large, dolts. His driver, a Vietnamese, his own unfortunate media experiences, and he puʲ down and barreled through.

But Hal Amsterdam was lurking outside the network anchor, you don't bicycle over.

his arms around the other two. In this one the middle figure's an octopus, and why—"

The phone rang before Mirabile had to ad-lib an explanation. This was the prearranged call. The Iluminado Castillo scenario was about to commence.

"What?" he exploded, feigning anger. "I gave explicit instructions—" He threw the phone down. "It's the usual story, divided authority. Castillo's being evacuated to Walter Reed. Maybe we can still catch him on the roof."

The compulsory weight-loss program had been Mirabile's own suggestion, but it didn't apply to contract civilians. He came out of rooftop security clutching his chest.

The scene had been carefully prepared, and except for one unforeseen hitch it went off as slickly as if they had rehearsed it for weeks.

The patient rolling across the yielding guano carpet was actually, of course, the Cat. Disguise technicians had given him a breakaway walking cast and Iluminado's mustache and skin coloring. Pushed by two medical corpsmen, he was heading for the Bell Medevac. Meanwhile, Warrant Officer Brady, in rain hat and fallout cape, was on her way to the Meadow Lark.

With five yards to go, the Cat staged a dramatic recovery. He leaped off the stretcher, waving a pistol. To get authentic performances from the corpsmen, Mirabile hadn't told them of the switch. Seeing their dangerous patient about to abduct a handsome young woman, one of them rashly ran after him, and the Cat had to shoot him.

It was pure reflex. When an enemy charges you—in this case, only an enemy of the scenario, true—you shoot, shoot to kill.

The young soldier, Andrew J. Hooper III, from Mobile, Alabama, had been in the army three years. He was unmarried, and had two girlfriends in different towns. He had once wanted to go on to medical school but he had changed his mind after being exposed to the underside of the profession. He was buried early next week at Arlington with full military honors, the bugles, the flags, the not-quite-synchronized rifle shots. By that time so much else had happened nobody gave the event more than a routine five or six lines.

Amsterdam had to be impressed. The Cat shouted something in Spanish and herded Brady into the Meadow Lark. Then he, too, was inside. An instant later, the helicopter was up.

Did Amsterdam buy it?

Yes, with most of his face. He had seen it, after all, seen the blood and the fragments of bone. Only his ironic muscle remained unconvinced. If you see it on the Pentagon roof, don't believe it even with affidavits, because to these people Winning Is Not Just the Main Thing, Winning Is the Only Thing (a slogan General McArdle had on his desk).

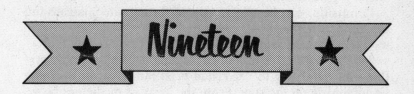

Nineteen

The Cat's cast, cunningly constructed in the Contract Abrogation property shop, came apart like a walnut shell. He dismantled the oxygen tent and checked Iluminado's pulse.

"Are you sure he's out?" Brady asked.

"He got twice the usual dose—damn right he's out. Another cc would have killed him."

The airspace over the Pentagon tended to fill up at this time of day, and Brady was being careful. At a sudden harsh noise, as though an enormous zipper had been pulled, she kicked hard at the left pedal. The Piranha again? It was only a blurred dot in the distance, climbing.

The sudden tilt had spilled Iluminado off his stretcher. The Cat ignored him; he had heard something he didn't much like.

He tried the lavatory door. It turned out to be locked on the inside. Whoever was in there was told to unlock and come out with hands in the air, or bullets would puncture the door.

Brady's antitorque rotor was chewing through starlings. She had her hands full for a moment. As soon as the air cleared and she was able to look, she saw a red-haired nurse in an overfull uniform.

"Wrong helicopter," this woman said cheerfully.

"No, it's the right helicopter," the Cat told her. "Aren't you the person who goes around breaking up knife fights? Some altitude, please, Brady. Our guest feels a compulsion to jump."

Iluminado, on the deck, groaned heavily in Spanish and threw out a hand.

"I thought you said—" Brady said.

The Cat was beside him in an instant. A suitcase, with everything he was likely to need, had been put aboard before the harlequinade on the roof. From the array of medicines he selected a throwaway syringe.

"This is one that I'm sure of, I loaded it myself. Instantaneous blackout. It has Lazy Bones in it, so when he wakes up, he'll want to help."

General McArdle had warned Hemlock that he was bringing bad news. Hemlock didn't understand how that could be. Circe was completely discredited. It would be months, perhaps years, before Admiral Marx would dare show his smug face again on the Hill. Shanahan had come limping into the Capitol, smelling faintly of fish, surrounded by aides to keep off the paparazzi. Like Circe, he was obviously through; he wouldn't pull a half dozen votes.

McArdle hawked and hesitated, and finally came out with it: Iluminado escaped, Warrant Officer Brady and the Meadow Lark hijacked.

The blood drained from Hemlock's face, leaving it the color of day-old bread pudding. Though his own military experience was nil, his bedside table was piled high with Military History Book Club selections, and he knew what was expected of honorary brigadier generals. First of all, not to start babbling. He managed to maintain a kind of shaken composure while McArdle begged him to go back on the Senate floor and demonstrate to their enemies that if they had hoped to rattle Diz Hemlock, Another Eight Billion, they had miscalculated badly.

"All five of us will be thinking of you, Diz."

After he left, Hemlock went to the top of the Capitol steps

to peer up at the sky. Sex, everybody thought, had to be at the bottom of any cross-generational relationship. They just didn't understand.

Until now, he had never refused a chairman's request, but what McArdle had asked him to do was impossible. Go back to the debate, pretend nothing had happened? Without considering the matter any further, he went down the steps at a slant, following a shortcut that had been taken by so many generations of legislators that a faint trail had been worn in the limestone. He arrived at a side street drinking establishment, now called Le Bar. It had once been The Inn Thing, and before that Top Hat, and before *that*, Clancy and Grogan's. Hemlock had stayed with it through all the ownership changes.

He found a welcoming atmosphere.

"Senator. Long time no see."

"Double Judge Taylor on the rocks."

That particular drug combination had probably never before been administered to anyone, even to mice. Certain clusters were telling Iluminado to wake up. Others told him to forget it, go on dreaming.

There was a flickering in his head, as though his closed eyelids had become the focusing point for many movie projectors, which were sending him overlapping images of America's military might: advancing tanks, what seemed like millions of airplanes, the war rooms and missiles and silos, brutal marines. He was only one man, half conscious, with his leg in a cast. How much could he do?

He couldn't have said how he came to be in a helicopter. With some part of his brain he continued to search and correct, and all at once he realized why his fellow passenger, who was also wearing a hospital garment, looked so familiar; in spite of the mustache and other small alterations in his appearance, this was the bogus Colombian captain, the assassin with whom he had crossed knives.

He heard a woman's voice saying, "Wrong helicopter." Commanding everything else to hold still, Iluminado parted his eyelids slowly. And saw Doris! Still in her nurse's uniform, still radiating good health and optimism.

But his enemy was holding a syringe, which he apparently intended to empty into Iluminado's arm without the usual ceremonial alcohol wipe. For what did it matter if the patient picked up an infection? He wouldn't be alive to be made sick by it.

The Yankee was thinking about only one thing, completing a successful injection, and Iluminado surprised him. One minute the patient was inert, more or less unconscious, the next he was exploding upward like a Jack coming out of its box. In his haste, Iluminado forgot that he knew karate. His fist clubbed the fellow back of the ear, sending him over. Before he had time to recover, Iluminado booted him in the head, using the leg with the cast. It was one of the most satisfying sounds he had heard since arriving in this violence-prone country: *clunk!*

He gave his own head a hard shake, to dispel the multiple images, retrieved the syringe and sank it into his enemy's forearm. Immediate anesthesia.

"Beautiful!" Doris cried. "Now all we have to do is land in a parking lot and look for a telephone."

"And call for help from some friendly army and navy? You're joking again, I think."

He found his adversary's pistol, examined the locking and firing mechanisms and took it around the mast cover into the cockpit. The pilot, on her high aluminum seat, was looking straight ahead.

"I don't remember your name."

"Brady, Warrant Officer Three."

He put the pistol against the side of her head. "In Colombia it is considered discourteous to shoot a woman, but women have more equality here. What I would do, I believe, as I can't fly a helicopter, is shatter one of your knees. Point-blank, not much would be left. What I want you to do now, Brady, is fly in a straight line to the nearest airport. Remember my finger is nervous. I'm thinking unkind thoughts about everybody. If you don't want to spend the rest of your life in a wheelchair—"

246

He was scaring her, he was happy to see. Doris, meanwhile, had dragged a black garbage bag out of the bathroom.

"Money?" Iluminado said. "Excellent, I'll need it for air fares."

"This was Shanahan's idea—show you some actual cash. We costed out Mr. G's offer sheet, and they're robbing you, dear. We can give you an equivalent airplane for two-thirds the price." She shook out a paper. "Letter of intent. It's legal gobbledygook, you don't have to bother to read it. What I want you to look at is the bonus schedule."

"Doris—"

She pushed on. "Roman numeral one. That's you, you personally, Iluminado Castillo. That number puts you up there with the Japanese prime minister, he holds the all-time record. Roman numeral two, the junta."

"Do you hear the Shanahan bid, Brady?" he called.

Doris said hastily, "These figures are confidential!"

An airplane flashed at them, rolled and passed underneath. An instant later, it was back. It didn't seem possible that an airplane could completely change course so quickly.

"And that's the John Wayne," Doris told him. "We arranged for a flyover. That is one terrific airplane."

Iluminado shook his head slowly. He was really beginning to admire this young woman.

"Doris, you're more impressive than any airplane. Only a moment ago you were about to be pushed out of a helicopter."

"So it's lucky for me you woke up, isn't it? On the other hand, I gave you the medicine that made you wake up, so I deserve some of the credit. Iluminado, don't you *see*? All you have to do is answer a few simple questions—"

"I know, about what happened in Cartagena. But I really and truly cannot, Doris, for it would get me into equally bad trouble with a whole different collection of people. Now you answer a question for me. Why does it matter so much?"

"I thought I explained that. Do we have time to go into it? If we don't show up wherever we're supposed to be going, they'll come looking for us with missiles."

"Nouns. Not pronouns. Who will come looking for us?"

"Everybody! You're the guy in the black hat. Not really your fault, of course. But the Joint Chiefs are finally getting a little respect back, after some tough years, and you can embarrass them. You can embarrass them *terminally*."

He continued to look at her steadily. She sighed in exasperation and explained further. Two multiple corporations, two weapons systems. The amount of money involved would run a medium-sized country like Colombia for the rest of the century. Presidential ambitions. Something that happened years ago in Gulf of Tonkin. Wherever the Gulf of Tonkin was, it had a faraway sound.

First Mirabile had to host Amsterdam out of the building. He didn't have to explain that negotiations with kidnappers are best conducted in secrecy; Amsterdam promised to put a twelve-hour hold on the story.

Everything seemed cool. Mirabile had staffed it out to the tiniest detail. This was to be a major production, with a cast of hundreds. He had taken the Cat through it again and again, until the abrogation man began to show irritation. But they couldn't afford any more slipups, so Mirabile wrote it all down, using numbered paragraphs and few subordinate clauses. His programmers translated it into language the W-3 computer would be able to understand. All the Cat had to do, basically, was remove one laser disk and load in another, programmed for Iluminado's destruction.

Why, then, as Mirabile told Amsterdam good-bye at the lower end of the mall, should he feel a sudden shortness of breath, a tightening of the scrotum, as though his precognitive receptors had picked a doomsday message out of the microwave flow?

He rushed to the monitors.

They had rigged the Meadow Lark with the same kind of two-way audio-visual circuit that enables the astronauts to carry on those jocular conversations with their buddies in Houston. To Mirabile's consternation, he saw the pilot and *three passengers*. He should have seen only two.

Clapping his close-work glasses over the pair he was already wearing, he put his face inches from the screen. The unwelcome passenger was one of those flamboyant women who always made Mirabile feel that he was about to sit for a crucial final exam without having taken the time to read over his notes. Could this be the same redhead who sweet-talked Harry Lord? Hard to tell, as the picture was black and white.

The Cat still wore the cast and his Iluminado Castillo makeup. The woman was taking packages of currency out of a garbage bag. Hundreds! The denomination of choice among givers of bribes! She was paying the Cat off—the preeminent combat soldier of his generation!

Mirabile's nostrils filled with the stench of disaster. Not for the first time in his career as a conceptual thinker, something had happened between idea and execution. Mirabile's Vietnam scenarios were still used as texts at the Command and General Staff College, but which Vietnamese are driving the Pentagon pedicabs? Not Charlie. Definitely not Charlie.

He hit switches.

Microwave control gave him a quick fix on the Meadow Lark. She was many miles off course, on the wrong side of Washington.

General Thorkill, the Air Force chief, was a short trot from Mirabile's office. Of all the chiefs, he was most in awe of Mirabile's intellect. And he did what the think-tanker told him, immediately, without asking for staff meetings or signatures.

Two and a half minutes later, the Air Assault choppers were up.

The Meadow Lark was holding over Baltimore airport, waiting for clearance, when there was a sharp change in the noise level.

Iluminado sprang to the window and saw gunships, the frightening weapon developed for use against backward peoples with limited surface-to-air capability. There were five he could count. A door gunner grinned at him and waved.

The radio crackled.

"Cat! Just what in God's name are you trying to pull? You better have a good explanation or I'm going to personally see to it that your Medal of Honor is expunged from the books."

249

Iluminado came up behind Brady and showed her his clenched teeth and the pistol. "Can they see us?"

She pointed. He punched out the lens with the pistol barrel.

"I have hostages," he announced. "I am prepared to do whatever is necessary to leave this country. We are about to land in what-is-it, Baltimore. Prepare a jet airplane with a full crew."

He heard only background noises. Then:

"Who am I talking to?"

"You must know the name Iluminado Castillo."

A grunt came out of the speaker, as though Iluminado had flown back to Washington and given the pudgy thinker a punch in the stomach.

Iluminado went on: "So the Medal of Honor is hardly in question. Tell your people to draw off. They are crowding me."

"How did you do it this time, I wonder. That guy's supposed to be *good*. Well, never mind. We have a policy, Captain. We don't give in to blackmail. We literally do-not-give-in-to-blackmail. Is that clear or should I say it in Spanish? Now why don't you just turn around and let us escort you to Fort Belknap? The Chiefs are on their way out. We want to sit down with you and settle our differences like civilized people."

They were being buffeted by the wash from too many rotors. These gunships carried two M-60 machine guns in each doorway, the new can't-miss Cottonmouth rockets in the nose, with their special affinity for the heat given off by gas-turbine engines. The soldiers aboard were pampered troops, given all kinds of extras because of their mission, which was to defend the seat of the government against rebellion and riot. They walked with a special gait, and were famous for brawling in bars. To keep them keen, their officers sometimes allowed them to fly over the Pentagon and fire into the birds.

"It's eyeball to eyeball time," Mirabile said. "Tougher people than you have tried to outstare us, Captain, and we didn't blink first. Now I'm going to count to fifteen. One, two—"

The door gunners were chewing gum, calling remarks to each other, projecting that special North American brand of reckless power. Starlings, Meadow Lark, why should they care what they shot out of the sky? Brady was a compatriot of theirs,

250

she knew their mentality, and Iluminado could see that they frightened her.

"How far is this Fort Belknap in minutes?" he asked quietly.

"About forty."

"Turn around, then. You are mixed up in serious things, Warrant Officer Brady. I must warn you—I have no intention of stepping out with my hands in the air. They didn't do all this to discuss things like civilized people. They could have done that at any time during the day."

They came about, climbing, the Meadow Lark in the center of a diamond formation six rotor-diameters wide, with the fifth ship overhead. The gunners had noticed Doris, and were clowning around for her benefit, inviting her to change helicopters in midair so they could fuck her.

"Not good," she said. "Jesus, Iluminado."

He was poking about in the assassin's suitcase, to see what weapons he could find. He found a remarkable knife with all kinds of folding blades, and with the help of its miniature sawblade, he had the cast off in moments. There were other interesting things in the suitcase, though nothing that would protect against 50-caliber machine-gun bullets: boxes of ammunition, a second and much smaller pistol, binoculars, three loaves of explosive, a flashlight and rod laser, a built-in rack of grenades, a makeup kit, a number of everyday objects which looked innocent but were undoubtedly deadly, a fountain pen, for example. A wrapped sandwich. A copy of the *Wall Street Journal*. A coiled rope and collapsible grappling hook. Cat, if that was the man's name, had been intending to change out of his hospital smock into a major's uniform with exotic patches, to be worn with a black beret. From the bulk of the man, Iluminado knew without trying it on that it would be sizes too big. But the uniform Senator Hemlock had worn that morning was there on its hanger. Iluminado put it on without underwear, and it wasn't too bad a fit, though Gabriella, for one, would have been appalled by those extra inches around the waist and the baggy seat. As for shoes, the choice was between flipflops from the sickbay and the Converse hightops Hemlock wore when he worked out at the Pentagon gym.

A moment later, dressed somewhat unconvincingly as a U.S. brigadier general, he decided he could use a drink. He poured a neat gin, omitting the Campari. Doris gave him a worried look.

"In the great days of the British navy," he told her, "sailors were issued a half pint of rum each day after breakfast."

"Damn it, Iluminado, if I hadn't tried to be so smart—"

"Don't reproach yourself. All you were trying to do was make me rich, and you've done that. Look at this bag full of money."

The Cat sat up, yawning. For the second time that day, with Lazy Bones in his veins he was feeling drowsy and happy.

"Anything you folks would like me to do?"

"No," Iluminado said shortly, then reconsidered. "Or rather, yes. Put on that cast again. And stop smiling. There is nothing funny about any of this."

The Cat snapped on the cast. In spite of what he had been told, the smile kept breaking through.

"Nurse, come here for a sec."

He beckoned her down and whispered something.

"Can I have your attention?" Iluminado said. "I speak as your superior officer. What were your plans for Castillo?"

"At Belknap? To lead him a dance! I mean, to lead him a *dance*! Mirabile may be a horse's ass, but the ideas that come bubbling out of that guy's mouth—"

"Tell me."

The Cat frowned. "I can't seem to remember right now, sir, but it's all written down."

He had Doris by the leg.

"Stop that at once," Iluminado said. "Talk to me."

"That's the army for you. Why does everybody have to be so *grim*?"

The suitcase proved to have a false lining. He worked an envelope out and passed it up.

"Read it yourself if you're so curious. But you don't fool me, you're no one-star. I know who you are, you're Castillo. I told Mirabile—give the guy credit. He's like the VC. Like the damn starlings, for that matter. Knock him down, stomp on him. He keeps coming at you. Nurse, where are you going?"

252

It was nearly dark.

Iluminado sliced open the envelope and spread out the orders. There were sketches, blueprints, aerial photographs. The text was largely initials and acronyms, and he was too impatient to puzzle it out. He tried to make the Cat hold still and explain, but the Cat was trying to corner Doris. The cast slowed him down.

If Brady had been right when she guessed at how long the journey would take, there was less than nine minutes to go.

Iluminado repacked the suitcase, taking out the rope and grappling hook and other bulky and arcane items and filling the empty spaces with packages of currency. He arranged the grenades on the bar, where Brady would see them when she looked back, which she was now doing frequently.

"You see what he's getting ready to do," Doris threw at the pilot, passing the cockpit. On the next lap: "So maybe something had better go wrong with the engine if we want to live through this. And pretty soon, don't you think?"

"Patton once said," Iluminado told everybody, "that if you know you're sure to be killed, take ten of the enemy with you, to keep you company in hell. Although Patton himself was careful never to get into that predicament. He was still alive at the end of his war."

Doris gave him a melting look. "Iluminado—"

They kissed. It started quietly, but in a moment she had one leg wrapped around him in a blind clutching grapple while the Cat looked on with approval.

But as usual, there was too little time. Their flankers were now within a half-rotor diameter, which meant that they must be nearing their destination. Iluminado took the binoculars to the window. This was desolate wooded country, apparently empty of people. The gunners facing him had let their machine guns tip all the way forward on the protruding pylons. One man was white, the other black. Hanging against the straps, they both looked ready to kill.

Brady looked back. "All right, damn you all. I guess the safest thing would be to run out of fuel."

"Not yet," Iluminado told her.

Remembering that he hadn't eaten all day, he unwrapped the sandwich he had found in the suitcase, causing Doris to worry about him again.

"You probably don't know about nitrites, Iluminado. And white bread! That's one of the worst things—"

He smiled at her and asked for some vitamins, which she was glad to supply. He washed them down with more gin.

They were skimming above one of the great divided highways which crisscross the North American continent: fresh ribbons of asphalt, licorice-colored, between smoky flares and orange-striped barrels. Off to the left was a heavy-vehicle park, at the foot of a slope being destroyed to get at its sand and gravel.

He motioned with his half-eaten sandwich. Brady very gradually cut power and began to give up altitude. The machine guns snapped to attention. Iluminado shook his head slightly when Brady looked at him.

Now he could see the gate, the big sign, sodium-vapor lights. Fort Belknap had been here for over two centuries. Unfortunately, the main post installations stood squarely in the path of an interstate connector. When the Department of Transportation puts a line on a map, usually everyone within a quarter mile on each side of that line packs up and moves. This time, however, the DOT had run into the DOD, Department of Transportation against Department of Defense, and both departments are equally stubborn, with equally powerful allies. The road crews had continued to build, refusing to believe that any mere army camp, no matter how long it had been there, could interfere with the *Interstate*.

Mirabile's voice from the radio: "Gently now, Captain."

A crowd of workmen in hard hats was massed at the gate, which was blocked by a picket line. Baby carriages? Iluminado tightened the focus. Yes, officers and their wives were pushing baby carriages back and forth in the glare of television lights.

Brady had slowed almost to a hover. The points of the diamond had collapsed around them. Two rotors overlapped the Meadow Lark from above and two from below, so it was locked at that altitude. In this close formation they proceeded, quite slowly, into Fort Belknap airspace.

Finishing his sandwich, Iluminado filled his pockets with C-4 and grenades while Doris watched.

"We'll make it," she assured him, and being full of vitamins and natural foods she may have believed it. "You've been lucky so far. Where will you go, back to Colombia?"

"Perhaps not at once," he said absently. "Could we meet somewhere first?"

"Yes!"

"And make love?"

"Oh, yes!"

The Cat was beaming at them. "And if you'd like to make it a threesome—"

Iluminado armed a lump of C-4 with an impact detonator. "Doris, you and Cat go one way while I go the other. Are you thinking?" he called to Brady.

"Hard."

Below and to their right, a long railway car hung from a single rail suspended on pylons. Here the Chiefs and their guests would gather soon for the W-3 demonstration. The post itself lay ahead—plain structures on stilts, a PX, a movie theater, and beyond, a low hill with officers' houses. Through public-address speakers, amplified bugles sounded retreat.

All the helicopter doorways now bristled with gun barrels. For the first time, the Cat noticed the tension.

"I'd hate to think it was anything I did—"

They were passing over what must have been at one time a thick stand of pines. Nothing was left but a forest of stumps in a bleak whitened landscape; apparently their starling problem had not been limited to the Pentagon. This gave way to a training area which reminded Iluminado of the one Military Assistance had constructed for his company outside Cartagena. Combat Orientation, it had been called: obstacles and ordeals of various sorts, a mud flat pocked with explosion craters and tangled barbed wire, an Asian village which had been taken by storm so often that nothing was still standing but bullet-scarred walls. The rotor wash whipped the long grass and further disturbed the branches of one small, disfigured tree.

On flat ground ahead, deuce-and-a-half Army trucks were drawn up in a circle, their lights pointing inward.

Mirabile: "You see the circle, Castillo. That's your LZ, your landing zone. No tricks."

The escorting machines were still very close. They had rearranged themselves so all their rotors were above Brady's and the only direction the Meadow Lark could go was down. It was delicate flying, a mutual hover slowly descending over the circle of headlights.

Zzzzzt!

They would be down in a moment, and the pilot of the Shanahan fighter had decided to make this one final pass. Thanks to its sophisticated guidance system, modeled on that of bats, this aircraft cannot be *forced* to collide with a low-level obstacle (according to the Am Tex sales kit). But the helicopter pilots didn't know that. Seeing an approaching thunderbolt, they did the natural thing. They dodged.

The formation opened like a flowering rose. The Meadow Lark whipped between them, as though out of control, flared up and back, bucking badly in the turbulence created by the others' feathering blades, across the mud, the barbed wire, and with a final convulsive wriggle, slammed down in the ruined village.

Bottles and glassware flew. Iluminado waited a moment to give Doris and the Cat their head start. Leaving a smoke grenade fizzing at the foot of the bar, he slipped out of the cargo door on the blind side and dropped into the rubble.

It gave way beneath him.

Twenty

Diz Hemlock had missed three roll calls in a row, the first time this had happened to Another Eight Billion since he was born again and started going to AA meetings. And the moment Mirabile thought of Alcoholics Anonymous, he knew where to look.

He found the senator drinking and dreaming in his old hideaway, a very gemütlich establishment a block from the Capitol steps. The bar seats were upholstered in buttoned black leather, to make congressmen feel at home and ordinary drinkers feel like congressmen.

Hemlock's drink was the color of sour-mash bourbon as it comes from the bottle.

"Do you put any stock in the Bermuda Triangle, Mirabile?" he said, looking up. "It's hard to swallow, I grant you, but there's a considerable accumulation of evidence to prove it exists. How can a helicopter just plain *disappear*?"

"We'll find them, Senator, don't worry. You can imagine the kind of search that's been mounted, within the parameters of no civilian involvement. A massive interforce effort."

Hemlock drank, sighed deeply and drank. "The Shanahans

are behind this. They must be. It's obvious what they're trying to do. They know they can't get me to turn my back on the Chiefs. No, they must want to distract me, make me forget my parliamentary procedure. But tell the guys not to worry. When the debate gets hot I'll be there in my war paint, whooping and hollering. And we'll whip ass, won't we, Mirabile, we'll drive them into the cloakrooms. Bet on it."

"Senator, if there were more people in this country like you—"

Hemlock was shaking his head. "No, I can't accept that. When you come right down to it, I'm a pretty ordinary Joe, Mirabile. Just a simple old-fashioned American, and there are more of us out there than you'd think from reading the *Washington Post* and *The New York Times*."

"Just what the Chiefs were saying. What we need at the Belknap demo tonight is some of that good Hemlock common sense. Senator Ziegler's going to be there, one or two others who still say they haven't made up their minds. It's a great chance to change a few votes."

But Hemlock had gone shimmering away, into some Bermuda Triangle of his own.

"I try to be charismatic like some of the others. I do try, Mirabile, but dull is the way it comes out. Whooping and hollering? Who'm I kidding? I'm a plodder and I always will be."

"I'll tell you one thing, Senator. The *Russians* don't think you're dull. About Belknap—"

Doris's eye was discoloring nicely, but otherwise she was fine. Declining further medical investigation, she climbed off the table and found a phone.

Senator Shanahan wore a device which bleated plaintively at him whenever his office wanted him to call in. He called in and they gave him Doris's number.

He asked how the flight had gone, and an unfriendly eavesdropper couldn't have told from his tone that the question had any special importance; that is what comes from three-generation wealth, a degree from a good university, consistent success with women.

"It's sort of a long story," Doris said. "We all got out before the chopper blew up. They chased the wrong guy at first. Iluminado's still roaming around, and you ought to be out here, Hughie. Bring some more cash. We're still a long shot, frankly, but the last time I saw Iluminado he had that glint in his eye—"

In peacetime, soldiers are trained to fight the preceding war. That is the way it has always been. The last battlefield enemy faced by American infantrymen had been, in effect, an army of woodchucks. Dig, dig was almost the only thing they knew how to do. Their tunnels went hundreds of miles in every direction. How could you beat an enemy that wouldn't come out of his tunnel so he could be bombed and rocketed? Well, it turned out that you couldn't. Still you had to try. Manuals were developed on how to seal, how to bomb out or flush out a tunnel. Replicas of the authentic article, built to exact VC or NVA specs, were added to all zone-of-the-interior Combat Orientation locations.

It was into one of these that Iluminado had tumbled. This might have been serious, but his would-be assassin, wanting to be totally prepared, had naturally put a folding entrenching tool in his suitcase, along with a flashlight and compass. Not everything works in the United States, Iluminado was beginning to discover, but this tiny flashlight, no bigger than one of his fingers, had been stepped up in some high-technology way, so it sent out a slender, very white beam as far as an automobile's headlights.

There was a whoosh overhead, a sudden sharpening of light. The Meadow Lark was on fire. There were alarming noises behind him, the spatter of falling dirt. If he wanted to go back that way, he would have to dig his way out.

The Vietnamese are a short people, even shorter than submariners. Knees bent, greatly hampered by having to tug the suitcase, Iluminado followed the flashlight beam, wanting to be out from under in case another section of tunnel collapsed. He

259

splashed through a shallow pool, slipped on the slick clay and lost his hat in the water. He didn't want to turn back and grope for it. For one thing, was it actually water?

He came to a fork. He hesitated only briefly before going left, the way that had had the heaviest use. It twisted back on itself, to come to a dead end almost at once in a sort of underground dayroom.

He darted the beam this way and that. He himself had been through Combat Orientation in Colombia more than once, and he had attacked the course with élan, flying over obstacles, swinging from ropes, crawling through muddy slop while machine-gun bullets (they were told) whispered overhead. This cave had been hollowed out by pragmatic soldiers who thought there were more agreeable ways to prepare for combat. It was a Yankee cave, not a Vietnam one, with enough headroom so Iluminado could stand nearly erect, on the midden of beer cans, cigarette filter-ends, trampled copies of *Hustler* and *Playboy*, with the naked ladies removed.

The place was so unthreatening, so homey and at the same time so comfortable, that he no longer felt he should be floundering in several directions at once. No one knew where he was. They would have to wait for the Meadow Lark's embers to cool before they could be sure he hadn't perished in the fire. He had noticed chocolate and bouillon cubes in the suitcase. If that had been water back there, he had water. Candle stubs in hollowed-out niches. He could sit down and consider, look at the maps again, perhaps distill some sense out of the Cat's orders.

He unfastened the suitcase and continued the inventory he had begun in the helicopter. A new identity awaited him—the Cat had passports in two different names, Diners Club and American Express cards. He unfolded a contour map of the fort and its installations, on a scale of one to ten thousand, and found the main gate, the structures they had passed over, the obstacle course, the battered Vietnamese village. A lightly crosshatched rectangle, six miles by four, was designated: PROVING GROUNDS, EXPERIMENTAL, W-3.

Very well. He unwrapped a chocolate bar and turned back to page one, designated fussily: "Page 1 of 4."

Each page carried the admonition: SUPERSENSITIVE, DESTA-BILIZATION EYES ONLY. The verbs were unequivocal, with no ifs or maybes: "You *will* proceed," "You *will* coordinate—" Iluminado, the protagonist victim, was referred to throughout as the MT, Moving Target. The moment the Meadow Lark touched down, the assassin was ordered to deactivate the pilot and disarrange her clothing. Having been given a powerful tracta-bility shot, MT might be persuaded to cooperate—teeth marks on her neck and breast would be helpful, flecks of Hispanic skin under her fingernails. To give the appearance of rape, appar-ently, which was preposterous, for Iluminado's experience with Yankee women had been precisely the opposite.

MT and escort *will* then proceed, rapidly but with the utmost caution, to W-3 command bunker, along a route delineated on the map by a dashed red line. The technician manning the computer tonight—Harlan Pettibone was his name—had just been put through his regular three-month psy/phys reevalua-tion, and the doctors had found an interesting and potentially dangerous personality flaw. Normal enough in other respects, he was strongly hypnosis-susceptible. All it took was a bright light and a few soothing words. They had had to return him to duty until they could train a replacement. It would be such a simple matter for the Cat, in the guise of an intelligence major, to (1) gain his confidence; (2) hypnotize him; and (3) reprogram the computer. The old program out, the new pro-gram in: there were sketches, with arrows and simple-minded directions that even a computer-illiterate would be able to fol-low.

All this was overture. The real opera would commence when the obs-car moved out from the starting pylon. At D-plus-13, still heavily LZ'd and so in the tractability mode, Iluminado would be turned loose with a roll of microfilm taped in each armpit. Blueprints, costs, performance figures—all the secrets, in short, that would show the Russians how to build a Wall of their own, and how to penetrate ours. At D-plus-16, the find-fix-annihilate systems, orchestrated by the Cat from the com-mand bunker, would explode into action.

Goaded by lasers and microwave emissions, the pitiable

Moving Target would be herded from station to station, to be annihilated, finally, by Porcupine, the definitive close-in anti-personnel weapon. Senator Ziegler, Zigzag Ziegler as he was often called, a notorious wobbler back and forth between treason and patriotism, would be invited to release the flechettes. This senator was a great stalker of animals, but until now he had never hunted a person. He would be bound to the Chiefs by blood.

This was Iluminado's blood they were talking about, and he could feel his scalp tighten. No matter; when the flechettes flew, Moving Target would no longer be in their flight path.

Heavy vehicles, possibly tanks, thundered overhead. Dirt sifted down from the ceiling. Iluminado not only needed a diversion to cover his departure, he needed a *colossal* diversion.

He continued to sort through the envelope, finding a detailed description of each W-3 component. He reread the Harlan Pettibone paragraph. Bright light, a few soothing words. No doubt this Wall of theirs, which seemed to be less an actual wall than a state of mind, was as great a folly as Admiral Marx's submarine. What if, with a screwdriver and a few well-placed lumps of C-4—

He was smiling, for the first time in this terrible tunnel.

Mr. G loved these Pentagon intrigues. He enjoyed setting group against group, usually ending up making enemies of both. Duffy, by contrast, believed that the facilitator's function was to bring people together. He lubricated, he didn't initiate. He provided a setting, so his clients and the underpaid bureaucrats they dealt with could locate their common interests.

But he was beginning to feel that mysterious forces were conspiring against him. Yes, he had made mistakes. He should have closed the deal the first night, when the young man was befuddled by too many Campari-gins. Later on, in the Pentagon, every time he and Iluminado were about to start talking business, someone had swooped down and snatched him away.

Quite a lot seemed to be going on, media snoopers wherever you looked. What had happened in E Ring? they all wanted to know. Duffy put on his all-you-get-is-name-rank-and-serial-number-even-if-you-torture-me look, and brushed past.

He walked the corridors until his heels were sore, tracing his quarry finally to the Pentagon sick bay. Small bearded men ran in and out, chasing the nurses. The scene gave Duffy a déja vu feeling, as though he had seen it before, perhaps in a Marx Brothers movie. Turning a corner, he came face to face with a bosomy, redheaded impostor, Doris, the turncoat who had defected to Shanahan.

Two security guards were some paces away. Doris got to them first. She pointed an accusing finger at Duffy.

"That man is a sicko, a well-known pervert! He tapes people to beds."

And she dragged them into a nearby room. There, sure enough, a bearded patient, snoring heavily, was taped to the bedposts. Duffy did some sputtering about damn lies and false nurses, but nobody listened.

They allowed him one phone call. He had to use it to call Mr. G, who was predictably disgusted. Fastening people to beds—couldn't he do that on his own time?

After two embarrassing hours, Duffy was turned loose without an apology, not because they thought he had been unjustly accused but because of a cash contribution to everybody's favorite charity, the Neediest Cases.

Doris was gone. Iluminado was gone.

The Pentagon's native-born doctors, hearing of the great Medicare gold strike, had long ago left for the private sector. Duffy found a Turk with an unsanitary mustache and little English, who had been up on the roof and seen it all happen.

When Duffy tried to find Mirabile, he was told that the thinker had left in a hurry for Belknap. Shanahan, Mr. G? At Belknap. Hemlock? Also at Belknap. Aha, Duffy said to himself, and looked for a helicopter that was going that way.

Sadists had designed this tunnel. Each easy piece was followed by a sudden drop-off or a cramped, difficult twist, to show the recruits what hunting undersized Asians through tunnels had really been like. Iluminado had to go to his hands and knees, then to his stomach. A sharp turn was ahead. He wormed his way toward it, pushing the suitcase. They would surely leave clearance for the occasional overweight soldier, he was telling himself. They wouldn't send their own men down here to die. But with North Americans, you just didn't know.

He negotiated that turn and to his dismay, saw the tunnel dip sharply downward. More heavy vehicles rolled overhead. With a soft plop, a large chunk of ceiling came down, half burying the suitcase.

There is a psychology to these things, Iluminado tried to persuade himself, as there is to a roller coaster. This dip must be the torturer's last twist of the screw, to make the unfortunate soldier fear that the tunnel will run on forever.

Backing off, he managed to open the suitcase and get out the folding shovel. It would have been simpler if he hadn't brought so much of the money. He scraped and burrowed his way through. Then, as he had hoped, the crawling was easier for a time and he tasted fresh air.

In a moment more he was out.

It was full dark.

He stood breathing hard at the edge of an unpaved road, feeling his blood surge and recede. The blazing helicopter and the confusion around it, the ring of truck headlights, were all a surprising distance away.

The map showed a motor pool a few k's away. He struck out across rather rough country, using the compass, and presently saw a lighted office and a number of neatly parked vehicles. The soldiers in charge, a private and corporal, readily surrendered a vehicle, although Iluminado was wrong for his story in a number of ways. For one thing, he must be the youngest general officer since Alexander the Great, and old or young, generals seldom go out in public bareheaded, wearing basketball shoes. But enlisted men who have any sense make a point of never looking an officer straight in the eye. Their eyes got no higher than the gold star on Iluminado's lapel as he told them he had broken a fan belt, and the mishap had made him late for an appointment with senators. An implausible story, but something else enlisted men don't do is argue with a disheveled brigadier general, smelling strongly of gin, during happy hour.

Iluminado signed for a jungle-camouflaged jeep and drove off.

A river of headlights was approaching. He cut his own lights and got off the road. Deneb, George S. Patton, Jr.'s, star, twinkled encouragement from a position below Orion.

It was a convoy of trucks carrying infantry. If they were going to the movies (but in that case why were they wearing steel helmets and holding rifles between their knees) they wanted to get there for the prevues of coming attractions. If they were looking for Iluminado, they were going too fast to notice the jeep and the hatless brigadier general crouching beside it in the dark field.

At the next intersection, he stopped to consult a pole studded with arrows. Not all were meant to be taken seriously: Las Vegas 2103 m., Havana 748 m., Elaine's Home Cooking and Cocksucking, 4 m. To confuse an enemy further, there was more than one Proving Grounds arrow. Iluminado oriented the map, located the dotted line and did what that told him.

Signs soon began: CONTAMINATED AREA, THANK YOU FOR NOT SMOKING, OFF LIMITS AND THIS DOES MEAN YOU, USE OF DEADLY FORCE AUTHORIZED. Then came a woven wire fence and a gate, which could be opened only with a coded card. Iluminado was equipped with this card, but the machinery hesitated, seeming to sense that it was being asked to open for an unauthorized person. And yet it had to obey.

The terrain on both sides, he was warned—a skull and crossbones means the same in all languages—was heavily mined and possibly radioactive. The starlings had left their traces among the stumps and the berry bushes. A dish antenna, a Toyota parked near a trapdoor, revealed the underground bunker's location.

He lifted the door. A dim light burned at the bottom. The stairs were steep and forbidding.

Well, he didn't want to go down. But he had programmed himself, and like the machinery at the gate, he supposed he had to. He was here to engage W-3 and destroy it, if possible, and light up the sky so they wouldn't notice one lone Latin American captain departing for some distant country where no one speaks English, preferably one without an extradition treaty with the United States.

The door at the bottom was marked: ABSOLUTELY NO ADMITTANCE TO UNAUTHORIZED PERSONNEL, with the inevitable penciled addition: "KGB Agents and Other Freaks Keep Out." A brigadier general of sorts, Iluminado entered without knocking.

Heavy rock was being played on a two-speaker system at maximum amplification. "I need it, I need it!" a woman's voice cried, and yet again, "I need it!"

The youthful soldier at the multiscreen console didn't realize that he was entertaining a visitor. Iluminado cleared his throat. The homey little sound cut through the musical clamor, and the soldier jumped to his feet, spilling crayons. Except for islands of acne he was mushroom-white, as though he spent even his days off underground.

Pettibone was the name on his badge. So far the assassin had been correctly informed; this was the Specialist Five whose psychiatrist had flagged him as a hypnosis risk.

He reached back to turn off the music.

"Good evening," Iluminado said in the crashing silence that followed. "But you're busy?"

The soldier's eyes jumped to his coloring book. "Killing time, sir, you might say."

"I will give you thirty seconds to get into uniform," Iluminado said, a remark Major Sadowski, in Cartagena, had often delivered to slovenly soldiers.

Turning his back, he examined the monitors. Only one screen was alive. This showed the main gate, the highway workers in their hard hats confronting the baby carriages. The signs said: ARMY BRATS PROTEST UNNEEDED HIGHWAYS, GO NOW AND PAVE NO MORE, STOP USING STARLINGS AS GUINEA PIGS.

Pettibone made a small noise to let Iluminado know that he had rolled down his sleeves and changed out of clogs, and was now properly dressed.

266

"It's bounced off the satellite, sir," he said of the picture. "Why it's so supersharp. The entire W-3 area gets saturation coverage, with zoom pickup and recovery. If a golf ball was laying out there in the grass somewhere I could locate it for you and read you the manufacturer's label."

"I have just arrived from three years overseas duty. From Southern Korea, in fact. These baby carriages—I don't understand what is happening."

"All right, the baby carriages. That's the married officers, sir, the married officers' wives. STOP USING STARLINGS—those are the starling lovers, you can forget about them, they're just piggybacking for the exposure. See, in the W-3 demo we showcase this pressure-sensitive minefield. And to show how sensitive, how those mines will go off if you look at them crosseyed, more or less, we use starlings. Kill two birds with one stone, I was about to say."

"The baby carriages, Pettibone?"

"Well, you know about the highway they want to put through, O.K.? Today they got some kind of court order. Our lawyers were out to lunch or something. Tomorrow we'll get it reneged, but they moved up their big machinery, and it's all right there ready to go. Unless we stop them tonight it's going to be fait accompli, if that's the way you pronounce it, right through Married Officers' Quarters, all right? We brought in the First Cav, and those guys don't give one *shit*, excuse me. But we want to try it the other way first, especially because it's all going out on TV. Those bulldozer guys are human, is the theory. You know you've got to be kind of a miserable human being to bulldoze a baby carriage."

Two immense recreational vehicles, the size of small whales, had pulled up at the picket line. A smartly dressed woman got out of one of them. Although the weather was fine she sported a fancy umbrella—and, in fact, looking more closely, Iluminado saw that it was his father's friend from the airport, Isobel Clancy. While she was negotiating for permission to pass, a convoy of red sports cars came up alongside. Pettibone twirled a knob and zoomed in for a better look.

"Look, it's Senator Shanahan! He's against the whole idea

of W-3, but sooner or later they all have to come out and see for themselves. If I say it who shouldn't, we put on a *show*."

"I am looking forward to seeing it. Perhaps you would explain it to me if you have the time?"

"Sir, all the time in the world. Everything seems to be behaving itself tonight, knock wood." He looked around, but there was no wood within view, only metal and plastic. "It's all totally experimental, you realize, and we've had our glitches, O.K. People have been pretty understanding, on the whole. Like the sheik of Saudi Arabia was here one night, king, probably, some kind of Arab, and we had a little short circuit and his robe caught on fire. Hey—no problem, I've got an extinguisher. He couldn't have been nicer about it. Gave me this tape deck to show there was no hard feelings. O.K.—it's all oriented to the monorail viewpoint. Usually when the Army's got something to demonstrate, the guests will sit in the grandstand and we bring the weapons to *them*. But here there's all this terrain to cover, we have to do it the other way. *They* move, the weapon stations hold still."

He was settling into the briefer's rhythm. He moved to a wall map, with overlay.

"Right here's your minefield, O.K.? We bait it with table scraps. Kentucky Fried Chicken sells us their organic garbage. Starlings really seem to go for that batter. Bang, bang, bang. Most everybody watching has been to the Pentagon, and you get very good audience response."

He stepped along.

"Because you don't know what level aggressor you're defensing against, is the basic idea. Could be a tank battalion. Could be some brainwashed kid with a bottle of gasoline, you know? We locate the target with heat-source, acoustical or olfactory detectors, and we lock onto that target *so* tight, General. Always before, it had to be line of sight. Now we've got that satellite up there, and your weapon can be over the horizon. You pick up the target, send pinpoint coordinates, and make all the corrections automatically via the bounce. Evasive action? Forget it. We've got missiles here that can turn somersaults and practically tap-dance, all right? I mean *on the way*. And we demonstrate that."

"With an actual target?"

"We blow up a Russian T-72, simulated. It's polyurethane, for budgetary considerations, but from the obs-car they can't tell the difference. The warhead is simulated nuclear, with the smoke configured in to give you your mushroom effect. Two-kiloton equivalency. Digs quite a nice hole. They let one of the guests work the remote. Know what I mean by a remote? That's this handheld clicker that will maneuver your tank for you. Back and forth, this way and that, according. You can really make it boogie out there. And the missile stays locked on, as I say. That's one thing we haven't had the least bit of trouble with, but there's a number two and a number three warhead in case of a fizzle. And of course I'm down here all the time backing up the automatic with the manual."

"The manual."

Pettibone picked up a flat metal box that looked like the keyboard of a no-frills portable computer, drastically downsized.

"One of the early objections, control was too centralized. One direct hit and there goes your ball game. So R and D came up with this baby. In real life, the computer and the various linkages are going to be down at the bottom of like a two-hundred-foot shaft. Very thick concrete. Five or six individual operators, ten or a dozen, however many you want, will be scattered around all over the place. Redundancy is the idea. Unless the enemy can blow a couple of square miles off the map, you're still in business."

"You have a great deal of responsibility, Pettibone."

"I'll say. I used to get so psyched out I couldn't go to sleep after. I've got more of a what-the-hell attitude now. Because the crazy thing is, it isn't that complicated."

He threw a master switch and all the screens lighted up.

"Like the car stops at Number Three station. I'm watching the screens for problems. If everything looks O.K., I hit the C on the keyboard. Third letter of the alphabet, that's all there is to it. Old man computer does the rest."

Iluminado was only half paying attention. One screen showed the still-burning Meadow Lark, surrounded by fire apparatus. On another, a motorcyclist was being chased by two helicopters with searchlights. He might have been Iluminado himself— one leg in a cast, the mustache, dyed hair.

Pettibone was saying, "Then I've got this whole library of visual effects to fall back on. Smoke, flame. Mock-ups of left-wing guerrillas, down to the last detail. Guy named George Segal does them for us, and you'd be surprised how lifelike. No kidding, they can fool you. Then there's a negative-field device that aborts any internal-combustion engine. I don't understand it myself—some kind of zapper, blows the inboard computers. You can use it to take out an individual vehicle or if you want to you can interdict a whole zone."

"Very interesting, Pettibone."

Iluminado used the assassin's powerful flashlight to check one of the instructional labels, and left it on.

"And we've got a towed drone," Pettibone continued. "That's one of our high spots. You know the heat-seeking concept. We have this baby blimp that tows a fake ballistic missile at two thousand feet. The machine-gun tracers go up and they can't seem to hit a thing. Then we turn on a twenty-five-watt bulb inside the target—twenty-five watts, this sort of dim glow, and the tracers converge, blow it out of the sky. Very impressive. Then a telemetrically controlled satellite-killer. That we do live, for a finish. And if anything glitches on you—as I say, it does happen—I can call in the chopper sweep. When all those choppers come over, I don't care who you are, it can scare the bejesus out of you."

"Pettibone, what is Porcupine?"

"Porcupine, O.K., that's APFs, sir. Antipersonnel flechettes. High velocity, range I believe of five hundred meters. We demonstrate that against some of the mock-ups, Vietcong usually, using the new targeting sensor that you program for individual bodily smells. You take your typical guerrilla, he's been sleeping out in the jungle for weeks. Primitive diet, primitive sanitary facilities. He's going to smell totally different from a GI who's

270

probably just had a shower and shave. And I'm not just saying that. It's been proved scientifically."

Iluminado could feel his own sweat beginning to gather, for Porcupine was the weapon they had been planning to use on him.

"You keep it hot down here, Pettibone. Doesn't it ever make you drowsy?"

"All the time," the soldier admitted. "They don't set the thermostat for my comfort, but to keep a constant environment for the circuits. Would you mind not doing that with the light, sir? It's only twenty minutes to blast-off. I've got to stay sharp."

"Soon the senators will vote on this wall," Iluminado said in a monotone. "If the vote is against, you will be given some less pleasant assignment. And so much can go wrong. If a missile wanders off course and blows up the railway car with all those generals and admirals—I'm not surprised that you're nervous."

"I'm fine, sir. Really fine."

"But I can't be sure of that, can I, if you won't look at me?"

Never look an officer in the eye: this enlisted man's phobia was now working against him. The little light searched along the console, trying to pick up a glint, a reflection.

"I know you are wondering why I am here," Iluminado said. "I specialize in psy-W, in other words psychological warfare. I am making a study of precombat tensions. To be afraid, to have the sensation that starlings are fluttering about in one's stomach, all this is entirely natural and in fact quite a good thing. It sets the, what is the medical term, adrenalin flowing. But if you allow it to take hold of you, Pettibone, you can fall to pieces, you can make mistakes. My advice to people when they feel this beginning to happen is: think of snow."

"Snow, sir?" Pettibone said, drying his forehead.

"Snowflakes." Having grown up only a few steps from the ten-degree parallel, Iluminado had had no direct experience of this phenomenon, but he had read about it many times in books. "In their millions upon millions. Large damp snowflakes. And they fall so softly. How insignificant, truly, is a single person compared to the majesty of nature. If you close your eyes you can see them come down. *Close your eyes.*"

This was an order, and Pettibone obeyed. Iluminado went on describing snowflakes. No two alike, it was said. Couldn't Pettibone see them?

"No, all I can see is these squiggly up and down lines, sir, like the stock market."

"Snowflakes," Iluminado insisted.

"No use, sir. I keep going back over my checklist, did I leave out anything."

The second hand of the big clock continued its steady advance. By this time Iluminado had a bad case of battlefield stomach himself, and thinking about snowflakes hadn't helped *him*.

A buzzer sounded. A message in large type flashed onto the main display.

ATTENTION ALL STATIONS! BE ON THE LOOKOUT FOR ENEMY AGENT DRESSED AS BRIGADIER GENERAL. BASKETBALL SNEAKERS.

Pettibone looked at Iluminado's feet, then, for the first time, into his eyes. Iluminado gave him a terrible glance in return, which hypnotized him in an instant.

"Funny," Pettibone said, "Weather forecast didn't say anything about snow."

"Yes, it's most unusual for this time of year. But otherwise it's been an ordinary night, wouldn't you say, Pettibone? No visitors."

Pettibone nodded agreement. "I worked on my coloring till the half-hour warning. Afraid I played with myself a little. A dirty habit, I know, but it helps to settle the nerves. Didn't come, though."

Iluminado gave him the crayon box. "You can relax now, Pettibone. If any problems come up, let me handle them."

"Good of you, sir."

Now Iluminado could open the suitcase and spread out the diagrams. Much would have to be improvised. He would take Pettibone's Toyota and leave him the jeep. The rod-laser, though small, was a formidable object, and would surely be able to cut through the fence. Undoubtedly the Toyota would have some kind of road map in the glove box—most automobiles do. Their excellent new highway went in the wrong direction, toward Washington. Iluminado would leave it as soon as he could, and work his way on back roads to the nearest big airport. Then—good-bye United States, have a good evening.

Following the step-by-step diagram, he gave the computer the program that had been prepared for use by the assassin. The remote-control keyboard would make it all simple. His last move before cutting the fence would be to work his way through the alphabet, setting everything off at once.

The be-on-the-lookout warning had already had an effect. On one of the screens a single-star general had been ordered out of his car at a checkpoint. Two MPs had him spread-eagled over the hood while they patted him up and down. Among the late arrivals being admitted to the observation car, Iluminado recognized the enigmatic Quimby, who no doubt had his own reasons for wanting to be present. On yet another screen, the only interior, a group of high-ranking officers stood huddled in front of a computer display. There were so many ribbons, so many stars, that these could only be the Joint Chiefs of Staff; Iluminado recognized several from seeing them together in the CCR. And what were they looking at with such interest and excitement? He realized too late that while he was looking at them on his screen, they were looking at him on theirs.

Quickly, back to the diagrams. But the small print was dancing around (the combat-jitters effect) and he had to consult Pettibone, who was shading in Goofy, the Walt Disney dog. Pettibone pointed out the little wide-open eye of the closed-circuit transmission, and Iluminado extinguished it with his laser. It was clear from the way the Chiefs responded to this that they were no longer getting a picture.

"Now, Pettibone," Iluminado said briskly. "Have you ever given any thought to becoming an officer?"

"Negative, sir. One hundred percent. I don't care for the chicken shit, coming or going."

"Think it over before you say no. I'm not suggesting that you waste any of your time at lieutenant or captain. Jump straight to general. Wouldn't you like that?"

"You know what," Pettibone said with a slow smile, "I think I just might."

"Fine. You'll need a uniform. You're welcome to mine. I've often wondered how it would feel to be a Specialist Six."

"Specialist Five, actually."

The exchange was quickly made.

"Just this one star?" Pettibone said doubtfully. "I don't want to seem ungrateful, Specialist, but while you're at it, couldn't you—"

"One star is all I want you to have at present."

The phone rang. Iluminado picked it up.

"Ten-minute warning, Pettibone," a voice sang. "Lots of big brass here tonight, so make it look good. Break a leg."

Iluminado hung up, and turned back to Pettibone. "We're encircled! Take my vehicle, General. If you break through, send helicopters. But watch your step—the enemy may be wearing American uniforms. If they capture you, tell them nothing."

"Naturally not, Pettibone. Nothing out of the ordinary happened tonight. No visitors. Worked on my coloring."

"Good luck, sir, and God be with you."

They saluted each other. Life would be simpler for a foreigner like himself, Iluminado thought, if he could hypnotize everybody.

But Pettibone turned back.

"Encircled, you say. We've got all this firepower. Why don't we use some of it?"

"Impossible, sir. Our one chance—"

"I don't mean fight from here, idiot. This bunker hasn't been hardened yet. It wouldn't withstand a direct hit from a forty-five automatic. A little something to cover our retreat."

Without sitting down he tapped a cluster of letters into the computer.

"Get those choppers in the air. They come over at three hundred feet, putting out a total of twenty thousand watts. If we're on the far side of that nobody'll see *us*, I can guarantee you."

The screen with the Joint Chiefs on it was pulling at Iluminado's eye. The Chiefs had sent everybody else out of the room. The Air Corps general was talking and waving his arms. The others nodded agreement. They armed themselves: pistols, one rifle, submachine guns. Iluminado zoomed closer still. He didn't need subtitles. The Chiefs had arrived at a mutual decision. No more delegation of responsibility, for that hadn't worked. They would have to do this themselves.

And that made it personal.

Iluminado spun around. He could run from an abstraction like the Pentagon or the United States Army and Air Force, or the Colossus of the North, but he couldn't run from these overdressed, overweight, foolish old clowns. His eyes were pounding. He was so mad he saw crooked. All right, they were armed. So was Iluminado. And he was armed with W-3.

Pettibone called, "You coming, Specialist, or what?"

"You go on, sir. I must remain at my post. I haven't been properly relieved."

"I'll take the responsibility."

"With respect, General, you belong to the psychological branch and you don't have authority. My place is here. But I'll need some help because I'm new at this, as you know. That was an excellent idea, the helicopters. And the missile that locks on, how do you change the target?"

"Just hit the erase. What do you want to substitute?"

Iluminado looked at the screens. The Joint Chiefs were ready to go. The Air Corps chief put out his hand, palm down, and the others clamped on. After some kind of incantation they flung their hands in the air and poured from the room.

At the main gate, the pickets continued to chant and circle: ARMY BRATS AGAINST UNNEEDED HIGHWAYS. Behind a parked truck on the Army's side of the fence, an officer was tucking some kind of angular object into a baby carriage. Iluminado zoomed in. It wasn't a baby, it was a submachine gun wrapped in a blanket to make it look like a baby. The cold war there appeared to be warming up.

He turned to the construction workers' vehicle park and picked out the largest and heaviest machine, a really enormous dragline shovel. Parked on a soccer field, its claw would be in one goal-mouth, its exhaust pipe in the other. The cab would tower above the topmost level of seats.

"This," he said.

"Ummm. The big enchilada. That we'd better do visually."

He brought the missile up out of its lair and showed it the shovel. The missile's controlling intelligence didn't approve of the change.

INAPPROPRIATE TARGET flashed onto the screen. RECHECK DATA.

"Nevertheless," Pettibone said cheerfully.

He typed a rapid command, and the display changed to LOCKED ON, READY TO FIRE.

"You've got those two backups, remember. I'll write it all down for you. I don't know how it happened, but just this one time, they didn't get too elaborate."

Using his red crayon and the title page from his coloring book, he printed a series of letters and numbers. The firing command was easy to remember, being the name of the system: W Slash Three Exclamation Point.

They exchanged another salute and Iluminado was left alone to go over the Cat's orders and put more surprises into the computer. Again he was smiling, probably looking a little like the happy dog in Pettibone's coloring book.

Then it was time to go.

The main door into the bunker was heavily reinforced. He made sure it was latched securely, and set off a medium-sized C-4 explosion at the top of the stairs, collapsing the stairwell. They would have to do some digging before they could reprogram the computer.

Pettibone, knowing his Toyota's failings, had parked it pointing downhill. Surrounded by the most advanced computer technology in the Western world, the engine refused to start. Iluminado set it rolling, leaped in and was off, being careful to stay within the free-passage lines marked on his map.

He pushed the little car to its maximum effort. A faint glow had appeared in the east, like a multiple sunrise: Pettibone's helicopters.

He was still some minutes short of the fence when they broke over the hill, giving off a terrible noise and an even more terrible light.

PORCUPINE STAGING AREA, he saw.

He braked hard. Nearby, the deadly steel slivers waited to be released. If they had already been programmed they knew how Iluminado smelled.

First to get rid of the Toyota. He dropped his last lump of explosive into the engine space and was fifty meters away, belly down in a gully, when the car blew apart. The light came on implacably, rolling over the dark ground like returning sunlight after a total eclipse. It would show every pebble, every weed.

Soldiers were stealing up through the grass!

Undeterred by the light, the noise, they continued to come, and Iluminado realized that these must be the dummies Pettibone had told him about. They were riding a flatbed. Central American by their look, they wore big countrymen's hats so from the air they would be mistaken for innocent farmers. They were hung with grenades and they carried the Soviet AK-47 assault rifle, so it was clear that they were up to no good. Jumping onto the flatbed just ahead of the light, Iluminado borrowed a guerrilla's hat and tried to think left-wing thoughts.

The light flooded into his skull and threatened to cook his brain. He had one of his companions by the shoulder, his fingernails deep in the imitation flesh. Suddenly, impelled by some inner mechanism, the figure lifted its gun to fire, giving Iluminado another serious scare. Snowflakes, snowflakes, he said to himself, but that was not what he saw. He saw a montage of exploding suns.

In time, it passed. Keeping the hat, he jumped down and struck off on foot. The fence was where he expected it to be. He applied the laser, and it was as easy as slicing zucchini.

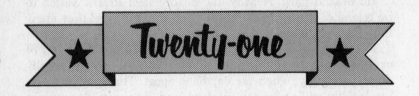

Twenty-one

"And just where the fuck have you been?" Mr. G demanded, giving Duffy no credit, as usual, for having been able to guess where his client could be found. "Lit Up. Iluminado God damn Castillo. He's at large out there somewhere, thumbing his nose at everybody. God damn it to piss-hell, Duffy, when I think of the way you keep letting him slip through your fingers—!"

He was waving in the general direction of the W-3 proving grounds, which, as Duffy had good reason to know, were heavily booby-trapped. He had watched the demo more than once, and knew what happened to starlings, for example, when they blundered onto that minefield.

"I want you to find that turkey," Mr. G said, "and if you let those Shanahans get ahead of you one more time—"

"Mr. G, I'm going out on a limb and say I don't think this is one of your better ideas. That's a good part of the world to stay out of, with the demo about to begin."

"No, keep your lights on and stay on the paved roads, you'll be fine."

A big diesel tank, one of a new line, the Tarantula, which Duffy himself had helped Mr. G unload on the DOD, was sitting there sullenly, waiting for Duffy to climb in. As a matter of fact, it was a pretty good tank, though its electrical system tended to conk out if it hit a pothole too hard. But as Mr. G said, on good roads it was perfectly O.K. Well, one of these days, Duffy told himself, he was going to surprise his client by saying no to one of his mad suggestions. *Me*? Are you kidding?

Iluminado heard flapping footsteps. Two parallel bands of light came swimming along the edge of the road like Circe's fluorescent fish. A purple-clad jogger labored past.

Iluminado ran after him. "Did you hear an explosion a minute ago, just before the helicopters went over?"

The runner grunted. If he stopped to inquire into every unusual sound, he might as well *walk*.

"Mind if I run with you?"

"Rather. You would. N't."

But Iluminado coveted that costume. If his enemies had caught up with Pettibone, they were no longer looking for a single-star general in basketball shoes, they were looking for a Specialist Five.

Because of the suitcase, his own stride was a little irregular. The jogger kept sending him irritated glances.

"Yes, running can be painful," Iluminado threw out. "Monotonous. I've found that only one thing helps. That is hypnosis."

"Pain. Live with it. Through the barrier."

Iluminado had battlefield superiority here, but all his weapons seemed somewhat excessive, in the Pentagon megamanner.

"I admire that shirt you're wearing. Will you sell it to me? I'll go as high as one hundred dollars."

He chopped stride, turning partially sideward. This broke the jogger's rhythm completely. He tripped and went down.

"Hurt yourself?" Iluminado asked solicitously, crouching.

Receiving no reply, he brought out his flashlight. He was

shocked by the runner's age. He must be thirty-five at least, much too old for such strenuous exercise. He had struck his head on a post, and seemed stunned.

Presently, wearing a gaudy outfit with an untruthful declaration across the shoulders, BELKNAP STRIDERS, WE RUN FOR FUN, Iluminado jogged into the construction camp. Pickups, the vehicle of choice among road workers, were everywhere. Perhaps he should go back to his original plan? Find someone who would sell him a pickup for some extravagant price, and make his escape before anything worse happened? In six months the Wall would be under way and Iluminado's name would be forgotten. He could go home and learn to live for pleasure, like his father. But having watched the Chiefs performing their mystic handshake, he knew this was no longer his fate. He had too much power in his suitcase, and power, as soldiers have always known, demands to be used.

Although Pettibone had boasted about the lock-on missile's reliability, Iluminado stopped a prudent distance away from the shovel, which the missile had taken into its memory. Unattended, the great creature stood in a shallow pit it had dug for itself. Iluminado circled it cautiously. There was no one nearby.

He took the portable keyboard into the empty cab of a grader, and tapped out the numbers that would bring the tube into firing position. Then, very gingerly, half expecting that in spite of every assurance he would set off the wrong kind of upheaval, he typed W, then slash, then three, and finally: *exclamation point*!

An enormous drum was struck deep within the prohibited zone. There was a kind of harsh sizzle, followed by an extremely ominous, long-drawn-out whisper. A bright object passed overhead, leaving a fiery trail. And suddenly, with another heart-stopping bang, the great shovel bloomed like a rose, passing in an instant from tight bud to full-blown flower. The light where it stood changed from very bright to black, and then back to bright. When this faded, the shovel had vanished completely and the terrible mushroom was rising.

When people with siren-equipped vehicles are taken by sur-

280

prise by anything, the first thing they do is turn on their sirens. The workers' advance guard surged back from the gate. Pickups dashed here and there. Iluminado was moving about, searching the disorderly scene for the commanding officer, "El Super," he would have been called in Colombia. El Supers, even without name tags or special insignia, are instantly recognizable. And a man of precisely this sort, beer can in one fist, phone in the other, came out of the command trailer, a long shed attached by various cables and other umbilical connections to the hot plant, an enormous raised caldron in which the top dressing was being cooked up for the new highway. He was built like a piece of his own heavy equipment, giving the impression that with a blade added in front he would have been able to move dirt.

Iluminado walked up to him and said abruptly, "Don't bother to look for your shovel because it isn't there anymore. Stray round from the firing range, will be the story they tell people. But that was no accident. Strike first is their policy. They expect us to panic and run."

"And who the hell are you?" El Super said, staring.

"From the office. We can go into that later. We have three minutes to prepare for the main force attack. Come, you can see for yourself."

To get the night-vision scope out of his suitcase he had to dig through two layers of currency. The blaze of green persuaded El Super that in spite of the outlandish costume, Iluminado must indeed be a person of consequence.

There was no time to waste, for he could hear the unmistakable sound of a helicopter. Without waiting to see what impression he had made on El Super, he started up the hot-plant ladder. El Super, a lover of melodrama like all his compatriots, was right on his heels.

The caldron, three-quarters full, was being kept warm in case the order arrived to force their way in through the baby carriages. Stepping out on the catwalk, Iluminado rested the scope on the caldron rim and looked for the tanks which were surely out there somewhere, in the dark. There was too much extraneous light. Bringing the laser to bear, he gave the globes over the gate a taste of some real illumination. They fizzed and went dark.

The superintendent was enjoying himself so far. "Hey, some kind of terrific stuff."

Now, through the scope, it was possible to make out clumps of infantrymen on the other side of the fence. Some were smoking, protecting the glowing ends of their cigarettes in cupped hands.

"You will notice the shoulder patches," Iluminado said. "Special assault troops. Extremely bloodthirsty, trained for close work with the bayonet."

A formation of trucks slept peacefully in a meadow. If this was the same convoy that had passed Iluminado earlier, he knew there were soldiers under the tarpaulins. He raked the lead truck with the laser, producing an effusion of men.

"Steel helmets," Iluminado pointed out. "Worn only in combat situations. Next on the schedule, they will put on a sideshow to draw off the TV cameras. Look more to the right."

While El Super had his eye to the scope, Iluminado slid out the keyboard and found and depressed one of the minefield keys, sending up geysers of dirt.

"It's beginning. And you know the United States Army. After they drive us back they will claim they had nothing to do with it. How to explain the casualties, the head injuries and smashed-up machines? A thing that happens often on Interstate highways. Fog. Two vehicles crash, then two more and two more."

Another key. Smoke could be seen rising.

"The weather is clear, but they can make their own fog."

Now for some spectacle. Three taps on the violet key at the end of the second row sent up the flares. They hung in the air, riding an updraft and giving off the same exceptionally pure light that had poured from the helicopters.

A tank column could be seen moving up. A Vietcong patrol in black pajamas and conical hats proceeded at an unhurried pace across an open field, occasionally firing or throwing a dummy grenade. At a crossroads, an armored personnel carrier

282

with a load of very high officers, ribbon accumulations nearly down to their navels, had sideswiped a camouflaged jeep driven by a hatless brigadier general. Who was wearing Converse basketball shoes? Undoubtedly. In the altercation, the lowest ranking officer, in his unhypnotized state a Specialist Five, was getting the worst of it, as was fitting.

"Now this should convince you," Iluminado said, giving El Super the binoculars. "Those men in the jeep are the Joint Chiefs of Staff, in person. Anything as delicate as this, they would want to handle themselves."

"Four fucking stars!" El Super exclaimed. "I think you've got to be right."

"Tonight I'm told we have the law on our side. Tomorrow their lawyers will find a new judge and get a new piece of paper. Continued stalemate. I suggest that we take advantage of the moment, and go in through the fence. Outflank them with payloaders."

"Payloaders against tanks? You're out of your fucking mind."

"No, I don't think so. Take them by surprise, draw circles around them. And if you don't agree," he added, "I shall be obliged to shoot you and take command."

And as though on cue, a helicopter swirled into DOT airspace, came about fast, dropping, and swooped down at them. Iluminado saw gunflashes. Without stopping to latch the suitcase, he gathered it up in both arms and leaped from the catwalk. He landed in a tall pile of sand and slithered down it, reaching the bottom as the gunship came back, almost on a level with the top of the caldron. El Super, caught in the searchlight, was clinging to an upright. There was blood on his khaki shirt.

Briefly, Iluminado was sheltered by the long side of the command trailer. He scrambled along it. When the helicopter came into view he was in among the machines. He crawled under a tall Euclid payloader. When the light passed on, he eased open the door on the far side and slipped into the cab.

The gunship wheeled and came back, fifteen feet or so from the ground, the fierce gale from its rotors kicking up whirlwinds

283

of dust. The powerful light fingered about, searching for Iluminado. They knew he was in there somewhere. The portside gunner was leaning far out, held by his overhead straps, machine-gun barrel erect.

Again, Iluminado was getting the gunship experience from the point of view of the target, and it was a frightening thing. He felt a rising anger. He had been slow to realize what these people were doing out here at Fort Belknap. They were preparing a major intrusion into Iluminado's part of the world, and who gave the *cabrones* the right—

He ran through the list of weapons controlled by his miniature keyboard. Nothing seemed appropriate for getting rid of this malevolent helicopter.

He could follow its movements by the sound. He thought it seemed to fade for an instant. No, it was coming back. Keeping all the way down, he started the engine.

He would have to back out. He selected a fragmentation grenade, the M-67, a twin to the one he had thrown in Cartagena, in the casino garage, and placed it carefully in an upside-down hard hat so it wouldn't roll. He stole a quick look.

The gunship was almost directly behind him, hovering, apparently about to land. He saw other faces inside the cargo space, gun barrels.

This Euclid was the top-of-the-line monster, with twelve forward gears and four in reverse. As the helicopter swung, the gunner was blind for an instant. Iluminado slid in behind the wheel, jammed the gearshift into number three reverse, and came back hard, shifting up almost before the power had reached the wheels. He came around in a very tight pivot, bucket a bit above eye level.

The construction-crew gringo in Colombia who taught Iluminado payloaders had claimed that roughnecks in the oil fields of Texas sometimes used them to chase armadillos. An exaggeration, possibly, but in spite of its great bulk and power, a payloader can be surprisingly agile, giving its operator the feeling that he has over-long arms and unusually massive fists.

The gunship was still turning, its tail down for the landing. The bucket hit well back on the tail. The blow was perfectly placed, and at the moment of impact Iluminado jerked upward so the sharp claws of the bucket tore through the helicopter's skin and put a bad crimp in the tail-rotor drive shaft.

The tail rotor stopped turning. Iluminado had had it explained to him: it was the overhead rotor that propelled the machine, but without the tail rotor pushing against the torque, everything hanging from the mast would spin crazily, out of control. And that was what happened now. The tail came around with such force that the gunner on the outside of the spin was flung out the door, to dangle helplessly at the end of his straps. The soldiers inside were undoubtedly being tumbled about like seeds in a dry gourd. On the third rapid rotation, the pilot managed to touch down. Iluminado's bucket, coming around, struck the tail another powerful blow. He smashed again, amidships, from above. Perhaps, after all, he wouldn't need the grenade.

Workers came running in from all sides. They didn't have to be told who had started the fight. All they needed to know was that a helicopter had angered a payloader, and they identified with the payloader.

One skid had crumpled. Alternating forehands and backhands, Iluminado cuffed the battered and now somewhat pitiful-looking helicopter ahead of him across the hard-packed dirt. One last shove sent it under the caldron. The overhead rotor, still spinning lazily, sheared off the bottom cock and the caldron emptied.

All right! By now, Iluminado imagined, the helicopter soldiers were regretting that they had gone into this murderous line of work. Next!

He pulled a cold beer out of a cooler and popped the top. Lifting it to acknowledge the cheers, he swung out onto the unfinished highway.

Like all payloader cabs, this one functioned as both kitchen and living room. Bottles rolled on the floor. A folded newspaper, the *National Enquirer*, lay on the seat— "I WENT TO A SEX ORGY

IN A UFO"—amid the litter from a fried chicken dinner. Wearing the hard hat, he arrived at the main gate honking. If anybody asked any embarrassing questions, such as who he was and what he was doing here, he would give them the same answer he had given the helicopter, a couple of hard backhands with the bucket.

"We're going in!"

But they weren't going in right this minute, for the baby carriages stood in the way.

George S. Patton, Jr., wherever you are, Iluminado said to himself, wish me well. He tipped the bucket forward and scooped up a baby carriage. He heard a scream.

If he was wrong about this, he knew that he could expect to be hauled from the cab and trampled to death. On the screen in the bunker, he had watched one carriage being prepared with a submachine gun instead of a baby. But was it this one? All baby carriages look somewhat alike.

The workers around him were backpedaling rapidly, disassociating themselves from the crazy man in the yellow hat and the purple costume. At the top of his arc, Iluminado jerked hard, jamming the drop lever forward. The baby carriage flew out, turning over, and everything spilled: the submachine gun first, a baseball bat, a nippled bottle, a box of disposable diapers.

And a baby!

No, thank God, not a baby. It was only a girl doll with pointed breasts and long golden hair. It batted its eyes coyly as it dropped to the pavement, where its head broke apart.

"Payloaders!" Iluminado shouted, coming about. "We go to Pittsburgh!"

He wasn't sure of this destination, but Pittsburgh or wherever, it didn't seem to matter. Drivers ran for their machines. Inside the gate, soldiers were moving up, most of them younger than Iluminado himself.

The major commanding the picket line was phoning for orders, using an outside booth. Iluminado lunged down at him, snatched up the booth in his bucket and sent it rolling away.

He snorted back and forth, as though having trouble restraining a spirited horse, and picked the transmitter off the steering column.

"It is Payloader One calling payloaders! Wink your headlights if you can hear me."

He flashed his own and began getting answers. The first compactors were coming out of the park, large, powerful machines though painfully slow. Iluminado whipped off the purple shirt and waved it like the battle flag of a division of joggers.

"We are attacking! They shot the super, the cowards, a shot from the dark. The last words he spoke were, '*The highway goes through.*' Blow your horns."

He was answered by a concerted blare. The graders were out on the pavement with their blades raised, the fifteen-tons, the dozers and backhoes.

"Bulldozers! Straight through the gate. I want four lanes staked out by sunrise. *¡Atacar!*" The Hispanics in the column would know what he meant, but he translated it for the rest. "Forward!"

Someone sounded four notes. "High, Ways, High, Ways," the horn might have been saying, and it was picked up by the rest.

The baby carriages had scattered, and by the time the bulldozers were ready the gate was blocked by a phalanx of army trucks, standing fender to fender. The dozers advanced three abreast. They struck with a crunch, drew back and slammed in again.

This was only the feint. Ranging back, Iluminado pulled the pavers out of the column. Their crews had been warned that the Fort Belknap fence carried a charge of funny electricity, the kind that will unravel chromosomes. They didn't want to go where he pointed. He positioned two compactors on a downward slope, and the drivers jumped out as the big machines started to roll.

They struck with an eruption of fireworks, taking out a ten-meter section of fence. Iluminado waved in the sand trucks, a new wave of compactors.

Now it was safe to advance, but before he gave the command he turned on his dashboard radio and looked for what his mother, who preferred Mozart, had called epileptic-fit music.

"I want your morning love, baby—"

He opened the transmitter and sent it out to the other machines, with the volume all the way up. It came back from a half hundred receivers, making a pleasant martial commotion.

He called, "Pittsburgh!" and honked: "High, Ways, High, Ways."

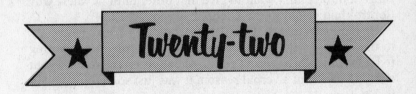

Twenty-two

It was the usual demo crowd, augmented tonight by a contingent of Revolutionary Dames. Wheat had his letter agreement from Hawk-Sisley, and this would be the final briefing of his career. It was also the final demo before the key Senate vote, so he was worrying about all the things that could go wrong.

Isobel Clancy's party swept up in two chartered Minnetonkas, the largest model, the Maxi-Minnie, which sleeps twelve. As the glittering guests thronged onto the escalator to the departure lounge, laughing and flashing their bracelets and fingernails, well aware that they were the most sought-after people in Christendom, Wheat had the terrible feeling that they had come out from Washington for the sole purpose of seeing him fall on his face. He would forget his lines, he would stammer and spit: the standard performer's nightmare.

When the choppers came over prematurely, not only early but *damn* early, he tried to get through to the control bunker. All circuits were jammed. He used the priority interrupt and still got a busy signal, which is the most dispiriting sound you want to hear in a crisis.

The media people had been herded into the monorail. They came reluctantly, for something ugly seemed to be taking shape at the gate. Wheat really ought to get them out of eyewitness range, but he didn't want to give that order until he knew why Control had called in the chopper sweep.

He had been told that the Chiefs would be here, to lend class to the event. They hadn't arrived. Mr. G stormed up, wanting to know why Wheat wasn't getting the show on the road. Wheat couldn't give him a verbal reason, it was just something he felt in his bones.

Mr. G was a bundle of superstitions himself, but he had a low threshold of tolerance for other people's. Several senators looked pointedly at their watches, then pointedly at Wheat. Harry Lord, who had come in the Clancy party, remarked that the Polish Army, too, never managed to get to a war on time. This was a pretty poor excuse for a joke, Wheat thought, but the Revolutionary Dames crowded around him laughed like madwomen.

Don't do it until you can get through to the bunker, Wheat's bones kept warning him. But those hardhats were definitely working themselves up to assault the married officers' picket line, and Wheat had seen them passing around buckets of gravel. And this was distressing to Wheat, because the outdoor unions were fanatically pro–United States, as a rule. Tanks were fanning out to prevent a breakthrough. Tanks against hardhats throwing gravel—if it had to happen, it had to happen, but please, not in front of all these opinion makers.

So, ignoring his instincts, he mashed the button. The car undocked smoothly and glided away on its single rail. Monorails—what a sweet way to travel, amazingly fast, with no sway or vibration. Why can't all trains be like this? Well, they can't, and that is all there is to it.

The Hawk-Sisley airframe division, given the monorail contract, had done its usual superb job, although at a three-hundred-percent cost overrun. Three rows of upholstered banquettes faced an uninterrupted window of tinted glass. Pretty young women costumed as pit girls—in other words, without very much on—moved about taking drink orders. Their eyes and eyelashes were works of folk art. Isobel's guests had tanked up on the way out. Senator Hemlock, celebrating his reunion with Brady, had opened one final bottle of champagne, after which he vowed to go back on the wagon for good. To hell with public appearances; he and the lovely warrant were openly holding hands.

As for the press corps, they had been drinking since lunch. Print people, Wheat didn't know why, seemed to drink more than TV people. More cynical, perhaps.

At the first station, he stepped up briskly, swagger stick tucked under his arm, and explained what they were about to see. His delivery was deliberately undramatic, for the drama was implicit in the situation. These weapons were still under test, and could you be sure they would do what they were designed to do, *every time*?

The minefield lights came up on schedule. One portion of the field had already blown; apparently some poor fool hadn't believed that a skull and crossbones means what it says. The starlings burst from their cages and fluttered about, confused by the lights. Smelling the feast that some kind person had spread out on the ground for them, they came down, to a messy death. Wheat's audience, who detested these dirty, unpleasant creatures because of the way they were defiling the Pentagon, set down their drinks to applaud.

Wheat allowed himself to relax. After all, everything was going to be fine.

New lights came on, revealing a menacing silhouette. This was an exact replica of the T-72, the enemy's main battle tank, a sight to scare babies with. It moved like a runway model, revolving to give the observers a sense of its single great cannon and flanking rockets. You wouldn't want to see a dozen of these things coming at you at once, and everybody in the obs-car knew that the Russians don't just have dozens, they have tens of thousands.

But look! Some five kilometers away, a long missile tube, *ours*, lifted gracefully into the light. As the tank moved, an artificial brain somewhere made the correction and the tube moved with it. On the board over the obs-car window, red lights were burning: LOCKED ON, READY TO FIRE.

Wheat offered the remote control to Shanahan, who declined with a smile.

"I might blow up the wrong thing."

Isobel Clancy asked to be permitted to try. Growling in her hoarse baritone, a sound she used in place of a laugh, she put the tank through its paces, controlling its speed by squeezing more or less hard on the sides of the remote, its direction by turning a dial. It darted one way, cornered, halted, reversed. Every move, they could see, was exactly duplicated by the tube.

Harry Lord took a turn. Suddenly an American tank, a Tarantula, appeared in the light. Wheat's grip on his swagger tightened. What was the imbecile doing? The T-72 continued to dance about, but apparently the Tarantula had broken into the line of sight; the tube was now tracking the wrong tank.

Wheat took back the control. He was tempted to fire anyway, to teach the intruder a lesson, but that wouldn't be right. He had the T-72 circle the Tarantula, zigzagging and bouncing around, until it recaptured the tube's attention.

The Tarantula proceeded offstage and Wheat called on one of the Dames to wind up the ritual. Giggling, she pressed her thumb firmly on the Fire button. They saw the missile emerge from the tube's mouth and describe its slow arc against the sky. Isobel had the remote again, and she squeezed and twirled. The target dodged this way and that, attempting to escape. To no avail.

The missile struck.

When the dust drifted off, the terrifying Russian tank had ceased to exist. Out of the pit where it had stood, a black mushroom sprouted. And a shiver ran through the car, a delicious, nearly erotic tingle. This came perilously close to forbidden ground.

Time for a change of scene. Wheat ordered the car to proceed. It stayed where it was.

Calm on the surface (inside was a different matter), he picked up the phone. A voice told him, "The number you have reached is not a working number. If you believe this announcement to be in error—"

Before he could try again there was a tremendous uproar on their blind side. They had to sit there on the comfortable banquettes, listening to the whine of transmissions, the roar of many powerful engines. Horns hooted in some ghastly code. And there was music, more frightening than the skirling of bagpipes.

> "Your morning love, baby
> Come on down—"

A payloader burst into view, followed by another payloader, another, a whole brigade of payloaders.

Quimby was beside him, scratching his bearded chin with his pipe stem.

"I'll be damned, that's Iluminado."

For simple subjective enjoyment, there has been no recent development in warfare to equal the old-fashioned cavalry charge, mounted men on the gallop with sabers, preferably against foot soldiers. (That is, if you are the one on the horse.)

Iluminado had alerted the computer to be ready to use its microwave zapper. Through the infrared scope, he saw tanks maneuvering to strike the payloader troop on the flank. W Slash Three Exclamation Point, and suddenly their electrical systems ceased to perform. Then the payloaders were on them, giving them hard raps with their buckets, until the tankers leaped out and ran, holding their ears.

The other payloaders went on, looking for more opposition to scatter or crush. But the brief battle seemed to be over. The heavier stuff was coming in through the fence. The surveyors were already positioning their bright little flags.

Iluminado was no longer needed, it seemed. He blinked a good-bye and went looking for further targets of opportunity.

After five minutes' hard driving along unlighted roads, he entered the proving grounds. He was hunting the Chiefs, and somewhere nearby, he knew, the Chiefs were hunting *him*. They must have reached the bunker by now, found its entrance rubble-choked and set off on their way back.

He found them at an intersection. Their personnel carrier had been damaged in the collision with Pettibone and they had changed to Pettibone's jeep.

Brake, downshift. The admiral was standing up trying to make sense of the frivolous directional arrows. "Moscow 3000 m., Blow Job 20 Rubles?"

While they were quarreling about which road to take, the very man they were after was approaching rapidly at the controls of a payloader, bucket all the way down, striking sparks. Fort Belknap was their stamping ground, United States Army property for over two hundred years, and one thing they could reasonably expect not to happen was to be swept up, jeep and all, in a payloader bucket. By the time they realized what was happening, they were all the way up. Iluminado corrected the tilt, unlimbered the laser and played a stream of highly charged particles lightly and rapidly across the back face of the bucket.

"Don't try to jump or I will cut you in two," he announced. "Throw out your weapons."

One came immediately, two more, a pause, then a fourth. There was a strong burning smell. The four sensible chiefs had to wrestle the last gun away from the holdout. When Iluminado saw it fly out, he closed down the laser.

"Now put your hands where I can see them."

Hands began to appear. When he counted ten, two to a chief, he ordered them to hold tight, then did the up-and-down trick with the lifting lever, and the jeep went flying.

He tilted the bucket so they could look into his eyes.

"The Joint Chiefs of Staff," he said, looking from one to the other. "I am the person you have been attempting to kill, so don't expect kindnesses from me, please."

They were trying to stand straight, and this was difficult on the sloping floor of the bucket. In various ways, their starched and usually immaculate uniforms had gone somewhat awry. The admiral's glasses were broken; he was holding them on with one hand. They all had name tags over their ribbons, and

294

the one labeled McArdle, in the middle with his fists on his hips, said bluntly, "I'll tell you this one thing right now, Comrade. We don't give in to blackmail."

They knew he had the laser, but perhaps they didn't know he had everything else? He wheeled and headed into open country, giving them a very rough ride. There were warnings everywhere, telling him to turn back at once, he had strayed onto the approaches to the supersensitive minefield. A *starling* could set off these mines, never mind a payloader weighing a number of tons. Iluminado was worried about many things but not about this, having just pressed the key that switched it all off.

He slewed to a stop. "I have your killer's suitcase. You shouldn't be surprised to hear that he brought many murderous things. Near here is where you planned it to happen, with the little steel barbs. So it would only be simple justice—"

They had drawn closer to each other, perhaps seeing the situation from his point of view for the first time, always a difficult stretch for anyone and especially for a soldier.

"You see," the chairman said, more reasonably, "the blackmail decision was arrived at on the highest security level. It's not just five men's idea, it's policy. Right now you have us at a disadvantage. Well, that's happened before in American history! But if we chicken out now the enemy's going to think he's discovered a character flaw, and he'll keep pushing and pushing, raising the ante. And if we chicken out the next time, the ante will go up again and finally we'll get to the point where the national interest is really at risk and we'll call their bluff and bring about the end of the world, and then we'll have that on our conscience."

"Don't worry about it," another said. "That won't ever happen, because the Russians are the ones who are chicken."

"Every time." (The marine.)

Dear God, Iluminado thought hopelessly.

He tried again. "Let me persuade you that this is not a question of blackmail. It will be easier if you use some different word. You must know by now that there are no guerrillas in or around Cartagena, and you're afraid I will announce this to the world. I've explained to Shanahan that I cannot do so, for personal reasons I don't wish to go into. There is no possibility whatever. Therefore I have turned down his offer of money."

"Well," the admiral said, "it would be nice to think you're telling the truth, but can we afford to take the chance?"

"Draft a statement and sign it," the chairman suggested. "That yes, there was a guerrilla attack. That yes, the commander was Cuban—"

"There have already been too many lies," Iluminado told him. "I have a different proposal. Cancel your foolish Wall."

"*Cancel?*" the chairman whispered, appalled. "*The Wall?*"

"Then no one will care if there were guerrillas or not that night, and you can tell your assassin to forget about me, go assassinate someone else."

They had stiffened, as though about to be photographed. "No way!" the Air Force chief declared emphatically.

"You realize, don't you," Iluminado said, "that where you intend to locate this wall was once Colombian soil? Oh, yes, for one hundred years. Every Colombian child knows the story of the so-called secession. In truth, you stole it from us, to have a place to dig your canal. Now you want to put weapons on it—weapons pointing at us! I cannot allow this thing, do you understand me?"

Another—again the marine—rapped out, "Nuts," the famous World War II response to a request for surrender.

Iluminado saw that they were all in agreement. If they had been speakers of Spanish, he would have tried to reason with them further, but this was too subtle a matter for English, the language of threats and demands.

He consulted Pettibone's crayoned list. After a quick petition to whatever saint looks after those who have never taken a course in computers, he tapped the three red keys in the uppermost row, crosshatched with black as a warning: keep your fingers off these unless you are prepared to suffer the consequences.

The sound, when it reached them, was a thunderous rumble. He had sent up the satellite killer.

The Chiefs watched it climb and dwindle. Its pea brain had been programmed to seek out and destroy a target with certain electronic characteristics, already in a stationary one-hundred-mile orbit. This object, however, had not yet been launched.

A tiny bright dot, it veered and dipped against the constellations, looking in vain. Then there was a sudden small puff of light, a profusion of meteors.

"Another malfunction?" Iluminado said. "Apparently. And I've hardly begun: OURS, THEIRS, on your board in the Pentagon—each time something goes wrong you will lose another few votes. Cancel, until you can get it to work properly. You'll astonish your public. When has anything like it ever happened before?"

"Nuts," the marine general said again, with contempt.

"You can make our job more difficult," the chairman admitted. "But Mirabile will think of something. A few years ago it might have been different but now we've got up off our knees, and people are proud to live in America. When the public hears we've been taken hostage, you'll see such an outpouring of national feeling—"

"A ball game's never over till it's over," the admiral said.

"And not only unreliable and dangerous," Iluminado persisted. "Easily penetrated. If one man can simply walk in and start pushing buttons—"

The chairman interrupted. "I don't buy the lone-gunman theory. Not for one minute. You had help. The KGB's full resources, to begin at the beginning. They deliberately set up that Cartagena affair to make us look like fools—"

"To make you look like fools," Iluminado repeated, again looking at each in turn.

"We have a reliable source, very high in the Colombian government, who tells us you were sent under Counter Coup cover to steal the W-3 secrets. Can you deny that? You've got those secrets right there in that suitcase. And now you suggest that to save our lives we let you walk away with all that material—"

"You can have it back as soon as I'm finished with it."

"You mean after you've memorized it! We've read the printout on you. The Jesuits say you were one of the smartest students who ever went to their school."

In another situation, Iluminado would have been glad to hear this; they hadn't said anything to him at the time.

"No deals!" another chief said. "We haven't begun to fight. You don't know the United States Senate."

"Good Lord," McArdle said, "we don't claim to be perfect. Maybe we didn't blow up the right satellite, but we blew up *something*. When you're operating at the cutting edge of technology there's no such thing as absolute certainty. Our friends on the committees understand that. They know we'll be back for a supplemental next fiscal year, to take out the bugs. You're missing the point."

"And what is the point?" Iluminado asked. "I am eager to hear."

"The point is to spend! To spend credibly! Listen, the Russkies have to match us dollar for dollar, or admit to the world that they're a second-class power. And their problem is, they can't really afford it."

The others' spirits had picked up considerably. Iluminado had been trying to keep their personalities separate but they kept running together. The voices overlapped:

"We'll potlatch them into Chapter Eleven."

"It's how we show our resolve. Our allies in NATO look at those dollar figures and they understand that we mean it."

"The way we keep score."

"The size of the appropriation! That's how history judges every generation of Chiefs."

"Contracts and jobs. Contracts and jobs. How do you think we finance our elections?"

"Take your average American citizen," McArdle was saying. "If we put the Pentagon budget on referendum, they wouldn't give us a dime. They want that money for themselves! For their cars and their summer vacations! That's why we've got to come in with this spectacular stuff, something new every year—but hell, I can see you don't appreciate what I'm saying. I've never had a whole heck of a lot of success explaining the American system to a foreigner."

Iluminado had heard enough. He threw the payloader into

gear and gave the lift lever a yank, tumbling his high-level prisoners into a five-man embrace. He was soon up to speed, making no effort to avoid bumps or depressions. If he totaled the payloader and they all perished, fine. Even Patton, with his flamboyant career, ended as a humdrum highway statistic.

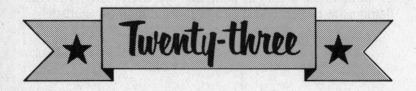

Twenty-three

All through the awful afternoon, Hemlock had been sure that his dear girl was being raped, again and again, by the insatiable Colombian captain. He had watched Iluminado check the terrain that morning: the perfect breasts with their nipples at perpetual attention, the long sweet curve of the belly, the ferny hillock where everything came together. A Latin, he wouldn't even consider it rape, probably! He would believe he was doing her a favor.

And then the miracle. There she was waiting at Belknap, with a few smudges and scratches, a heel off one shoe—but alive!

They shed tears together. It didn't matter to Hemlock that people were watching, though crying in front of strangers is one of the worst things an American politician can do.

He was almost afraid to say it. "Did he—"

"No, thank God," she whispered. "There wasn't time."

Hemlock called for champagne. He should be working the obs-car aisles on behalf of W-3, but that would have to wait. For now, he and Brady sat side by side on the middle banquette and he was enormously happy. Their hands were together, in full view of the media. He knew that his enemies, who were also the Pentagon's enemies and therefore the country's enemies, would circulate rumors, but if he couldn't hold hands with the only woman he had ever been able to love, what had it all been for?

Something had happened to the monorail power. The lights were down to half strength. Hemlock was a trifle annoyed because with so many fence sitters present everything ought to be perfect, but electricity has its own reasons.

The cocktail girls continued to hustle the product. In the darkness a battery of 155s unexpectedly opened fire. To be precise, as they weren't using real ammo on this one, there was a loud noise and out of each howitzer's mouth came a long paper tongue, an effect copied from New Year's Eve party favors. This was another annoyance—the howitzers were supposed to be part of the finish, to demonstrate acoustical targeting, harass-and-interdict fire set off by the merest whisper in Spanish. And then the satellite killer went up. Hey, Hemlock thought, what's going on?

Some kind of bulky vehicle was approaching across open country. Only headlights at first, then an ungainly shape, shimmering like a desert mirage, then color: a yellow payloader.

Hemlock squinted under his hand. *The Chiefs!*

They were disheveled, without dignity. Two were hatless. Admiral Green—or Brown, which was it?—had lost his glasses, and his face looked less than half finished. It was a terrible tableau for Hemlock, who worshiped these men. Well, not the men, in fact they were nonentities, much like Hemlock himself, but he worshiped the symbol.

He called for binoculars. For a moment, everything trembled. He made a tripod with his elbows on knees, and the driver's face came into focus.

The rapist! (For Hemlock hadn't quite believed Brady's disavowal. How much time does it take, after all?)

Wheat, an ice cube as usual, was huddling with Mirabile. Hemlock sent him a look he couldn't ignore.

"Where are the tanks, Wheat?"

"Engines won't start, sir. I think we have to assume that he's taken control of the full W-3 capability. Sharpshooters are moving up. A minimum of eight minutes to get in position."

"And in eight minutes he can slaughter a considerable number of folks. What's he want?"

"Unconditional surrender, I believe, sir."

Brady, beside him, said hesitantly, "Diz, it didn't seem to me—"

Hemlock patted her hand, telling her in the fondest possible way to shut up for a minute. This was the Patty Hearst syndrome, of course, where the captive identifies with the captor, something which is more likely to happen when the captor is young and dashing in some exotic way.

"Does Mirabile have any bright ideas?"

"His advice is to stall, sir. The guy has five major hostages. If he asks for an airplane, let him have it, but plant a bomb in the tail so he'll blow up over water."

"Sacrificing the Chiefs?"

"Cross that bridge when we come to it, sir. The important thing right now is to keep those W-3 specs out of unfriendly hands."

The payloader prowled back and forth, facing the window. Through the binoculars, Hemlock saw the eyes of a fanatic. A desperate enemy—if he thought it would advance his cause, he would snuff out the Chiefs as though slapping five troublesome mosquitoes.

And something unfamiliar began to happen to Hemlock. He began to feel hatred. Senators are not known for their feelings, having had to cork the ordinary human reactions in the interests of reelection. Whatever this Iluminado Castillo's political beliefs, there was one thing he wasn't. He wasn't *blah*.

"Wheat," Hemlock said quietly, "rustle me up a side arm."

"*Sir?*"

"I don't know about you hombres, but I can't sit here like a bump on a log witnessing the humiliation of the Joint Chiefs of Staff. Mr. G carries a thirty-eight."

Both Brady and Wheat said no, emphatically.

"I'm the only one who can pull it off," Hemlock told them.

"He won't let anybody else near him. We had a good chat this morning. I could tell that he liked me."

They continued to protest. He understood what they were trying to say, and it made him smile. They thought that because he'd had a few drinks the kid would be able to outdraw him. But the sight of the Joint Chiefs huddled helplessly in the bucket had shocked him totally sober. When Hemlock made up his mind that it was his duty to do something, get out of his way! Grit and determination, muleheadedness if you will—these were the qualities that had carried Another Eight Billion from scoutmaster to mayor, to congressman, to senator, to possible secretary of defense, perhaps even—but better say nothing about this even under your breath.

"You mustn't, you mustn't," Brady was saying.

"It's something I have to do if I want to go on living with myself."

Lines spoken by generations of film heroines came to her lips. Hemlock continued to smile and shake his head. He was going to put a bullet between those fanatical eyes, and then he was going to take Brady to her new apartment in the Watergate and claim his reward.

He buttoned the pistol inside his shirt. Brady was hanging onto his arm, pleading with him to leave it to the military, whose business it was (and what a mess *they* had made of it, right?). Wheat pretended he could see the sharpshooters taking their positions. But Mr. G told him gruffly, Go ahead shoot the mother, but make it a good one so he wouldn't have a chance to play any more tunes on the W-3 keyboard.

Hemlock freed himself gently from Brady's grasp. He had always wondered about courage, how he would stand up under fire, and he was delighted to find that he was entirely without fear. He felt healthy and fit.

There was an emergency hatch behind the bar. The car was twenty feet from the ground, not much of a drop for a pole-vaulter, but there was no foam rubber down there to break Hemlock's fall. Using a lemon-peel knife supplied by the barman, he cut several long strips of carpet and knotted them loosely together.

Brady was crying. "Diz, you're a stubborn old mountain rat—"

He took her in his arms and exacted a real kiss, with a meeting of tongues. The barman opened the hatch and let down the carpet.

"Not to worry," Hemlock told everybody.

A little clumsily because he didn't claim to be much of a trapeze artist, he lowered himself.

It was an accident, everybody agreed later. Nothing inherently wrong with the design, just a mysterious atmospheric disturbance that sent ghost clues into the sensing system. The people sniffer, which had worked so well on the Ho Chi Minh trail and in all previous exercises, was programmed to react, like a bloodhound, to particular smells. Specifically, within W-3, to the funky smell of dark-skinned, chili-eating peoples. For this reason, troops handling the Porcupine components were all white Anglo-Saxons or North German–Scandinavians. To be on the safe side, they bathed frequently, sudsing up well with brown soap, and then sloshed on the deodorants.

Diz Hemlock's whiteness went all the way back. He took a morning and often an evening shower. Was it a whiff of something Brady picked up from Iluminado and then passed on to Hemlock in that final embrace? In any event, the sensors blew the incoming data completely, tripped the triggering mechanism, and Porcupine found him.

The group in Iluminado's bucket was still exchanging sports wisdom and declaring that Joint Chiefs never give in to blackmail.

Iluminado said sharply, "Now be quiet and listen. Here we have deadlock, trench warfare, nothing to do but grind back and forth or surrender. Be quiet, I tell you. I've heard it said that it is businessmen who rule your country, not Congress or the generals. Is this true?"

"You're joking," McArdle said.

"Tell me about an airplane called the John Wayne."

"Named after one of our great Americans," the Air Force general said. "Aggressive. Can do. Beautiful fighting aircraft."

"The Piranha?"

"Another damn fine flying machine. I recommend them both without reservation."

"I heard someone say that Circe was to be built by Senator Shanahan's firm. And this Wall? By Mr. Sam Green?"

They looked at him with suspicion.

"I don't know about Shanahan, but Mr. G will back us up, don't worry," McArdle said.

Iluminado returned his attention to the keyboard. On command, distant floodlights came on, and the long missile tube rose into view. It had used one of its rounds on the shovel, a second on the look-alike Russian tank. It had one missile left.

He gave it a new target. It came around smartly and its wide-open mouth lowered to gape at the lighted car, carrying so many important persons that if it chose to speak a third time, there wouldn't be room on the front page for all the obituaries.

Isobel Clancy was using the binoculars.

"Looks like another intelligence boo-boo," she announced in her carrying baritone. "That's a cute-looking boy, but Iluminado Castillo he's not. And that can be easily checked, because the real Iluminado Castillo is one of my dinner guests."

A middle-aged gentleman with a cavalryman's mustache was leaning against the bar. Hearing his name mentioned, he lifted his glass in an ironic salute.

"Present. Accounted for."

Irony would be the theme of this trip, Castillo had decided. Certainly it had got off to an ironic start with the delightful evening in Bogotá. The truth was, he was a little ashamed of himself for having let the beautiful Señora Alvarez delay his departure. What he should have said, what he *would* have said if he had been a totally different person, would have been, "My dear Gabby, dinner? How I would love it. But it's Nado, you see, I promised to ride up to Washington with him. He's afraid he will be laughed at for his inexperience. It's a father's duty—"

And yet to be realistic, when had he let fatherly duties keep him away from a party? That was the man he was, take him or leave him! Nado had the good genes, the right instincts. He would be better off in the long run if he was made to stand on his own two feet.

A full twenty-four hours late arriving in Washington, he found Isobel Clancy's invitation waiting at his hotel. Would he come to her Taurus dinner? He had snoozed on the plane, and "of course" was the only possible answer. Isobel gave fabulous parties. Who else would think of serving a movable feast in a recreational vehicle?

A gnarled stump of a man, under a cowboy hat that had seen many changes of weather, was peering up at him from less than a half foot away.

"I don't believe this. Iluminado Castillo?"

This must be Sam Green, the legendary Mr. G of Hawk-Sisley. Having been impressed over and over with the confidentiality of the mission, Castillo took the little man to the far end of the car and urged him to lower his voice.

"That prick Duffy, I guess he fucked up again," Mr. G said in a hoarse whisper. "I thought there was something screwy when the kid turned down that great broad. Redhead, six feet one in heels. You'll be crazy about her. Listen, I've got to go to the can. Haven't had a movement all day. How's one million six strike you?"

To cover his surprise, Castillo used the ironic eyebrow-lift. The colonels had been hoping for a million and a half, maximum, and they would settle for less.

"One seven five," Mr. G said, misinterpreting the eyebrow, "because my belly is griping me. Deal?"

More and more dazzled by the fast pace of the negotiation, Castillo didn't know how to respond. And that proved to be the perfect response. The price rose to one nine, to two. There the bargain was struck. He was wondering: did he have the stomach to pocket that extra half million? No, he decided regretfully, probably not.

A bearded civilian in an excellent jacket, which Castillo had already admired, had noticed that his glass was empty and brought him another Campari-gin.

"If you're Iluminado Castillo, who's that driving the pay-loader?"

Payloader? Castillo fished out his glasses, which he hated to wear. He had seen the payloaders pass in review, but he had assumed, without worrying too much about it, that this had been laid on as part of the entertainment.

Generals in a payloader bucket? Castillo had learned not to be surprised by North Americans, but this was truthfully a little surprising. An admiral? And *Nado*? Under the yellow hat, bare-chested, that was definitely who it was, and the boy looked mad enough to eat those high officers raw, without salt or pepper.

Something was vibrating, Castillo realized now; there was a strange kind of juice in the air. Even the cocktail girls had extinguished their smiles. Isobel, very pale, was fingering the lift scars under her hair. Was Nado in some kind of trouble? He had needed a father's guidance, and what had the father been doing? Screwing around, listening to Cole Porter tapes.

The payloader came about, and father and son looked at each other, or so it seemed to the older Castillo. He interpreted the look as saying, "I have important fish in my bucket. These are life-and-death matters, too heavy for you, old man. You got me into this but it is my affair now."

The boy had grown up in thirty-six hours!

Since his previous visit, Castillo had been affecting the loose-jointed cool of black North American basketball players, the easy locutions, the wonderful handshakes. He lifted a shoulder and opened his wrists.

"That is Iluminado Castillo in the payloader. I? Well—" he said to Mr. G with the shrug, "I thought it was worth trying."

The payloader arrived at the observation car at the end of a long controlled skid. At Iluminado's signal the door slid open. A jerk on the lifting lever, and the Chiefs ended on the floor of the car like a loose throw of jackstraws.

"Shanahan!" Iluminado cried. "Mr. Sam Green! Into the bucket!"

At one time he had mistaken these two for homosexuals. He knew now that he had been wrong about that. Fearless in conversation, they nevertheless didn't want to get into Iluminado's bucket, and he had to give the side of the car one or two bangs. When Shanahan came out empty-handed, Iluminado sent him back for the additional cash which Doris had surely advised him to bring.

Mr. G, meanwhile, had made sure that several thicknesses of people were between him and the door. "Not getting into any payloader bucket with *that* sidewinder. What do you think I am, crazy?"

To the surprise of all, the unflappable Colonel Wheat hit his prospective employer with the swagger.

"Get in."

But Mr. G still refused. Iluminado received help from an unexpected source. To his surprise, his own father emerged from the crowd, took the smaller man by the scruff of the neck and the seat of the pants and walked him into the bucket. The rough handling had loosened Mr. G's grip on the flight bag he had been carrying all day, and he had lost his big hat. Iluminado's father swept them both up and threw them in after him.

Iluminado backed off and drove rapidly away. Hearing noises from the bucket, he stopped and adjusted the tilt so he could see what was happening. His two passengers were wrapped in each other's arms, and this was definitely not a homosexual embrace. Shanahan was younger and stronger, but Mr. G was a dirtier fighter. Given another moment, he would have had one of the senator's eyes.

Iluminado applied laser heat to the bucket until they pulled apart.

"There will be time for that later. First to get business out of the way. Colombia must have up-to-date airplanes, it seems, or people will think we are only a banana republic. I don't quite remember. How many planes did we order?"

"Forty," Mr. G told him.

308

"I have decided," Iluminado said, "to recommend the John Wayne. I don't see the difference myself but I like the saleswoman better."

"That plane is a widow maker!" Mr. G shouted. "A Mach Two coffin! You'll regret this, Lit Up! It's throwing your money down the toilet!"

"But your Joint Chiefs have explained it to me. The point is not how long the wings will stay on the airplane. The point is to spend. I'm sure some United States bank will be glad to lend us the money. But we've argued too long about this. Don't start wrestling again. I'll take twenty-five of each."

"Half and half!" Mr. G cried indignantly. "That's no kind of deal! The Shanahans have never done a penny's worth of business north of the bulge."

"But this is the year that will change. You ordered my death, and that is your punishment. Now hand me the money."

The senator and the businessman both tried to speak at once.

"I know, you brought more than you expected to pay," Iluminado said. "Please stop thinking of me as a rug to be auctioned off. Look on this as a mugging. A mugger takes everything. But you can keep whatever you have in your pockets, for taxi fare."

"Can you deliver your junta?" Mr. G said after a moment, pronouncing it with a *j*.

"I believe so, if you brought enough money."

The two men in the bucket, deadly competitors for so long, measured each other.

"Does your daddy let you wipe your own ass?" Mr. G wanted to know.

"Never till now," Shanahan said pleasantly, "but now may be a good time to start. What the hell, G—we can pass it through. At the count of three."

He counted and threw his bag. Mr. G was unable to let go of his, and Shanahan had to chop it out of his hand.

"Next," Iluminado said, "you will have to forget this Wall in the jungle. It will never be built. We don't want that gringo nonsense so close to our border. One of these five old men I have had in my bucket kept saying 'Nuts.' I think what he meant by it—if he does something sensible his enemies will think he is afraid of them. Well, I can be equally stubborn, and equally foolish if necessary. Latin Americans were the inventors of macho. You have borrowed our word for it. So I say to you, Nuts. If you must build some kind of wall, build it on your own property."

"They've been R-and-D'ing that thing for years," Shanahan said. "You won't get them to dump it in ten minutes."

"But ten minutes," Iluminado announced coldly, "is the amount of time I am willing to allow them. The point is to spend? You two will be partners in the Colombian contract. Think of something else, very expensive, that you can manufacture together."

"I've been saying all along," Shanahan said slowly, "a wall—it's too passive, G. Doesn't catch the mood of the country. And Circe. I went along with it, I didn't have much of a choice, did I, but a *jellyfish*, for Christ's sake—it strikes the wrong note. Everything's defense, defense nowadays, Department of Defense, sit on our ass, let the other guy make the first move. Let's *be* a little macho for a change. We've got the tonnage, we've got the accuracy, we've got the delivery system, the only question is, where do we base it?"

"Don't look at me," Mr. G said. "I don't know shit about all that first-strike, first-use counterforce countervalue equivalent throw-weight shit. The difference with me is, I'm willing to admit it."

The helicopters were overhead, with their horrible lights. Iluminado had turned on the radioactive warnings: CONTAMINATED AREA. DO NOT LAND.

Shanahan was massaging his forehead, using the big shoulder muscles and all ten fingertips. But no matter how hard he massaged, he was unable to rub up an idea. They would have to fall back on the experts. Luckily one of the country's foremost strategic thinkers was only a short distance away, Michael Mirabile. But somebody would have to pay him, Shanahan said, looking at Iluminado, because this was one mercenary bastard.

He would want cash in advance. Shanahan and Mr. G, having just been mugged, were temporarily penniless.

"If he wishes to live," Iluminado said, bringing the payloader around, "he will do this thinking for us for nothing."

But having suspected that they might be coming for him, Mirabile had holed up in the lavatory. He was dragged out and forced to enter the bucket. So it was this unprepossessing fellow, Iluminado thought, who was the architect of the various kill-Iluminado scenarios. Iluminado gave him a bounce or two before letting Shanahan outline the problem.

He could be seen to begin to think—with Mirabile never a pretty process. Veins throbbed in his temples, his glasses almost seemed to fog over. There wasn't much time. Iluminado thought he heard helicopters, and the pilots might not have been warned that if they attempted to napalm or door-gun or defoliate or otherwise interfere with Iluminado, all those in the monorail would die.

Mirabile continued to strain for the needed idea. He was dramatizing a little, Iluminado thought, and to hurry the process he gave the bucket a touch with the laser.

"Got it!" Mirabile said hastily. "How about helter skelter dispersal? MIRVed RVs on the Interstate. Restless, incessant movement. Call it hardened mobility. A real consensual system, Senator—Am Tex contributes the punch, Hawk-Sisley the vehicle. And totally noncontroversial. We step on nobody's toes. I don't have an ounce of vanity in my makeup, but give credit where credit is due, gentlemen. This one is a *pearl*."

Both Mr. G and Shanahan seemed to agree with the thinker's assessment.

"Why didn't *we* think of that?"

"By the balls, Mike."

However, Mirabile added, talking the Chiefs into it might be more of a problem. Damn the torpedoes, only one life to give for my country, fight it out on this line if it takes all summer, live in fame go down in flame—they grew up on such sayings.

"Try," Iluminado said coldly.

LOCKED ON, READY TO FIRE— The letters throbbed with new urgency. For three months Wheat had conducted these twice-a-week briefings. Other systems had faltered occasionally, but the missile had never missed. It was overengineered for its mission. It didn't just cripple, it pulverized. Out in the pay-loader, Wheat was sure, the crazy Hispanic had already fed three-quarters of the firing command into the computer, the W, the slash, the three. The only thing lacking was the exclamation point at the end.

Mirabile did the talking at first, then Shanahan took over, then Mr. G. After only a moment Mr. G was stamping on his hat, waving his fist under McArdle's nose, calling him bunkhouse names. The chairman went on shaking his head. Here they'd been telling everybody for months that without this Wall the nation's underbelly would be dangerously exposed. Now they should call a press conference and take it all back? They would look like absolute nitwits.

Without warning, the car moved. Wheat felt a flash of hope, but their enemy was merely reminding them of how matters stood. As the car moved, the tube also moved. When the car stopped, the tube stopped. Ironic; when you wanted something to fail, that was the time it worked.

The Chiefs were still adamant. Shanahan tried taking them one by one for hands-on persuasion. Mr. G brought out his checkbook. What was their favorite charity? No way! The Guard dies but never surrenders. The spic had to be bluffing.

And as though Iluminado, studying their changes of expression through binoculars, had been able to read their minds, he drove slowly past. Bluffing? Let them look into his eyes and decide.

Wheat gripped the swagger stick with both hands, trying to recover his calm. It is the briefer's job to reduce the terror and confusion of combat to a comprehensible pattern. You may not have the least idea where your people actually are, but still you have to pretend; you give them their usual designations and put them on the board or the battle-control table so the commander, for his part, can pretend he is still in control. Good briefers have answers for everything. This is only possible because the briefing room, with its arrows and numbers and little flags, is physically removed from the battlefield. Here the battlefield was right outside the long picture window, and Wheat was able to look death in its single, wide-open, unblinking eye.

Panic: it is never far beneath the surface of nuclear politics. Isobel Clancy, who had had such fun playing with the Soviet tank, was now the target herself, and it was much less enjoyable. A believer in the tarot deck and astrological signs, she was checking her amulets, the copper bracelet against bone decay, a diamond and emerald shamrock, a gold eye from Tibet. A cocktail girl turned three times and spat through her fist. Shanahan, known for his sophisticated polling techniques and computerized mailings, had taken a Saint Christopher medal from beneath his Paul Stuart shirt. The Revolutionary Dames had their flags, Mirabile his pocket calculator, on which he added and subtracted meaningless sums. General Thorkill stroked the rabbit's foot that had carried him safely through many a dog-fight over Korea. Hal Amsterdam had been given gold cuff links for his birthday. His sweeps ratings were in his left cuff, his market share in his right; he was fingering these.

For this was stalemate, a small replica of the more important one between the two superpowers. Destruction was mutually assured. If your nukes fly, mine fly, and among other disastrous consequences, winter will arrive a bit early that year.

Infantrymen were now scattered about the slope, crouching behind pine stumps in their dappled uniforms, examining Iluminado through the sights of their scoped rifles. Iluminado had surely seen them. He was bending well forward, his hands in the light, fingers grazing the keyboard. Even a perfect shot, killing him instantly, would drop his finger onto the exclamation point, and if by some unlucky chance he twitched prematurely, he would regret that move for the rest of his life, a matter of seconds.

Two minutes left. Wheat's swagger snapped under the pressure.

Iluminado could see that the Chiefs, for what they must feel were sensible reasons, were really not going to give in to blackmail, for if they did, to preserve their own skins, the enemy would test them again, then yet again, each time on a more serious level, until finally—

Impulsively the marine general turned toward the chairman and put out his hand. The others clamped on, in the five-man handshake. Five is a favorite number among mystics, and it struck Iluminado all at once that in one way or another, these *civilizados*, these presumably rational people, were all doing magic.

Mr. G, his eyes shut tight, was straining to levitate. Warrant Officer Brady, a Catholic, probably, had her hands clasped and her heels tucked up in the serenity straddle, praying to more than one god. There was the Cat, who had more reason than most to know what destructive power Iluminado had under his fingertips. His lips were pursed in blowing position; the tune in his head was undoubtedly melancholy. Iluminado's father had reached out to rub the knuckles of his dice hand against Doris's nipple, an old crapshooter's hex. As for Doris, she was carrying pills to her mouth, as though to persuade the warhead to pass her by and strike instead the two-pack-a-day smokers, the eaters of fatty snacks. Quimby, using a camera only half as long as his thumb, was recording it all. He wouldn't be blown up, surely, while he had undeveloped film in his camera? Colonel Wheat, so unemotional usually, had broken his swagger stick. A look of extreme revulsion distorting his handsome features, he pointed the pieces at the missile tube in the form of a cross. And there on the seat beside Iluminado headlines glared up at him: miracle deathbed recoveries, UFO orgies, a woman who had given birth to a mouse.

Gringos!

And seeing his father doing his black crapshooter imitation, Iluminado remembered the synthetic Indian village the Yankees had built on the Río de Oro, the fertility rite, the witch doctor's bone dance. His father had handled the political permissions. In fact he was the one who suggested hanging crutches and hearing aids on the bushes around the dancing ground, and seeding the forest litter with discarded Anacin and Tylenol bottles. The Yankee tourists had swallowed it all, with enthusiasm.

The dashboard radio was still muttering softly. Iluminado turned it up. They liked magic so much? He would show them some magic.

He worked for a moment from Pettibone's list, putting new commands into the computer. Ten minutes, he had told them. The final minute was ticking away.

A lone American tank approached, not realizing that it had entered the zone controlled from the payloader. Fine. Iluminado needed covering fire, for this was a dangerous thing he had decided to do.

He let go the heat-seeking fifties. They rushed at the intruding tank and put out its headlight, causing it to swerve into the path of an advancing Red Army patrol. An interesting collision ensued. Dummies went flying. Iluminado started a highway flare. Reaching up to the roof, he laid out his props. He went into the Cat's suitcase for the makeup kit. Two vivid smears of red across his cheekbones were all he had time for. Before leaving the cab he did a bit of remembered magic himself. For the first minute or so, he was the one who would be needing supernatural protection.

"Virgin Mother, blow smoke into the riflemen's eyes." He crossed himself sketchily and threw a smoke grenade. "Confuse them, make them hesitate."

He put the bucket on lift. As it rose he stepped onto its lip and it carried him to the roof.

When the smoke cleared, the sharpshooters saw him out in the open, but still holding the keyboard. He scaled his yellow hat into the darkness.

"I cannot murder so many!"

With the radio roaring beneath him, he knew they wouldn't be able to hear him inside the sealed car, but if he did it broadly enough, someone would surely grasp the idea.

"This has gone far enough. We must step backward and find

a solution. But something has happened that I don't understand. I have asked too much of the computer. The missile remains locked. I cannot unlock it. I have drawn closer, you see, and I, too, am now part of the target. We are one keystroke away from total erasure. Don't try to jump, for Porcupine, too, as you saw, has gone crazy. The circuits are sparking and spitting. Wait. Let me try—"

And taking up the flare, he began the dance.

There was nothing pretty about the music this station sent into the world. All it had was the beat and the energy. Iluminado could feel the beat deep in his brain.

> "Streets full on a hot night
> Whiskey fight in the neon light
> On a hot night
> Hot night in the city—"

Inside the car, the Chiefs were still deeply involved in their mystic handshake. The others watched Iluminado with what might be the beginnings of hope. He was the only thing that stood between them and the nuclear mushroom. The Chiefs, in their five-sided ivory tower, had made a typical twentieth-century mistake. They had thought they could base a computer-driven, super-high-tech system in a primitive rain forest, where it would be most vulnerable to dampness and mildew and all kinds of extrasensory interference. There were strange things out there in the jungle, strange reversals and silences. Iluminado was not, as they had been led to believe, an enemy agent, a spy from the evil empire. He had come up from the rain forest, at the risk of his own life, to point out their foolishness.

That was the gist, and it seemed to be getting across. Wheat lowered his improvised crucifix, Quimby his camera. Mr. G's gnarled body lost some of its tension.

> "Honey hug me it's a hot night—"

Unzipping the flight bags, Iluminado sent a cascade of packaged currency into the bucket. Packages broke, and those in

316

the car could see that the bills fluttering downward like butterflies were hundreds—the true United States currency, which all the world craves. Using his flare, he touched off the expensive bonfire.

Everyone had noticed that Shanahan and Mr. G, on their return from the payloader, had left their flight bags behind. It was obvious what kind of transaction had taken place: Iluminado had been bribed to call off his counterdemo. And a glance at the two money-men showed that this surmise was correct.

Iluminado had taken the money; who wouldn't? But tampered with one time too often, W-3 had gone out of control. It wanted blood. Wanted it now, not at some undetermined time in the future. To propitiate the gods of the microchips, who were perhaps also (who knew?) the gods of the rain forest, he was destroying the bribe. Green scraps swirled up to sting his naked shoulders and chest. He shook them out of his hair.

> "Hot to the touch on a hot night
> Sizzle and steam on a hot night—"

Then he was dancing again. It was a wild performance, with something for everybody. As he whirled and leaped, he punched keys, being very careful to stay at the far end of the keyboard from the exclamation point. Three-stage rockets rose and blossomed, with sudden bangs. Howitzer tongues darted out and curled back. More starlings fluttered down to be blown to bits. High overhead, the Piranha and the John Wayne, their pilots unaware of the deal that had been struck by Shanahan and Mr. G in the payloader, stunted and swooped. Two helicopters came up from the east, towing a flag as large as a football field. Innocent-looking but sinister campesinos, mullahs with bundles of dynamite, proceeded serenely on flatcars amid the smoke and fiery effects. They fired their assault rifles, got rid of their dynamite and were cut down by swarms of flechettes.

Through it all, the same American tank continued to blunder about, nobody's friend.

Still the tube remained locked on the car.

317

As the fire flickered down, Iluminado knelt and reset the keyboard. Time now for the real magic.

He came back up with a leg bone from the fried chicken dinner. The Río de Oro witch doctor had used a much larger bone to effect his remarkable cures, but this one would have to do.

He raised it over his head. All his strength, plus some powerful rain forest magic, flowed up his arm and into the bone. The bone seemed to become denser, charged, almost too heavy to hold. If those in the car had looked closely they could have seen that he wasn't relying entirely on magic; he was also pressing keys, telling the tube to forget what he had said some minutes earlier, he had changed the target again.

He pointed the bone at the tube, as Wheat had pointed his crucifix. Slowly, the knotting of deltoids and triceps showing that the bone was putting up considerable resistance, he lifted.

And the terrible mouth came up, up, locking finally on the absolute vertical.

"Oh, baby, so hot, so hot—"

And now, at last, the exclamation point. The thing understood that Iluminado had told it to destroy itself, and that went against every program. The keyboard trembled violently. Was he sure, was he one hundred percent *sure* that this was what he wanted?

He did the sequence again, no longer bothering to hide his movements from the watchers in the car. W. /. 3. !!!!

With enormous reluctance, the missile flew. It rose, did a sudden reverse, and cleaved its own trail coming down.

Flash. Concussion.

★ Twenty-four ★

"So this is what everybody talks about all the time," Iluminado said sleepily.

"So nice," Doris murmured.

"It was that way for you as well?"

The flesh around Doris's injured eye had turned the same shade of purple as the jogging pants, which had been hastily discarded and now lay in a sweaty heap on the hotel carpet. She rolled toward him with a contented sigh, fitting her forehead into the hollow of his shoulder.

"No," he insisted. "I truly wish to know, in order not to settle for less. This will be my last stupid question."

But the self-sufficient young woman, so forthcoming on all other matters, refused to talk about this, leading Iluminado to believe that she, too, had found it extraordinary.

In every way it had been a continuation of the dance on the roof of the payloader. Iluminado's last move before he collapsed had been to fling the keyboard into the grass. After all the frightening things they had witnessed, no one inside the car wanted to touch the stop-and-start button. Iluminado may have slept briefly. The earth shook—an airplane engine and bits

319

of a wing had landed amid the pine stumps—and he raised his head, dazed. Had any of this really happened, he wondered, had he changed the flight path of the missile with a *bone*? No, he answered himself, of course not. (On the other hand, maybe.)

He stood aside and declined to do anything to help. A soldier was found who knew payloaders. He off-loaded the crowd. The barman came last, bringing champagne. More bangs followed as the bottles were opened, and these proved to be the last of the night. Harry Lord grabbed a fuming bottle and doused some of the Dames, the old victory ritual.

The cocktail girls were busy around Iluminado. Wanting something tangible to recall the occasion, one of them dampened a cocktail napkin in the sweat from his flanks. Isobel Clancy, speaking in tongues, fastened herself on him, and had to be pried off, a limb at a time. His father approached, palm outturned for the ghetto handshake. They exchanged a look.

"Papa, there are some things I would like you to do."

Corks and flashbulbs continued to pop. The radiation warnings had shorted out and the Hueys now decided that it was safe to come down.

The tough helicopter troops broke Iluminado out of the crowd. The Chiefs, needing privacy to decide just what it was they had seen, rode back by themselves. The news flew ahead of them and a disorderly media mob was waiting to greet them in Washington.

From the Chiefs, who still hadn't agreed on an attitude, they got No Comment and some soldierly abuse. From Iluminado, even less. They followed him to his hotel and upstairs to his room. He had to put on the look he had recently learned, the look of a man who has had the Joint Chiefs of Staff in his bucket, before they would leave him alone. He and Doris fell into bed with the door double-locked, the telephone silenced, Do Not Disturb on the outside knob.

Almost at once, a quivering began, a clenching and calling out, and except for occasional small interruptions, to visit the bathroom, to eat some apricot flakes and instant vitamin F, it never really stopped until morning.

F, the sex vitamin, here was proof that it worked. Doris

traveled with lubricants, which she was generous with, a capsule which she invited Iluminado to bite down on when his countdown neared zero. He did as she suggested, and his head filled with the same light that had come from the helicopters. He thought he heard angels playing electric guitars.

Time telescoped and expanded, in a combination of jet lag and Lazy Bones. A moment came finally when he was far inside her, doing variant bone magic. They were locked closely together, warhead and target.

Her fingers wandered across his chest. When they stopped at his nipple—he hadn't even known he possessed one—it was like pressing one of the crosshatched buttons on the W-3 keyboard. Waves ran the length of his body, activating hidden connectors, entered Doris and continued upward to Iluminado's hand holding her breast. There the circle closed.

Again, flash and concussion.

She was crying, he noticed. The interior space altered subtly, and soon they were doing wild things again, with bursts of intense pleasure; and what he was asking her, now that it seemed to be over, did this happen every time someone gave her his input, if that was the way to say it in English?

"For hours and hours? Of course not. That was a major disturbance. About fifty on the Richter scale."

He moved pillows so he could see her in her total dishevelment.

"There may be other things we can discover together. No one will miss me at Counter Coup school. Come on a trip with me. New York, Paris. My papa says Leningrad is spectacular at this time of year."

She looked vaguely uncomfortable and failed to reply.

"Mr. Sam Green," Iluminado went on, "has a Mercedes convertible he would like me to lease from him for one peso a year. Or we can travel in our own private airplane if you wish. It appears that I will end with a great deal of money."

"But—you burned it?"

"Yes, it appeared so. But it's not that easy to burn money in packages. The top few bills, the bottom few. The rest are merely charred at the edges."

"Baby, the trouble is. *Hell*. I told Hughie I wasn't busy this weekend."

"Shanahan."

"Some people he wants me to meet. And not only that." She hitched up in bed. "Mr. G has just about had it with Duffy. Remember the skateboard? Sure you do, I mean how could you forget? That's the kind of service Mr. G expects from his Washington rep, not just now and then but *every day*, and would I be interested? That gives me two major contracts and I haven't even opened an office."

"And yet our lovemaking has been so remarkable for you."

"Yeah, well." She put her face down and embraced his legs. "That's how it is, I guess. You said you weren't going to ask any more stupid questions."

Again, it seemed, he had a large adjustment to make. The radio was playing a familiar tune.

"Your morning love—"

But Doris decided, all the same, that perhaps she had better explain. She was measuring herself for a whole new identity, did he see what she meant? She had been offered a chance to break into a profession that had always been totally male. After all, Shanahan might be the next president. Access—fees in the high six figures. No guarantee of similar astonishing Richter-scale readings in the future. The payloader dance was what had done it this time. And Iluminado himself—different worlds, different cultures. He would go home and amaze his own countrymen. But they would still meet—weekends, vacations. Because he was so—

The trouble was, she was trying to explain these difficult ideas at the same time as she was doing fellatio, as Gabriella had taught him to call it. After a moment Iluminado decided that he would never understand these North Americans.

She looked up. "But we could have dinner Monday. And spend the night?"

Mirabile came out of sensory deprivation after an excellent float, feeling secure and appreciated. He had brought the United States through another very bad crisis.

The Chiefs were waiting for him.

"You're wondering who we hang the rap on for this," Mirabile said with that infuriating smugness of his. "My recommendation is, nobody."

"I'm black and blue from that ride he gave us," the chairman complained. "We weren't just humiliated, we were *publicly* humiliated. Property damage in the tens of millions. The CBS satellite shot down—you know CBS is going to give us grief about that. Then poor old Diz Hemlock. I could never warm up to the man personally, but we'll miss him at budget time, believe me. We've got more than enough to deep-fry that spic."

"In principle I couldn't agree with you more," Mirabile answered. "But I'm thinking practicalities now. Did you notice the way those cocktail chicks flocked around? Those gals are blasé, they've served drinks to some top glamour people. If we could do it off the record, I'd be tempted to say sure, go ahead. But too many people saw it happen. We'd have to bring him to trial. Some of that stuff last night would be tough to explain in a courtroom."

"The top enemy agent since Alger Hiss, and we just let him walk?"

"The legal process would take two years minimum, with bad PR damage all the way. Spec. Five Pettibone would make a terrible witness. 'Ordinary night. No visitors. Worked on my coloring.' And he's not the only one, the computer can't remember a thing. All wiped out in that last big power surge. It'd be a different matter if we'd caught him with the playbook, even with the keyboard. Somebody saw his daddy toss a couple of parcels into the hot plant, so I'm guessing that by now it's all been paved into the highway."

"But what do we say *happened*, Mirabile?" General McArdle said, a bit plaintively.

"I want to suggest something brand new, General. Why not say we don't know?"

For Michael Mirabile, the know-it-all, to make such a suggestion silenced them momentarily. Then several chiefs spoke at once.

"Yeah—good identification values."

"Something the public can relate to."

"Everybody's been asking for new ideas."

Mirabile went on (this was the moment he lived for): "Why did so many W-3 components go bananas at exactly the same time? Search us! Nonnuclear, thank God. I'll tell you who's going to come out of this wearing a halo, that's Another Eight Billion. Ol' Diz saw the Joint Chiefs in jeopardy and he didn't hesitate for an instant. We knew what we were doing when we made him brigadier general. And the sniffer goofed. The irony is, Porcupine's manufactured in Hemlock's home state, he pushed through the appropriation. How could such a thing happen? Well, what makes the stock market go up and down? Why are some people smarter than others? What really went wrong at Three Mile Island? Why did the starlings come to roost on the Pentagon, of all places in the world? The fact is, *we really don't know*."

"But what do we say about Castillo?" McArdle asked, being the one who would have to answer questions at the news conference.

"I'm coming to that. A young Latin American captain, one of Isobel Clancy's dinner guests, showing machismo above and beyond the call of duty, brought the accident under control. Don't ask us how he did it because that's another thing we don't know. But we owe him a debt of gratitude and I think we'll have to give him the Distinguished Service Cross."

They didn't like that. Grudging forgiveness was one thing, but the DSC! Wasn't that going a bit far?

The deferential young man from Senator Shanahan's staff—beautiful suit, beautifully polished cowboy boots—found Gabriella at her finca and asked her to comment on a sensational

324

story that had appeared in the North American press. Alarmed by the fact that he had flown all the way from Washington for this purpose, she asked if anything had happened involving anyone she knew, Captain Iluminado Castillo, for example. And he gave her extremely grave news.

Apparently those few innocent half-truths about guerrillas and so on had had unfortunate consequences. She didn't listen too carefully, being busy throwing things into a traveling bag. Her black linen. As the United States was her destination, definitely no bra. Airplane reservations were no problem—the young man had come in the Shanahan Learjet.

On the flight north, after ordering her thoughts, she made certain small adjustments to her story. The shootings in the casino, she had now come to believe, had had something to do with a jurisdictional dispute between the casino people and the salesmen of lottery tickets. As for the Cuban Communist newspaper, well, the first persons on that scene had been members of the security forces, with their hush-hush Yankee connections, and wasn't it possible that they themselves had arranged for this newspaper to be found?

The young man was delighted with what she was telling him. If she would repeat these statements in front of a TV camera, Iluminado's difficulties would vanish. While the interview was being arranged, she would have an opportunity to take instruction in microphone technique, to visit the hairdresser, if she wished.

"Oh?" she said icily. She had had her hair cut in a new style for the inauguration, and she had been given compliments on it by everybody. Did he consider it overly frizzy to be fashionable in the United States, or not frizzy enough?

Their landing was briefly delayed while a baby blimp, towing a paper kite in the shape of some kind of projectile, was maneuvered out of the pattern. A dim lightbulb burned in the kite. There were tanks on the airport approaches, a plague of helicopters making conversation nearly impossible, people running around with signs.

"What is happening, are you having an uprising?" she asked her companion.

Her command of English, learned largely from *Time*, was not good enough to make sense of his explanation. Bards were a factor. Poets, did he mean? Oh, *birds*. That didn't make sense either.

He needed to call his office. He stood in a transparent booth, and at first she thought she would have to summon medical assistance. He went deathly pale. Then he went red, then half red and half white. Then he jumped up and down. Hanging up, he told Gabriella that her statement would no longer be necessary, thanks so much for her willingness to cooperate. She could have the limo, and Senator Shanahan would be glad to defray her expenses while she was here. And now if she would excuse him—

He had given her the name of Iluminado's hotel. The limousine stretched toward its goal, moving much too slowly for Gabriella. Also the hotel elevator. She urged it to hurry, to hurry. Would she find her lover's skin sleek and intact, or punctured with bullet holes?

A number of rough individuals, some holding cameras, had gathered around one door which must be Iluminado's. The door was guarded by an athletic-looking person wearing various bandages and Band-Aids. His nose had recently been broken. The eyes separated by the nose bandage were a frightening shade of blue, the blue found at the deep end of a swimming pool. When she told him her name he gave her a look that nearly straightened her hair. Meanwhile, the others were taking photographs and asking about Iluminado. Where did he spring from, was he pro-democratic or what?

A very small woman said, "I'm from *People*. We've heard a rumor he's gay. Can you give me something on that?"

Gabriella could have given her plenty, if she had cared to, but why on earth should she? It was all very strange and confusing.

The doorkeeper patted her swiftly in the various places where a female assassin might be carrying a pistol. It was over before Gabriella had time to object. He knocked twice, paused, then twice more.

A peephole clicked open and she saw an eye. She would have known those lashes among thousands.

She heard an exclamation, the sound of bolts being thrown. The door flew open. In his eagerness, Iluminado hadn't stopped to put on clothes. He looked perfectly heavenly. She sprang into his arms.

"My darling, are you all right? They told me you were in terrible danger—"

"Yes, for a time. Now not so much anymore." His shyness seemed to be gone. He was looking at her with none of the protégé's gratitude which had always made her so angry. "I had nearly forgotten how beautiful—"

But he was getting massage oil on her Perry Ellis sheath. She smelled sex suddenly, and her eyes jumped to the canopied bed.

A redheaded woman with a bruised eye lay between designer sheets that had clearly received a great deal of recent use. Her hair was arranged in short ragged spikes. Was this the fashion, then, so new that *Time* hadn't got around to it yet? And the eye. Had Iluminado given her that? Something, the air conditioning perhaps, made Gabriella shiver.

An explosive situation, which Iluminado defused competently by pretending that this was a drawing room, not a bedroom, and they were all fully clothed. (Though she could see that his old self was lurking just under the skin.)

"I would like to introduce Doris. Doris, here is the lady you read about. Do you wonder that I find her irresistible? I rescued her from a terrorist band, it seems, although I confess that next morning I couldn't remember anything about it."

"I thought that was rather clever, myself," Gabriella said, showing that she too could do this kind of theater. "Who could have predicted that people would take it so seriously?"

"Though it has ended happily."

Only two days had gone by? It seemed a lifetime.

The woman in bed sat up with a rearrangement of pillows. Gabriella might be wrong, but she strongly suspected that this redheaded Doris had experienced more than one major orgasm during the night, which might account for the surprising alterations in her young man. Precisely as Gabriella had intended when she sent him to Washington, and yet—

"Time for *Good Morning America*," Doris said. "Turn on the TV, why don't we, maybe something's happened at Fort Belknap."

"This may interest you, Gabriella," Iluminado said. "And we were about to telephone for breakfast?"

Nothing for her, she told him; she had been given coffee on the airplane. He put on a pair of shapeless purple trousers with fluorescent bands on the cuffs while the screen brightened, bringing the face of a blond young woman, unnaturally composed except for trembling earrings. She told them the news, smiling more than people generally do when talking about death and catastrophe.

Doris's eyes were shining, even the injured one. "Sweetie, you're superfantastic."

"I think so," he agreed.

Gabriella couldn't believe the things she was hearing. "Iluminado, you did all that?"

"More," he said simply.

"But *how*?"

He considered. "I was holding the bone. And from somewhere, a kind of *tingling*—"

A glance passed between the two lovely young people, and all at once they were laughing. Gabriella felt a little left out.

The newswoman excused herself for a moment, promising to return. After messages about cures for constipation, ways to remove troublesome stains from dentures and the like, there she was again, shaking her earrings at them. For reasons no one had been able to explain, one of the newly developed W-3 weapons had run amok and cut down a prominent senator. Two experimental fighter planes, the Piranha and the John Wayne, had collided at ten thousand feet. That generation of airplanes, with those wonderful guidance systems, aren't supposed to collide. The mishap was being blamed on unusual emanations coming up from below. The pilots ejected safely.

Almost down, they were netted by a giant American flag being towed by helicopters. Wrapped in the flag, they landed hard. Like W-3 in the Senate this morning, they were both on the critical list.

And a CBS satellite—one minute it was there, the next minute it had unaccountably disappeared. But good news for motorists. The controversial I-183 connector was going through, though not without bloodshed. Unusual atmospheric disturbances had been reported up and down the Eastern seaboard, strange lights in the sky. The president had suffered bruised elbows in a fall at the Pentagon, and had been ordered to take no phone calls for twenty-four hours. Rumors of a major structural collapse in that building were being denied by Pentagon spokesmen. "Routine maintenance" was the reason given for corridor closings. The birds were still on the roof, for the hundred and sixty-fourth day, but ornithologists thought they could detect a restlessness among some of the females, as though they might at last be thinking about moving.

Two sharp knocks, a pause, two more. Iluminado put his eye to the hole and unbolted.

It was like opening the door of a furnace. The crowd outside shouted questions. A bearded gentleman came in smiling. On a thin golden chain, he wore a tiny scissors and spoon, cocaine apparatus as Gabriella happened to know.

"Quimby," Iluminado said. "I wondered how soon you'd show up."

"A security feel from a Medal of Honor man. What I call a thrill. The last I heard, he was trying to abrogate you. Did you kiss and make up?"

"They gave him a dishonorable discharge. I needed someone to beat off the journalists. I'm told he once shot a congressman?"

"Long ago now. Purple looks good on you, Captain, but you can't wear those pants to the White House. General McArdle's sending over his tailor."

"The White House?"

"One of the main things about American presidents, they

like to be in the photograph. You're getting the DSC. And not only that, the Finns are making you Knight Commander of the White Rose."

"He already has—" Gabriella started to say, then decided to keep quiet about the decoration she had borrowed from her husband.

Tap, tap. Tap, tap.

The famous Hal Amsterdam was outside, not requesting but demanding an interview. Iluminado looked at Quimby.

"Tell him to get lost," Quimby advised. "After last night everything's anticlimax. Don't talk to anybody. In fact, I think you ought to get on an airplane and go home, right away if not sooner."

"No, I don't think I can do that. I hope to persuade Señora Alvarez to accompany me to some scenic location for the weekend. Then I have an appointment with Doris on Monday."

"In any event," Gabriella put in, "it might be wise to stay out of Colombia until tempers have cooled. Hernán Vega is still stamping up and down, making threatening noises."

"I'm taking my new bodyguard," Iluminado said, "and he's quite an impressive person. A little bad luck is all. But I don't expect bullets, Gabriella, I expect compliments. I have some money to give them. I'm not sure exactly how much, my papa is counting it now."

"What I recommend—" Quimby began.

"One moment."

Iluminado picked up the phone, and asked the hotel operator to get him the Pentagon, the chairman of the Joint Chiefs of Staff.

"McAddled, I think, or McArdle. Tell him Iluminado Castillo is phoning."

The call was put through at once. And this was Gabriella's young man from the provinces, who had come to her in too narrow a necktie, not knowing much about foreplay or how to open champagne. She came closer, wanting to hear. With Iluminado on hold, canned music came out of the phone: "—for spacious skies, for amber waves of grain—"

Then a voice, loud enough to be heard across a parade ground.

330

"How you doing, *amigo*? Got everything you need?"

"I have a question. Who does Quimby work for?"

"Run into Quimby, have you? To tell you the truth, Captain, he's sort of a mystery man. Can you trust him, is that what you're asking? Sure you can trust him. As far as you can throw him!"

A laugh was heard in the background. Another voice: "If you find out anything about him, let us know!"

The chairman again: "You've given us a lot to think about, Captain. We've got the same kind of standoff in just about everything else. Like the nuclear thing. If you talk to the arms control people—"

"They're all so God damn *rational*!" (Another voice.)

"One hundred good reasons why we can't give an inch."

"And it's the same on the Russian side of the table."

The chairman: "Maybe what we need to do is get rid of the experts and call in, well, not a witch doctor but somebody along the same general lines. Tell everybody to knock it off, game's over, go home. Swords into plowshares kind of thing."

They were still talking when Iluminado hung up. He went to the door and called in the formidable doorkeeper.

"I am about to ask this man Quimby a question which I expect he won't want to answer."

"What's the question," Quimby said, "who I work for? The fact is, I'm between jobs and if you could use an administrative assistant—"

Iluminado made a sign. A knife flashed and the middle button of Quimby's jacket fell to the floor.

"Hey! Guys! These days there's no such thing as hundred-percent affiliation. Everybody doubles or triples. I'll tell you a story. This is an actual historical case. Colonel Rudolf Abel, you probably never heard of him. Russian spy in the fifties, and he had such great cover. He was a pretty good Expressionist painter, studio in Brooklyn, fucked all his models, sold out his shows, had a really wonderful life. Back home in Moscow they wouldn't have let him paint modern, and the girls there aren't nearly so free and easy. So I always wondered: which was the cover? What if running a spy network out of a

Brooklyn art studio was the only way he could paint as he pleased? Be serious, Iluminado, what does it matter whether I'm developing intelligence assets, or cruising for boys? You might consider the possibility that I don't know the answer myself."

A lot of this was over Gabriella's head. Had this good-humored creature been trying to seduce her young man?

"You need somebody like me," Quimby continued. "You need *me*. You have the instincts but you don't have much experience. Don't take my advice if it doesn't sound right to you. Just listen to it."

"All right, I'm listening."

"Go back today, before the counterrumors get started. They'll give you a nice press. Computers raging out of control, barefoot boy from the boonies comes up with some down-home magic, saves top U.S. officials. For the first day or so you can have anything you ask for. You need a base and a bankroll. Ask for the governorship of the Department of Boyacá. The guy there now is disasterville, hard to do business with."

Gabriella didn't understand this at all. Boyacá? It was an impoverished part of the country, about all they had there was coca and emeralds.

Quimby had taken a bone from his side pocket.

"Let's do a little work on the myth. That chicken leg last night was such a miserable little thing. This is actually from a Stop 'n' Shop turkey, but why don't we say it came off an eagle?"

He held it out to Iluminado.

Gabriella was completely at sea. The bone must be a symbol, but what did it signify? Iluminado had gone back half a step. He was pale, even more beautiful. His hands were at his sides, but they weren't hands, they were fists.

For a long moment, Quimby and Iluminado looked at each other.

"Take it!" Gabriella said impulsively, and regretted the impulse immediately.

"History," Doris said softly from the bed.

"Sky's the limit," Quimby said.

Iluminado relaxed his fists and accepted the bone. He weighed it thoughtfully, gave Gabriella a glance which started the shiver again, and dropped it on the table beside the bed, where it joined a squirt bottle of oil and a box of apricot flakes.

The Pentagon tailor arrived, bringing what was left of the lovely uniform which had been Iluminado's going-away present, an eon ago in Cartagena. It had been badly mistreated since then, Gabriella saw. The man thought the coat could be salvaged but look at the condition of the trousers, they would have to go back into the trash.

Gabriella felt a localized prickle of excitement when the tailor's hand went into Iluminado's crotch to measure the inseam. She wanted to do the same thing herself, at the earliest opportunity.

Knock, knock. Knock, knock.

This was the senior Castillo. He advanced on his son with one palm raised to be slapped. The fingers were smudged from counting charred bills. After accepting the slap he made a thumb-and-forefinger *O*. While he didn't want to go into detail in front of outsiders, the count had been *better* than satisfactory. Some for the colonels, some for Iluminado, perhaps some left over for Papa.

His eye, restless as always, lighted on Doris, obviously naked under the flowery sheet. A long-legged redhead, the kind he admired most, and hadn't he stood next to her last night in the obs-car? Been having carnal connection with Nado, had she? Excellent. He noticed the bottle of Campari and the bottle of gin, which his thoughtful son had provided for breakfast. And finally he noticed Gabriella.

"Gabby!" He came toward her in his ghetto walk, rolling his shoulders to get the effect of tumbling water. "And it was only night before last that we had that splendid dinner together. You didn't say you were coming to Washington."

A spark flared in Iluminado's eye. She could see that he understood it all in an instant. It was Gabriella who had arranged the whole thing, delaying the father so his innocent namesake would be given an education in international politics. That look told their future. Starting this moment, he was nobody's client or protégé. Not Quimby's. Not Shanahan's or Mr. Sam Green's. Not Gabriella's.

But meanwhile, she consoled herself, there were shivery moments ahead, long slippery nights, many interesting things.

In the middle sixties, when General McArdle's contemporaries were moving into procurement or counterinsurgency, McArdle had opted for social engineering. It was a wise choice, and he rode it all the way to the top.

The Pre-Poll was McArdle's personal baby. In classic polling technique, first something has to happen and then the poll takers get on the phone to find out what people think about it, or indeed whether they care. The Pre-Poll gets in ahead of the news. If the responses are negative, the event can often be modified, sometimes called off altogether.

This morning, the questioners opened the phones before most people were up. Based on the answers, ranging from no-comment grunts to an astonished "No shit!" it was decided that Senator Hemlock should be given a gold-plated funeral.

Every public-disturbance control force in the District was put on full alert. They had had to wear kid gloves the day before, but today it was crack-head time and no fooling. Not that they had any intention of interfering with the public's right to dissent, they just had to clear the avenues for Hemlock's funeral procession.

Because of the downed satellite, parts of the country were unable to watch. That was their hard luck, for raters of funerals gave Hemlock's a ten: an entire division of foot soldiers, eight bands, numerous black-draped Tarantulas, a sky full of stacked helicopters. The ground-level action wound five times around the Pentagon—that number again—over the river, past the monuments and the White House, up the Hill, at a slow, slow one hundred paces a minute. Flags were carried at the mourning angle, declined out of respect for the man who manipulated all that money out of Congress (and in the end, out of the taxpayer). Twenty-one-gun salutes were let off at intervals, using blank ammo and uncurling tongues.

The caisson bearing the coffin was drawn by six matched gray horses, recalling the days when horses, too, had a place in warfare. Then came Black Jack, the riderless stallion. Hemlock's own boots, reversed, stood in the silver stirrups. Instead of the traditional black-handled sword, a .357 magnum, Hemlock's personal handgun, hung from the saddle.

A freight elevator carried Black Jack and the coffin up to the Great Rotunda for the lying-in-state. There the catafalque waited, the noble platform that had sustained the weight of six presidents. The Joint Chiefs themselves stood honor guard. They were wearing new uniforms, the old ones having been pretty well wrecked during their ride in the payloader bucket. Some of the seams had only been basted, so they had to be careful to stay at parade rest and not make any sudden moves.

Duffy had hated to go into the W-3 proving grounds with all that funny stuff going on, but naval officers are trained to take orders even when they would prefer not to. After a number of undignified adventures, his Tarantula was belatedly brought to the attention of the microwave zapper. Its motor gulped twice and died.

He put his head out. Clouds of smoke and tranquilizing gases were being blown into his face by gigantic fans. A formation of flechettes approached. Luckily they were satisfied with the way Duffy smelled, and continued past.

He was very close to the missile tube. It was pointing straight up, which couldn't be right. Duffy's old mishap flashed into his mind, the time gremlins were fooling around in the bowels of his sub and the Poseidon escaped. He leaped down and ran. Hearing the unmistakable whoosh of a small-scale launch, he flung himself to the ground.

There was a rising whisper, a falling whisper, and his clothes were blown off, everything he was wearing down to his shoes and socks. And that was the moment he decided he was no longer working for Mr. G. Too many headaches.

The next day he met Doris in the Capitol Rotunda.

"Doris—"

"Duffy—"

He made her go first. She said she would miss him. Probably she had been unladylike at times, and she apologized for that. She had gone into business for herself, she told him, and she had more on her plate than any one person could handle. Am Tex, Hawk-Sisley. She would be making frequent visits to Colombia, to service the John Wayne–Piranha account. She was thinking of taking an associate. Could Duffy suggest anybody?

His spirits lifting, Duffy suggested himself. They loved him at the Pentagon still, and he loved *them,* loved the Command and Flag Officers' Mess, the drowsy afternoons in the sauna, exchanging tales of old wars.

She quickly agreed, and they went back to the office to begin rearranging the furniture.

Hal Amsterdam swallowed another Valium. He had been talking for four hours, as anchors must on historic occasions, and the day was still far from over. He had an instant documentary scheduled, and the writers were driving him crazy. He had *been* there, after all; did that handsome Hispanic kid actually burn three million dollars and turn a Sidewinder missile aside by waving a bone? Amsterdam thought that was what he had seen, but perhaps it would be better to omit the supernatural angle.

The Valium was causing his blood to rush back and forth. He felt hot on one side of his body, cold on the other. The air became harder to breathe, as before hurricanes.

The majority leader wound up the eulogy. It had been flattering, probably, but no one had heard much of it because of the terrible echoes.

The president came through. Everybody else had the usual three dimensions, but as so often lately, the poor man only had two. Being offered the microphone by Amsterdam, he praised Hemlock for a moment, managing to remember his name correctly.

Most of the country's top military men were on line, but apparently Admiral Marx had decided not to attend. Amsterdam could understand that, for Hemlock and Marx had fought many a bitter battle. In actuality, Marx, too, was dead. His submariner's heart, weakened by all the rages, the impatience with subordinates who couldn't come up to his expectations, had stopped pumping after the Circe debacle. The Navy decided to put him on ice, literally put him in ice cubes. They would thaw him out and bury him later, for this was Diz Hemlock's day.

The widow appeared, arm in arm with Chief Warrant Brady, the Meadow Lark's pilot, looking lovely in black. Amsterdam murmured his sympathy.

"Mrs. Hemlock, I have a bulletin. The governor has just announced that he intends to appoint you to fill out your husband's term?"

She blotted her eyes. Yes, she had heard this rumor, and she did want to say that she would do her darnedest to make W-3 Hemlock's memorial. She would be out there whooping and hollering. (There hadn't been time to bring her up to date on the latest developments.)

And Brady? She had been piloting Hemlock for what was it—five years? The memories, the associations—

True, Brady said, and everything would conspire to remind her of that great man, the small part she had played in his life. She had almost decided that she might have to leave the service. Perhaps she would try her luck in some different country. She had been hearing great things about Colombia lately.

In his office on the other bank of the river, Mirabile was watching. He hastened upstairs to the big computer, which was constantly being fed bits of raw data from terminals all over the country. There was nothing new in the Brady file. But Am Tex, Mirabile read, was leasing Iluminado a personal helicopter and that meant that he would be needing a pilot. The son of a bitch was making off with all the good-looking women.

Back in the Rotunda, Amsterdam was chatting with Senator Shanahan. What *bout* W-3, which Shanahan had been opposing so strongly? Shanahan's public-relations Steve had warned him not to say, "I told you so," because that is not the remark of a statesman. W-3, Shanahan mused. A magnificent vision, a great shot in the arm for certain procurement companies. But didn't it pose unacceptable risks? Look at what it had done to the satellite, to the great shovel, in fact to Ol' Diz, and how about that threat to the Joint Chiefs of Staff? For long moments Harry Lord, Shanahan himself, Isobel Clancy and others, Hal Amsterdam too, had had to confront basic reality at unbearably close range. We are all aware that we are part of a target population. Those Siberian missiles aren't pointed at anybody else. But they are so far away that we don't have to think about them unless we actually want to.

Well, the Pentagon planners had worked through the night and come up with a new proposal; and Shanahan was behind this one a hundred percent. In a nutshell, the new idea was to take some of the heavy accurate stuff, which can cross an ocean and come down on a given kopek in the Kremlin cafeteria, and build it into specially reinforced Maxi-Minnies, the oversize Minnetonka recreational vehicle. Because of these creatures' desperate thirst, they are no longer as popular as they were once, and without government help the factories would have to close down, putting thousands of workers on the streets.

The Minnetonka, as it happened, was manufactured by a Hawk-Sisley subsidiary. The missiles were part of the Am Tex line, so Shanahan could vouch for them personally. At one stroke, money was spent, jobs were created, the basing problem was solved. Instead of being dense-packed or racetracked, or immobilized in sitting-duck silos, the missiles would prowl the Interstate, and enemy satellites would be unable to distinguish these particular Maxi-Minnies from all the others lumbering about with vacationers at the wheel. The Army drivers would be permitted to take the wife and the kids, and they could wear Bermudas or whatever they liked, anything but Army clothes.

Unfortunately, he added, like any other sophisticated new weapons system, this would cost money. Amsterdam asked for a ball-park projection.

The answer, sepulchrally distorted by the Rotunda acoustics, might have come from inside the coffin, from Diz Hemlock himself.

"Over the life of the contract, perhaps another eight billion."
It echoed away—eight billion, eightttt billllion—and Am-

sterdam understood what was causing the barometric disturbance that had bothered him earlier. It was the beating of wings.

The starlings had left the Pentagon and moved to the Capitol.

All along, the cameraman filming the file-past had been uncomfortably aware that Black Jack, the riderless stallion, was a part of his picture. The rustle of wings was beginning to bother the horse. Its tail lifted.

The director, in the trailer outside, cut hastily to Amsterdam as the famous Amsterdam twitch, usually confined to a single muscle, took over his face. This was no longer irony, but total dismay.

Again the director cut away. Iluminado Castillo, the media's latest celebrity, had been handed a floral piece and was placing it against the catafalque. His nostrils flared slightly as they caught the scent of manure. And this was the picture that was widely reproduced in Colombian newspapers after his return, and some years later, on the stamp.